ABOUT PENELOPE JANU

Penelope Janu lives on the coast in northern Sydney with six wonderful children and a distracting husband. She enjoys exploring the Australian countryside and dreaming up travelling and hiking breaks. A lawyer for many years, she has a passion for social justice, and the natural environment. Whether coastal or rural, Penelope's novels celebrate Australian characters and communities. Her first novel, *In at the Deep End*, was published by Harlequin in 2017, and her second, *On the Right Track*, in 2018. Nothing makes Penelope happier as a writer than readers falling in love with her smart and adventurous heroines and heroes. She loves to hear from readers, and can be contacted at www.penelopejanu.com.

Also by Penelope Janu

In at the Deep End
On the Right Track

PENELOPE JANU

Up on Horseshoe Hill

mira

First Published 2019
Second Australian Paperback Edition 2020
ISBN 9781867218388

UP ON HORSESHOE HILL
© 2019 by Penelope Janu
Australian Copyright 2019
New Zealand Copyright 2019

Published by
Mira
An imprint of Harlequin Enterprises (Australia) Pty Limited (ABN 47 001 180 918),
a subsidiary of HarperCollins Publishers Australia Pty Limited (ABN 36 009 913 517)
Level 13, 201 Elizabeth St
SYDNEY NSW 2000
AUSTRALIA

® and TM (apart from those relating to FSC®) are trademarks of Harlequin Enterprises (Australia) Pty Limited or its corporate affiliates. Trademarks indicated with ® are registered in Australia, New Zealand and in other countries.

A catalogue record for this book is available from the National Library of Australia
www.librariesaustralia.nla.gov.au

Printed and bound in Australia by McPherson's Printing Group

To Peter

CHAPTER

1

My brother's plot is in the third row of graves at the Horseshoe Hill cemetery. Dad made his cross from a red gum branch, which fell near the cottage in a storm.

Railway sleepers, faded dusky grey, mark the end of each row of graves. The timber is dusty and rough but my jeans are dirty from work, so I sit and stretch out my legs. At the top of the rise is a tiny stone church, weathered and golden with age. My ute is the only car parked there today; more people will come on the weekend. Some pray at the church, or chat with the loved ones they've lost. Others take shelter from the sun. Our wheelbarrow and gardening tools are stored at the back of the nave.

The land beyond the graveyard is mostly cleared for crops, and sheep and cattle grazing. I can't see the river from where I'm sitting, but paperbark trees mark the flow.

'So, Liam, I guess you know it's the second of August.' Tears blur my view of the cross. 'You would've been sixteen.'

I saw Liam once, when he was only two days old. Mum was holding him closely and rocking him gently, her eyelashes spiky and wet. She opened the blanket and showed him to me, his little nose and mouth, and skinny arms and legs. Besides the paleness of his face and the stillness of his body, he was perfect.

There are gums around the cemetery, thick silver trunks and grey-green leaves, but very little shelter for the graves. In summer and autumn, they're peppered with grass; sometimes in winter they're draped in white frost. For much of the year Liam's plot is like the others.

In spring it comes to life.

We planted the daffodil bulbs the day that he was buried. The soil, ruddy red-brown and freshly dug up, was soft because of the rain. We made divots in the earth with our trowels, pushed the plump brown teardrops into the ground, and pressed the soil firmly around them. The rain was falling sideways in gusts and we were all cold and wet. When I said that planting a bulb was like tucking a baby into bed, Mum smiled bravely, and then cried even harder. I started to cry too, and so did Dad, but later he said it was a good thing I'd spoken. The rain and our tears, the moisture and warmth, fell into the dirt together.

Mum died two years after Liam. That was thirteen years ago, when I'd just turned fourteen. I was familiar with loss by then, and knew better than to quip about tucking things in. We planted daffodils on Mum's grave too, and jonquils as well. Liam's grave was more difficult to sow the second time around—it was March and it hadn't rained in months. Dad softened the ground with water from the bore tap, and we planted the jonquils one by one, taking care of the bulbs that were already there. Mum used to say that nothing smelled better than a jonquil, even the scent of a baby, my freshly washed hair or clean saddle leather.

The freesias I planted a decade ago won't have tall, straight stems like the daffodils and jonquils, but they'll shoot earlier, spindly stalks with knobbly heads. At the end of the winter they'll flower milky white, ruby red and pink—sweet-smelling colour that'll tangle with the grass. A lot of the shoots are peeking out already, bright green and glossy.

Something glistens—I see it from the corner of my eye. I get to my feet and watch a car, a white four-wheel drive, pull off the loop road and follow the pot-holed lane towards the gums where I parked. I can't see who's driving, but the car is unfamiliar. Dubbo, the biggest town in the district, is only an hour away. Maybe it's a day-tripper from there, checking out the church before heading into Horseshoe Hill. The town, named for the final peak in the crescent-shaped Horseshoe range, gets occasional visitors in winter. In addition to the pub, there's a row of shops, a primary school and a doctor's surgery.

I squat at Mum's grave, being careful to keep my boots clear of the shoots. Her headstone is lined up with Liam's cross, and I look at the letters, twisting and turning in front of my eyes. 'Dyslexia is a blessing,' Dad always said. 'It gives you a special way of seeing things.' He also said, 'It's lucky you were born with the memory of an elephant.' I run my fingers over the words. In addition to the way they move around, it's hard to recognise the letters and symbols. And things get worse when I try too hard. A word I read one day, I can't read the next. But the words on Mum's grave? I know them all by heart. *Abigail Laney died at thirty-nine, doing what she loved. She was married to Ross Kincaid and had two beautiful children, Jemima and Liam.*

'Hey, Mum,' I say, wiping my eyes with the palm of my hand. 'Chili Pepper's doing well. He gets a gallop occasionally, just to stretch his legs, and I take him to Follyfoot almost every week.'

It took me years to tell Mum I didn't ride any more. And even then, I didn't give her the real reason, just told her I'd lost interest. A lot of teenage girls do that. If she was listening, I hope she believed it.

'Mrs Hargreaves called this morning. She knew it was Liam's birthday, and so did Sapphie and Gus. It's good that people remember about Liam, isn't it? After so many years.'

I blink back tears again. Sapphie tells me not to do this to myself, that I can think about my family just as well from a distance as I can here, that they wouldn't expect me to visit. But the only time I cry is on their birthdays. A few days a year isn't going to kill me. When I wipe my face with my shirtsleeve, dark blue tracks mark the fabric. I trace them with my finger.

'See, Mum, blue is still my favourite colour.' She used to laugh when I competed at horse shows and waved first-place ribbons happily under her nose.

Wheels crunch on the gravel as the four-wheel drive does a three-point turn, before heading east on the highway. The wind picks up. When my hair, long and fair, flies into my eyes, I twist it into a rope and flip it down my back. Then I crouch by Dad's grave. It has daffodils too, and jonquils and freesias. And there's a headstone. Not that I can read those words any better than I can read Mum's.

'Hi, Dad.' I shade my watch with my hand and make out the time. 'I'll be back on the weekend.'

I follow the pebble path to the first row of graves near the church. These are the oldest plots, with weather-beaten headstones, intricate crosses and tiny ornate fences. Dad used to chart my growth against the statue of the angel. I run a hand over her outstretched wings.

'How're you doing?' I say quietly.

As I walk through the space in the fence where the gate used to hang, I kick through the leaf litter, breathe in its scent. There's an ironbark tree at the front of the church, and its roots jut out of the ground. I balance on one and stand on my toes to get a closer look at the black slate roof. More tiles have come loose and slipped into the gutter. It's bound to rain soon. On Sunday I'll bring a ladder, rearrange the tiles and fill in the gaps.

The cabin in my ute smells of smoke from the forge, so I wind down the windows to let in the breeze. Behind the trees, the sun dips lower, casting brightly coloured spirals on the dash. I put the car into gear and check the rear-view mirror.

The cemetery, the crosses, the headstones.

Liam, Mum and Dad.

I turn off the road towards home, driving through the pillars and over the cattle grate. Bushes and shrubs scrape against the ute as I round the bend in the driveway. My weatherboard cottage, built decades ago for a housekeeper, nestles beneath the branches of a towering gum. Barely twenty metres away, at the end of the drive-way, sits Kincaid House, the homestead owned by Dad's cousin. It has a pitched roof, chimneys, wide verandahs and fifty hectares of grazing land that slopes down to the river. I pull over near the shed. And it's only as I shut the door behind me that I notice the car I saw at the cemetery, parked beneath the peppercorn tree on the far side of the homestead.

Chili Pepper, my mother's warmblood cross, is at the gate, as are my ponies, Freckle and Lollopy. Where is Vegemite? And where is the driver of the car?

'Hello!'

Silence. But then I hear a long, loud bellow. Only horses are kept in this paddock, but my neighbour Gus grazes cattle on the far side of the river. More bellows ring out, increasingly distressed. I climb through the gate and run down the hill, towards the trees that grow along the riverbank. Finally I see Vegemite. He has his back to me but turns his head and pricks up his ears when I get close.

I press the stitch in my side. 'What's going on?' Vegemite rubs his head against my legs as I stroke behind his ears.

There's another bellow, not as loud as the others. And then, apart from the sounds of rustling leaves and the rush of water, it's eerily quiet.

I climb through the wire fence and step carefully around the trees and undergrowth towards the six-metre cliff that drops to the river. It's impossible to cross at this point, but I can see to the other side, where the slope rises steeply. A cow stands at the base of the slope, close to the water, her calf tucked in by her side. He's small, probably only a few months old. His body is trembling; his legs are wobbly. His woolly coat is rust-brown and curly and I suspect it's sopping wet.

I walk closer to the edge, wrap an arm around a sapling and take my phone from my pocket. I wave the phone around but can't pick up reception to call Gus. So I walk a little further, back to higher ground. Which is when I see the man.

He's not far from the cows, and is leaning forwards with his hands on his knees, as if to catch his breath. His hair is short and dark, his shoulders are broad and, when he straightens, I see that he's tall. His blue shirt pulls tightly across his back and his navy pants cling to his legs. His feet are bare. He's just as wet as the calf.

He opens his arms and walks towards the cows. When the mother gazes at him, wide-eyed but motionless, he picks up a branch. Taking care to stay between the cows and the river, he swipes the branch against the ground, until finally the mother gets the message, pivoting and scrambling frantically up the riverbank, her calf at her heels. As they crash through the undergrowth, the man runs up the slope behind them. A minute passes, maybe two, and then I hear a series of bellows, some loud, others soft.

I think they've found their friends.

There's little brightness in the filtered sun, and the cliff shades the river. A tall wedge of rock divides the water, making a pair of fast flowing streams. Rocks beneath the surface glisten black.

'Jemima?'

My head jerks up. I don't know his name; how does he know mine?

He stands on the opposite riverbank with his hands on his hips. I can't see his face clearly, but I'm certain he's young, maybe thirty. He runs a hand through his hair.

'Are they okay?' I shout.

'Back with the herd.'

'Was the calf in the water?'

One side of his shirt has pulled out of his pants. I see a flash of white teeth as he yanks the rest free and pulls it away from his body. 'Unfortunately, yes.'

'Is that your car at Kincaid House?'

'Yes.'

'Did you cross down there?' I point downstream, to the kink in the river. 'It's much harder to find the path back. Walk a few hundred metres through the paddock behind you, as far as the paperbark trees. The riverbank levels out down there. It's the best place to cross to this side.'

'I'll come back the way I came.'

He's not Australian—his words are clipped. Maybe English? He climbs halfway up the rise before turning and facing me again.

He pushes back his shoulders as if he's taking a breath. Surely he wouldn't …

He runs as far as the distance allows, then leaps over the water, at least two metres wide, and lands with both feet on the rock that splits the river. For an instant he teeters, but then he pitches forwards, taking hold of the rock with both hands. I suck in a breath as he climbs to the top. His body tense, he jumps, legs scissoring in midair, over the second stretch of water. He lands with bent knees, on the plateau of rock at the base of the cliff.

My heart is beating fast as I walk to the edge of the cliff and, once again, wind an arm around the sapling.

I look down. He looks up.

His eyes are blue, bright as summer skies.

CHAPTER

2

'What were you thinking?' I say, swallowing hard when the words come out croaky. 'Now you're stuck.'

He crosses his arms. 'I'll retrace my steps.'

I open my mouth and shut it. I look up and down the riverbank, considering whether a landscape that's been the same for tens of thousands of years has suddenly changed. *No.* Everything is just as it should be. The plateau he's standing on is a few metres long. The river is behind him. Directly in front is a sheer rock wall. He climbed down six metres? Even if he did, there's no way to climb up.

As if he reads my mind, he raises an arm, finding a handhold. 'It's not quite vertical.'

'Don't!' I lower my voice. 'You'll fall.'

'I won't.' He's not looking at me; he's surveying the cliff.

'Listen to me.' My voice catches. 'Swim back to the other side and cross upstream.'

'It's far quicker this way.' He lifts a foot to an outcrop of stone, and places his hand in a crevice. 'It's not that high.'

'I'll call my friend. She abseils, she has ropes.'

He shakes his head. 'No need.'

I can't climb down there if he falls, and it would take more than an hour for paramedics to get here. I don't want to watch but I can't look away.

He takes hold of another chunk of rock. He finds a second foothold, and then a third. The muscles in his arms tighten, and so do the cords in his neck. Sometimes he moves sideways, putting his limbs at impossible angles. Often he tests a hold, only to dismiss it. When he's halfway up the cliff, a slender ledge gives way beneath his foot, sending rock shards tumbling.

'No!' I cry out.

He curses under his breath as he hangs from two hands, with one foot wedged into a crack. He tips back his head as he extends his other leg, searching for a foothold. As he climbs higher, he disappears from view.

Only a few minutes must have passed. Even though it feels like an hour. Or a week or a month. I crawl closer to the edge of the cliff. One of his hands is close to the top. I lie on my stomach and reach down.

'Take my hand.'

'No!' His eyes flash with anger. 'Get back!'

I scurry away like a crab. And not long afterwards, his hand appears over the top of the cliff. A muscular forearm follows, then an elbow. He hauls his body over the edge and rolls onto level ground.

My breathing gets back to normal as he rests for a count of three, before pushing himself to his feet. He rolls his shoulders. His fingers clench and unclench. Wincing, he wipes his hands down the front of his pants. He clears sweat from his forehead with his sleeve.

His clothes are wet and dirty. He has blood on a knuckle and a scrape on his cheek. But his chin is firm, his mouth is nicely shaped, he has a well-defined jawline and his cheekbones are high. His hair is darkest brown. I've seen plenty of good-looking men, but none that look like him.

He holds out his hand. 'Finn Blackwood.'

I shake his hand automatically. It's much bigger than mine. His grip is firm. 'You could have fallen.'

'Had I taken your hand, we both would have fallen.' He looks me up and down. 'You couldn't hold half my weight.'

I cross my arms. 'It was a stupid risk to take.'

He runs a hand through his hair. 'I know what I'm doing.'

So did my mother and she broke her neck.

He narrows his eyes as he stares into mine. What does he see? My eyes are brown, unusual given my colouring. And my face will be paler than usual. He turns away abruptly, reaching into the fork of a tree to retrieve his boots. He's lost the top two buttons of his shirt. It gapes when he takes his phone from a boot, shoving it in a back pocket. He puts his wallet into a front pocket and sits on the ground.

He pulls on socks. 'You are Jemima Kincaid?'

'Jet. No one calls me Jemima. How do you know my name?'

'Your uncle described you.'

'Edward is my father's cousin, not my uncle.'

'He said uncle.'

'You were at the cemetery.'

'I couldn't find the homestead. When I saw your car, I intended to ask for directions.'

'But you didn't.'

'I was reluctant to interrupt.'

Did he get out of his car? Listen as I talked to my family? Are my eyes still red and puffy? I look away.

'Why were you looking for Kincaid House? Why did you come down here?'

He smiles stiffly. 'I heard the calf.' He sits up straighter and tugs at his shirt. His face and throat are tanned.

'They're Gus Mumford's cattle. He owns the neighbouring property. I'll let him know what you did.'

'One of the stakes is down, the wire has snapped. What I cobbled together won't last.' He ties the lace of his second boot. 'Tell him that.'

He follows me through the undergrowth to the paddock. Vegemite is still there, leaning over the fence. He whickers softly when he sees us. I climb through the fence and wrap my arms around his neck.

'Hey, boy. Ready to come home now?'

'A thoroughbred? How old?'

'Ex-racehorse. He's twenty-eight.'

He points to the top of the hill. 'Are the others yours too?'

'The ponies are Freckle and Lollopy. They're retired as well.'

'The warmblood?'

'Chili Pepper. He was my mother's eventer.'

'Edward said you're a blacksmith.'

'I shoe horses. I'm a farrier.' When I walk away, Vegemite follows and Blackwood walks beside me. His boots aren't old, but they're comfortably worn in. They're an expensive brand, as are his pants and shirt. I increase my pace but he's much bigger and keeps up easily. I study our shadows as they move side by side. I'm five foot five; he has eight inches on me, maybe more.

'Do you know Edward well?'

'We met last month.'

'Where do you come from? England?'

'I was educated there. I grew up in Scotland.'

'Are you on holiday?'

'I'm working on a project at the open plains zoo.'

'You're at Dubbo? What sort of project is it?'

'A scientific one.'

'Are you a vet?'

'Yes. But not for dogs and goldfish.'

'You never said why you were here.'

'You don't know what's happening, do you? Edward told me he'd emailed.'

I have a series of responses on a document I keep on my desktop, to use when I know who the sender is and I don't have time to decipher the words. I would have copied and pasted response number five, the one I generally use for Edward: *Thanks for the email. Content noted. Jet.*

'I must have missed it.'

'You live in the cottage?'

'I've been there all my life.'

'I've leased the homestead.'

When I trip, he grabs my arm. My heart thumps, my breath quickens. He leans in close, our forearms touch. He searches my face and frowns into my eyes.

'What's the matter?' he finally asks. When I take a step back, he lets me go.

'The homestead is in the middle of nowhere. Why would you want it?'

He looks around slowly, from the valley to the top of the ridge. The sun glows fiery orange as it sinks behind the hill. He shelters his eyes with a hand.

'The zoo arranged accommodation in a serviced apartment in Dubbo. I don't want to spend my weekends there.'

I close my eyes, only to look straight into his when I open them again. 'Look … I'll speak with Edward.'

'What about?' His voice hardens. 'He's signed a lease.'

'I keep my horses on his land.'

'I don't need the land.'

When we reach the gate, I push the horses back so we can get through. Something glistens at my feet, a piece of foil in a dandelion weed. I stoop to retrieve it.

'Edward had no right to do this.' I look from the cottage, painted white, a corrugated water tank perched on one side, to the homestead, broad verandahs and sandstone foundations. 'The houses share a driveway, and a garden. Like I said, I'll talk to Edward.'

'I won't change my mind.'

I nod stiffly when we get to his car. 'Thank you for helping the calf.'

He yanks open a back door and rifles through a bag. When he faces me again, he rolls down his sleeves. He undoes a shirt button, and another. What is he …

'Oh!' I'm walking quickly towards the house when he calls out. 'Jet?'

He's shoving his head through the neck of a T-shirt when I turn. His abs line up in neat rows like blocks. The T-shirt is black. His stomach is flat.

'Yes.'

'I understand you worked at Thornbrooke Stud.'

I haven't eaten since lunch, and I shod five horses after that. I was forced to watch him climb a *not quite vertical* cliff. Is that why I feel sick?

'Eight years ago, yes.'

'Edward said I should ask you some questions.'

'What about?'

'The day the horses died.'

CHAPTER
3

Edward Kincaid inherited Thornbrooke Stud from his father five years ago. Why would he have questions now? And what has Finn Blackwood got to do with it? I didn't give him the chance to explain, just left him standing, feet apart and hands on hips, as I bolted to the cottage.

The landline at home is in the hallway, cluttered with boots and hats and a stand filled with umbrellas and walking sticks that never get used. I sit on a dining chair with a worn leather seat and reach for the phone. Edward answers immediately.

'Jemima. I thought you might call.'

I told Blackwood that no one calls me Jemima. It would have been more accurate to say that no one in the district calls me that. All of them, ever since I can remember, have called me Jet. Dad told me I got the nickname when I was four years old. He hoisted me onto my pony and let go of the reins. By the time he'd shaded his eyes from the sun, I'd trotted clear out of sight.

'Finn Blackwood said you'd emailed. Why didn't you call about the lease?'

Edward is sixty-three, five years older than Dad would have been if he'd lived. He thinks we should be closer than we are. But I don't know that either of us can do much about that. He's a banker and lives in Sydney. We have little in common.

'If I had called, there would have been immediate opposition. I hoped that, once you'd had the opportunity to digest the information in my email, it might dispel your reservations. Dr Blackwood will live in the house irregularly, and primarily on the weekends.'

'That's not the point. Why did you do this?'

'Kincaid House is mine, Jemima, just as the cottage is yours.'

'I look after the homestead. Doesn't that count for anything?'

'It gives you somewhere to keep your horses. How many do you currently have?'

'Only four. Just give me some time, Edward. I'll put up a dividing fence, grow a hedge.'

'I'm afraid it's too late. The lease has been signed. You'll barely know that he's there.'

'What? I saw him at the cemetery this afternoon. And he's been up and down the cliff already. He pulled Gus's calf from the river.'

Edward laughs. 'He's an extremely well-regarded scientist, who's clearly not afraid of a physical challenge. He might be a useful fellow to have around the place.'

I squeeze my eyes shut. 'This is my home, Edward, and I like my privacy. He didn't even care I didn't want him here. Why did you give him a lease?'

Edward clears his throat. 'I wanted him to do something for me, something he had no interest in taking on, to be frank.'

'He mentioned Thornbrooke.' I take a deep breath. 'What's going on?'

'He's agreed to investigate the death of the stallion, Rosethorn, and the other horses.'

I press the phone closer to my ear to steady my hand. 'It happened so long ago.'

'Testing is more accurate than it was. If Finn can access suitable samples, he might find something new.'

'What will that achieve?'

'You know the answer to that. The horses in Rosethorn's line, his descendants, aren't worth as much as they should be. If we can find a definitive reason for his death, it will clear the air.'

'You can't bring the horses back.'

'I appreciate that.'

'The autopsies said food contamination.'

'So why did only some of the horses die, the stallion and colts, and not the others?'

'Rosethorn's offspring still do well on the track.'

'That doesn't stop the questions. He dropped dead, and so did three of the horses he'd sired. A problem with the genes? Food that kills some horses and spares others? It's a niggling doubt at the back of people's minds.'

'Why Blackwood?'

'He's a specialist in genetics, amongst other things, so whatever he concludes about Thornbrooke will carry additional weight. And he'll be going back to Europe early next year. He won't mind trampling on local toes.'

'I was there, Edward. You know how hard it was for me.'

'I'm not doing this to upset you.'

'I want to leave it behind me.'

'You knew more than you let on at the time, that was obvious. It might be a positive thing to bring things out in the open.'

I endeavour to speak calmly. 'Darren Morrissey was the stud manager, Dr Schofield the vet. They were in charge.'

'Schofield has passed away. I tracked Morrissey down in Perth. He refuses to add to the statements he gave at the time. Which is why I've decided to take this on myself. You were with the horses before and after it happened. Your recollections will be useful.'

'It's all a blur.'

'Give Finn what you have, a first-hand account.'

A wave of heat spreads through my body. I lean back in the chair and stare at the ceiling. A daddy-long-legs spider hangs from a gossamer thread.

'I don't have anything.'

'Four horses, Jemima. Worth millions. Unexplained deaths? In what used to be a reputable stud?'

'Your father got an insurance payout.'

'It wasn't nearly enough. And that's hardly the point. I want to find out why they died. The stud's reputation, and possibly its future as a viable concern, is at stake.'

I stretch out my legs. There's a hole in the heel of my sock. 'Schofield did autopsies.'

'His testing was rudimentary. But, luckily for us, the colts and Rosethorn were tested on numerous occasions before they died. And my father was a stickler for detail and ensured the samples were properly stored. Finn will analyse those, and look at any other information we can gather.'

'I refuse to get involved with this.'

'You won't answer a few simple questions?'

'No. And I don't want him living next door, either.'

'Please, Jemima, don't make things difficult.'

'The homestead is well cared for.'

'Is it? The entrance is evidently overgrown. Finn said it was barely visible from the road.'

'I'll cut back the shrubs on the driveway.'

'Good, because he'll be there on Friday morning to pick up the keys. What time shall I say?'

'I'll be gone by seven-thirty.'

'I shall let him know.'

Suddenly I'm tired, so tired it's an effort to keep my eyes open. When I slump in the chair, the timber crossbar digs into my back.

'All I want is to live in my home—in peace.'

'Forever? While you tend the graves at the cemetery? You're a popular young woman. It's time you left the past behind and created your own family.'

'I'm happy as I am.'

The spider dangles in midair, before climbing to the ceiling again. He scurries to the cornice.

I mumble goodbye and quietly hang up the phone.

Persephone, Poldark, Blackjack, Rosethorn.

The conclusions in the horses' autopsy reports were all much the same: *Death attributable to cardiac arrest and asphyxia. Possibly caused by food contaminant. Source unidentifiable.*

I was barely eighteen when I got the job as a stablehand at Thornbrooke. I was a full-time apprentice farrier by then, so only worked weekends at the stud. The work topped up my salary, and included lodgings and board a few nights a week. I'd been there a year.

There were usually two stablehands on duty at night, but it was Easter Sunday, and I was the only one who put their hand up. It was just after midnight when I heard something over the stable monitor, loud enough to wake me up. I rolled out of bed and pulled clothes over the top of my nightie. The first horse I found was Persephone, the youngest colt at Thornbrooke, but big for his age. He was brown and sweet tempered with a small white star on his forehead. I opened the stable door and found him on his side and fighting to breathe. He was sweating and trembling, and his coat was soaked through on his neck and flanks. I called Morrissey, the stud manager, and screamed into the phone, telling him to contact Dr Schofield and the veterinary hospital, and to come to the stables. I sat at Persephone's head and felt for his pulse, which was beating so quickly I couldn't keep up. The pupils of his eyes were wild with fear and completely surrounded by white.

It didn't take long for him to die. Afterwards, I sobbed into his neck as I gently stroked his face. I rubbed around his ears. But then I heard Poldark, who was kept in the stable next to Persephone. He was walking restlessly and lifting his hind legs, kicking at his belly. The only thing that made sense was that he had colic, meaning he had to be kept on his feet and walked around. I tried to get him out of the stable but he collapsed into the wood shavings. He writhed on the ground, his legs thrashing wildly.

I grasped his halter but he was far too strong to hold on to for long. He rolled, from his side to his back and to his other side, again and again and again. I stood in the corner of the stable and fumbled with my phone. Morrissey didn't pick up. I looked at my contacts but couldn't make sense of them. So I talked to Siri, asked for Dr Schofield and Sapphie and the veterinary hospital and Gus. Nothing she suggested was right. I closed my eyes and took deep breaths and tried to still my panic. But when I opened my eyes again, the letters, symbols and numbers on my phone were even more jumbled up than before. They darted, twisted and turned.

Sweat darkened Poldark's deep chestnut coat. His cotton rug was twisted around his legs. His forelock and mane were matted with wood shavings, as was his tail. His nose and eyes were streaming. He sucked in breaths, wretched gasps. His body convulsed in a spasm. He groaned, a deep keening sound that bounced off the walls. And then, like Persephone, he died.

Afterwards, I pulled the shavings from his mane and smoothed it down. I neatened his forelock, combing through it with my fingers. I wiped my face on my shirt and staggered to my feet.

Blackjack was next. I found him fidgeting in his stable, his dark coat stained with streaks of sweat. I clipped a rope to his halter, led him out of the stable and walked him up and down the aisle. I talked to him in whispers, telling him the vet would be here in no time, he'd be taken to the veterinary hospital, he just had to hang on a little while longer and then everything would be okay. I called Morrissey again and this time he answered. I told him about Persephone and Poldark. He sounded odd, distant, but said he had things sorted, that help was on its way. Before I could ask where Schofield was, I had to disconnect.

Rosethorn was down.

He had his own section of the stable block. It was made up of a large stable, and a barn and yard where he covered the mares. Owners and managers would bring them in once, twice, sometimes ten times a week. He'd been standing on the far side of his stable last time I'd seen him, but now he was on his side, his powerful body heaving and shuddering.

I tied Blackjack to the tethering ring in the aisle. I threaded the rope and threaded it again, trying to do a slipknot, sobbing and blinded by tears.

My family went on a holiday once. It was mid-summer and every day we went to the beach. On our last afternoon, I was playing in the surf and was hit by a wave. It tossed me off my feet and sucked me under the water. I couldn't breathe. There was sand in my eyes, in my mouth and in my throat. I barely knew up from down. The roaring in my head when I was under the water was the same as it was that night. Grating, pumping, grinding.

Paralysing.

Even so, I heard Blackjack outside, the sounds of his hooves on the concrete. He was still tied up, but his haunches had sunk to the ground and he'd dropped to his knees. His head and neck were twisted, yanked up by the halter and rope. His eyes were enormous.

Terrified, tortured.

I tugged uselessly on the buckles of the halter, pulled tight by Blackjack's weight. I tore frantically at the knot I'd tied. I broke my nails. I skinned the ends of my fingers. The knot became sticky, smeared and stained with my blood.

I'm not sure how much time passed by. Seconds? Minutes? A sharp crack of splintered wood and the ring pulled out of the wall.

Blackjack, finally free, fell at my feet.

Thornbrooke.

I want to keep things in the dark. I want to forget.

CHAPTER
4

On Friday morning, the mist, soft and white, hangs in the valley like a cloud. A herd of sheep, sheltering under trees on the boundary, huddle together for warmth. I roll up my sleeves and angle the metal pail so the lip slides under the tap. I catch my thumb on the handle.

'Ow!' A sterile pad, held in place by strapping tape, hides my broken thumbnail. When it bleeds through both coverings, I hold it in the palm of my hand. I glance at my fingers. The quick on the little finger is red and swollen, but the skin isn't torn. Unlike the ragged top of my index finger, which is tightly wrapped up like my thumb.

Hidden from view.

It's been years since I've dreamt about Thornbrooke. But the nightmares came back on the day I saw Blackwood. When I dream, I toss and turn. I bite my nails.

Shielding my eyes from the rising sun, I look past the cottage to the driveway. It's just gone six-thirty. There's no sign of him yet.

Chili Pepper, tied to a piece of string that's looped through the ring that hangs from the post, a folded rug tossed over his rump, turns his head and pricks up his ears.

'Back to it.' I lean against his shoulder and grasp his fetlock. 'Come on, boy, give me your foot.' When he finally lifts his leg, I pull it between my knees, resting it on the leather apron that hangs from my hips. I wrench off his shoe before throwing it on the pile near the shed with the others. When I straighten, he turns towards me. I rub his snowy-white blaze.

Chili was Mum's favourite horse, a warmblood crossed with a thoroughbred. He had the best of both breeds—willingness, strength, spring and power. Dad wanted to give him to one of Mum's teammates after her death, but I wouldn't let him. When I was with Chili, I imagined how Mum used to be, how she'd laugh as she flew over jumps. The image of her lying on her back, breathless gasps and frightened eyes, was pushed to the back of my mind.

When Chili presses his face against my stomach and nudges, I take a step back. 'You're such a soppy horse. Let's get your shoes on.'

My ute is reversed up to the shed. A portable forge, a cast-iron box attached to the tray and heated by a gas bottle, glows fiery hot. My toolbox is at my feet, and I've set up the anvil and stand. I lift Chili's foot again, laying a pre-cast shoe against it—as if I need to confirm the size is right, even though I shoe him twelve times a year.

After half an hour, Chili's hooves have been trimmed and two shoes are nailed to his feet. I grasp the third shoe firmly with tongs, plunging it into the fire until it glows bright orange. Then I lift Chili's near-hind leg and position it over my knee. When I lay the shoe over the bottom of his hoof, thick white smoke wraps around me. I look to the side so my eyes don't stream, count to three and then lift. Chili's hoof is charred with a shoe-shaped mark. It tells me what I need to do to fit the shoe to the hoof, not the other way around. I work at the anvil, hammering until the width of the shoe narrows a touch, before lifting Chili's foot to test it again. The shoe is cooler now and the smoky cloud is thin. Through it, I see the new mark. I murmur under my breath. 'Perfect.'

'Jet.'

My head snaps up. I let go of Chili's foot, releasing a breath as I straighten. Blackwood is dressed up—white shirt, grey pants and laced-up black leather shoes. He fixes a button on his dark grey jacket as he walks around the ute. He nods politely.

'Good morning.'

'Morning,' I say as I pass, plunging the shoe into the pail of water to cool. I pick up a handful of nails and examine them closely; straight and long, sharp and smooth.

He scratches under Chili's forelock as I nail the third shoe into place. I scrabble in my toolbox for the nail cutter, quickly trimming the ends of the nails that jut through the hoof.

He smiles, a glimpse of teeth. 'You start early.'

'Yes.' When I look around him, I see his four-wheel drive. It's parked to one side of the driveway, between two bottlebrush trees.

'I'm taking the float out today. It won't get past your car. You'll have to move it.'

'I didn't like to park at the homestead until I'd spoken with you.'

'Why not? Edward confirmed you have a lease. You're taking the homestead whatever I think.'

His lips tighten. 'Correct.'

I line up the nails on the anvil. 'I've cut back the shrubs at the entry. I'll do more on Sunday, reduce the undergrowth so two cars can pass.'

'I can assist.'

'That's okay.' I tighten my ponytail. 'I do whatever needs doing around here.'

I freshened up the inside of the homestead last night, getting rid of the dust that'd settled since I'd done it a fortnight ago, lighting the hot water system and turning on the fridge. After breakfast this morning, I raked bark and leaves from the lawn. I filled up a barrow with timber, stacking it in the nook in the lounge room, and setting a fire in the grate. Then I swept the balcony, cleaned the cobwebs away and watered the jasmine in the pots at the door. It had just gone six and was barely even light when I went to the home paddock. I caught Lollopy, the Shetland cross I rode as a child, putting him in the small paddock next to the cottage because I'll be taking him to Dubbo with Chili.

'You live alone?' he says.

'That's right.' I wipe my hands down my faded blue work jeans. The strapping tape was white, but now it's dusty grey. I make a fist. My thumb is bleeding through the tape again. 'Just me and the horses.'

He's rubbing around Chili's ears now, slow strokes of his hands. My smile feels stiff and strained.

'I left two sets of keys at the homestead,' I say. 'They're hanging on a hook behind the green shutter, near the back door. I've marked which key is which. There's a shed near the old outhouse, filled with timber and tools mostly. I don't have a key for that, but it's open.'

'Thank you.'

'Are you staying tonight?'

'No. I came today to pick up the keys and see what I might need.'

'Edward occasionally sends people here for weekends. Pretty much everything is in the homestead except for food. There's linen, kitchen and laundry appliances, things like that.' I look at my watch, run my hands over Chili's rump. 'I have to get to work. I'd better finish up.'

He hesitates. 'When can we talk about Thornbrooke?'

I walk past him, pick up the tongs and grasp the final shoe, shoving it into the forge. I stare into the fire, my hands on my hips, and wait. He steps back when I stalk past, the fiery shoe hanging from the tongs. I tap Chili's nearside foreleg and he lifts it easily, as if that's the way he always behaves. I position his leg between my knees and place the shoe on his hoof, carefully, so it's in the exact right place, shaky hands or not. But I turn my face away too late. Thick white smoke gets in my eyes and goes up my nose. I sniff and squeeze my eyes tightly shut, but a minute passes before I can see properly again. I feel Blackwood's eyes on my back. Maybe Chili's eyes too? He knows the drill. Why am I taking so long?

I didn't notice the stillness before. There's no wind rustling through the trees, no baaing of sheep or mooing of cows from neighbouring properties, no cars on the road. I return to the anvil, compressing the shoe at the inside heel with strokes of the hammer. I measure it against Chili's foot but it's still not right, so I go back to the forge and heat it again. Back and forth between the forge and my horse and the anvil. When I dunk it into the pail for the final time, there's a hiss and then silence again.

I wipe my forehead on my sleeve. It's only just gone seven, too early in the day to sweat, for my hair to stick to my face.

'I'd like to make a time that suits you,' he says.

I speak over my shoulder as I take more nails and bunch them into my hand, loosening my grip when a pointed end juts into my palm.

'Like I told Edward, the answer is no.'

'He's contacted others who worked there. They'll talk if you don't.'

I face him. 'Is that a threat?'

'Edward would have explained the circumstances. I don't need this work. I'd like to get it done.'

'So do it.'

'Mike Williams defended you.'

'Leave Mike alone. He had nothing to do with Thornbrooke.'

'Didn't he?' He frowns. 'I simply want to ask him what he saw.'

'Didn't you hear what I said?' I lower my voice. 'Mike is elderly, he's been unwell.'

Blackwood shakes his head. 'Jet, what the hell is going on?'

I reach for the tongs and throw them in the toolbox. 'Call me Jemima.'

'You said no one calls you that.'

'No one I'm close to.' I wave my arm around, taking in the hill, the valley, the river, the town. 'No one from here.'

He curses under his breath. 'I need information about the horses, the condition they were in before they died, the circumstances of their deaths. I'll analyse available samples, then I'll write a report. That's it.'

'Do what you have to do.'

'It was Easter Monday, wasn't it? Only the stud manager and you were there.'

'Write what you want to write.' I pick up nails, putting them into my pocket. 'I have nothing to say.'

He runs his fingers around the back of his neck. His hair looks different when it's dry. It's short at the sides and slightly longer at the top.

'Damien Schofield, the vet, was called in later.'

I skirt around him to get to Chili. 'You're wasting your breath.'

'Anything other than eyewitness accounts are simply conjecture.'

'Are you sure you're a vet? You sound like a lawyer.'

I hammer in the nails, eight of them, and trim the ends that come through the hoof. I tidy Chili's feet with a rasp while Blackwood stands at his head, watching me closely.

'All I want is the truth.'

Squatting in the dirt, I wipe Chili's hooves with an oil-dampened sponge. His feet catch the light, glisten and sparkle. I stand and look up, shading my eyes with a hand. The sun is climbing higher, a bright yellow orb in a cloudless blue sky. It will shine again tomorrow, and the next day. I'm not in my bed, in the middle of a nightmare. I'm fully awake and know what to say. I won't break down here, not in front of him. Blinking hard, I turn abruptly.

And collide with his chest, hard and unmoving. He puts his hands on my arms to steady me, his grip above my elbows firm but impersonal. He smells nice. Masculine. Soap and fresh clean clothes. His fingers are long and lean and his nails are nicely shaped.

My hands are dirty and oily. There's blood on the tape on my thumb. An ache hammers deep in my chest.

'Let me go.'

He opens his hands.

I rub my arms.

His voice is quiet and measured. 'Talk to me, Jet.'

Talk to me, Jet? I want to shove him in the chest with my dirty broken nails, rip off the tape and show him what he's done. It's almost impossible to speak through the tightness in my throat.

'I told you to call me Jemima.'

He stiffens. 'As you wish.'

I throw tools into the box—the nail cutter, wire brush and rasp. I carefully place my hammer on the top. It was a gift from Mike. The day after my final exam, he tied a blue ribbon around the handle, drove all the way to Horseshoe, knocked on my door and gave it to me.

Blackwood reaches into an inside jacket pocket and pulls out a business card. His eyes are frosty blue. Our fingers touch. We both pull back.

'Should you wish to contact me about Kincaid House,' he says. 'Or Thornbrooke.'

The card is made of textured cardboard. The zoo logo is clear—a circle with three rhinos. A line of bold black letters stretches across the middle of the card. I suppose that's his name. There are a series of letters on the next line, most of them tall. They'll be capitals. It might be his credentials, his university degrees. Vets have a bachelor of science, but if he knows about genetics, he might have other qualifications as well. At the bottom of the card is a long string of digits. That'll be his numbers. I'd usually be able to make them out. Not today.

'Jemima?'

How long have I been staring at his card? Should I tell him to keep it? That reading's not one of my strengths? I put it in my pocket.

'Thanks,' I say, picking up the pail and pouring the murky grey water down the drain. When I straighten he's still there, his hands behind his back. 'I meant what I said about Mike. Leave him alone.'

'You trained under him, didn't you?'

'Only the last two years of my apprenticeship.'

I turn my back to squeeze soap on my hands from the dispenser in the ute, then rinse them under the tap.

'I'll be overseas for a couple of weeks,' he says. 'I'll see you when I get back.'

I stand on my toes to reach into the tray for a hand towel. 'Sure.' I fiddle with knobs on the forge, switch off the gas supply and disconnect the bottle. I lift it into the tray.

When he pats Chili's neck, I hear it. But not the words he mutters. He walks to the homestead and up the steps to the verandah, disappearing around the corner. The paint on the shutter is fresh, but the hinge is old and rusted. It'll squeak when he pulls the shutter aside to access the keys.

Twenty minutes later, after I've hitched the float to the tow bar and walked Chili and Lollopy up the ramp, his car turns out of the driveway and sweeps onto the road.

He's gone. For now.

CHAPTER
5

After I've finished my work at Follyfoot, a riding and therapy centre for children, I'll have to drive to Warrandale to warn Mike. I don't want to tell him about Blackwood, because he'll worry, but Blackwood said he'd be back in two weeks. I don't have much choice.

I've trimmed three horses' feet already. Dasher, a Welsh Mountain pony, is my fourth. When I release his hoof, he flicks his tail and turns towards me, as if wanting me to hurry up. I run a hand over his dappled-grey rump before walking to the edge of the concrete slab that's adjacent to the shed. The slab is protected from the weather by a corrugated-iron roof, held up by four metal posts. I have a clear view of the horses, riders, therapists and volunteers from here.

I shout to Chelsea on the far side of the arena. 'Great riding!' She sits even straighter on Cascade's back, and pushes down her heels as she rises to the trot. 'Keep it up.'

Chelsea is fourteen, and started riding at Follyfoot years ago. In her first session, she had trouble sitting astride because her legs were so stiff and painful. But she was determined to stay on a horse for longer next time, so worked on the exercises her physio suggested. Now, if she were allowed, she'd ride ten hours a day.

All the children at Follyfoot have challenges, physical or intellectual, sometimes both. Eight-year-old Darcy has a spinal deformity and needs help from three volunteers, one either side of him and one leading the horse. He leans forwards in the saddle over Lollopy's neck, supported by cushions at his chest, his fingers tangled tightly in the pony's thick black mane. Lollopy slows to a stop when a physio steps in front of him and holds up her hand. She adjusts Darcy's position a little, bringing his arms closer to his body. When he stiffens, she massages his back while Lollopy patiently stands. A minute passes, maybe more. But then Darcy nods and moves his heel, signalling he's ready to walk on. The only time I've seen him in tears is when it's time to get off his horse.

The arena has equipment in the middle, forty-four gallon drums used for games, poles fashioned into obstacles, and purpose-built mounting blocks. Some parents stay with their children and watch the sessions from the tiered seating at the far end of the arena; others use the opportunity to take a break. The program only runs once a week, but I reckon we could be fully booked every other day if the children had their way. On the first Friday of the month, I shoe the horses that need it, mostly those taken beyond the paddock and arena, and trim the others. On the other Fridays I prepare the horses and warm them up, and lead them around for the rest of the morning.

Chili Pepper stands out. He's over sixteen hands tall and strongly built, with a powerful head and neck. His coat, a rich red-brown, is just as glossy now as it was when Mum was alive. We're all amazed he's worked out so well. He's tolerant of unsteady weights on his back, unpredictable children who screech, and being led around at a snail's pace. We'd never have tried him out if Laurence, now nineteen years old and six feet tall, hadn't grown out of the other horses. He had a stroke when he was thirteen, no warning, just collapsed out of the blue in a maths exam. By the time the doctors worked out what had happened, he was paralysed down one side. He's now at university but the younger children love him, which is why we talk him into coming back every year.

'Jet!' he yells, his words a little slurred. 'What did you think of *Lethal White*?'

Laurence and I have a book club for two. He reads whatever book we choose, and I listen to the audio version of mine.

I point my file in his direction. 'For a crime book, it wasn't too bad.'

He laughs as, one handed, he shifts his body in the saddle, signalling to Chili to turn towards me.

'Your turn to choose next,' he calls.

There are straps attached to each side to the belt around his body, so the volunteers walking either side of him can, if needed, help keep him upright on the horse.

'How about *Great Expectations*? Have you read it?'

He laughs. 'Dickens again?'

'I like Dickens.'

My reading was as bad as it had ever been when my primary school librarian, Mrs McNab, put me onto audio books. Audio wasn't as accessible as it is now, and there were only limited CDs in the local libraries, so she introduced me to her personal collection. Her CDs were made up of nothing but classics, most of them English but many of them Scottish. There were novelists like Dickens and Robert Louis Stevenson, poets like Byron and Burns.

I found them hard to understand when I first started listening, but somehow the words drew me in. I guess it was the rhythm of the passages, the tone of the narrators, the ebb and flow of beginnings and middles and ends. I didn't have to decipher the look of the words; all I had to do was guess what they meant. The language made pictures in my mind.

I finally understood what books were all about.

'Jet?' one of the volunteers calls out. 'Have you finished with Dasher yet?'

By the time I lead Dasher out to the arena, Andreas, ten years old with big brown eyes, is pacing impatiently in front of the mounting block. He yells in excitement and throws his arms in the air when Dasher gets close. Dasher doesn't even blink; he's been at Follyfoot for years and is more or less bombproof.

I stand at the pony's head as helpers supervise Andreas, who doesn't like to be touched. They shadow Andreas's movements, guiding him up the mounting block without physical contact, while making sure Dasher stays perfectly still. It took months to get to the point where Andreas could learn, on his own, to safely mount a horse. Sometimes he'd get so agitated and angry about following directions, or wearing the safety belt, that we had to give up, and his mum would have to take him back to school. Now he climbs carefully onto the block and presses his body against the saddle. The helpers watch closely as he grips the pommel and cantle to haul himself onto Dasher's back. He places his feet in the safety stirrups and leans forwards, rubbing his face against Dasher's neck, draping his arms over the pony's shoulders, stroking and whispering.

'I think Andreas is happy to see you, boy,' I say, scratching under Dasher's chin.

Magda, a middle-aged woman with a generous smile, has volunteered at Follyfoot for years. She's an aunty to many members of her community, and like a favourite aunt to many here as well. She hands me a page to sign when I get back to the shed. It was only a few hours ago I couldn't read Blackwood's card, but on this piece of paper, a lot of the words are clear. Follyfoot. Farrier. Disbursements. But smaller words, the words most people would barely notice, I struggle with. An. It. Do. The harder I try, the worse that it gets. The letters reverse, turn upside down; often it's like they spin in the air. Should I have worked harder at reading when I was a child? Done more to unravel the mess in my mind?

Before Mum died, she encouraged me. And she threatened me—I wasn't allowed to ride my pony until I'd done the exercises set by the therapists. Dad had a different approach, doing whatever he could to make me happy. Which meant he did most of my homework. I suspect I missed my chance.

'Should I read it to you?' Magda says kindly, as I continue to study the page.

'It's listing the supplies that Follyfoot needs for the horses, isn't it?'

She pulls me against her, hugging me tightly. 'You're a good girl, Jet. Real good girl.'

I pull back and smile. 'If you've written size three shoes for the ponies, strike it out. Mike Williams has a stash he's keen to donate.'

She pushes her black curly hair off her face. 'How's Mike doing?'

'I'm heading out to Warrandale now. He's in remission again, but ...' I take a shaky breath. 'He's saying, whatever happens, he won't have more treatment. It made him so sick last time. He was in hospital for weeks, and he hates being away from home. And you know how he likes to be useful. It's taken months to get his energy back.'

'You send him love, won't you, from Follyfoot?' She sweeps an arm out wide. 'And from my family.'

'I'll let him know we all miss him. If I said the l-word, he'd get cranky.'

She smiles and wraps me in another hug. 'Mike is a lucky man, having a girl like you.'

I sniff as I hug her back. 'It's the other way around.'

CHAPTER
6

Mike and I met for the first time at a hotel in Armidale, at a gathering of farriers and apprentices. I didn't know many people, so was sitting by myself at a small table at the back of the lounge. Mike couldn't stand the noise near the bar, so he asked if he and a friend could join me.

Jackson McAdams was around twenty-five then, only six or seven years older than I, but he was making a name for himself already. He'd studied in England and the US, and was working at well-regarded racing stables. Not only that, he looked like Chris Hemsworth. I sat quietly while he and Mike talked and attempted, mostly unsuccessfully, to get me to contribute to the conversation. It turned out Mike's niece competed in three-day events like Mum, and he'd often seen her, and later me, on the competition circuit.

'Abigail Laney was a brilliant horsewoman,' he said. 'Won everything worth winning, and all with horses locally bred and trained.

She could've been selected for the Olympics, everybody said so, but she would've had to live in Europe to do that, and compete in more international events. She wouldn't do it.'

'Why not?' Jackson asked.

'It was hard for my father to travel,' I said. 'Mum refused to leave him.'

Jackson frowned. 'Why couldn't he—?'

'Right then!' Mike jumped to his feet. 'The barman's called last drinks. My shout.'

As I said goodbye, I overheard what Mike said to Jackson. 'Ross Kincaid never had luck on his side, but he'd give you the shirt off his back, and never had a bad word for anyone. He had guts. A damned good bloke.'

I didn't see Mike often in the next few months, but whenever I did he always pulled me aside and asked how I was doing. Mum and Dad's names sometimes came up, and he'd always have something nice to say.

U

Warrandale is almost two hours south of Dubbo, and well off the highway. It's a quiet little town with a picturesque street of shops and offices, and a pub. The park is large and well kept, sharing the same river that flows at a much faster rate through Horseshoe.

Mike's house, one of the few old Federation weatherboards still standing, is close to the centre of town. The porch is just as it always was, cluttered with odds and ends. I doubt Mike has ever thrown anything away that could, sometime in the future, be useful. When he doesn't answer my knock, I walk around the back. The shed doors are open and Mike is welding something at one of the benches. Rows of tools are stacked on shelves and hanging from hooks around him. I lean against the doorjamb until he notices me.

Last year he had radiotherapy. The year before that it was chemo. He was relieved when his hair, thick and white, grew back.

He takes off his protective glasses. 'Hello, Jet.' A smile creases his craggy old face, much thinner than it was. 'How long have you been there?'

'Not long. I didn't want to interrupt.'

'Ah, get on with you. Now I'm out to pasture, there's not much going on.'

I gesture to the muffler and pipe on the bench. 'What are you doing?'

'Tom's exhaust system is up the creek.' He wipes his hands. 'Time for a cuppa?'

'Sure. I told Mr Romano I'd be there at three to trim his alpacas.'

'It's good of you to step in for Jackson. It's a busy time of year for him.'

As we cross the yard, Artie Jones, who must be ninety by now, walks towards us. His back is rounded and he has a stick in each hand.

'Good afternoon, Miss Kincaid,' he says, nodding repeatedly before turning to Mike. 'Could we have a chat about the fete? And …' he pulls a torch from his bag, 'perhaps you can help me with this? The screws are rusted in place. I can't get the battery out.'

'No worries, Artie,' Mike says. 'I'll take a look.' He waves towards a bench under the tree near the gate. 'Put your feet up while I have a natter to Jet. Won't be too long.'

'Mike,' I say, as I follow him to his house. 'I can wait.'

He shakes his head. 'He's lonely, is all. The fete's not for months, and I looked at that torch last week. It must be as old as he is, which means he needs a new one. I'll make him a cuppa when you and me are done.'

Mike was born in his cottage, and is determined to die here. His laundry hangs over the backs of chairs, paperwork and newspapers blanket the dining table, and a radiator and various other car parts are spread out on a blue tarpaulin in front of the fireplace in the lounge. The only thing orderly in Mike's life is his shed, his farrier box and the tray of his ute. He looks around as if surprised to see so much stuff in the room, and then he harrumphs.

'Let's go into the kitchen,' he says.

He's never married, and doesn't have children of his own, but is close to his sister and her family. Unfortunately they live in Queensland, but I don't think he's lonely. He was apprenticed as a farrier at fifteen, but can make or fix just about anything. Long before I started working for him he mentored young men, giving them work experience in metalwork so they'd have a chance of employment in the bigger towns. And sick or not, he's always volunteered with the fire service.

After he's made the coffee, he joins me at the table in the kitchen. 'Everyone at Follyfoot says hello,' I say, 'especially Magda. And those pony shoes you offered? Remind me to take a few sets with me when I go.'

He stretches out a leg. 'I'll be back at Follyfoot soon.'

'You feeling okay?'

'I'm not dying this week, if that's what you're asking. The docs say the cancer will be back, there's no stopping that, but until it gets me proper, I might as well tick items off my bucket list.'

'What's on your bucket list?'

He frowns over his coffee cup. 'What are you looking so worried about? No Kilimanjaro for me, Jet. I want to work for as long as I'm able. On the social side, I'm keen to do the BBQ at the fete, and go to old Chambers's Christmas party, all dressed up with you on my arm.'

'So this year is sorted?'

'And so is next year, that's what I'm hoping.'

'It's good to hear that.'

'I'm sure it is, but I said much the same to you last week. You didn't come all this way for a cup of instant coffee and pony shoes. What's going on?'

I wrap both hands around my mug. 'It's Thornbrooke. Edward's looking into it.'

Mike wipes a hand over his face. 'Give it to me straight.'

'He's asked a vet, Finn Blackwood, to help him. If he can work out what happened, Edward thinks it'll increase the value of the horses in Rosethorn's line, and that'll make the stud more valuable.'

'Reckon it will,' Mike mutters, lowering his voice even further, as if we can be overheard. 'Who's this Blackwood fellow?'

'He's a scientist kind of vet, and he'll be at the zoo until early next year. I've told him and Edward that I have nothing to tell them. And that you don't have anything to say either.'

Mike's wrinkles deepen further. 'This was always on the cards.'

'After eight years?'

'People still talk about Thornbrooke.'

'Edward won't back down.'

'So back to the hornet's nest for you?' He slowly shakes his head. 'I did you a wrong turn, Jet.'

'You were trying to protect me.'

'That didn't work too well, did it?'

Morrissey, the stud manager, and Schofield, the vet, arrived at the stud not long after the fourth horse, Rosethorn, had died. None of us expected Mike to turn up at six in the morning on Easter Monday, to give a second opinion on a horse with a problem foot. When he arrived, I was sitting on a stepladder with a bowl in my lap, in case I threw up again. Morrissey and Schofield were asking me the same questions over and over.

Had I added the vitamin supplements to the feeds? Yes.

Which horses? All the horses stabled that night, twelve of them.

How much had I used? Whatever amounts were written on the chart.

Did I read the doses correctly? Yes.

Read this, then, just to make sure. They were standing either side of me. I was a quivering wreck by then. I couldn't have read a word to save my life.

All the horses at Thornbrooke had a pre-mixed bottle of supplement. It was one of my Sunday afternoon jobs to measure the amounts specified, combine the liquid with a small amount of feed, and give it to the horses. Dr Schofield must have made the supplements from legal substances, because the horses were often tested. But something had gone wrong.

I couldn't think straight any more. I knew I hadn't done anything wrong, but I couldn't articulate that. Mike had no way of knowing whether I'd done anything wrong or not, but whatever had happened, he didn't think I should be held responsible for it. He demanded to be shown the supplements, kept in a box in the feed room. And before anyone could stop him, Mike turned the box upside down and smashed all the bottles.

Morrissey argued that destroying the bottles made it appear that we had something to hide—that there was something wrong with the supplements, or I'd poisoned the horses by giving them too much. That's why he and Schofield came up with a plan. They worked out what the autopsy reports would say:

Death attributable to cardiac arrest and asphyxia. Possibly caused by food contaminant. Source unidentifiable.

I was so shaken by what had happened that I could barely see the rights or wrongs of it. The horses were dead. Nothing could bring them back. And I'd had a part in that, whether I'd administered the right dose or not. And then there was Mike. He got dragged into going along with the cover-up—the false autopsy reports, the destruction of paperwork.

Mike puts his coffee cup down and twists his hands together. 'I should never have started it. You're careful. If you can't read something yourself, you ask what it says. A leopard don't change its spots. You did nothing wrong.'

'When they were dying, I should have called others in.'

'You did your best. Anyway, Morrissey told you to wait until he got there. But …' He shakes his shaggy head. 'Whatever this Blackwood finds out, we'll both look as guilty as sin.'

'You were protecting me.'

'You were barely out of the schoolroom. You worked eight-hour weekdays shoeing horses. And then you laboured on weekends, for chicken feed, at the stud.'

'Morrissey didn't have to give me that job; I was happy to get it.'

'You paid a high price.'

I reach for my coffee. 'Blackwood mightn't find anything new. Morrissey isn't talking either. He'll want to protect his reputation.'

'What about your reputation?'

'I just want to forget it ever happened.'

'And how are you doing with that? You're peaky as hell.' When he glances at the tape on my hands, I hide them in my lap. 'You still getting those nightmares?'

I was working for another farrier when I was at Thornbrooke. He was good to me, and gave me leave after the horses' deaths. He was patient as well. But most of his work was at racing stables, and I couldn't face going back. When Mike worked that out, he offered me a job so I could finish my apprenticeship. When we had early starts near Warrandale, I used to sleep on a camp bed in the closed-in verandah at the back of the house. My screams would wake him up in the middle of the night.

'They've come back. I'll deal with them.'

'There's a woman I know, a psychologist; she often has a yarn with the young blokes in the fire service.'

'I'm okay, Mike.' I peer at his face, paler by the minute. 'Are you?'

He gets to his feet. 'Bit of a shock, that's all.' He tries to turn on a tap but doesn't seem to have the strength to twist it. With shaky hands, he puts the mugs in the sink.

'I figure Schofield was up to no good,' he finally says, 'the way he mixed those supplements. Maybe Morrissey too. That makes us, at best, accessories after the fact. You see it in the cop shows all the time.'

I join him at the sink and touch his arm. 'I only told you about it in case you heard it from someone else.'

He attempts a smile. 'It's not on my bucket list, Jet, going to jail.'

'You won't go to jail.' I take a deep breath. 'I'm not going to say anything and neither will Morrissey. Dr Schofield is dead.'

Artie Jones waves his stick in greeting as Mike and I walk to the shed to collect the shoes. I stand on a stepladder to reach them, and Mike holds it steady. Last year's surgery left a mottled circular scar at the side of his neck, and the arthritis in his hip is playing up again. He's not nearly as strong as he was.

I pat his arm, and he pats mine when we get to my ute. 'Try not to worry,' I tell him. 'Edward has leased the homestead to Black-wood. He told me he's going away for a while, but he's bound to turn up at the homestead after that. When I see him, I'll let him know you don't want to talk to him any more than I do.'

CHAPTER

7

My stores of horseshoes are kept in boxes in the shed, stacked in size order from smallest to largest. I pack the ute with the ones I'm likely to need for horses booked in for tomorrow and Tuesday, before checking the gauges on the gas bottles. The landline, wired up so I can hear it from the shed, rings loudly as I walk along the path to the cottage. I take the steps two at a time.

'Jet Kincaid.'

'Finn Blackwood. I'll be at Horseshoe soon. I thought I should let you know.'

When he didn't turn up yesterday, I'd hoped to avoid him for another weekend. 'How long will you be staying?'

'Two nights.'

'Right.'

'I presume you're working tomorrow.'

'Yes.'

'May I speak with you this afternoon?'

'What about?'

'Thornbrooke. It won't take long. I'll come to you. Four o'clock?'

'I'd prefer to see you at the homestead.'

After I take my washing off the line and sweep the verandah, I wash my hands, squeezing my fingers on a towel to get the moisture out of the strapping tape. I smooth down my hair, tightening the ponytail and putting loose ends behind my ears. I'm not sure why I make the effort, when my shirt is so faded the blue has turned to grey, and my jeans are stained with rust and threadbare at the knees. I'm folding the washing when I hear Blackwood's car on the gravel. By the time I've made a salad for tonight and a sandwich for lunch tomorrow, it's almost four.

I rub my arms as I walk to the homestead, and up the steps to the verandah. The skies are clear blue, but a breeze cools the air. I watered the jasmine this morning and the earth in the pots is still damp. Wisteria vines, thickened with age, twist around the posts. Come October, less than two months away, there'll be leaves and purple blooms. I take a deep breath, raise my hand and knock.

When I hear footsteps, I imagine him striding down the gunbarrel hallway. He opens the door.

My breath catches. 'Oh!'

'Jemima.'

He has a black eye, the upper lid swollen and red, the lower lid marked with blue-and-purple shadows. I hide a wince as my gaze slides to his mouth. A jagged red line runs through his bottom lip and an angry blue bruise marks the top.

My hand lifts involuntarily. 'What happened?'

'I was mugged on Friday night.' His lips barely move.

'*What?* In Dubbo?'

'Around ten at night.' He touches his eye and flinches. 'Three men. The hotel manager called the police. Alcohol, drugs. It happens.'

'Did they get your wallet? Your phone?'

'No.' He fingers his lip.

'Three against one?'

'It was nothing.'

If you think you're indestructible. 'Did you run?'

'I defended myself.'

'What?'

'They were men, not adolescents.' He frowns. 'I'll take a few days off.' He stands back. 'Come in.'

'I … can we talk here?' I wave over my shoulder. 'I always put the horses in the home paddock in the evenings. I don't have long.'

'It won't be dark for over an hour.' Even bashed up, his eyes are brilliant blue. Is he paler than usual? His lashes look particularly dark. 'I won't keep you.'

The homestead is at least three times the size of my cottage. The original lounge and dining rooms, and two bedrooms, are off the hall, and there are three other bedrooms, with en suite bathrooms, in the new part of the house. There's a modern living area and kitchen in that wing as well, with views across the valley.

Blackwood walks into the lounge room and I follow. The kindling is layered on top of the newspaper in the fireplace grate, just as I left it. I add to the pile, taking twigs from the basket. When I feel his eyes on my back, I slowly stand upright.

'I guess I'm not responsible for this.'

'No.' He shakes his head as if to clear it, and gingerly touches his eye. 'Sit down, Jemima.'

I cross my arms. 'I'd prefer to stand. Say what you want to say.'

He leans on the back of an armchair. He's informally dressed, a thin black sweater with a V-neck, jeans and boots.

'I have serum samples and test results from racing authorities, and a number from the stud.'

'Right.'

'Damien Schofield, and probably Darren Morrissey, appear to have destroyed much of the data, but they didn't get all of the records.' There's a dot of fresh blood on his lip, and I try to focus on that. 'Edward has found information kept by the accountants, invoices and receipts.'

My face feels stiff when I speak. 'He's given this to you?'

He runs his hand around the back of his neck. 'He intends to. It may be significant, it may not.'

I look through the window, the way it frames my cottage. Sapphie says that because I take care of the homestead, I might as well live in it. And if I'd ever asked Edward if I could, he probably would have agreed. But I've never aspired to live anywhere else but home. I don't need fancy furniture and appliances, en suite bathrooms.

'Was there anything else you wanted to say?'

'Yes. What are you hiding?'

The lump in my throat expands. 'Edward said you were reluctant to take this on, you didn't want to help him.'

'I didn't.'

'So why are you looking at invoices and all those other things?'

He touches his lip, grimaces. 'We have to go with what we have. There's little scientific evidence. You've never said anything. Morrissey insists Schofield's investigation was adequate.'

'Thornbrooke is over.'

'It's not. Edward's been inundated with messages, so have I. From racing people, equine vets, breeders. They all want to know what happened.'

I gaze out of the window again. Cotton-ball clouds, white and thick, blow in from the west. They hide the sun. I shiver.

'Can I go? I have work to do.'

He takes a step towards me. 'All I want is to get to the truth.'

'Or your version of it.' I walk to the fireplace and grip the mantelpiece. Blackwood is reflected in the gold-framed mirror. Our eyes meet.

'Was there a cover-up?' he says.

I turn. 'I have nothing to say to you.'

'Edward isn't going to let this go.'

'He cares about his investment.' When I link my hands in front of me, my knuckles turn white. 'I should have done more than I did. When the horses got sick, I should have called others in. That's the truth.'

'What was Morrissey doing? Wasn't he there too? What about Schofield?'

'I don't know.'

His face is set. 'You're lying.'

'I don't care what you think!'

'Mike Williams. I want to see him.'

I count to ten as I look around the room—polished floors, a rug in front of the fireplace, an antique partner's desk with a leather-cornered mat, old-fashioned armchairs.

'Mike came to Thornbrooke after everything was over,' I say quietly. 'I was upset. He took me away. That's what he said at the time. It's all he'd have to say now.'

'You seem sure about that.'

'I saw him a couple of weeks ago.'

'To get your stories straight?'

'Leave Mike alone!'

He touches his lip with his thumb, before walking to a painting that hangs on the far side of the room. Sheep, their wool sparse and scrappy, forage for grass near a creek bed. He tilts his head as if closely examining the brush strokes. Finally he turns.

'You never went back to Thornbrooke, did you? Or to the farrier you worked for at the time?'

I walk to the door. 'I'm going.'

'Jemima! Tell me …' He touches his lip. 'Fuck!'

He holds his fingers against his lip, bleeding properly now. He opens the desk drawers one by one. They rattle when he slams them shut.

I push him out of the way as I yank paper from the desk mat, folding it before grasping his arm and angling it over his lip. He stands as still as a statue. His breath is soft on my fingers.

'Am I pressing too hard?'

'No.' He covers my hand with his much larger one. He frowns as he touches the tape on my thumb. 'I can do this.'

I ignore the heat that spreads from my hand to my arm. 'You can't see the split.'

When I reposition the paper, he lowers his hand and looks into my eyes as if searching. For information? Evidence? The truth? As soon as I lift the paper, the bleeding starts again. I can't walk out. Not yet.

He speaks quietly. 'I met Mr and Mrs Hargreaves.'

'I don't think you should talk right now.'

'How long have they run the general store?'

'Pretty much forever. Thanks for shopping there. I know Dubbo is cheaper.'

'They've known you since you were a child?'

I look away. 'Since I was born.'

He puts his hand over mine again. His is much cooler. 'Do they know anything about Thornbrooke?'

'No more than anybody else.'

'Nothing, then.'

One of my hands is trapped under his. My other hand is on his chest. The fabric of his sweater is soft beneath my fingers. His heart thumps strongly against the inside of my wrist. Or is that the beat of my pulse? I know why his eyes are so dark. Steel grey shards shoot through the blue.

'Did you go to the doctor about your mouth? Your eye?'

'No.'

'Maybe you need stitches.'

'I don't.'

'How do you know?'

'I'm a vet.'

'You should get a second opinion.'

He hesitates. 'Why do you care?'

'Because …'

Frowning, he pulls the paper from under my fingers. And then he folds it carefully, before pressing it to his mouth again. The bruise on his top lip is raised and round. A knuckle?'

'I can't make you out,' he says quietly. 'Thornbrooke. Don't you want to settle it?'

'That's what you want to do.' I curl my fingers into my palm, feel the bulkiness of the tape. 'All I want to do is to forget.'

CHAPTER

8

The following Saturday afternoon, Blackwood's car bumps over the cattle grate and up the driveway. As he passes the shed, I balance the bucket of soapy water on the bonnet of my ute and wave vaguely over my shoulder.

He stops and winds down his window. 'Jemima.'

I turn. The bruise on his eye has faded, as has the redness of the split in his lip. 'Dr Blackwood.'

'Finn, please.'

'How's your mouth?' The words are out before I think them through. *Why didn't I ask about his eye?*

'Healing.' He looks from me to my ute and back again. 'How often do you wash your car?'

I stand on the step of the passenger door and pull the sponge from the bucket. 'Every couple of weeks when there's water. Mike had a thing about it, cleaning bugs from the bumper and windscreen.'

By the time he drives on, I'm scrubbing marks off the roof, and the front of my hoodie is wet. Doors slam. He disappears into the homestead. Ten minutes later, as I wipe the windows and dash, my heart rate slows to normal.

'Jet!' I turn to see Sapphie, riding Chili in the paddock by the river. Chili pricks up his ears as he nears the fallen red gum. It was a tree I leapt over when I used to ride, and one of its branches marks Liam's grave. Sapphie leans forwards as Chili jumps, clearing the log by a mile. The sun is still out and his chestnut coat glistens.

Sapphie sits back in the saddle, slowing Chili down, and waves as they canter up the well-worn path. Her hair, dark brown and plaited, flies out behind her.

'You're home early,' she shouts. 'Won't be long.'

I rode from when I could walk. The first time Sapphie climbed into a saddle she was sixteen years old, and had only just moved to Horseshoe. Mr and Mrs Hargreaves, her foster parents, couldn't afford to buy her a horse of her own, so Dad told her she could come to him for lessons. She was a year younger than me, but much too big for Lollopy, and we'd sold my other horses, so he put her on one of Mum's retired showjumpers. Sapphie had gentle hands and a good seat, determination and grit. Within a year she was good enough to ride Chili.

It took a long time for us to trust one another. It was hard to understand how someone as beautiful and smart as she was could be so withdrawn and unhappy. But after Dad died, she still came to the cottage, even when the weather was bad or it was too dark to take Chili out. We tiptoed around each other. She didn't like to talk about her family, and why she came to Horseshoe, so I did my best not to pry. When I spent weekends at Thornbrooke, she used to look after my horses. We cried together when her birth mother died; when she did well at school, we celebrated. She boarded with one of my clients when she studied at university. Now she's a teacher and works at the primary school in Horseshoe.

I rest the broom against the open-sided stable and walk through the small fenced yard. Lollopy blocks my way to the paddock, leaning against the wire in the hope of being fed. He bustles past as soon as the gate swings wide, pausing near the tap to eat the shoots of new grass growing near the drain.

'Good ride?' I say, closing the gate behind Chili.

'Always.'

Sapphie's real name is Sapphire, and she has the darkest blue eyes I've ever seen. She smiles as she leans low to pat Chili's neck, sticky with sweat. Throwing her long leg over Chili's rump so she's facing me, she jumps to the ground and takes his rein. 'When he's cooler I'll brush him down, then we'll do your accounts.'

'Thanks. Coffee?'

She takes off her hat. 'Please.'

I'm sitting at the kitchen table, bills spread out in piles around me, when I hear Sapphie's voice, and Blackwood's. I take a deep breath and try to refocus. When the front screen door slams shut, I jump.

'Jet!' Sapphie calls.

'In here.'

She throws herself on the chair next to me, stretching out her legs and crossing them at the ankles. 'I met Finn.' She whistles. 'Why didn't you warn me?'

'About what?'

'Ma Hargreaves said he was handsome, but she says that about any male under eighty. When you told me he was a friend of Edward's, I pictured something different.'

'Not bashed up?'

She grimaces. 'In Dubbo of all places. But that's not what I meant and you know it.'

I pour the coffee. 'He's good-looking.'

'You *could* say that.' She whistles silently. 'And he's fit. He's got great gear.'

'What?'

She raises her brows. 'Climbing equipment. He was heading down to the river.'

'Right.' When I put a pile of invoices in front of her, she picks them up and lines up their edges.

'Pa told me what he's doing with Thornbrooke,' she says, tipping her head to the side. 'Can't you let it go?'

I pour milk into my coffee and stir until it spins. 'I have let it go. He wants to bring it back.' I push more papers her way. 'There might be nothing to find, but it scares me anyway.'

'I'm sorry it's so hard.'

'I don't have words a lot of the time, you know that.' I take a deep breath. 'But images, pictures in my head … I have a lot of those.'

Sapphie pretends an interest in my paperwork. 'Let me know if I can help.'

'Thanks.' I clear my throat. 'What have you got for me to do this afternoon?'

She looks up and grins. 'Really? Do you mind?'

A lot of people know that Sapphie is involved in just about all of Horseshoe's community activities, and is also good at sports. Not everyone knows that she makes flowers. She opens her bag and gets out a stack of crepe paper, each sheet a mottled shade of burgundy.

'How did you make it this colour?'

'A tea wash.' She hands me a small cardboard template, shaped like a wobbly hourglass, and scissors. 'Trace around it thirty-six times. And then cut out the pieces.'

'Thirty-six?'

She smiles. 'Six flowers, six outer petals. Thirty-six.'

'How many different-shaped petals will each flower have?'

'Four or five. But we won't get to the others today.'

Sapphie explained it to me once—how flowers made petal by petal are perfectly imperfect, just like real flowers are.

'What type of flowers are you making?'

'Dahlias. Next month it's red-gum blossoms. We're doing plant groups in geography.'

'How's your class?'

'My senior kids? Ten to twelve year olds? You know they're the best.'

'You say that whatever age group you have.'

When I pick up the scissors, she raises her brows. 'What have you done to yourself?'

I carefully thread my thumb through the hole. 'I had a difficult day at work. I broke a couple of nails.'

Sapphie is good at reading people. I'm not much of a liar. She frowns. 'It's Thornbrooke, isn't it? Nightmares again?'

'I thought they'd gone.' I shrug. 'I'll be okay.'

She sorts through my accounts, making sure I've paid my debts and correctly ordered the supplies I'll need for the next few weeks. When she writes anything down, she prints in large rounded letters, widely spaced. She tells me she does it like that because she's a teacher, even though we both know the truth.

By the time Sapphie puts fresh cups of coffee on the table, the sun is going down. Before she sits, she flicks on the lights.

'You're not seeing anyone, Jet, are you?'

I add a petal to the row in front of me. 'Luke Martin and I have been out a few times.'

'Just as friends?'

'That's right. Why do you ask?'

'Finn said something about you being busy all the time. I think he was curious. Does he like you?'

'No way.'

She laughs. 'When was the last time you dated?'

'I don't know … last year I guess. I went out with Rob.'

'I never saw him here.'

'He never stayed over or anything.' I shrug. 'He was getting his flying hours up, crop-dusting in the north a lot of the time.'

'Isn't he engaged to Sally now?'

'I introduced them. I'm going to be one of her bridesmaids.'

'No heartbreak then?'

'Rob and I were never serious.'

'Have you *ever* been serious?'

'I have a lot of friends. Like you do.'

'You have platonic relationships with men who turn into lifelong friends. I have sex with men I never want to see again. What will become of us?'

I put down the scissors and paper and stretch out my fingers. 'I'll paraphrase Mrs Bennet from *Pride and Prejudice*. No one could be as good and kind and pretty as you, without a very good reason.' When she opens her mouth to interrupt, I hold up my hand. 'And that means, if you ever wanted a man to spend more than a night with, there'd be a queue a kilometre long.'

She laughs. 'In the meantime, I'll make flowers from Italian crepe paper, and you'll listen to audio books.'

'And what's the problem with that?'

She picks up the petals and stows them carefully in an envelope. 'The problem for you is, I think you'd like a family.' She smiles sadly. 'I'm not sure I'll ever be ready for that.'

When I walk Sapphie to her car, a chorus of kookaburras laughs from the red gum.

'Will you be at trivia next Saturday night?' she asks. 'It's starting up again. I can't believe winter's almost over.'

'Sure. I'll be there.'

She glances at the homestead. 'How long will Finn be staying weekends?'

'He'll be at the zoo until early next year.'

'Why don't you go away for a while, have a break? It could do you good.'

'I have a business to run. Anyway, I want to be here for Mike. Thornbrooke upsets him too.'

'You've seen Finn down at the river, right?'

'Yes.'

'He likes to climb.'

'You said he had climbing equipment?'

She opens the door. 'Ropes, carabineers, pulleys, all European.'

'He didn't use ropes last time.'

'He free-climbed?'

'Assuming that means climbing without ropes, yes.'

'It's better to do it in pairs. He must have known what he was doing.'

'Which is exactly what he said. When he was near the top, I offered to take his hand. I don't think that impressed him.'

She grimaces. 'That's not how climbing works.'

'I wasn't thinking straight. I was scared he'd break his neck.'

Abacus was a warmblood, black except for a startling white sock on his near front leg. Dad stood at his head as Mum swung onto his back and tightened the reins.

'Keep him steady at the wall,' Dad said. 'He'll need to take his time over it.'

Mum smiled. 'Don't worry. I know what I'm doing.'

She blew us a kiss, and then tipped her hat. She bent low over Abacus's neck and patted him firmly. They walked away, out of the clearing under the ironbark trees where Dad had parked the truck.

Dad hadn't been well, so Mum had insisted he rest after lunch, at least until it was time for her to compete in the showjumping round, day three of her event. The junior competition had taken place earlier in the morning and my blue ribbon hung from the rear-view mirror. Sunshine, my horse, wearing a bright red rug to keep off the flies, was tied to the rear of the truck and greedily pulling hay out of a net. I was sitting like Dad was, in a deckchair with my feet up on an esky. I didn't want to stay behind while Mum warmed up on the jumps, but she and I knew that if I got up to follow, Dad would get up too.

Like Mum said, he had to rest. He even got sleepy after a while and closed his eyes. His breathing was raspy, but that was nothing unusual. It was lucky I sensed something was wrong in the arena, because nobody came to find us. I guess they were too busy calling the paramedics, and making sure the emergency doctors would be available at the hospital. Everyone said it was good we didn't see the accident. As it turned out, I saw plenty anyway.

We were parked on the far side of the ground in the shade; the leaves skimmed the roof of the truck. The loudspeaker was so far away that you couldn't hear what the announcer said, unless you listened carefully. But all of a sudden, there was nothing to hear anyway. Maybe that's how I knew. Because Mum and the other riders should have walked the course already and finished warming up. The competition should have started. Abacus was ranked second after the first two rounds, so would have been competing second last. That's why I'd let Dad snooze—I'd thought we had plenty of time.

It's not often that so many people make so little noise. As I got closer to the arena, I saw the paramedics, a man and a woman, sprinting ahead of me. And then I saw Abacus. He was less experienced than Chili, but Mum had thought it would be good for him to compete in a first-class event. It didn't matter whether he did well or not, because she'd already qualified for the overall championships at the end of the month. But as it turned out, Abacus won the dressage—unusual for one of Mum's horses—and completed the cross-country course with only a handful of penalties. Showjumping was his weakest event because he was easily spooked by the jumps, but it was Mum's favourite. She reckoned they balanced each other out.

Someone held Abacus's rein, I'm not sure who, and had wound up the stirrups on his saddle. The big black horse was standing perfectly still, looking down at the ground like he was curious about something. So even if I hadn't caught up with the paramedics, I would've known exactly where to go. No one held me back, how could they? I was fast for my age. Not only that, the paramedics cleared my way. I was snapping at their heels like a kelpie after sheep.

Mum had snapped her neck.

I overheard a conversation afterwards, how she should have died immediately, but didn't. I crouched in low beside her. She looked straight at me, her blue eyes wide. She didn't make a sound, she couldn't. But her mouth opened slowly. Her lips formed a word.

Jemima.

CHAPTER
9

I'm pulling onto the road on Thursday, after shoeing my fifth horse of the day, when my phone rings. It's eleven o'clock and the sun is high in the sky.

'Hello, Jet. Andrew Martin here.'

'What's up?'

'Can you look at one of the takhi colts? Batu hurt himself last week, mucking around with one of the other colts. We anaesthetised him and stitched the wound, but he's still favouring the leg. We've got him in a yard at the enclosure.'

'I could be there in an hour and a half.'

'Great. We'll sort Batu out, then I'll shout you lunch.'

Andrew is one of the most senior vets at the zoo. The specialists there know just about everything about the animals, but sometimes want a second opinion on a hoof problem, or the best ways to go about treating it. I used to tag along with Mike when he worked on the zoo animals, but since he's been unwell, Andrew has been calling me more and more often. Except when an elephant is in trouble: Mike has a special relationship with them.

As soon as I get to the zoo, I change into a keeper's uniform, because when working on the zoo animals, I have to guard against contamination from domesticated animals. Andrew, in his late fifties and wearing a crisply ironed shirt, meets me at the animal clinic. We hop into a buggy, like a golf cart, and drive to the takhi enclosure, accessed via the kilometres of bitumen paths that wind around the zoo.

'Will Batu be anaesthetised?' I ask.

Andrew shakes his head. 'He's sedated, and remarkably cooperative. He was treated regularly as a foal because he had gut problems, and that's paying off now. You'll be able to examine him safely.'

Takhi horses are kept at the zoo because they're endangered, and part of the zoo's conservation and breeding program. Most of them look like Batu, a light beige colour with darker chocolate markings on their legs and along their spines, a stiff mane like a zebra, and a short bushy tail. Batu's eyes are big, brown and anxious.

'I can't find a problem with the leg,' Andrew says, passing me a box of sterilised farrier tools.

'You can see it's his foot from how he's standing.'

There's another vet, and four keepers, in the yard. It takes a little manoeuvring, but Batu eventually lifts his hoof. I squat next to him and carefully pare away at the rough underside of his sole. When I get to a section near the frog, the soft triangle of thickened skin that acts like a pump, pushing blood up through the hoof, he flinches.

'That hurts, boy, doesn't it?'

I continue to work as Andrew watches on, looking out for signs of discomfort. We can't handle many wild animals like this, even though keepers work hard to encourage them to cooperate in their treatments. The alternative is a full anaesthetic, which always carries risks. I scrape some more, finding a section of sole that's slightly darkened. I rub at it with my thumb.

'See the bruise?' I say. 'Could be he's just landed awkwardly on a stone, or something sharp.'

'You don't think there's an infection? We couldn't see any cracks or punctures in the radiography.'

'I wouldn't dig deeper with a horse, so I'm not going to do that with him.'

'What next then?'

'Continue to restrict his movement, and poultice him for twenty-four hours. If there's an infection further up the hoof, the poultice should draw it out. If there isn't, if it's just a bruise, no harm done.'

Andrew smiles. 'Let's get to it then.'

An hour later, we drive past the rest of the takhi herd, grazing in their enclosure. When a stiff wind whistles through the trees, stirring up leaf litter and dust, the herd takes flight, charging across the ground. Most of the large animals at the zoo are kept in their enclosures by moats, broad steep trenches with fences along the spines. It's a more natural environment for the animals, and the visitors get a better view.

'Busy afternoon ahead?' Andrew asks.

'Thursdays are always busy, but not as bad as Fridays. I'd better change before lunch. Can we go back via the clinic?'

We drive past herds of addax and eland, different breeds of deer. An adult male rhino, part of the African exhibit, lies in the shade of a tree. I change quickly, but by the time we leave the clinic, my stomach is rumbling every few minutes.

The café is adjacent to a picnic ground. A group of school children gather in a circle on the grass, eating from lunch boxes. We order at the counter and sit at a small round table on the terrace.

'Delicious,' Andrew says, fifteen minutes later, as he finishes the last of his pie. 'How was the sandwich?' I have my mouth full, so nod and hold up my thumb. Andrew waves as he looks over my shoulder.

'Finn! Catriona! Over here!'

I take a napkin from the stand on the table and, without looking up, carefully wrap the remaining half of my sandwich.

'I'd better get going.'

'Don't rush off.'

Finn, an iPad in his hand, walks into the café and lines up at the counter. He's only at the zoo temporarily. Is that why he's dressed in a dark blue shirt and pants, not the khaki shirt with a logo that the other vets wear? The woman he's with is about his age, tall and attractive, dressed in a zoo shirt like Andrew's. When she laughs, Finn laughs too.

Andrew brushes crumbs off his lap. 'Have you met Finn?'

'Yes.'

'We couldn't believe our luck when he agreed to join us, if only temporarily. He has a doctorate in genetics and a first-class reputation in the field.'

'We didn't talk about the zoo.'

Andrew grimaces. 'Ah. Thornbrooke.'

I nod stiffly. 'You know about it?'

'Edward Kincaid is a zoo sponsor, and a generous one. He asked for a recommendation and I supplied it. Finn is eminently qualified to look into what occurred.'

I push my chair back. 'I bet he is.'

Finn's shadow crosses the table. 'Andrew, Jemima.'

The discolouration under his eye has faded and the swelling has gone down, but his eyelid is purple. A narrow red line marks the split through his lip.

'Jet?' Andrew says.

Am I flustered because I didn't see Finn's outstretched hand? Or because of the press of his palm?

'Dr Blackwood.'

He frowns. 'Finn.' And turns to the woman. 'Catriona Webb. Jemima Kincaid.'

'Jet to her friends,' Andrew says, as she and I shake hands. 'Catriona is one of our newest vets on staff. She specialises in ungulates.'

'Giraffes, right?' I say. 'Mike Williams mentioned you. I work with him sometimes.'

'He wasn't too well when I saw him last,' she says. 'How's he doing now?'

'Much better, thank you.'

Andrew stands. 'Please, join us,' he says.

Catriona shakes her head. Her hair is shiny and brown, cut short with a fringe. 'Duty calls. I have to get back to the clinic, lend a hand with a cheetah.'

'Lardosa?' Andrew says. 'I wanted a word about him, so I'll walk you out. Finish your lunch, Jet. Keep Finn company until I get back.'

Finn picks up another chair, positioning it between Andrew's and mine. 'You were working here today?' he says.

I thought I'd imagined the shade of his eyes. I hadn't. 'Yes.'

His brows lift. 'In what capacity?'

'Batu is lame. He's a takhi.'

'What other animals do you treat?'

'Deer, occasionally giraffe. I've helped Mike with zebras a couple of times. I only look at their hooves, that's all. Obviously.' I reach for my bag. 'Look, I'd better get back to work.'

He leans forwards in his chair, linking his hands and placing them on the table. 'I won't be at Horseshoe this weekend. We could talk now, or make a time for the following weekend. Which would you prefer?'

My long-sleeved shirt has been washed a million times, so the denim is pale and soft. But the cuffs are worn, and one of the buttons near my belt has fallen off. I overlap the folds of fabric, hiding the gap.

'I may as well get it over with. Hurry up before Andrew gets back.'

He nods towards my sandwich. 'Are you going to eat?'

'Later.' I put the sandwich in my bag.

Andrew and Catriona are on the path now, Andrew nodding intently as they talk. A few of the school children bundle onto the terrace, talking and laughing. The waiter holds Finn's coffee aloft as they pass, then puts it on the table with a flourish.

Finn picks up his spoon, before putting it back in the saucer. 'Analysing the samples will take time.'

I reach for my glass, wrapping my hands around it. 'Right.'

'The way the horses behaved in the lead-up to the deaths—Morrissey is sticking with his original statement. You've never said anything.'

When he sips from his cup, I put my glass to my lips. My thumbnail is a mess from last night and I meant to tape it before I left for work. The quick at the side is torn and a strip of skin beneath the cuticle is angry and red. He watches me put the glass onto the table. There's a crease between his brows. I hide my thumb in my fist.

'Others who worked at the stables have told me what they know,' he says. 'When Edward's papers come through, I'll look at them.'

'Okay.'

When he opens his iPad and sits it between us, a large rhino appears on the screen. His feet are planted firmly in the dirt. His head is down. He has two horns at the front of his head, one large, one smaller.

Rhinos are brutal. Dangerous. Finn? I suspect he's not afraid of anything either.

When he touches keys, the rhino disappears. I see a document, pale green in colour, covered in handwritten words.

'This is Morrissey's statement,' he says. 'It was also signed by Schofield, and records their version of events. It was written the day after the deaths.'

I look away, to the elderly couple sitting at the table next to us. The man pours tea from a teapot into the woman's cup. She smiles her thanks.

'It's only a page, Jemima. Read it. Tell me your thoughts.'

There are a series of paragraphs; many are short, others are long. The words are … Roman? Arabic? Cantonese? I'd be too anxious to make sense of them even if I wanted to. The movement of the symbols, the way they bounce and sway, makes me nauseous. I focus on the children at the counter. One has a Coke, another a juice. The third child, a little boy, unwraps an ice cream on a stick. When my vision clears, I turn back to Finn.

So now he's the quiet one? Watching, waiting. I could tell him I can't read, not right now, anyway. It's no secret. Most people who live in Horseshoe, and many outside of it, know I have a problem—that words that make sense one day, don't make sense the next.

'Jet? I want to get to the truth.'

I can't read Morrissey's story, but that doesn't mean I don't know what it is. Every letter, every word, every sentence. Every variation of the truth. He and Schofield only arrived after the horses had died, but they didn't want people to know that. I'd sobbed details of some of what I'd seen. Morrissey made sure this was consistent with the autopsy reports that Schofield would write.

'I don't have any thoughts.' I slowly rotate the glass. 'And call me Jemima.'

He slams the iPad shut. *'Jemima.'* He stretches out the syllables. 'Is that better?'

'Yes.'

'Edward often refers to you as Jet.'

'I wish he wouldn't.'

His mouth is firm. 'Tell me what's going on.'

I grip the table and stand. 'You'd better get back. Edward will want a report. I have clients waiting. If you see Andrew, tell him I said goodbye.'

He stands too. 'I'll report to Edward when I have something to say.'

The lump in my throat expands. Blackwood's not confused and unsettled. He's clever and powerful. Just like Edward, Morrissey and Schofield. I'm in their shadows, trapped like a mouse.

When I step back, my chair scrapes the concrete. My eyes sting. I reach blindly for my bag and bundle it under my arm. The elderly couple looks towards me, then quickly away. A café worker hovers in the background.

'Why does this scare you so much?' His voice is quiet. His expression is wary, cautious, his eyes are dark. I study the weave of his shirt, the narrow threads of linen. When I held the paper against his mouth, I put my hand on his chest. I felt the steady beats of his heart.

'Maybe I'm not very brave.'

When he holds out his hand, I take it automatically. But he doesn't shake as I expect. He holds on, palm to palm. We're close, so close I see a hundred shades of blue in the bruising of his eye. His gaze slips to my mouth. I stare at his.

'Does it still hurt?' I whisper.

He lifts my hand with his. And then he runs his knuckle along his lip. I feel his breath on the backs of my fingers.

'A little,' he mumbles.

An ache thrums deep in my abdomen.

'Ready to go?' Andrew waves from the counter.

I tug my hand free and take a giant step back. Finn calmly picks up his iPad. His nails are short, with neat white tips.

'I'll see you the weekend after next,' he says.

'Right.' I turn away.

'Jemima? One last question.'

I face him again. 'What?'

'Morrissey said the stallion, Rosethorn, was the last to die. Is that correct?'

When I grasp the back of the chair, my bag slips down my arm and dangles from my wrist.

Since breakfast, I've eaten half a sandwich.

It rises up my throat and gags me.

U

I was outside Rosethorn's stable, sitting on the ground next to Blackjack. The tethering ring had pulled out of the wall and he'd collapsed. I stroked his neck, his cheek, rubbed around his ears. But just as it had been with the other two horses, there was nothing I could do. Nothing. *Not even get his eyes closed.*

When I'd left Rosethorn's stable, he'd been on the ground. I hadn't heard him while I'd been with Blackjack, but now I could. I dragged myself to my feet and walked across the aisle. I'd closed the bottom half of his stable door, but the top half must have shut too. I put my hand on the latch. My fingers were scraped and bleeding from trying to undo the knots. I remember thinking, *They must hurt.* But I couldn't feel a thing.

I heard Rosethorn's hooves as they crashed on the walls. *I didn't open the door.*

I heard his moans. *I didn't open the door.*

I heard his snorts, his laboured breath. *I didn't open the door.*

Tears and snot ran down my face. 'Shhh. Shhh.'

I could have been brave but I wasn't.

Rosethorn died alone.

CHAPTER
10

The next eight days pass by in a blur, so the next time I see the takhi it's after four o'clock on Friday afternoon. My boots scuff the ground because I'm tired. And even though the collar of my jacket is up and my hands are in my pockets, I'm cold. But it's impossible not to smile when Batu, spooked by the wind, tosses his head, swishes his thick bushy tail and canters around the enclosure with the other colts.

'He looks sound to me,' I say to Andrew.

'You were right about the bruising.' He puts an arm at my back. 'Are you okay to drive home?'

'What do you mean?'

'You're shivering and holding in yawns.'

An hour later, when I turn off the road and into my driveway, I see Gus's ancient green tractor through the gloom, parked in the paddock near the gate. Gus is in his late seventies but, except at shearing time, runs his property more or less on his own. When I was a child and there were no lambs or pregnant ewes in his herd, he taught me how to round up sheep on my pony. He still keeps an eye on me, but he never usually comes to the cottage after dark. Maybe he wants to borrow something?

I'm walking up the path, my bag slung over my shoulder, when he comes into view. He's on the cottage's verandah, leaning on the railing with his back to me. All that's left of the sun is a fuzzy golden line, a halo on the hill. But the verandah light is on, as is the spotlight at the side of the house. When Gus moves sideways I see Finn, on his knees and leaning over something. It's …

'Ruby!' I run up the steps and crouch next to Gus's black-and-tan kelpie. She's lying on her side, barely moving except for the twitching in her legs. As I stroke her face, she shudders a breath and her eyes slip closed. I look from Gus to Finn. 'What's happened?'

'Her heart's failing,' Finn says.

'What?' I run my hands down her shoulder, along her side. 'Ruby?' My voice breaks.

'She's been under my feet all day,' Gus mutters sadly. 'Didn't know what was the matter with her.'

Finn speaks quietly. 'She's thirteen, Jemima.' It's only then I see an open bag, packed with medical supplies.

Tears fall in tracks down my face. 'I know how old she is.'

When Mum died, Ruby was barely eight weeks old, a fuzzy ball of energy. Gus brought her to the cottage after the funeral, because she was too little to leave alone with his other dogs. After that, for months, Dad took me to visit her once or twice a week. She'd chase me around Gus's garden and clamber all over me. When she fell asleep, I'd rock her tightly in my arms, like Mum rocked Liam when I saw them in the hospital.

Finn's eye is a lot less bruised. The split in his lip has faded even more. He puts his hand on the top of Ruby's thigh. His brow creases. 'There's barely a pulse.'

I sniff and wipe my nose on my sleeve. 'You said you don't look after dogs.'

He points to his stethoscope. 'Listen to her heart.'

'I don't know about those things. I don't …' I swallow a sob. 'I don't know!'

Gus pats my shoulder. 'Easy does it, love. Better to happen like this, when Ruby's with friends. I feel a bit of a fool, truth be told. A farmer all my life, and I can't see when my own dog's time is up.'

'You came on the tractor?'

'To beg a lift from you to the Dubbo veterinarian.' He looks at Finn. 'I can't drive on the roads any more, eyes not what they were.' He pats my shoulder again. 'Who do I find when I get here? Dr Blackwood, the vet who's already helped me out, fishing that calf from the river.'

'Her breathing was laboured,' Finn says. 'She was anxious. I gave her a sedative. We can take her to Dubbo, but it's likely she'll die before we get there.'

As she matured, Dad and I watched Ruby with the sheep and cattle, learning from the older dogs how to keep them together, chase down the stragglers, round them up without alarming them too much. She still got excited when she saw me, but not in the way she used to. She wanted to be in the paddocks with Gus, the live-stock and the other dogs. Dad sat next to me on a hay bale in Gus's shed about a year after Mum had died. He explained it was time for Ruby to do more growing up, learn new skills and be independent.

It was only years later that I worked out he was talking about me.

I sniff back tears as I stroke. 'When you were a pup, we played together.' I hiccup a breath. 'You were the best, Ruby, the best. But now …' I swipe at my face with my sleeve again. 'But now we're older, you and me. So if you're tired, if you want to sleep, you go right ahead.' I look over my shoulder, down towards the valley. 'Do you remember Dad, Ruby? He said he'd enjoyed enough days to last him a score of lifetimes. He said it was time he had a rest.'

Gus's joints creak when he sits next to me. He lifts Ruby's head and rests it on his lap. 'Thirteen years,' he says, 'almost fourteen. Not a bad innings for a working dog, that's for sure.'

I lean against his arm. 'Do you remember the first time you brought her here?'

''Course I do. It was the day your mum was buried.'

'Ruby jumped into my lap and licked my face, didn't she?'

'She did, love. And what did you say to that?'

'I said I didn't think I would ever laugh again. But I did.'

I stroke Ruby's ear, soft as velvet. I rub beneath her jaw where she always liked a scratch.

My words are shaky but clear. '*The friend of man, the friend of truth, The friend of age, and guide of youth.*'

Finn touches my arm and I look up. '*Few hearts like his, with virtue warm'd. Few heads with knowledge so informed.*'

'Oh,' I whisper.

'Robbie Burns.'

'Yes.'

Ruby takes a deep breath. She trembles and shakes.

Finn holds her steady.

Gus strokes her head.

My tears wet her black-and-tan fur.

I get home early on Wednesday afternoon, so visit the cemetery before it gets dark. The pebbles on the path crunch underfoot as I make my way to the graveyard. We had occasional frosts in winter, and very little rain, so the grass is thin and pale. I bend low over the freesias on Liam's grave. Fresh sweet scent, bright green stalks, colourful flowers.

'You're doing better than the others.'

A few of the stems of the jonquils and daffodils, which should be straight and glossy, are yellowing already. I press the ground on Mum's grave.

'Damn.'

When it rains, the bulbs look after themselves. When it's dry, water is precious. Too precious for plants not meant for these conditions. The year before last, we were in drought, and there were barely any flowers. I dug compost and leaf litter into the dryness, and hoped that things would improve. And they did.

We've had a dry winter, but the rains last autumn were good, and rain is forecast for later in spring. The river is high. There's plenty of town water, and the levels are good in the dams and tanks.

I make a vow to Sapphie, who's on Horseshoe's sustainability committee. 'I'll water the flowers today, but only this once.' And then I walk quickly to the church and rummage through the tools until I find the watering can, hidden by the barrow. I fill the can from the bore tap, and water Liam, Mum and Dad's graves, and the other plots that people take care of. Gus's wife's grave was planted with banksia roses over twenty years ago. The bushes are cut back at this time of year, but in summer they'll bloom like a bright yellow cloud. After the first few trips to the bore tap, I warm up and take off my jacket.

It's easier to pull out the weeds with moisture in the ground. I shake them free of dirt and throw them into a bucket. Mrs Hargreaves can't weed her father's grave with her knee the way it is, so

I pay much more attention to his plot than I do to Dad's. He was never much of a gardener.

When I've finished, I stand back and smile. The freesias will keep flowering for another few weeks. And with any luck, the jonquils and daffodils will follow. A daffodil stem on Dad's grave is much taller than the others. I gently touch the bright green leaf.

> *The friend of man, the friend of truth,*
> *The friend of age, and guide of youth.*

Last Friday, Finn helped Gus load Ruby's body into the tractor so he could bury her under one of the flowering gums in his garden. I offered to go with Gus but he refused, insisting his younger kelpies, Banjo and Patty, would keep him company. When Finn said good night, I mumbled thanks for what he'd done and went back to the cottage. I worked most of Saturday so barely saw him then. And on Sunday, I wasn't even out of bed when I heard his tyres on the gravel.

Last night, Tuesday, he left a message on my phone.

Jemima. I'll see you on the weekend. Finn

CHAPTER

11

By the time I get to Horseshoe on Saturday evening, it's well after seven and the car spaces in the main street are taken. I park in a spot near the library, on the far side of the park, skirt around the rose beds and walk through the grass, doing my best to avoid the puddles left by the bore-water sprinkler. When I reach the pub I yank off my sneakers, shoving them into my bag, and pull on short boots with high heels. As I adjust my sweater, a gusty wind blows up the road and tosses my hair around.

Leon Wang, the publican, modernised The Royal when he bought it a few years ago. The poker machines were relegated to a separate room out the back, and the patterned carpets were ripped up in the bar area, revealing wide blackbutt floorboards. In the lounge, tables and chairs are grouped around the open fireplace, over a hundred years old like the building. There's a poolroom off the bar, and a private dining room that's sometimes used for parties.

'Thanks for arranging my lift,' Gus shouts from the bar. 'I would've waited for you.'

'No point in us both being late.'

'Jet!' Sapphie appears around a pot plant and hugs me. 'Have you heard? Trivia is cancelled. The trivia guy's car broke down.'

I hide a yawn. 'An early night for me, then.'

She laughs. 'No, you don't. Luke is here. He was asking where you were.'

As if on cue, Luke Martin, the youngest son of Andrew, the vet at the zoo, waves from the bar. He's with a large group of people.

Sapphie leans in close. 'Just a warning,' she whispers. 'Finn is here as well, and also asking after you.'

'What does he want?'

'No idea.' She squeezes my arm. 'I'm sorry about Ruby.'

I'm looking at the dinner specials, on a board behind the bar, when I see Finn. He's dressed casually in a T-shirt and jeans, and sits on a stool with his elbow on the counter, talking to Leon and the barman. He'd stand out even if he weren't a newcomer to Horseshoe. It's not his black eye, which has pretty much healed, but his confidence and height and … Everything stands out with Finn.

'Jet?' Sapphie says. 'Are you ready to order?'

Finn swivels on his stool. He nods politely and I nod back. It's suddenly difficult to swallow.

'I'm not that hungry.'

'Why not?'

'I had a late lunch. I'll get a juice.'

Gus circulates, speaking to people he knows well, and to those he's never met until this evening. A group of women, who must be from out of town because I don't recognise any of them, are having a hens' party. They talk and laugh, loudly and often, in the lounge. I'm at the bar, with Mr and Mrs Hargreaves and Sapphie, when Luke joins us. He's a year older than me, fair haired, tall and lanky with a boyish smile.

'Dad gets to see more of you than I do,' he says as he hugs me. 'Have you no taste?'

'Andrew complains you're still under his feet.' I step out of his arms and pick up my juice. 'You've got a degree in town planning and a job with the council. Why don't you settle down?'

He laughs. 'What is it with him? He forgets he got divorced at forty-five.'

'Young people wait too long these days,' Mrs Hargreaves says, smiling at Mr Hargreaves. 'We were married at twenty-two, and that was forty-three years ago.'

'Quite right, love,' Mr Hargreaves says. 'And for thirty years we've worked side by side at the store.'

Mrs Hargreaves adjusts her position on the stool. She had a knee replacement a few months ago and is recovering very slowly. When she was young she had thick brown hair. Now it's peppered with grey. Mr Hargreaves, thin and tall, has barely any hair and almost always wears a cap.

'I'd like more grandchildren,' Mrs Hargreaves says, looking pointedly at Sapphie.

Sapphie shakes her head. 'You already have ten.'

'What?' Luke says.

'Foster grandchildren,' Sapphie explains.

Mrs Hargreaves smiles. 'No difference to us.'

'Quite right, love,' Mr Hargreaves says.

When Mrs Hargreaves nods to someone behind me, beckoning with an outstretched arm, Sapphie's eyes widen in warning. I sense that it's Finn before he stands next to me.

'Hello.' My gaze slides from his eyes to his mouth. The split is barely noticeable now.

He nods. 'Jemima.'

Mrs Hargreaves beams. 'Jemima,' she says. 'Your mum gave you such a pretty name. I can't remember the last time I heard it.'

Heat moves up my neck. 'Do you know everyone, Dr Blackwood?'

He shakes Luke's hand, looks from him to me. 'Finn.'

'We've seen Finn at the store,' Mrs Hargreaves says, smiling at him. 'Sapphie and I are looking forward to the cocktail party next month.'

'What cocktail party?' Luke asks.

'A fundraiser for the zoo,' Mrs Hargreaves says. 'Finn is giving a speech.'

I whirl ice cubes around in my glass. 'I'd better get going.'

'No way.' Luke bumps his arm against mine. 'Another drink? A game of pool?'

'No thanks.'

There are shouts of laughter from the group of women in the lounge. Sapphie groans. 'It's going to be a big night. They're just getting started.'

Mrs Hargreaves peers at my face. 'Have you been working too hard again? You're a little pale.'

'I'm fine.'

'Why not get an apprentice? Mike usually had one.'

'I prefer to work on my own.'

'How is Mike? I haven't seen him in an age.'

'He's back to doing everyone's odd jobs in Warrandale. He's not shoeing horses any more, but still has work at the zoo.'

Finn glances at me. 'I spoke with him yesterday.'

I open my mouth and shut it, tear my gaze away. When I put my drink on the counter, I miss the coaster and the glass clunks onto the bar. I lift my hair off my neck, twist it, and throw it down my back. I pick up my bag.

'I have to go.'

'You just got here,' Luke says, hugging me again. 'I'll call you, let's meet up.'

Just before I get to the door, a man steps in front of me. He'd be in his mid-thirties, with heavily muscled arms and a vaguely familiar face. When I try to walk around him, he blocks my path.

'G'day, Jet.' The light is dim, but when he holds out his hand, I notice his tattoo. It's an eagle with a small black eye and a long curved beak. He lifts his thumb and the beak opens wide. When he pointedly looks me up and down, it sets my teeth on edge. Who is he?

I take a jerky step back. He's Jason Caruthers, one of the stable-hands at Thornbrooke. I don't think I've seen him since then. He always fancied himself, and used to have a beard. He didn't have the tattoo at Thornbrooke. I would have remembered it.

'How're you doing?' he says.

'I'm well, thanks.'

When I walk away, he follows and opens the door. 'It's been a few years.'

'Yes.'

'We should catch up, have a drink.'

I nod automatically, and then walk quickly down the steps to the footpath. The winds have strengthened. The moon, a wafer thin crescent, hovers in the sky above me. I've only made it as far as the general store when I hear footsteps. I look over my shoulder.

It's Finn.

CHAPTER
12

'Jemima.' He catches up easily.

I turn and face him. 'I told you to leave Mike alone.'

He runs his fingers through his hair, black in the shadows. 'Can we discuss this at home?'

'My home? No.'

His lips firm. 'It will have to be here then.'

'What do you want?'

'I'll walk you to your car.' He looks around. 'Where are you parked?'

'Near the rose gardens.'

As I walk down the hill, carefully because of my heels, he falls in beside me. The streetlights are mostly behind us now, but there are lights at the entrance to the park.

'Like it or not, we have an association,' he says, as we pass the cenotaph and step onto the grass. 'You're related to Edward. He requested my help. I've leased the homestead.' He jerks his thumb over his shoulder. 'We see each other socially.'

'So?'

'You're hiding something. So is Mike.'

'You had no right to contact him.'

'Is he dying?'

'No! What did he say?'

'Nothing, because you'd told him not to.'

'So now you can leave us alone.'

'Mike was frightened.' He hesitates. 'Like you are.'

I step onto a soggy patch of grass and my heels sink into the ground. When he reaches for my arm, I shy away.

'I have other shoes.'

He follows me to a long timber bench in front of an oak tree. I feel his gaze on the side of my face as I pull my sneakers out of my bag and place them on the seat between us. I unzip my boots and shove them into the bag. The tree has lost most of its leaves. But the few that are left, and those on the ground, rustle and dance in the breeze. Other than that, it's quiet and still. No cars on the road, no words.

I pick up one of my shoes. The double-knotted bow is damp from my walk to the pub, and the fabric clumps together. When I bend low over the lace and pick at it carefully, it appears to get even tighter. So I place the shoe back on the bench and put the other shoe on my lap. The harder I try to unravel the laces, the tighter the knots become. One of my fingers feels sticky. Blood? When I'm working, I need the tape. When I'm not, it draws attention to my hands, so I leave it off when I can. Now I wish I'd hidden my fingers completely. I put both shoes on the ground.

'I'll do it later,' I say, sitting upright again and squeezing my hands between my knees. 'Have you said what you wanted to say?' My socks are almost worn through at the heel. I look up at the clouds, drifting in front of the moon. 'Why are you still here?'

'Fucked if I know.' When I turn towards him, he expels a breath. 'You and Luke Martin. How close are you?'

'Why do you care?'

He mutters under his breath. 'Forget it.' He picks up my shoes, puts one on the bench between us and the other on his lap. Then he methodically works at the laces, slowly untangling one knot after the other. The thin white strips drape over his knee and he draws them out, lining them up so they're parallel.

The silence between us is suffocating. I pick up the other shoe; create tighter knots and additional tangles. The clouds shift above us. A moonbeam lights my hands. The side of my thumb is swollen and the tips of my fingers are red.

He puts his hand over mine. I wish I hated his touch, the way it warms me inside and out.

'Leave it, Jemima.'

'I bite my nails.' The words spill out, weak and croaky.

'I noticed.'

He places the shoe he's untangled onto my lap. 'This one's done. Put it on.' He takes the other shoe.

When my hair blows into my eyes, I pin it under the neck of my sweater. I push my foot into the sneaker, tying the laces loosely into a bow. By the time I've finished, he's unravelled the other lace. He puts the shoe back on the bench. I reach for it.

He captures my hand again. He looks at my nails. He frowns.

I should pull my hand away. I should … 'It's a bad habit,' I say.

He tightens his hold, covers my hand completely. 'There are worse.'

'I get nightmares. I do it when I'm asleep.'

He strokes the back of my hand with his thumb. 'Is that why you leave the lights on?'

'Do you want to know everything about me?'

He looks down at our hands, then uses both of his to open mine up. He sandwiches it. 'Is that what you think?'

'It … no.'

He's intent, serious. He lets go of my hand and tilts my chin with his fist, setting off nerve endings down to my toes.

'You're so fucking complex.'

'I have to go,' I whisper.

He releases my chin. 'Do you?' The wind whistles through the oak tree. My hair blows around my face. I turn away, grabbing my second shoe from the bench and bending down to put it on with shaking fingers. When I straighten, my knee bumps his thigh.

'You don't like me, do you?' he says.

'I have no reason to.'

'Same. It makes no difference.'

I'm not sure who moves first, but my thigh is suddenly pressed against his. 'You were kind to Ruby.'

'Gus is a good man.'

'Thank you for helping with my shoes.'

'Is there anything else?'

'What do you mean?'

'You're listing reasons to like me.'

Our eyes meet. I swallow. 'Now it's your turn.'

He slowly shakes his head. 'You don't want to know my thoughts.'

He picks up my hand again and opens my fingers, placing his palm against mine. He lifts my hand to his mouth, puts his lips against my thumb. He peers at me through the darkness.

When I shuffle closer, he cups my face. He touches my bottom lip with his thumb, slides it back and forth. And when I release a shuddering breath, he lowers his head. His lips are a millimetre from mine, maybe even less. He whispers words, lots and lots of words, against my mouth. It's nice. The movement of his lips, the promise of his kiss. His careful hands, his unsteady breathing.

'What are you saying?'

His forehead rests on mine. He smiles without humour. 'This is a stupid thing to do.'

My body is hot and restless. I put my hands against his chest. It's hard and muscular. I feel the thumps of his heart.

'It's no big deal.'

He covers my hands with his, keeping them still. He stares at my mouth. 'Isn't it?'

Our mouths touch properly, silently. I run my tongue along the crease between his lips. I wrap my arms around his neck to bring him closer. I stroke his silky hair. He lifts his head again. He groans softly. 'Fuck.'

'Does your mouth hurt?'

'Not as much as it should.'

My breasts press against his chest. He runs his hands up my sides as we kiss again. I mutter a complaint when his mouth slides to my cheek, across it. He buries his face in my hair, kisses my neck. I soften against him. I shudder.

He lifts his head. 'Are you cold?'

I tighten my arms; bring his face so close our noses almost touch. 'No.'

He pushes hair off my face, tidies it behind my ears. He lifts one of my legs over his lap and puts his hands on my waist, lifting me higher. When I feel his erection against the inside of my thigh, a shock passes through me. The warmth in my veins heats my blood. I spread my fingers wide against his chest.

I move restlessly against his body. I need to feel his breath, his lips, his tongue in my mouth.

'Sorry, you two!' A woman's voice. 'Sorry about this!'

Finn's arms are bands around my body. His jaw is clenched tight. He turns his head and I follow his gaze. A group of women, the hens' party, is gathered at the rose garden. They're talking over each other and laughing. One of the women, unsteady on spiky heels, holds a bottle of sparkling wine. A long white veil is tangled on a shrub near a timber trellis, and two of the women tug at the folds. The bride-to-be, anchored by the tiara in her fiery red hair, finally pulls the veil free. The women cheer, and the one holding the bottle lifts it in salute. They all totter back towards the cenotaph.

Just like before, the wind blows through the tree. Somewhere in the distance, probably the pub, music plays. Between Finn and me there is silence. My leg is on his lap and my hands are on his chest. His hands are warm on my waist. If I looked up, his mouth would be close. Close enough to kiss. I count my breaths and I'm up to eight when his hands grasp my waist more tightly. I feel the tension in his body, the indecision.

He stands in one motion, lifting me with him. And as soon as I have my balance, he steps back and lets me go. We face each other without making eye contact. I smooth down the legs of my jeans. I blow into my hands. I wrap my arms around my middle. He picks up my bag.

'Are you all right?' he says.

I don't have any words yet. I check that the bench is still there. Yes. So I didn't imagine sitting on it, my leg flung over his legs, my hands splayed on his chest. A gust of wind whips hair around my face. *Intimacy*. I didn't imagine it. But it's an ephemeral thing.

'Thornbrooke,' he says, perfectly calmly. 'We have to get it out of the way.'

An elephant steps on my chest. 'Piss off.'

'Jemima!'

I snatch my bag. 'What?'

He speaks through his teeth. 'Don't pretend this didn't happen.'

'Were you deliberately nice? Did you hope to soften me up so I'd talk about Thornbrooke?'

He mutters under his breath. 'I'll walk you to your car.'

'I can look after myself.'

His gaze moves pointedly to my shoes. 'Can you?' When I try to walk around him, he holds out an arm, blocking my way.

'What now?'

'I shouldn't have said that.'

'Why not, when you obviously think that it's true.'

'Don't put words in my—'

'I haven't finished!' I cross my arms. 'You value the truth. Do you want to know another one?'

'Do I have a choice?'

'Before you came to Horseshoe, I didn't dream of Thornbrooke. I didn't get nightmares. I didn't bite my nails.'

'What?'

'I could even untie my laces. And as soon as you're gone …' I clear my throat. 'As soon as you're gone, I'll do it again.'

When I take a jerky step back, he lifts his hand. I shy away so sharply, I glance it with my elbow.

My shoes are tied in single bows, not doubles, so the laces are too long. I keep my eyes on my feet, careful not to stumble as I walk across the grass.

CHAPTER
13

Paddocks either side of the narrow roads are ploughed in lines, ready for spring and warmer weather. It's nine o'clock and the sun is rising quickly on a breezy hazy day. When my phone rings, I pull over under the shelter of a solitary gum.

'Jet Kincaid.'

'Morning, Jemima. It's Edward. Are you all right?'

'Fine, thanks.'

'I received a call from Finn Blackwood last night.'

'Right.'

'He told me you won't talk to him about Thornbrooke.'

Gripping the steering wheel tightly, I count how many fingers are sore. One. Two. Three. And a thumb. Finn wants a recount? Let him tap into my dreams.

'He didn't waste any time informing on me.'

'Jemima ... He's anxious to get his report done as soon as possible. That's why he wanted your input. He wants my paperwork too.'

Knotted laces, stolen kisses. Did he mention those to Edward?

'I'll let you get onto that, then. I have a client waiting.'

'On a Sunday?'

'I'm trimming alpacas out of Wellington.'

'How long will it take to drive back?'

'An hour at least. But I won't be finished until late this afternoon.'

'Can you leave earlier? I'm at Kincaid House.'

A flock of cockatoos fly onto the branches of the gum tree, their white and yellow feathers bright against the green.

'You're with Finn?'

When one of the cockatoos takes off, all the others follow, screeching and squawking together.

'Correct. Will you come back?'

'When I've finished what I have to do here.'

He sighs. 'Give me the address. I'll drop by on my way back to Sydney.'

U

Dad used to say that he and Edward got on well—even though they had little in common—because each of them was happy with their lot. I've never thought of Edward as particularly happy. My father? It was inevitable that he would die young. But he was almost always cheerful.

'Every day is a gift,' he said. 'Treasure it.'

Mum and Dad had been married for a year, and I'd just been conceived, when Edward's father gave them the cottage. It gave Mum and Dad a home, and somewhere to keep Mum's horses. But even more importantly, it was only an hour away from a large regional town, and medical help.

Dad needed daily treatment to break down the fluids that built up in his lungs. Simple infections were potentially fatal, so he had as many medications and as much physiotherapy as his body could tolerate. He often went into hospital—sometimes for the day, but often for much longer.

Cystic fibrosis almost always leads to infertility, so Dad had his sperm frozen, and stored, when he was young. I was conceived through IVF, to ensure I didn't have CF or carry the gene. Liam was conceived naturally, which, even though Dad's reproductive tract was okay, was considered a miracle given what he'd been through. Mum was tested when she fell pregnant, so knew the baby would have CF, but wanted to keep it anyway. As it turned out, Liam was born so prematurely he never took a breath on his own.

Dad made me a promise on the day Liam died. 'You'll have your Mum when I'm gone.'

He did his best to introduce me to my extended family after Mum died, because it was only a matter of time before he'd die too. Mum had been born in England. Her parents had retired to Spain, and Dad sent me to stay with them, where I also met Mum's brother and his children, who still live in England. But after that first visit, Dad's health got worse and I refused to leave him, so I talked to Mum's family by phone on our birthdays, and on Christmas Day. We still do that. On Dad's side, his father had already died. Nan was in Sydney but she had dementia and lived in a nursing home.

Edward did his best to get to know me, and I occasionally stayed with him in Sydney in the holidays, but he was divorced and had no children. I missed Dad and home anyway, so my visits got shorter and shorter. When Edward came to Horseshoe, it was awkward. His interests were so different to ours.

Dad wasn't in palliative care for long. I was seventeen and allowed to stay with him. We had a ground-floor room with wide French doors that led to the gardens. It was October and the roses were out. Stakes supported the tall standard roses that bordered the path. Small thorny bushes with sweet scented flowers circled a birdbath. The climbing roses, with pink and orange flowers, formed an arch between broad posts.

On his second day at the hospice, a nurse and I wheeled Dad around the grounds. He was on oxygen by then, because he couldn't breathe without it. When he saw the flowering bulbs at the bottom of the garden, his eyes filled with tears that tumbled down his face. The nurse was concerned, and squatted by his chair. But I knew that Dad was happy.

When I squeezed his hand, he squeezed mine right back.

'It's time to say goodbye, isn't it?' I said.

'Treasure every day.'

'You have to go to Mum and Liam.'

He pulled me close, his words were whispered. 'Every day's a gift.'

U

When I run my fingers through Flopsy's woolly coat, up to the soft brown mop on the top of her head, she stares at me with round and trusting eyes. 'You're such a good girl.'

Robbie has a gangly fifteen-year-old body, and could do with a hair wash. He stands at Flopsy's head, holding her halter and lead rope, as I wipe my sleeve over my face and pull my hat lower. I look over the paddock towards the gate. Edward's not here yet, but he's bound to turn up soon.

'Almost done.' I stroke down Flopsy's leg, lean my upper arm against her shoulder. 'Give me your foot, Flopsy.'

'Mum shouldn't have let me name the alpacas,' Robbie says. 'I was a kid. I didn't know what I was doing.'

'Flopsy is a good name. It suits her.'

Robbie points towards the alpacas I've already trimmed. They're waiting to be let out of one of the yards and into the paddock.

'What about Mopsy, Cottontail, Bunny and Bouncer?'

I'm laughing as I rest Flopsy's foot over the leather on my knee. 'It's a good way to keep track of them. I always remember they're siblings.' I clip Flopsy's nails, two on each foot, with cutters. 'You forgot Peter.'

He grins. 'Peter's an okay name.'

I straighten, standing back to see that Flopsy's four sets of nails are lined up and she's standing square on her feet. 'That'll keep her going for another month or two,' I say as I roll up my sleeves. 'Who's next?'

He rolls his eyes. 'Montague.'

Robbie's father bought Montague from a stud in Tasmania. He's pitch black and tall, with beautiful confirmation, but he also has attitude, and wasn't handled regularly when he was young. Robbie's mum will name his offspring, and she's already made a list. Romeo, Juliet, Mercutio, Tybalt, Capulet. My school librarian, Mrs McNab, would approve.

'Will you be all right to hold him on your own?'

'No problem. I'll paddock the others first.'

I'm filling my bottle from the tap when I see Edward's Range Rover on the driveway. By the time Robbie walks Montague into the yard, Edward has parked on the gravel next to my ute.

'Be there in a minute,' I shout.

When I hold out my hand to Montague, he backs away and flattens his ears.

Robbie grins. 'I think he remembers you from the other times, Jet.'

I offer my hand again. Montague looks at me with suspicion, but lets me run my hand over his neck, thick with wool. 'You don't much like a pedicure, do you, boy?'

This is the third time I've trimmed him. The first time it took an hour, with three members of the Nickola family keeping him steady. They tried to handle his legs and feet more regularly after that, so the next time, besides spitting on me twice, he behaved well.

'I won't be long with Edward,' I tell Robbie, untying my apron and hanging it over the fence, and picking up my hat, slowly so as not to spook Montague. 'Just keep him calm, walk him around. Don't lift up his feet though. He's bound to strike out until he gets used to it again.'

Edward, tall and fit, is dressed in navy pants and a polo shirt. He walks around my ute, kicking the tyres as if checking the air pressure. His hair used to be dark and wavy. It's still thick, but is now almost white. He wears it a little long, pushed back from his face like a Hollywood actor. It's not surprising he's photographed at city race days.

He takes his sunglasses off when I get close. 'You look well, Jet.'

I wipe my hands on my jeans, take off my hat and brush hair from my face. 'Thanks. You too.'

He holds my shoulders and kisses both cheeks.

Dad was a modest version of his cousin. He was much more slender because of his illness, and not as tall. But the deep brown colour in their eyes was the same.

Edward looks around, taking in the ramshackle yards and sheds, the Nickolas' nineteen-sixties blonde-brick house, carport and neglected garden.

'So this is where you spend your Sundays,' he says.

'That's right.'

'No regrets? You wouldn't change anything? It's never too late to improve your education, to—'

'No regrets.'

Edward has never got over the fact that I refused to move to Sydney after Dad died. He'd had a meeting with a private girls' school headmistress, who had told him I'd had inadequate support in the past, but her school had excellent teachers and resources, and, at seventeen, it wasn't too late to improve my literacy.

I open the back of my ute and hoist myself onto the tray, sitting next to the forge. It's not needed for trimming; there's no hiss or heat from inside. I point to the space next to me.

'You can sit here.'

He raises his brows, then leans against the ute and crosses his arms. 'This will do, thank you.'

I look over my shoulder towards Robbie and the alpaca. 'I don't have long, Edward. Why did you come out of your way?'

He frowns. 'It worries me, Jet, your reluctance to talk about Thornbrooke. Finn suspects a cover-up of some sort. If you were involved, I'd rather know about it now.'

'I refuse to go back, so does Mike. You already knew that.'

'Finn's no fool. He appreciates it was traumatic, as do I. Even so, we can't comprehend your reluctance.'

I look towards the road, shade my eyes from the sun. 'That's because you weren't there.'

'I merely want to clear the air.'

'You hope your stud, the horses, will be more valuable.'

He harrumphs. 'Reputation is important too.'

I jump to the ground. 'You said Finn called last night. Is that why you came to Horseshoe?'

'I simply arranged to deliver the documents. And, to be honest, we hoped the three of us could have a civil conversation. That you might see sense.'

'Two against one?' I fight the sick feeling churning in my stomach. 'You and Finn thought that'd improve your odds of making me do what you want?'

'Jemima …'

'Goodbye, Edward.'

I focus on putting one foot in front of the other as I walk to the yards. Robbie looks away as I clench my jaw, swallowing hard. I balance my hat on a post and fasten my apron, smoothing the leather over my jeans. I stroke Montague's neck firmly, as if I'm in control. I run my hand down his leg, lean against his shoulder and—

U

'I'm fine, really I am.' I press the cold, wet cloth against my jaw. 'Just a scrape. It was my fault, totally, really. I rushed him.'

When I picked up his foot and leant over it, Montague kicked out, grazing my cheek. He barely touched me, but the shock of it threw me backwards and onto the ground. Before I'd managed to get to my feet, Robbie had called his parents. They came rushing from the house.

His mother brushes dirt from my arm. 'Come up to the house, Jet. Or should I drive you to the hospital?'

'No way. Like I said, I'm fine.' I take the damp cloth, marked pink with blood, away from my face. I gingerly touch my jaw and open my mouth. 'It's nothing.' I hold out my hand. 'Pull me up, Robbie, let's get back to work.'

Robbie stands at Montague's head and Robbie's parents stand at his shoulders. 'I'm sorry, boy.' I stroke his neck, across his back. 'It was my fault. No harm done. I won't rush you again.'

U

It's late afternoon by the time I get home, but Finn is still there. He's sitting on a chair on the verandah with a book in his hand, an overnight bag at his feet. He looks up as I drive into the shed.

I'm reaching into the back seat of the ute, going through the checklist in my head and making sure I have everything I'll need for tomorrow, when I hear footsteps. My heart rate quickens.

'Jemima?'

'Yes?' I turn without thinking.

'What the hell?'

In a few strides he's standing in front of me, a crease between his brows. 'What happened?'

I can look after myself. 'An alpaca called Montague. It's nothing.'

'Bullshit.' He tilts his head as he stares. He lifts his hand and puts it to his side again. 'A hoof?'

When I bend to pick up my toolbox, my jaw aches. But the tightness in my throat is far more painful. I was right not to trust him.

'Occupational hazard. He barely touched me.'

He holds out his hand again. 'Let me look at it.'

'You already have.' I turn my back and load the shoes I'll need for tomorrow, putting sets of four in the divided sections of the box. 'It's fine.'

'It's dirty. You're risking an infection.'

I spin around. 'My shed isn't part of your lease, even Edward knows that. So leave me alone. I have work to do.'

He rubs a hand around the back of his neck. 'You're angry I called Edward.'

'Funny, that.' I scoop up a box of nails. The cardboard lid comes loose and a bunch slip out, falling onto the concrete at my feet. 'Shit.'

He squats on the dusty floor next to me, picking up nails one by one. My hand is much smaller than his, and grubby. His hair is damp. He's cleanly shaven. And so close I can smell him. Fresh pine and ... Our hands touch. My stomach flips. Our eyes meet.

His arm moves slowly. So slowly I could swat it away, or tell him not to touch me. But I like the feel of his hand on my shoulder, the pressure of his fingers on the side of my neck. There's concern in his eyes.

His thumb rests against my jaw. 'Let me clean the wound.' He speaks slowly and quietly. 'Nothing else. I won't ask questions.'

'No.' My voice is a croak. 'No, thank you.'

'It was a hoof. Anything could have been on it. Your skin is broken. It's important that it's sterilised.'

'I have to bring the horses in.'

'Please, Jem, listen to what I'm saying.'

Jem? What sort of name is that? I'm suddenly tired—tiredness that has nothing to do with getting up early or working all day. Finn exhausts me. How can I be attracted to him, given what he's up to? When I shuffle backwards, his hand drops to his side.

I start loading again, wedging my toolbox securely into the tray. 'I'll clean my face.'

'You think I should have warned you that Edward was coming?'

'I guess.'

'And when would that have been? Late last night? At dawn this morning?'

I ignore what he says, skirting around him while avoiding his gaze. I wipe my hands on my jeans as I walk up the path to the cottage. His car door opens and slams shut. Footsteps again. When I turn, he holds out a handful of slender white sachets.

I take them and study the small red print. I can't make out the words. 'What are they?'

He frowns. 'Antiseptic swabs. Use them after you shower, tonight and tomorrow morning. If the wound gets red or inflamed, go to a doctor. I presume your tetanus is up to date?'

'Yes.' I nod jerkily. 'Thank you.'

'I'm going home on Wednesday, to Switzerland.' He smiles stiffly. Besides a tinge of yellow under his eye, there's no sign of bruising, but there's still a red line on his lip. Will it scar?

'How long will you be gone?'

'I'll be back for the zoo function at the beginning of October.'

'Only a couple of weeks then.'

'I'll do what I can when I'm away, but my report will take time.'

'Right.'

'The nightmares you spoke of last night. I hope—'

'You going away, that'll help. I'll be fine.'

His lips thin. He nods abruptly and then he walks away, strides down the path without looking back.

There's a hollow feeling deep in my chest as I trudge up the steps. A high-backed pew, given to Dad when the church at the cemetery was decommissioned, sits on the verandah beneath my bedroom windowsill. It was once stained dark mahogany, but has faded in the sun. I sit and pull off my boots, lining them up on the floorboards.

It was only last night he untangled my laces. It feels like a lifetime ago.

CHAPTER
14

When I arrive at Follyfoot on Friday morning, Jason Caruthers, the stablehand I worked with at Thornbrooke, is leaning against the fence that separates the carpark from the shed and arena. He was at the pub a few weeks ago—the first time I'd seen him in almost eight years. And here he is again. As I undo my seatbelt, I try to convince myself this is only a coincidence.

He walks towards me as I step out of the ute. He tips his hat. 'G'day, Jet.'

When I saw him in the pub, I noticed the tattoo of the eagle on his hand. It's still cold in the mornings, but his shirt is short-sleeved. Darkly inked feathers wind around his forearm.

'Jason,' I say, skirting around him to the back of the horse float.

'Didn't get a chance to catch up at The Royal.'

When I release one of the latches on the tailgate, Chili impatiently stamps. Lollopy leans over to Chili's side of the float, trying to reach the lucerne in his haynet.

'No,' I say.

'Been up in Queensland. Darren Morrissey got me the job when the shit hit the fan at Thornbrooke.'

'Everything has settled down now.'

'That's not what I've heard.'

'Were you waiting for me? I'm pretty busy.'

He trails his hand over the wheel rim as I release the other tail-gate latch. After I've lowered the ramp, he leans against the side door of the float. He scratches an ear.

'I'm on the lookout for work. Heard of any jobs at the racing stables?'

'I don't work with racehorses, there are specialist farriers for that.'

He nods towards the shed. 'Nothing here, then?'

'At Follyfoot? We're all volunteers.'

He holds out a card. 'Just in case.'

I throw the card in the glove box and face him again. 'Can you move out of the way? I want to untie the horses.'

He crosses his thickly muscled arms, blocking the door completely. 'I've been talking to Darren Morrissey.'

I take a step back. 'Right.'

He kicks a clump of grass. 'He doesn't like the sound of what Edward Kincaid is up to; asking questions about Rosethorn and the colts. Blackwood's a problem too.'

'I have nothing much to do with either of them.'

'Kincaid's your uncle.'

'He was my father's cousin.'

'Whatever.' He smiles, his lips stretched tightly over his teeth. 'Morrissey said you had a deal. He wanted me to remind you of it.'

'What deal? Why didn't he call me?'

When I reach around Caruthers for the door handle, he grabs my wrist. I smell cigarette smoke on his breath.

'I haven't finished.'

When I yank my arm, he tightens his hold. 'Let me go!'

'No worries.' He opens his fingers wide. 'Now that I've got your attention.'

I rub my wrist. 'Why would Morrissey send you?'

'You walked out years ago, and no contact since. It'd look suspicious if the two of you started talking now, especially with him living in Perth.'

'You said Morrissey and I had a deal. What do you mean by that?'

'That no one talks about Thornbrooke.'

'Right.'

'I saw you with Blackwood at The Royal.'

'What are you? A spy?'

'Morrissey reckons you and Mike and him, none of you did anything wrong, but you've all got to keep your mouths shut.'

Laurence's father pulls up on the far side of the carpark. 'I haven't said anything. And I won't. You tell him that.'

'What about Mike? I can have a friendly word, remind him.'

'I've done that!' I shove Caruthers out of the way, wrenching open the door. 'We don't need reminders.'

'I'll pass that on to Morrissey.'

'You do that.'

I pull at the safety knot on Chili's lead rope so hard that when it releases, my hand hits a bolt. Biting my lip, I swallow a curse.

I've been at Follyfoot for most of the morning when Magda walks into the shed. She holds out a mug.

'Here you go, love. Sorry, we've run out of biscuits.'

'That's okay.' I take the coffee gratefully. 'I'll pick up a sandwich and milkshake before I leave town.'

'Jet?' Chelsea shouts, as she trots past on Cascade. 'Is this okay?'

Chelsea is as horse-mad as many fourteen year olds. As horse-mad as I used to be before Mum's death.

'You're doing great,' I say, as I walk up the steps to the tiered seating area. Laurence, towering over everyone else, is riding Chili Pepper. Darcy rides Lollopy, leaning low over his neck with three volunteers supporting him. Bringing up the rear are Andreas and Dasher. Andreas is in a jubilant mood, talking to one of the volunteers at a hundred miles an hour about different breeds of horses. The volunteer is elderly, nodding and exclaiming patiently.

My phone rings. 'Jet, it's Sapphie.' She coughs and splutters.

'You sound terrible.'

'I can't shake this virus. I have a favour to ask.'

'What?'

'At the hotel a while ago, did you hear Ma talking to Finn about a cocktail party, a fundraiser at the Dubbo Convention Centre?'

'Yes.' I touch my cheek. There was a graze there last time I saw him. My skin is smooth again now. 'He's giving a speech.'

'I was supposed to take Ma, but there's no way I can go like this. And I don't want to give her a lift in case I pass on my bug. Pa can't get her there on time, because he's stuck at the store until seven. I hate to ask but—'

'Sure, I can drive her.' I take a sip of coffee as I stand.

'It's more than that. Her knee's been playing up so she'll need help up the stairs. And she's not comfortable going to a social function by herself, not in Dubbo anyway. That's how I got dragged into this.'

'I … I guess I can stay.'

'She'll be so grateful, Jet. She's even bought a new dress.' Sapphie coughs again. 'I know how busy you are on Fridays, and you'll be up early again tomorrow, but I can't think who else to ask.'

'What time do we have to be there?'

'Six forty-five.'

I have four horses to shoe at a riding school out of town, and then I have to double back to collect Chili and Lollopy before I drive home. I'll be too busy to think about Finn. Too busy to think about anything but work. I take the steps two at a time.

'Tell Mrs Hargreaves I'll pick her up at five-thirty.'

'You'll have my ticket, so you'll get a drink and something to eat.'

'I don't have to buy a new dress, do I?'

She croaks a laugh. 'No, but it is kind of formal so leave your jeans at home. Pa's promised to head out to Dubbo as soon as the store closes, so he'll be there around eight. As soon as he turns up, you can leave.'

Chelsea trots diagonally across the arena, her concentration fierce as she manoeuvres Cascade around the drums. The curve in her spine means she can't sit quite straight in the saddle, but she relies on her knees and calves to guide Cascade, leaving her hands light on the reins. When she gets to the far side of the arena, she slows Cascade to a walk.

'Did you see?' she asks.

Cascade is agisted at Follyfoot, meaning Chelsea can ride him whenever her mum and the volunteers can organise it. But he's twenty-two now, and increasingly stiff in his shoulder, so it's only a matter of time before he joins the other retirees at Horseshoe. Which horse would Chelsea ride then? Chili would be perfect, but he's only here on Fridays.

'You're riding really well,' I say. 'And next week you'll be even better.'

'Are you going already?'

The sun is high in the sky now and warm on my back. 'Something's come up. I'll see you soon.'

CHAPTER

15

Mrs Hargreaves holds onto my arm as we walk up the steps to the brightly lit function room. A large white screen takes up one wall and giant easels, holding photographs of African animals, rhino, elephant, hippo and giraffe, are grouped in each corner.

We're slowly making our way around the guests, who are talking, laughing and drinking, when I see Finn, standing near the podium. He's taller than the men around him and, unlike some of them, looks comfortable in a suit. The mayor is on his left, and the owner of one of the biggest thoroughbred studs in the country is on his right. Andrew Martin, the vet from the zoo, is in the group too. He waves, gesturing that I join him. I shake my head, walking with Mrs Hargreaves to the chairs near the front.

After she's eased herself into a seat, I perch on the chair next to her.

'Now I'm settled,' she says, squeezing my arm, 'you go and get something to eat. I've heard the grumbles in your tummy all the way from Horseshoe.'

I drove straight to the riding school after I left Follyfoot, skipping lunch to save time. One of the horses had a bruised sole and it took me a while to fit a special pad and shoe. By the time I collected Chili and Lollopy from Follyfoot it was already after four, and I had to drive home, settle the horses for the night and shower. I arrived at the Hargreaves's house ten minutes late.

I point to a group of people who are snatching canapés from a tray held by a harried-looking waiter. 'Unless I crash tackle them, I doubt I'd have a chance.'

She titters. 'The men should stand back for the ladies.'

How Mrs Hargreaves has hung on to her old-fashioned manners while raising abused and neglected foster children is a mystery, especially to them. Maybe it's because she treats everyone the same, as likely to lecture a police or probation officer, social worker or magistrate, as one of her own kids.

I leave my jacket on the seat. 'I'll get us a drink. Bitter lemon?'

She smiles. 'Thank you, Jet. But take your time, talk to a nice young man or two. You look lovely tonight.'

'Thank you,' I say, smoothing down my dress. It's pale blue, short and tight, the fabric clinging to the few curves I have.

As I'm walking to the bar I see Finn again, standing on the slightly raised stage and talking to a woman fiddling with a microphone, adjusting its height. When our eyes meet, he adjusts his tie, silver and blue, and says something to the woman. Soon enough, he's standing in front of me.

'Jemima.'

He holds out his hand and I take it, stiffening my fingers, afraid of holding on for too long.

'I came with Mrs Hargreaves. Sapphie is sick.'

I can't complain that he's staring at my face, not when I'm staring at his. There's barely a mark on his mouth now. I bite my lip, desperately thinking up something to say.

'Did you have a good break in Switzerland?'

He frowns. 'I was working.'

'Right.' My shoes match my dress, but they're ballet flats. I wish I had heels. I wish I were taller. 'Are you nervous?'

He opens his mouth and shuts it again, like he's not sure how to respond. 'Nervous?'

'About your speech. I would be.'

'I won't speak for long.' He angles his head, looks at my cheek. 'No complications?'

'From the kick? It was nothing, like I said.'

'Edward had no idea it had happened.'

'I wouldn't tell him something like that.'

A waiter offers us canapés, mushrooms stuffed with prosciutto in a creamy chilli sauce.

Finn shakes his head. 'No, thank you.'

I'm tempted, but worried I'll make a mess. 'No, thanks.'

Finn's eyes look darker than usual. Is it his grey suit?

'Has Edward given you an update on Thornbrooke?' he asks.

'He knows I wouldn't want to hear it.'

'Pretending there isn't a problem doesn't get rid of it. Edward is right about that.'

'Don't you two have better things to do than talk about me?' I look across the room. 'I promised Mrs Hargreaves a soft drink.'

I don't wait for a response, but walk straight to the bar. My throat is tight, so is my chest.

U

'I'm happy to stand,' I say, picking up my jacket and offering my chair to an elderly woman.

Mrs Hargreaves touches my hand. 'Thank you, love. I'll see you after the formalities.'

I stand at the back of the room, next to an easel with a photo of two hippopotamuses, a mother and her young. The mayor makes a speech about funding and an environmentalist talks about the importance of conservation. A zoo director introduces Finn, lists his qualifications, and spends an age reading out his achievements. Finn looks mildly annoyed, and walks to the podium the moment the director finishes. He takes a small device out of his pocket and points it at the screen. An image of a large male rhino appears, similar to the one I saw on his iPad at the zoo. Behind the male are two more rhinos, a mother and calf. The three of them are on a savannah but sheltered by a tree, its branches hanging low over scrappy green grass.

Finn adjusts the microphone and faces the audience. 'All of us come from somewhere,' he says. 'I was raised in a council flat on the outskirts of Glasgow. My father is a railway worker, my mother a hairdresser. When I was a child, they supported my interest in wildlife, particularly megafauna like elephant and rhino, with books, David Attenborough documentaries and zoo excursions. As I grew up, particularly after a teacher suggested I sit for a scholarship and go to university, and told my parents I could be a doctor, I suspect they hoped I'd get over my obsession.' He smiles. 'Sadly for them, I never quite did.'

No one is whispering or filling their glasses. The room is quiet. Finn changes the image on the screen to a herd of elephants at a waterhole. He tells us he studied veterinary science at Oxford, but in the university breaks he worked in Kenya, Namibia and Swaziland. While completing his doctorate, which had something to do with genetics and rhinos, he lived mostly in South Africa.

'I used to spend my days in the field,' he says. 'Now I spend a lot of time at a desk or in a lab. Occasionally,' he taps the podium, 'I stand at one of these. Why? Because conservationists and other scientists, geneticists like me, endeavour to preserve species for the next generation, while protecting them from the current one.'

An image of a rhino male comes onto the screen. He's a light-grey colour, with a large head and two weathered horns.

'This Northern White rhino was the last male of his subspecies. His kind won't die out because they fail in evolution, but because of habitat loss, trade in animal parts, political upheaval, and other issues directly attributable to all of us.'

The next image is of another rhino, lying dead on his side. His horns have been hacked off. Five dead elephants, their bellies swollen, fill the screen after that. There's a pile of bullet shells on the dusty ground next to them.

'These animals were killed by poachers,' Finn says, 'victims of poverty and conflict, often desperate to feed their families. If one is arrested, there'll be ten to take his place. That's why it's vital that the traffickers are caught. Organised crime syndicates may start out in guns and drugs but, with less risk of prosecution and a greater pay-off, they often branch out into animal parts.' He takes a sip of water and looks around the audience. 'The authorities need sophisticated methods, intelligence-based forensics, to take these people on.'

Another image comes onto the screen, a crash of rhino feeding on grasslands.

'At Pretoria University, we've taken DNA samples from thousands of rhinos, the endangered black rhino, and also the white rhinos you see on the screen, to find their genetic fingerprints, and set up a database. Rangers are trained to treat rhino deaths as crime scenes, to retrieve blood, tissue and hair samples. They learn about "chains of custody", to ensure samples aren't corrupted. That way we match rhinos to blood found on poachers' clothes and equipment, and to horns found in markets overseas.

We use the database to identify where horns come from and track the means by which they get to their destinations. This information is used to prosecute the people at the top, the organisers, the ringleaders.'

Waiters walk past with trays of food, but I ignore them. I listen to the tone of Finn's voice, his words and sentences, the power and passion of them.

When another image appears, I reach for the easel next to me and grasp it tightly. The rhino on the screen is on his knees and seems to be staring into the lens of the camera. His horns have been gouged out. A trail of thick dark blood runs down his cheek. A dart is lodged in his head, just behind his eye.

'I didn't take this photograph,' Finn says. 'I didn't have the stomach to. The rhino had been tranquillised to stun it, then shot with a rifle—in his flank, legs and chest—thirteen times. Even then, he didn't die. The poachers took his horns while he was paralysed. He managed to get to his knees as the tranquilliser wore off, and this is how we found him.'

A man raises his hand. 'Did the rhino die?'

'He was bleeding to death.' Finn hesitates. 'I fired the shot that killed him.'

He points at the screen again and the first image, of the three rhinos on the savannah, appears.

'That's him, taken the week before he died.' A woman gasps. 'His territory was in Kruger National Park. We'd been concerned ever since he'd moved his herd to the north, near the border to Mozambique. For good reason, as it turned out.'

'Did you catch the perpetrators?'

'Unfortunately not, but we have his DNA. If his horns turn up in Asia, or the Middle East, we might be able to prosecute.' He looks around the room. 'Any more questions?'

The zoo director clears his throat. 'I have one. Much as we're delighted to have you here, you're now based in Switzerland. Do you miss living in Africa?'

Finn hesitates. He frowns. The question seems to be a difficult one to answer. 'I miss the people and I miss the wildlife. I miss the physical challenges of working in that environment.' He smiles stiffly. 'I don't miss the politics. Your climate, your big open skies, the browns and greens in the landscape, they remind me of Africa.'

He patiently answers questions about conservation, explaining the role that modern zoos play in maintaining genetic diversity, which is like an insurance policy, or a safety net, for the protection of vulnerable species. People in the audience are still putting their hands up when the director tells them there's no more time for questions. After the applause dies down, a number of people move towards the stage. I watch Finn talking, shaking hands.

When someone touches my arm, I jump.

'I see I wasn't the only one hanging on every word,' Mr Hargreaves says. 'Sorry to give you a shock.'

'I … He's a good speaker, isn't he?'

'That he is. I wonder if we could tempt him to be our guest for the Follyfoot fundraiser, to talk to the children and parents. It's not until February, but this might be a good time to ask, get in early, so to speak.'

'Getting in early is a good idea.' I catch a waiter's eye and put my glass on his tray.

'Can I find you another drink?' Mr Hargreaves says.

'I'd better get home. Mrs Hargreaves is sitting in the front row, three seats in.' I stand on my toes and see her deep in conversation with the woman sitting next to her. 'Can you tell her I said goodbye?'

Just before I reach the exit, another waiter walks towards me, holding out a platter of tiny desserts.

'A basket made of Belgian chocolate,' he says, raising his brows, 'and filled with a caramelised cluster of nuts.'

'Thank you.' I carefully pick up a basket. 'I'm starving.'

He smiles. 'Take another for the road.'

I eat the first dessert in just a few bites as I walk down the stairs, but take my time over the second one. As I chew the crunchy filling, the basket melts on my fingers, so I'm licking them one by one as I step onto the footpath. Daylight saving has started, so the days are a little longer, but the sun must have gone down an hour ago at least. I stop under a light to check there's no chocolate on the tape on my finger, and then button my jacket against the cold. It didn't rain today but the air is damp, the moon obscured by clouds.

I dropped Mrs Hargreaves at the entrance to the Convention Centre so she didn't have far to walk, and parked a few hundred metres away. I jump over the low brick wall that borders the city park and walk across the gardens. There's a long and narrow pond, brimming with rushes and grasses, but other than that, the garden beds are like bigger versions of those in Horseshoe's park, with old-fashioned plants like roses, lavender and salvia. There aren't many lights, but the streetlights from the main road glimmer through the trees.

I'm getting close to the steps that lead down to the road on the far side of the park when I hear footsteps behind me. The stride is long; I think it's a man's.

'Jemima!'

CHAPTER
16

Finn slows his pace, but within a few seconds he's standing in front of me. There are deep, dark shadows all around us.

'What do you want?'

'Why did you leave?' His jacket is open, his shirt starkly white. He's taken off his tie.

'I've had a long day.'

'I wanted to talk to you.'

'There were people lining up to talk to you.'

'I'll go back shortly.'

My shoes have less height than the boots I wear for work, so he seems even taller than usual. He buttons his jacket and then unbuttons it again.

'I wanted to apologise. I shouldn't have raised Thornbrooke, not tonight.'

'You don't seem to be able to help yourself.' The sandstone path is only metres away; I walk to it quickly.

'Jemima.' When he calls out, I pull up at the top of the steps, but don't turn around. 'Please come back.'

I grasp the wall that runs either side of the steps. The sandstone block is cold beneath my hand. I squeeze my eyes shut.

'I've been up since five. It'll take me an hour to get home. I want to go to bed.'

He mutters something under his breath. Then he overtakes me, walks down two steps and turns, so we're at eye level.

'It's been almost three weeks. May I see you tomorrow?'

'If you're staying at the homestead, there's nothing I can do to stop you.'

He sighs. 'So fucking obstinate.' He touches my forearm. 'You're intractable.'

'What do you mean by that?'

'You're set on your course.'

Even through my jacket, I feel the warmth and strength of his hand. 'You do what you want to do, too. You live in England, South Africa, Switzerland.'

His hand slides up to my shoulder. 'It's Horseshoe I've missed.'

A scratching breaks the silence. A possum's tail, long and bushy, disappears into the branches of a gum tree at the bottom of the steps.

'Oh.'

He touches my earlobe, sets off a million nerve endings I never knew I had. He strokes my cheek with his thumb. When I look up, it's into his eyes.

'No infection?' he says.

'I've already told you.'

'I was concerned.' His clean, soapy pine smell scrambles my brain. I should push him out of the way and run, but my hands flutter between us, brushing his lapels.

'I'm sorry about your rhino,' I whisper.

He picks up a lock of my hair, lets it slip through his fingers. 'I find you impossible to read.'

'Except for obstinate and intractable. Why do you try anyway?'

He leans forwards and anchors my hands against his chest. He frowns. 'I can't stop myself.' He runs his hands down my sides to my hips and pulls me even closer. He mumbles against my mouth. 'Jemima?'

My body is soft and heated—my lips, breasts and stomach. 'Mmmm.'

'Say my name.'

I draw back a little. 'Dr Blackwood?'

He slowly shakes his head. 'You can do better.'

I sigh against his mouth. 'Finn.'

'Try to trust me a little.'

'I can't do that.'

He draws back. 'Which is why I should walk you to your car.'

'I don't need to be walked anywhere.'

'Because this is Dubbo?' He picks up my hand and lays my finger against his lip. 'I thought that too.'

'Oh.' The scar might have faded, but I know where it was. I press against it, and then trace a path to his eye.

'Have you found anything else to like about me?' he says.

My finger trails from his temple to his jaw. 'I like your face.'

He groans a laugh. 'That's it?' His erection is long and hard against my thigh.

'I liked your speech. I like the way you say your words, how you're so proper.' When I kiss along his jaw, his bristles are rough on my lips.

He pulls back. He stares into my eyes. 'But nothing more?'

I must smile because he gently touches the dimple at the side of my mouth. He kisses it as he runs his hands up my back, under my jacket.

I feather my fingers over his lips, between them. I touch his teeth. He dips his head and bites the pad of my thumb. Then he stills. He raises his head and frowns, just for a moment. Is he thinking this is a bad idea? Given I won't tell him my secrets? Given there's no trust?

I wrap my arms around his neck and thread them through his hair. I touch his bottom lip with my tongue. When he growls I feel it, from my lips to my toes. I stroke under his eye and study his mouth up close. I gently kiss his lips, feel their contours, find his tongue and stroke. He's holding back. I raise my face and murmur.

'It's just a kiss.'

He lifts my chin with his knuckles. He razes my neck and softly bites my earlobe. His voice is gravelly.

'What about tomorrow?'

I thread one of my legs through his and secure it with my calf. 'No tomorrow.'

He stiffens; his grip firms on my hips. And then, as if he can't help himself, he lifts me up and moulds my body to his until I'm on my toes. His thumbs brush the sides of my breasts. I want his hands on my body, against my skin. Our breaths are loud in the night.

He teases me with kisses, light, tempting, gentle, firm. Our tongues dart and flick. Until, when I'm impatient with need, he takes my face in his hands. He explores my mouth, every millimetre of it, outside and in. It's sweet and intense, heated and hungry. When he lifts his head, I moan a complaint.

His eyes are black in the night. 'You're sure about this?'

'Yes.'

He kisses me again until his touch, his taste, his scent, they're all that I'm aware of. I run my hands over his biceps. I grasp his shoulders. He slides his tongue so far down my throat that I can only breathe through him. My heart hammers, my legs are unsteady.

Intimacy. Desire. Passion. I'm flushed and shaky and want much more.

But then he stills. Lifts his head. Grabs the tops of my arms. His grip is far too tight. His fingers dig into my skin. He pushes me away.

'Finn?'

He takes a clumsy step backwards. He touches his mouth with his fingers. He rubs it harshly with the side of his hand. His eyes are wild.

I shiver and wrap my arms around my body. 'What's the matter?'

He clutches the sandstone wall at the side of the steps. A moment later he sways. He staggers.

'Finn!' I grab onto his arm and push with all my weight so he doesn't fall down the steps. His legs buckle and he collapses, slumping onto a step. I shove with my shoulder, wedging him tightly against the wall to stop him from falling. He puts his head in his hands. His whole body shudders. He wheezes and gasps. I force his head up.

'What's happening? Tell me!'

'Ep …' He's sucking in breaths. His hand goes inside his jacket. His movements are jerky and clumsy, imprecise.

'What are you looking for?' I push his hands away and search the pockets. 'An inhaler? Is it asthma?' My hand connects with a hard plastic cylinder. I wrench it out of his pocket.

'Epinephrine,' he whispers. 'Get …'

My world goes deathly quiet. His lips move, but I can't hear a thing. The wind isn't rustling in the trees any more. No car horns. No squawking birds, no scratching possums.

It must be an allergic reaction. I shut my eyes and picture the shed at Follyfoot, the ambulance officer who visits every year to train us in first aid. *Anaphylaxis*. Finn's tongue and lips will be on fire. His trachea will be swollen, narrowing the airways, restricting his breathing.

I'm not strong enough to carry him up the steps, or to support his weight to come down them.

'Listen to me, Finn. You have to lean back.' I push and shove until his back is against the wall with his legs stretched out on the step. My hand shakes as I tear the wrapping off the auto-injector and pull out the safety release.

'Finn, are you listening? I'm giving you the adrenaline. Okay?'

He croaks a yes.

I hold the EpiPen against the outside of his thigh. 'Here? I can do it through your pants, can't I?'

'Hard. Push it …'

I hear the click that goes off when the adrenaline shot is released. We worked in pairs last time we did the first-aid course. My partner read the instructions on the packet, and I gave the shot to the dummy.

Finn is so pale. He forces air in and out, but his chest is barely moving. He's tall. He's powerful. He needs a lot of air, not a tiny stream, a trickle, of it. I brush hair from his face. His skin is clammy and cold.

He swipes at the EpiPen and vaguely rubs his thigh. What if adrenaline isn't enough? The Follyfoot instructor said CPR is next, but air has to get through his throat for that to work. A tracheostomy? I don't have my tools. If I have to cut a hole in his throat, what will I use? A key? I turn my bag upside down.

My phone clatters onto the step. And suddenly sounds come back. The wind blows through the trees. A truck rumbles in the distance. My shoes scrape on the sandstone. Someone has switched the sound back on in my nightmare.

I don't need to read the numbers, just to punch them in. Fourth row, middle number. Zero zero zero.

'Ambulance!'

CHAPTER
17

'How can I do CPR if he's allergic to me?'

The woman on the emergency line speaks slowly. 'We'll cross that bridge if we come to it. He's still breathing, isn't he?'

I've undone his shirt buttons. He has a thin leather cord around his neck with a medical disk attached. My hand is flat on his chest so I can feel every breath. They're rapid and shallow. Tortured.

'Only just. I'm sure his pulse is much too fast. He's barely conscious. His eyes are shut. He can't talk.'

'You're doing well, Jet, really well. The ambulance will be there any minute. Just keep him calm.'

'He's cold.' His jacket is bunched up under him, so I take off my jacket and drape it over his chest. When I hear the siren I don't dare look up, willing Finn to keep on breathing. But finally I see the ambulance lights, garish red and ghostly blue. They illuminate Finn's face. Two paramedics appear. Even before they run to the top of the steps, open their cases and crouch, they fire questions.

'He's already had adrenaline?' the tall one says.

I look at my watch. 'Six minutes ago. He's worse than he was.'

'Still breathing, love. That's good.'

'There was no one else to help.'

'You did fine on your own.'

'Do something.' My voice breaks.

'We'll look after him. Finn, right?'

'Nut trigger?' the short one says.

'I think it was hazelnuts and almonds. I don't think it was peanuts. I don't know!'

'Easy, Jet, doesn't matter what sort.'

The tall paramedic listens to Finn's heart and takes his blood pressure and pulse. He unwraps a syringe and gives him another adrenaline shot. He speaks into his radio. The voices are muffled but easy enough to follow. Finn is in trouble; it's too risky to wait until he's at the hospital to intubate him. It'll have to be done here.

The tall paramedic puts down the radio. 'Finn,' he says, 'my name is Simon. I'm a paramedic. I'm going to put a tube down your throat and attach it to a ventilator. You okay with that?'

Finn doesn't respond. His face is so pale. I rearrange my jacket over his chest as the short paramedic rips open a packet.

'He can't hear you.'

'You're a local, Jet, aren't you?' Simon says. 'What do you do?'

'I'm a farrier.'

'Really? In that case, you must be stronger than you look. A good thing, given the job I've got for you. I want you to lie across his feet and legs. Don't want him rolling down the steps now, do we?'

Finn gags when the tube goes into his mouth. He passes out completely when it's pushed to the back of his tongue. The paramedic keeps changing the angle of the tube but can't get it down. He takes it out and repositions it.

'Take two,' he says.

Finn's eyes are closed like he's sleeping, but he's much too still for that. Has he stopped breathing? The paramedic slowly rotates the tube.

'Sorry, mate. Not much room to manoeuvre down here. Swallow if you can.'

'He can't hear you.'

'Yes, Jet,' Simon says, taking the tube out of Finn's mouth again. His eyes meet the other paramedic's and he raises his brows. He's even more worried than he was. I sense the tension in both of the men.

'Pulse no good,' the other paramedic says, reaching behind him and pulling another wrapped packet from the case. 'I've got the tracheostomy needle.'

Simon tips Finn's head back even further. 'We're losing you, Finn. Let's try one more time.'

The short paramedic readjusts the portable light set up at the top of the stairs. Then the tube goes back in Finn's mouth. 'That's the way,' Simon mutters. 'You're doing great.'

I swallow for Finn. Again and again.

And, moments after they lose his pulse, the tube goes down. Simon connects it to a ventilator, purring softly on the step. Other than the movements of his chest, as the air is forced in and out, Finn lies perfectly still, just like the dummy in the first-aid course. I turn to Simon when the short paramedic runs to get the stretcher.

'What now?'

'This'll keep him going till he gets to the hospital.'

'Right, then.' My voice wavers.

He touches my arm. 'They said it was you who ate the nuts. I've heard about kissing cases. First one I've seen.'

I see the tall paramedic more clearly now. *Simon*. He must be sixty at least. The woman on the phone said she'd send someone who'd done a tracheostomy before, just in case.

'Thanks for what you did.'

'He's a strong young fella. He'll come good.'

I follow the leather cord around Finn's neck with my fingertip until I find the disk. I rest it in the middle of his chest and clumsily fasten the buttons on his shirt. I pull my jacket further up his body. His lashes form semicircles, dark and even, under his eyes.

'The shock is making him cold.' My voice wobbles. 'He needs a blanket. Do you have a blanket?'

Simon pats my arm. 'There'll be one on the stretcher. Don't you worry about that.' He reaches for his radio. He speaks quietly. 'We're coming in. It was touch and go. Line up a medic.'

'Tell them about the disk,' I say. 'Should I take it off?'

'It's safer where it is. They'll find it.'

Finn wakes up as they're manoeuvring him onto the stretcher. He grasps his throat.

'Easy, Finn,' the short paramedic says, holding Finn's arms to his sides. He nods to Simon. 'Better sedate him.'

'You're on a ventilator,' Simon says, as he takes out a syringe. 'They'll take the tube out when we get to the hospital, and this will help you rest in the meantime. Won't be long. You're doing great.'

I stroke Finn's forehead. 'It's okay, Finn. You're okay now.'

His eyes stay open, glazed and dull, as the paramedic wheels the stretcher towards the back of the ambulance. The short paramedic opens the front passenger door and motions I get in. I touch Finn's cheek. I think he'd like to say something, but can't speak through the tube.

'Can I sit in the back with him?'

'You'll see him soon enough,' Simon says kindly, 'and my mate will keep him company. I'm good company too. Ride up the front with me.'

CHAPTER
18

A team of medical people appears as soon as the ambulance pulls up at the hospital. They surround Finn's stretcher when it's unloaded, then wheel him towards double swing doors that lead to the emergency ward. When I follow, one of the nurses holds out her hand.

'Wait for us here,' she says, indicating a row of seats in the corridor. 'I'll keep you posted.'

'Will he be okay?'

'He should be.' She's very pretty, with black hair, tightly pulled into a bun. 'I'll be out soon.'

I spend the next hour pacing the corridor and looking up every time the doors open. When the nurse finally returns, she puts a hand on my arm.

'Sorry that took so long. We've taken the tube out. He's comfortable and breathing well on his own. He was asleep last time I saw him.'

'Thank you.'

'You were with him when it happened?'

I jerk a nod. 'Yes.'

'The ambos said you did well. You're Jet, right?'

'Yes.'

Her eye shadow and liner are gold and bronze, and show off her beautiful eyes. 'Would you mind taking a call from his parents?' she asks. 'We're flat out in there.'

When I follow her to a nurses' station just inside the emergency room, she hands me a phone. I press it to my ear as I perch on the edge of a chair.

'Hello, this is Jet Kincaid.'

'This is Annie Blackwood, Finn's mam.' Her voice is tight with anxiety but she doesn't sound old. Maybe fifties? 'How is Finn? Is he all right?'

'I spoke to the nurse a minute ago. She said he's doing well.'

'It was you who helped him, wasn't it?'

It was me who almost killed him.

'Jet?'

I swallow. 'Sorry, Annie. Yes, I was there. He's asleep now, and the nurse says he should rest. But he's going to be okay.'

'Are you sure? When the doctor called, she said they had to put a tube down his throat. That hasn't happened since he was a boy.' Her voice breaks. 'A very wee boy.'

'Things were bad for a while, but now he's much better. He's at a really good hospital; there are doctors and nurses everywhere. They know what they're doing.'

'Can you see Finn now?' She bursts into tears. 'We're so far away.'

I feel like crying too. And my hand is shaking so much I have to support it with my other one.

'I'll see him as soon as he wakes up. I promise.'

'Thank you, Jet.' A man's voice. 'This is Finn's dad, Findlay Blackwood. I've put you on the speaker so Annie can hear. We don't want to make a fuss, but, just as Annie said, we're so far away.'

'I'll stay here, I promise. And I'll make sure he's looked after.'

'Thank you, lass. That's very kind of you, particularly as it'll be the middle of the night in Australia. Can you give our lad a message? Would you mind?'

'Of course not.'

'Tell him to call the landline at home, because we don't want to miss him on our mobiles, just in case the reception goes. He's to call us as soon as—'

'No, Findlay.' Annie sniffs. 'First of all, tell him we love him very much. And we know how busy the medical folk are and don't want to be a bother, so we'll be sitting by the phone, waiting for his call when he's feeling up to it. It doesn't matter what time it is, we'd just like to hear his voice.'

I speak to his parents for a few more minutes, reassuring them as best I can. Another hour goes by before I see the nurse again.

I get to my feet. 'Is he awake?' My head swims and I hold onto the chair. 'How is he?'

'He's nauseous, his throat is sore, and he's bound to feel like he's been hit by a truck, but that's to be expected. All things considered, he's not too bad. Even so, it's important someone keeps an eye on him until morning.'

'He'll stay here, then?'

She grimaces. 'That was the plan until he woke up. He's fed up, and adamant he wants to go home.'

'To Scotland?'

She laughs. 'To Dubbo. He said his apartment is in the centre of town.'

'Can't you make him stay?'

'Not without his permission. He can stagger out of here whenever he chooses.'

'Does he have someone to stay with him?'

'He told me this is no one else's business.' She rolls her eyes. 'He also said if I won't order a taxi, he'll do it himself.'

'Can I see him? I promised his parents I'd give him a message.'

The nurse walks me through the emergency ward. There are rows of beds, separated by curtains. Most of the patients are elderly but one little boy has his arm in a sling, his parents sitting either side of him on the bed. Doctors buzz around, leaning over patients, talking quietly to each other, typing in front of computer screens.

'Good luck,' the nurse says, pointing to a curtained-off section in the corner.

Easing the curtain aside, I slip through silently. Finn is lying on a bed, stabbing at his phone with his thumbs. His mother said he was a little boy the last time this happened. He's a man now, with stubble on his jaw, inky dark against the paleness of his face. Even so …

I'd like to push his hair back from his forehead. Rest my hand on his chest to feel his heartbeat. Put my ear to his mouth to hear his breath. Is he warmer now? I'd like to—

He looks up, straight into my eyes. 'Jemima.' His expression is watchful and guarded.

'Finn.'

'Go home.' His voice is croaky; he massages his neck as if it hurts. 'It's late.'

'I wanted to see you were okay.'

'I am.'

'You should stay here at the hospital.'

'No.'

He picks up a remote, joined to his bed frame by a curly white cord. He presses a button and props up his bed until he's sitting. There's a cannula in the back of his hand. The tube, running from the needle to a bag on a stand, doesn't seem to worry him when he reaches for a cup. He sips very slowly. Whenever he swallows, he winces.

Our eyes meet. 'Would you like more water?'

He ignores me, pointedly pushing the *nurse* button on the remote. I stand at the foot of the bed.

'Your parents want you to call.'

He tips back his head and addresses the ceiling. 'Who told them?'

His hospital gown hides the leather cord he wears around his neck, but when I point to a spot in the centre of his chest, he tightens his lips and nods his understanding.

'They're recorded as next of kin,' I say.

The disk also listed his allergies. Tree nuts. Legumes such as peanuts. Crustaceans. *A Belgian chocolate basket filled with a caramelised cluster of nuts.*

'They shouldn't have been called.' He takes another sip of water. 'The staff knew who I was.'

'Because I told them. But I didn't know your birthdate, or your blood type. They found the information on the disk, but wanted to make sure it was accurate.'

'My parents. How much do they know?'

'The doctor told them about the tube.'

'Fuck.'

'I spoke to them. I told them they shouldn't worry. And I promised that ...'

'What?'

'I'd pass on a message.' I focus on the wheels of his bed. 'They said they love you very much and they'd like you to call them when you can. They're sitting at home by the landline because they're worried about the reception on their mobiles. Maybe if they spoke to you, they'd—'

'I get it.' He winces, massages his neck. 'I'll call.'

'I'll go with you to your apartment.'

'No.'

'Why not?'

He hesitates. 'This …' He looks around the curtained-off space. He gestures to the gown, the cannula. He narrows his eyes. 'This is personal.'

Wasn't kissing him personal?

The pretty nurse with dark hair pulls open the curtain. 'Have we sorted everything out?'

'Yes,' I say. 'I'll take him to his apartment and stay with him.'

His eyes fly to mine. He shakes his head. 'I don't need that.'

I grasp the end of the bed with both hands. A clipboard hangs from a hook. What does it say? That he's obstinate? Intractable? *He thinks he's indestructible.*

'I promised Annie I'd look out for you.'

He closes his eyes. He opens them again. Bruised and battered blue. 'I'll tell her you did.'

'That would be a lie.'

He frowns. 'She won't know the difference.'

'I will.'

'And you never lie?'

'No!'

'You avoid the truth.'

Thornbrooke. I'm swallowing compulsively. He can barely swallow. The monitor above his bed flashes numbers. What if I'd had to read the EpiPen instructions? Or the street names so the ambulance knew where to go? I look at the screen again, a foggy blur of mysteries.

'Jet?' The nurse touches my arm. 'It's been a long night. You're exhausted. Maybe you should go.'

'I promised his mother.' My voice wavers. 'I feel responsible.'

'Bullshit,' Finn mutters.

'I'll leave as soon as it's light.'

Finn talks to the nurse. 'I'd like to speak with Jemima alone.'

'Sure,' the nurse says, 'but I want to speak to her first. You almost died, Finn. The paramedics lost your pulse. You could've gone into cardiac arrest. A relapse isn't likely, but you have to be monitored, and Jet needs to know what to look for.' She walks briskly to his side, her shoes squelching on the linoleum, and fills his cup with water. She smiles as she hands it to him. 'After I've briefed Jet, I'll help you to dress, and then I'll process your discharge.'

CHAPTER
19

You almost died, Finn. I want to shout the words into his face as he walks, slowly and unsteadily, by my side. The taxi is parked in the laneway at the front of the hospital. The threatened rain has finally arrived, just a drizzle but enough to dampen our hair. I run ahead to open the door and stand back as he gets into the car, before going to the other side and sliding in next to him. There's a beeping sound as the driver pulls into the road, but it's not until he looks in the rear-view mirror and jerks his head in Finn's direction that I work out he hasn't fastened his belt.

I'm not even sure he realises what I'm doing as I reach across him for the belt and click it into place. He's opened the window. His head rests against the frame. His fists are clenched and he's breathing through his teeth. He's deathly pale, and there's sweat on his forehead.

'You want to throw up, don't you? Should I ask the driver to stop?'

He shakes his head. 'Speed up.'

The apartments are only a few storeys high, but probably the best that Dubbo has. Finn clings onto the railing in the lift. I reach for his arm as we walk down the hallway but he steps away, using the walls for support. When he leans against the doorframe to get a key-card out of his wallet, I snatch it out of his hand and open the door myself. As I turn on lights, he staggers a few steps and crashes into an armchair, putting his elbows on his knees and hanging his head.

I shut the door quietly behind me. The sitting room has a two-seater sofa as well as the chair. There's a separate bedroom. The bathroom must be off that.

The kitchenette is next to the sitting room. There are cupboards and appliances, and a narrow bench with stools.

'The nurse said you have to drink a lot. What would you like?'

'I don't care,' he whispers.

I hand him a glass of orange juice, then search through the cup-boards. 'Would you like fruit and toast? Cereal? That's all I can find, and nothing will be open this late.'

'Anything.' He stands and puts the glass on the bench. 'I'll shower.'

I hear him foraging around in the bedroom, opening and shut-ting drawers. I think I hear his voice. Is he calling his parents? The shower starts up and runs for so long that I worry he may have fallen over or passed out. I'm tiptoeing into his room to listen when the water stops running. I freeze for a moment. Then rush around his bedroom, finding a spare pillow and blanket in the cupboard and throwing them onto the sofa. I use the rubber gloves from under the sink when I cut up apples and oranges, and make a pile of toast and marmalade. I boil the kettle. When he walks out of the bedroom, I'm leaning on the bench, drinking instant coffee with lots of milk and sugar.

His hair is wet and brushed back from his forehead. His face has a little more colour than it did. He always smells good. He sits on a stool opposite me.

'Wouldn't you be more comfortable sitting in the armchair?'

'No.'

His T-shirt, grey like his trackpants, stretches over his biceps, even more when he leans forwards to take a piece of apple. He pushes the plate towards me, but I shake my head.

'I don't feel like … I'm not hungry.'

He slowly drinks his juice, wincing when he swallows. And when the glass is empty, he pushes back the stool. He looks me up and down.

My lids are so heavy I can barely keep my eyes open. My clothes are creased and dirty from the gardens, and damp from the rain. I push my hair back.

'You're dead on your feet,' he says.

'Can I clean myself up in the bathroom?'

'What time is it?'

I look at my watch. 'Just past one.'

'You said you were up at five.'

'Yes.'

'Fuck.' He turns and walks out. A minute later he comes back, putting a drawstring cloth bag on the bench in front of me. It's stamped with a logo I recognise. British Airways.

'What is it?'

'Pyjamas. They'll be too large.' He throws a toiletry bag on the bench too. It has the same logo.

'Can you spare them?'

'I get them all the time.'

'You called your parents, didn't you?'

'Yes.'

'I'll have a shower when you go to sleep.'

He pours himself another glass of juice. 'Jemima?'

'Yes.'

'This wasn't your fault.' He uses both hands to rub his throat. 'It's just ...'

'Personal, I know.'

'I've been a bastard. I'm sorry.'

I go to the sink and run the water. My back is to him when I speak. 'No one likes being sick. And you ...'

'What?'

You like to be in control. 'I hope you sleep okay.'

I feel his gaze as I rinse the plates, but he doesn't reply. He puts down his glass and walks away, leaving his bedroom door ajar. I think he does it to give me access to the bathroom, not so I can watch him sleeping. But that's what I do ten minutes later, when I stand at the foot of his bed. He lies flat on his back with his head turned to one side. His lips look soft, his breathing is deep. I tiptoe to the bathroom and close the door behind me.

The British Airways pyjamas are much too big. I fold the sleeves up to the elbows and roll onto my side. The pants twist around my legs so I wrench them off and throw them over the back of the sofa. I lie on my back.

The bedroom door is open, but I can't see him. I can't hear him breathing.

The standard lamp in the corner of the room lights my way to the bedroom. But all I can make out is his outline. I move silently around the bed and peer into the gloom. He's so still. Too still? His arm is outside the sheet. When I lean over and feel for his pulse it's strong and steady, but I can't let him go. I have to keep counting. My hair falls in front of my face. It smells of his shampoo. The scent of his soap clings to my skin. I scrubbed myself all over, especially my hands. I brushed my teeth and tongue, inside my cheeks and the roof of my mouth. I retched when the toothbrush went too far down my throat. I think I'm clean but …

I let go of his wrist. Tears clog my throat. Every time I close my eyes I see him, lying on the sandstone step. I thread my hands together and watch the rise and fall of his chest.

Dad relied on oxygen when he had an infection or his lungs got too clogged up. He'd breathe through a mask or spikes in his nose. Sometimes I stayed up all night. I'd sit next to his bed and cry quietly so I wouldn't disturb him. I'd shed silent tears. They'd roll down my cheeks and drip onto my hands.

'Jemima?'

I jump. 'Oh!' And spin away. But not quickly enough. Finn captures my hand. My fingers are wet. He whispers.

'Baby?'

I yank my hand out of his grasp so violently he has to grab the side table so he doesn't fall out of bed.

'I'm not … we're not … Don't call me that!'

He pushes himself to a sitting position and leans against the headboard. He tips back his head and closes his eyes.

'I … can you get me a drink?' His voice is so hoarse I can barely make out the words.

When I hand him a glass of water, he drinks slowly until it's empty. He moves into the middle of the bed and indicates the space next to him.

'Sit down.'

I sniff and wipe my nose with a tissue. 'I'm okay here.'

'I said sit.' He takes a weary breath. 'Please.'

I reach for fresh tissues and blow my nose. 'You were awful in the hospital too.'

'I hate the attention.' He pats the space. 'Please, Jemima. Sit.'

I don't want to be alone, so perch on the side of the bed.

'Why were you crying?' he asks.

His face is in shadow. All I can see from the corner of my eye is his profile. He rubs his hands over his eyes as if he's just woken up. He *has* just woken up. He was so still.

I clear my throat. 'At the park … you stopped breathing.' My voice wobbles. 'I thought you might be dead. And then …' I hiccup.

'Ba—' He cuts off the word, leans forwards and puts his hands on the tops of my arms.

He's alive. He smells nice. I'm exhausted. When he pulls me towards him I go willingly. I rest my head against his chest and take a deep breath, shuddering as I exhale. He rubs his cheek on the top of my head.

'Listen, Jemima. I'm far from dead.'

Thump-thump. Thump-thump. Thump-thump.

I hear the beats. I feel them against my face and hands when he unravels my fingers and lays them flat against his chest. He runs his hands across my back with long firm strokes.

Stupid fat tears roll down my cheeks. He pulls my legs onto the bed. He shuffles until he's lying on his back with his head on the pillow. I lie down too, resting my head on his chest again. His T-shirt is soft against my face.

He slides his fingertips across my skin, beneath my bottom lashes. He wipes my cheeks with the palms of his hands.

'I didn't mean to do it.'

He tips up my face. He shakes his head. 'You think I don't know that?' He settles my head against his chest where it was. 'Sleep here.'

Before we kissed, when I touched his lips and teeth, he stilled. Did I poison him with my hands as well as my mouth? I spring upright so quickly he sucks in a breath. And before he draws another one, I'm half off the bed.

He takes my arm. 'Jem!'

'What if it happens again?'

His hand slides down my arm, he tangles our fingers together. 'It won't,' he whispers. 'Don't run away.' He searches my eyes. 'Lie down. Let's go to sleep.'

My eyes sting with tears I've already cried, and tears I haven't cried yet. I lie on my back as he reaches for the sheet; stiff white cotton, bunched at the end of the bed.

'Which side do you like?' he asks.

'What do you mean?'

'Do you prefer to sleep on the left or right side?'

'I think I sleep in the middle.'

'I meant when you're sharing a bed.'

'I've never slept with anyone.'

He blinks. 'Never?'

There are two pillows, lined up side by side. I lie on one of them with my back to him. 'You said we should rest.'

He pulls the sheet over both of us. He touches my shoulder. 'Jem?'

'What?'

He hesitates. 'Will you be warm enough?'

I nod. 'Yes, thank you.'

Maybe I doze, because when I open my eyes again I'm lying on my back. It's quiet in the room. I'm not touching Finn, but we're close. When I turn my head to check on him, he comes up on an elbow.

'You okay?' he says, putting hair behind my ear.

'I guess.'

'May I hold you?'

'I'm supposed to be looking after you.'

When he opens his arms, I fold myself into them. 'You can do that from here,' he says, lying on his back and pulling me with him.

'You're still breathing.'

He croaks a laugh and loops his leg through mine, threading us together. He rubs my back. He spreads my hair across his chest, drawing out the strands and stroking them smooth, just like he did with my laces. My body softens.

'Your hair is different shades,' he says. 'Like a lion.'

'It's always been like that.'

'Jemima?'

'Yes.'

'If you've always slept alone, does that mean you haven't had sex?'

'That's none of your business.' My voice is muffled.

His hand slips from my head to the small of my back. He tightens his hold. 'We'll talk tomorrow.' He kisses the top of my head. 'Night, Jem.'

I mutter into his chest. 'I'm sorry I kissed you.'

He whispers. 'I'm not.'

U

I'm back at Thornbrooke, running from stable to stable, untying knots, tearing frantically at buckles.

Something wakes me. A car horn? I'm still in Finn's arms but my body is trembling. I'm whimpering. My hands are near my mouth. My fingertips are wet. I bunch them up.

'Baby?' He mumbles the word.

I squeeze my eyes shut, feigning sleep, as he prises open my fingers and wipes the moisture away. He lays my hands against his chest and covers them.

He keeps them safe.

CHAPTER
20

My head is cradled in the dip between Finn's neck and collarbone. One of my arms is curved possessively over his body, my fingertips on his shoulder. My knee is bent and nestles on his thighs. My top has ridden up. His hand scoops my hip, skin against skin. His breaths are deep and steady.

Filtered light streams through the blind. When I ease myself out of his arms and stand by the side of the bed, he stirs and frowns. But soon he's fast asleep again, his lashes thick and dark. Imagine if he'd died? When a sob rises up my throat, I walk to the window and grasp the sill. There are gaps either side of the blind. The rain slides down the glass, drips onto the window ledge and trickles away.

Dad was born before some of the modern CF treatments had been developed, so his body had been irreparably damaged before he'd turned thirty. We always knew he'd die early. It was just a matter of when. Mum? That was different.

Loss. I know all about it.

And how to avoid it.

I creep to the bathroom, wash my face and brush my teeth, dress in my grubby dress and jacket and comb through my hair with my fingers. There's a pad and pen on the table next to the television. Sometimes writing is easier than reading. I print slowly and carefully.

> Finn,
> *I hope you feel ok. Sorry about everything. I'm going home. Thank you for the pjs and toothbrush.*
>   Jemima

The note looks all right to me, but there are bound to be spelling and other mistakes, so hopefully Finn can decipher it. He's kicked the quilt off one long leg. His stomach is flat. His shoulders are broad. His lips are slightly open but there's no sign of swelling or redness on his mouth. I place the note on the side table, under a glass of water. His eyes spring open.

'Jemima.' He winces and grabs his throat. 'What are you doing?' His voice is raspy.

'You were asleep.'

He sits slowly and leans against the headboard. He runs a hand through his hair as if to straighten it out, even though it's already smooth. He rubs his eyes. There's no need to do that either, they're clear and deepest blue. He focuses on my bag, tucked firmly under my arm. He frowns.

'You're dressed.'

I take three backward steps and point. 'I left you a note.'

He massages his throat when he speaks. 'Where are you going?'

'To pick up my ute, to drive home.'

He reaches for the glass. He swallows. 'Fuck.' He swallows again. 'What did they do to me last night?'

'They couldn't …' *After I kissed you, after you collapsed and stopped breathing …* 'They couldn't get the tube in.'

'Forget it.'

He swings his legs off the bed and his feet hit the floor. He's rumpled yet brutally handsome. Dangerous.

'I have to get to work. I'm late. It's seven already.'

He picks up the note and rises to his feet. 'Stay.'

I raise my chin. 'You didn't even want me here.'

He rubs the back of his neck and his T-shirt rides up. A dark line of hair trails from his navel to … He yanks the shirt down.

'We slept together,' he says.

I've never slept with anyone. My voice is strained like his. 'So?'

'We need to talk.'

I turn my face away and look longingly at the open door to the sitting room. 'I was in shock. You were … Nothing happened anyway.'

'Didn't it?'

'No.'

He presses his fingers against his forehead, rubs in circles. The nurse said he wouldn't feel good for a couple of days. Is a headache normal?

'You kissed me in the park,' he finally says.

When I walk to the kitchenette, he follows. I fill another glass from the tap and hold it out to him, keeping my distance. '"No tomorrow", remember?'

He drinks slowly, puts the glass down on the bench. He squeezes his eyes shut and massages his temple.

'Are you running because of Thornbrooke?' he says quietly.

'Not only that.' When I bunch my fingers together, he looks at them pointedly.

'What then?'

'Mind your own business.' Heat moves up my face. I said the same thing last night, when he asked …

He narrows his eyes, as if he's read my mind. And then he looks at my note. Seconds pass. He frowns. He opens his mouth and shuts it. He looks at the note again.

'The last sentence,' he says. 'You thanked me for something. What?'

I clear my throat. 'The pyjamas and toothbrush.' I point towards the bathroom. 'I put the pyjamas in the washing machine, but I didn't think you'd want the toothbrush.' I indicate my bag. 'I took it. I hope that's okay.'

He scrunches the paper into a ball. 'This is all you were planning to leave me?'

'What else?'

He throws the note in the wastepaper basket. He's paler than he was. 'You said last night you don't lie. You're kidding yourself. You hide the truth.'

I take a step back. 'You have secrets too.'

'My allergies? They aren't a secret.'

'Just personal?'

'I handle them.'

'Like I handle Thornbrooke.'

He looks at the bed. 'You want to forget you slept there?'

My hair was still damp when I lay in his arms. He ran his fingers through it and laid it on his chest. He said it had shades like a lion.

'Yes.'

'We go back to how we were?'

'Yes.'

His eyes are navy, his body tense. He brushes past me as he walks to the door. I wish I could tell him he's as white as a sheet, that after

I've gone he should go back to bed. I wish I could tell him how life can be short. I wish I could tell him he's never to kiss me again.

But I slip through the door without saying a word. When he slams it shut behind me, I swipe at my eyes.

Is refusing to tell the truth as bad as telling lies?

It can't be, can it?

It's been raining on and off for almost three weeks. And it's the best type of rain, not floods that wash the topsoil away, threaten the stock and ruin the crops, but steady rain that soaks the land and fills up the dams. Green shoots appear—in the paddocks, at the sides of the roads, in the cracks in the footpaths in town. Pebbles squelch underfoot as I make my way to the third row of graves in the cemetery. I straighten my hood and tighten the drawstring.

Most of the freesias are already spent, but some are still perky and bright. The daffodil flowers are yellow and sunny. The jonquils are scented and white. Mum's grave is flowering the best. I cut a bunch of blooms with my penknife. When I get home, I'll put them in the blue and white vase that sits on the windowsill above the kitchen sink.

Weeks of rain and no sign of Finn. I didn't expect him that first weekend, but he hasn't shown up for the last two weekends either. Today it's Tuesday. I ease out the last of the weeds and wipe my hands on my jeans, dirty from work already.

By the time I turn off the road and drive over the cattle grate, Sapphie's car is parked out the front of the cottage. She left a voice-mail an hour ago, accusing me of avoiding her and telling me she was coming to dinner, whether I wanted to see her or not.

She's sitting on the pew on the verandah. 'I brought a casserole,' she shouts.

I yell back from the shed. 'Thanks, Sapphie. Let yourself in.'

'I already have.'

'I'll be as quick as I can.'

I've been keeping the horses in the home paddock because of the rain. Chili Pepper and Lollopy usually take shelter in the hayshed at the back of Kincaid House. Vegemite, in a blue waterproof rug, and Freckle, his coat still thick even though we're well into spring, huddle together with the windbreak of pines at their backs. Because they expect it, I take a few biscuits of hay from the back of the shed and throw them into the wheelbarrow, manoeuvring it through the gate and spreading it over a patch of higher ground. Vegemite is walking particularly stiffly. I run my hands over his body and feel down his legs. When I take his halter in my hands and look into his eyes, he blinks right back at me. 'You all right, mate? I can't find anything wrong.' I stroke under his chin. 'Is your arthritis playing up? We'd better go back to two rugs at night.'

By the time I get back to the house, Sapphie is in the kitchen, bending over the oven. 'That smells good,' I say, filling the vase at the sink.

'Chicken casserole. Ma made it.'

'I'll clean myself up.' Drips from my jeans fall onto the linoleum. I wipe them away with the toe of my sock. 'Won't be too long.'

She looks me up and down and laughs. 'Take your time.'

∪

An hour later, our plates are scraped clean.

'More?' Sapphie says.

I shake my head. 'That was great, thank you. Mrs Hargreaves is a gem.'

'It was a thank you for taking her to Dubbo.' She looks towards the homestead. 'Will your neighbour be here this weekend?'

I twirl my glass around. 'No idea.' I nudge her foot under the table. 'And stop fishing.'

She grins. 'Put me out of my misery.'

'I was telling the truth. I have no idea whether Finn will be here or not.'

'Finn? What happened to "Blackwood"?'

'I was the only person in Horseshoe calling him that.'

'He's the only person in Horseshoe who calls you "Jemima".'

Unexpected tears spring to my eyes. I reach across the table and pick up her plate. 'I don't want to talk about it.'

'I'm sorry.' She puts a hand on my arm. 'He's hurt you, hasn't he?'

I stand. 'We wouldn't be good for each other.'

'Finn followed you out of the cocktail party, Pa told me that. And when I came to ride Chili early on Saturday, it was clear you hadn't come home. You spent the night with him, didn't you? That must have been a big deal.'

'For someone like me, you mean?' I carry the plates to the sink. 'It's not what you think. He wasn't well, he was … It's personal, private. I can't say more.'

'Everyone likes him but you. Is it because he's helping Edward?'

'I wouldn't be having nightmares if not for him.' I fill the sink and squeeze in detergent. 'He doesn't let up about Thornbrooke. And there's other stuff as well.'

She folds the tea towel and unfolds it again. Her big blue eyes are wide with worry. 'What?'

I hand her a bunch of knives and forks. 'It's … remember when I met him down at the river? Right from the start, I could see he was dangerous. There's something about him. He's a risk-taker.'

'He's smart, fit and *very* attractive. Can't you just focus on that?'

'I don't do risk.'

She blows out a breath. 'You used to. According to Gus, you weren't afraid of anything.'

'Yeah. Well, now I am.'

Her eyebrows lift. 'We have an assembly every Friday in the primary school hall. I presume you remember the trophy cabinet?'

I shrug.

'You're still the only child who won the sports prize four years running. You excelled in swimming, athletics, cross country, just about everything.'

I rinse the glasses. 'It was lucky I didn't win the academic prizes, that would've made me big-headed.'

'You were school captain, so you must have been competent at the microphone. Did you memorise your speeches?'

It's been a long time since I stood behind a podium. I lean forwards and smell the jonquils.

'Mum encouraged me to learn them by heart, in case I wasn't able to read on the day.'

'You won the public speaking prize.'

'It was for poetry. Thank Mrs McNab for that one.'

'You won the citizenship award too.'

'I'm still friendly. That hasn't changed.'

'You don't try anything new any more.'

'I'm not twelve years old.'

'After what happened to your mother, you stopped riding. I understand that, everyone does. But do you have to pull back from other things too? I'm pretty sure Finn likes you.'

I wipe around the rim of the plate, even though it's clean. 'He doesn't belong here, not really. Anyway, we had a fight.'

'A fight?'

'An argument.'

'What about?'

Rain falls on the cottage's roof, pounding on the corrugated iron. There's another sound too. I was aware of it last night, the steady thud of water on the homestead's verandah. The gutters are overflowing. A downpipe must be blocked.

'Jet?'

'Do you hear that?' I point through the window. 'I'd better check the homestead's roof and gutters. Edward won't be happy if water gets under the eaves.'

'Okay, ignore me.' She threads the tea towel through the oven door. 'But think about what I said. You get on well with men, and they like you too. I don't see why you can't take things further sometimes, get a little closer than you do.'

'You're right.' When I smile, I feel the stiffness in my face. 'But not with Finn.'

We had a fight. It sounds so simple. Like a lovers' tiff.

We weren't even lovers.

So why did it feel like we were?

CHAPTER
22

The rain has eased, so it's merely overcast on Wednesday when I pull over at a picnic spot at Dundullimal, and take out my lunch box. The sandwich is filled with leftover chicken from last night's casserole. I'm finishing the coffee from my thermos when I get a call.

'Jet, it's Mike. You in the neighbourhood?'

'Your neighbourhood? Warrandale?'

'Dubbo. Andrew Martin called. He wants me to take a look at Precious. I'm back behind the wheel but my leg's a bit dodgy. Could you meet me at the zoo in case I need a hand?'

Precious is an elephant, over fifty years old, and Mike has known her for almost half her life. They met for the first time when she lived at Taronga Zoo in Sydney. One of the Dubbo vets thought a lot of Mike, and arranged for him to fly there to look at her. Portable radiography wasn't available then, so Mike watched her for days, trying to work out what he'd be in for before she was anaesthetised. And he guessed right. Precious had developed an infection behind one of her toenails, which was cracked, and necrotic tissue was trapped inside her foot, so Mike drilled a hole, drained and treated it. Many years later, he was at the Dubbo zoo to see one of the takhi horses. Precious had just arrived at Dubbo, a better environment for the management of her arthritis. When she spotted Mike walking on the path, she charged up to the barrier and looked directly at him, trumpeting her recognition. She's often cantankerous, and being in pain makes her moods worse. But she's never a problem with Mike. The vets appreciate that, as do the keepers.

'I'll have to put back my next client,' I say, 'but it should be okay.'

After I've made the call, delaying my appointment until five, I do a U-turn and head back to Dubbo. Last time I was at the zoo I saw Finn.

I grip the wheel more tightly as I turn off the road and into the carpark. If I see him today, I'll act like nothing happened.

We didn't kiss. I didn't almost kill him.

U

By the time I walk out of the staff area, changed into clean clothes in case I have contact with Precious, Mike is sitting on a seat outside the veterinary clinic. One of his legs is stretched out and resting on his bag. A watery sun peeks through the clouds. He shelters his eyes with a hand.

'Your hip hurts, doesn't it?' I say. 'You shouldn't drive when it's like that. I could've picked you up if I'd had more notice.'

He raises his brows. 'Elephants don't make appointments.'

'Then you should have asked Andrew to send a car to collect you.'

He pats the seat. 'Sit, Jet, until Dr Martin gets here in the buggy. And stop your fussing. Anyone'd think I was poorly.'

My shirt cuffs cover my hands. I turn them up a few times, smooth out the creases. 'Do you know Jason Caruthers? He was a stablehand at Thornbrooke and then moved to Queensland.'

'Never heard of him.'

'Unfortunately he's heard of you. He told me Morrissey sent him to give us a reminder not to talk.'

Mike shuffles closer on the seat. His fingers, calloused, knobbly and bent, twist together.

'About Thornbrooke? What's going on now?'

'It was a few weeks ago. I didn't want to worry you by telling you over the phone, not when I think I got rid of him. I told him we weren't saying anything, to Finn or anyone else.'

'You know Dr Blackwood called me?'

'He said you'd told him nothing.'

'It wasn't easy, Jet. Seemed a reasonable sort of bloke, quietly spoken, respectful like Dr Martin.' He lowers his voice. 'But that's not the point. Who's this Caruthers?'

'He says he's a friend of Morrissey's. He saw me at The Royal, talking to Finn, and didn't seem to like the idea.'

Mike pulls off his hat and shoves it into the bag at his feet. 'I don't like the sound of this.' He had a little colour in his face, but now it's back to grey.

I squeeze his arm. 'Caruthers is a creep, so I don't know why Morrissey is using him as a go-between. But at least it confirms that Morrissey wants to keep quiet. That suits all of us.'

The wrinkles between Mike's brows get deeper. 'Accessories after the fact, Jet. That's us.'

'To be an accessory, you need a crime. We don't know what happened, why the horses died.' I help him to his feet when Andrew, driving the buggy, appears around the bend.

'I was the one who broke the vitamin bottles and dragged you away like a criminal.'

'It's over, Mike. Please don't let it upset you.'

He grips my arm. 'I've been thinking. I reckon Morrissey and Schofield might've had it in their minds right from the start, to set you up in case something went wrong. It always seemed odd, those horses getting their vitamins once a week, and on a Sunday.'

'We don't know that the supplements were to blame.'

He drags his hat out of his bag again, turns it in his hands. 'Maybe you've got that right. Let Dr Blackwood do his testing. But he won't find a genetic problem, I'd bet on that.'

Andrew waves. 'I'll drive you there.'

Mike hobbles stiffly beside me. 'Let's get this elephant sorted out.'

Precious has been moved to a small yard at the rear of the elephant enclosure. She has her ears back and looks unhappy, but when she sees Mike, she seems to perk up, ambling towards him and threading her trunk through the railings. He doesn't only do farrier work with the elephant. Andrew calls him in when the vets need Precious's cooperation for X-rays, checks on her arthritis, blood sampling and other things.

'Hello, old girl,' he says, leaning against the railing. She feathers her trunk over his face and snowy-white hair. 'You got dodgy legs like me. Want to show me what's going on?'

Precious's keeper encourages her to back up to the railing and lift her hind leg. She rests it on a block that's positioned on our side of the railing, so Mike can safely work on it.

By the time Precious arrived at Taronga Zoo from another city zoo in Nairobi, her toenail was deformed. When her skin grows around it, it causes her pain. If she didn't allow Mike to pare away the skin without anaesthesia, she'd have to be knocked out every few months, and that always carries risks, especially for an elephant her age. I climb onto a railing a few metres away and watch Mike at work. Every movement is careful and precise, and he talks the whole time, about getting old, and knowing when it's time to call it quits.

By the time he's finished, I have a lump in my throat, and he's ghostly pale. 'May as well see to the rest of her feet as I'm here,' he says.

Andrew steps in before I have the chance to. 'I think that's enough for today, Mike.'

'Precious don't want to be mucked around again for no good reason,' Mike mutters. 'And I'm not dead yet.'

I jump down from the railing. 'Do you think I could help out? Would Precious mind? You'd still be in charge.'

Mike looks from me to Precious. 'Jet's a good girl, and handy with her tools,' he tells the elephant. 'What do you reckon?'

The arthritis in Precious's front legs makes it harder for her to bend them at the knee and put them on the blocks, so I start with her back legs, working with a paring knife on the undersides of her feet and scraping away the thickened skin layer by layer. Some elephants don't need this treatment at all, even in a zoo, particularly when they have large areas to roam around in. But Precious spends a lot of time standing. If a stone or other object gets wedged in her foot, it could lead to an infection that passes to the bone. That would be particularly serious with an elephant as old as she is.

Mike keeps talking as I work, telling Precious what's going on, giving me direction, and praising my efforts. It's not easy, working on elephant feet with Mike and one of the zoo's senior vets watching every move, but by the time I put the knife in the toolbox, the soles of Precious's feet are relatively smooth. Probably more importantly, she's allowed me to do it, cooperating by raising her feet and standing perfectly still.

'Thank you, Jet.' Andrew shakes my hand, sore from wielding the knife. 'That went well.'

'It's about time you stepped up,' Mike says gruffly, hiding a smile. 'How's it feel to be an apprentice again?'

I smile too. 'Strangely familiar.'

Andrew rubs his hands together. 'Can I trouble you both for another few minutes? We've radiographed one of the giraffes. Afaafa is five months' pregnant and footsore, but damned if we know why. Mind dropping by the clinic on your way out to have a look at the slides?'

I glance at my watch. 'I'd better change first. I have a client to get to by five.'

The non-surgical and treatment part of the clinic consists of a large open-plan area, crowded with desks and partitions, plus a few offices and labs. The head of pathology looks at a computer screen with two other employees. Lorenzo, an animal dietician, is at a standing desk with a bundle of papers in front of him.

'Jet!' he says when he sees me. 'My daughter Francesca, she tells me you are the prettiest, cleverest farrier in the world.'

I laugh. 'She's as easy to like as her pony. Congratulations on being a dad again.'

He beams. 'You have seen him, little Marco?'

'After I shod Batman last week, Luisa and I had coffee. Marco was fast asleep when I held him.'

'I have a beautiful wife, beautiful children.'

'Hurry up, Jet,' Mike grumbles.

I've almost caught up when Finn walks out of a room a few metres away. I pull up so quickly my boots scuff the carpet. He isn't pale like he was the last time I saw him. If anything, dressed in black jeans and a thin blue sweater, he looks even healthier than usual. His eyes are bright, but guarded. When he speaks over his shoulder, I see a second man. He's fair-haired, almost as tall as Finn and about my age. He's wearing a suit and tie.

I press back against a desk, leaving room for the men to pass. I don't think Finn intends to stop, but has little choice when the other man does.

'Jet? Is that the name I heard?' He has an American accent.

'Yes.'

'It's great.'

'It's short for Jemima.'

The man thrusts out his hand. 'Nate Gillespie.' He smiles broadly. 'It's amazing here. What a fantastic place to work.'

'I don't really work here. I'm just a farrier. Are you a vet too?'

'Nah, I'm with the UN.' He smiles at Finn. 'We met in Switzerland. We're climbing buddies.' He whistles. 'I've had my life in his hands too many times to mention.'

Finn's smile is stiff. 'Nate is now based in New York.'

Nate grins. 'Indoor climbs have inferior scenery, that's for sure.'

'Jet!' Andrew calls from the other side of the room. 'Ready when you are.'

'I'd better go,' I say, shaking Nate's hand.

'Jemima?'

I turn around again. 'Finn.'

'I'll be at Horseshoe this weekend.'

His eyes are cold. What expression does he see in mine? Trepidation? Regret? I look down at my boots, damp and streaked with mud. 'Right.'

I stop at the doorway that Finn and Nate walked through. Finn's office? Under the window is a desk, stacked with papers and books. A stainless-steel bench takes up one wall, with a microscope and different sized boxes. On another wall is a whiteboard. There's a hand-drawn diagram that looks like a spine with a ladder inside it. There are arrows, and reams of words either side. The writing must be Finn's, neat and black with capital letters. Often I'm better with longer words than short. And sometimes words I've never seen before, words I don't understand, light up in my mind like beacons. *Paternal chromosome. Homozygous. Heterozygous. Adenine. Maternal chromosome. Thymine. Guanine. Cytosine.*

I swallow the constriction in my throat. He was cool and reserved. Angry. I shouldn't be hurt or upset. *It was me who told him we had to go back.*

Back to how we were before we kissed.

CHAPTER

23

As I haul the extension ladder up the path to the homestead, dragging it over the sodden ground, Vegemite looks forlornly over the fence.

'Go into the hayshed with Chili and the other horses,' I tell him, wiping my hands on my jeans and stretching out my fingers. 'I'll feed you after I've cleaned out the gutters.'

It's Friday afternoon and the rain, only a light drizzle now, dampens the air. The last time I saw the sun was Wednesday at the zoo, and that was through a break in the clouds. Right now they're dense, but are a paler shade of grey than they were last night. I can't put this off any longer. Every night I lie in bed and listen to the rain dripping onto the verandah at the homestead. When I brush past a tree branch, a spray of water wets my face and trickles inside the neck of my jacket. I drop the ladder, pull up my hood and fasten all the press-studs. It was hardly worth having a shower and cleaning myself up. I'll have to do it all over again.

The roof of the homestead is high and steeply pitched. I lean the ladder against the verandah railings and extend it by pulling on the ropes, until the top rails rest against the gutters. There's little slope where I'm standing, but enough to make the ladder tilt slightly, so I find a brick near the tool shed and wedge it into the soil, under the rubber foot. I struggle to pull on gardening gloves; my hands are clumsy, cold and wet.

Halfway up the ladder, I pause for a break, bracing my feet and looping an arm through a rung. The lounge room curtains are open. Everything looks the same as it usually does except for the large, blue cardboard box on the desk. The lid sits alongside the box, which is full to the brim with papers. Is this the box that Edward brought from Thornbrooke? I guess it must be. Though Finn can't have spent much time looking through it because he hasn't been to Horseshoe in over a month. Is that because the papers aren't important? What would they …

Mike's words from Wednesday flash through my mind. *It always seemed odd, those horses getting their vitamins once a week.* What was he getting at? That the supplements were dodgy, even though the horses were regularly tested for prohibited substances? It doesn't make sense. I rest my forehead on the metal rung. The rain is heavier now, spitting on my hood. I climb again, putting one foot carefully in front of the other.

As I get closer to the gutter, the force of the wind tugs at my hood. When I swipe it back, my hair gets wet, but visibility is better. Another six steps and the gutter is adjacent to my waist. I wind my arm securely through a rung. The sky has darkened, with steel-grey clouds moving in from the west. Twigs and leaves hide the top of the downpipe and the mesh that protects it. Half the gutter is blocked up too, all the way to the middle post of the verandah.

It's slow work, hanging onto the ladder with one hand and removing debris from the top of the downpipe with my other hand. But eventually I get to the mesh, rubbing it clear. As the water starts to flow down the downpipe, the pull of it drives the leaves in the gutter towards me. I scoop them up as they pass and throw them to the ground.

The water is flowing freely along the gutter when I hear a distant rumble. Thunder. The skies darken further as I clear the last of the leaves. There's more thunder, much closer. A flash of lightning. Damn.

I'm halfway down the ladder when I see the headlights. Twin beams bounce along the driveway, taking the bend around the shed and lighting up the homestead. A door opens wide and slams shut.

Another flash of lightning, closer than the last, brightens the sky. Finn runs, his strides long and sure, from the car to the ladder. Feet apart, he grips the vertical rails, one hand either side. Why didn't he put on a jacket? He'll be sodden. When he looks up, I swipe rain from my face. Our eyes meet.

'Jemima! Get down here! For fuck's sake!'

I'm standing on a metal ladder in an electrical storm. Of course I'll get down. But I don't want to break a leg. There are two more flashes as I slowly descend. As I reach the bottom few rungs, he stands back. My feet touch the ground but I keep hold of the ladder, reluctant to turn.

'Jemima?'

I swing around, forgetting about the brick at my feet. My boot catches and I stumble.

When he grasps my arms and hauls me against his chest, I swear I feel his heartbeats through our clothes.

CHAPTER
24

Finn's hands move from my upper arms to my forearms and then to my wrists. There's a gap between the top of my glove and my jacket. His thumb, cold but firm, slides into the space.

I keep my head down. 'What are you doing?'

'What I told myself I wouldn't do.' His voice is rough. He strokes the skin at my pulse.

Rain drips from my hair. I'm not cold, but I shiver.

He frowns into my eyes. 'What the fuck were you thinking?'

I pull my hands away and release the ropes on the ladder to reduce its length. He reaches above me to grasp it, and then lays it onto the ground. Thunder rumbles behind us and there's another fork of lightning. His shirt sticks to his skin. His hair, pushed back, is glossy and dark. His mouth is wet with rain.

'Come inside,' he says.

'No.' I tug off my gloves, shoving them into my pocket before pointing to the shed. 'I have to feed the horses.' I hesitate next to the ladder, wondering whether to pick it up, but he mutters under his breath when I reach out, so I leave it where it is. It's only fifty metres to the shed, but seems to take forever. When his arm bumps mine, I skitter away. It's dry and warm inside and smells of hay. My ute is parked at an odd angle because I needed to take the ladder out. I pull the band off my ponytail, comb my fingers through my hair and retie it. I face him.

'Thanks for your help.'

He opens his mouth and shuts it. He runs a hand over his face. If it weren't so wet, his shirt would be pale blue. He's wearing suit pants and brown leather shoes. Has he been in his office all day, writing words and drawing diagrams on his whiteboard?

'Is that a dismissal?' he says.

'It … did you have something to say?'

'We could talk about your death wish.' He points towards the homestead. He frowns. 'What the fuck?'

'I was clearing the downpipe. The weather got worse.' I turn my back and walk to the bales of hay neatly stacked to one side of the shed, taking one and dragging it across the floor to the wheelbarrow. 'I was on my way down.'

'You were alone.'

'At least I had a ladder!'

'What?'

I point towards the river. 'The cliff?'

He mutters a curse. 'Why tonight?'

'I'm responsible for the maintenance of Edward's house.'

'For fuck's—'

'Stop swearing!' I focus on the wheelbarrow. 'The thunder was a long way away at first. I thought the lightning would be too.'

He walks slowly towards me, lifting a hand before putting it back to his side. 'I could have helped.' He undoes his cuffs and rolls up his sleeves, pulls at his shirt where it sticks to his skin. The movements of his body, his strength and grace, double my heart rate whenever I see him.

'I didn't expect you until tomorrow.'

'I left work early.'

Because of the blue cardboard box in the lounge room? Will he go through its contents? Ask more questions? There's a scratching on the roof. It'll be the bottlebrush trees, the ones Dad planted.

'You probably have things to do. And I …' I glance outside at the rain, like a veil in the half-light. 'I have things to do too.' I lift the hay by the strings, resting it on my bent knee before tipping it into the barrow.

'When will you stop running?'

I grasp the barrow handles. 'I haven't had a chance to check the gutters at the back of the homestead, but I think they're all right. Let me know if they're overflowing.'

'So you can climb a ladder in a thunderstorm and sort them out?'

'I'll wait until the weather improves.'

'You do all the work on your own?'

I let the barrow go, and straighten. 'It wouldn't be fair to ask Gus to help, not in this rain.'

'How long have you looked after Edward's house?'

'I keep my horses on his land. It's a fair exchange.' The top press-stud of my jacket feels tight. I undo it, and the next one. And then, as he watches, all of the press-studs. My sweater's neck is wet, and so are my boots and the bottom half of my jeans, but the rest of my clothes are dry. He's wet through. 'I guess you'll want to get changed.'

He looks down at his shirt as he comes closer, stopping in front of me. 'It can wait. Jemima?'

'Yes.'

'Do you have any questions for me?'

'About what?'

'Anything.'

When you touch me, my blood heats up. Why is that? How come your eyes are so blue? I suspect you could break my heart. But why would you bother with that?

'Why are you in my shed?'

The wind finds us, stirring up dust on the floor. A crack of thunder. A bolt of lightning.

'Because you are.'

I bunch up my hands and blow against my fingers. 'I don't have any more questions.'

His forearms are nicely shaped. Even wet, his rolled-up sleeves are neat and even, just like his writing.

'This is untenable,' he says.

'What?'

'You, me.' He flicks the toggle at the neck of my jacket. 'Especially you.' When I take a step back, he reaches for my hands. His are cold. His grip is light. I could pull away but don't. He threads his fingers through mine.

'What are you doing?'

'It's been three weeks. I go away again on Sunday, for a fortnight at least. Do you think we could settle this beforehand?'

'Settle what? I want to be left alone.'

He squeezes my hands. 'They're cold.'

'Yours are frozen.'

He smiles, a flash of white teeth. Then turns my hands over and studies them—the callus on my index finger, the torn ends of two fingernails, and the narrow bloody line on the side of my thumbnail.

'They must be painful.'

'Not very.'

'Bullshit.' He runs his thumb across my fingertips. He dips his head and kisses my knuckles. His lips are hot on my skin.

Aching warmth seeps down my arms to my breasts. 'Why do you do this?' I whisper.

'Don't make me wait two more weeks.'

'For what?'

He lowers his head, rests his forehead on mine. 'Whatever you're ready to give me.' His voice is quiet but gruff.

Another gust of wind, stronger than the others. It rattles through the roof and whistles. I take a deep breath and close my eyes, conjure up words in my mind.

'*The wintry west extends his blast, And hail and rain does blow.*'

I feel his smile against my cheek. '*The stormy north sends driving forth, The blinding sleet and snow.*'

I'm not sure how long we stand there. The wind drops, the rain eases. A kookaburra starts up, and another one.

I lift our hands to his chest. 'I'd better feed the horses.'

'Let me help.'

When I take a breath—a shuddery, shaky, *I give up* breath—he lets go of my hands and slides his arms around me, linking them loosely at the small of my back. I rest the side of my face on his chest. It's damp, but warm.

'You were sick when I left you at your apartment. I felt really bad about that.'

He tightens his arms. His body is hard, he smells nice.

'Forget it.' He runs his lips up my neck.

There are butterflies in my stomach, thousands of them, fluttering all around. His breath is warm on my ear, my cheek, my lips. The tip of his tongue flicks the corner of my mouth. I open for him on a relieved kind of sigh and draw him in. I snake my arms around his neck, bringing him closer. He runs his hands down my back and deepens the kiss as if he can't get close enough. That happened last time we—

'No!' I jerk my head away and push against his chest. When his arms stiffen, I push again. 'No, no, no, no, no.'

He opens his arms and takes two rapid steps backwards. He spins around, shoves his hands into his pockets and stalks to the other side of the shed. Maybe only a few seconds pass, maybe a minute. But I've counted ten cobwebs in the rafters by the time he's turned around again. His expression is guarded. He speaks quietly.

'I wouldn't do anything you didn't want.'

'I know that.'

'You can trust me.'

The words hang between us, the untruthfulness of them.

It's my turn to walk away. I stand next to the wheelbarrow again, pull out strands of hay.

'Trust you with Thornbrooke?'

'That's not what I meant.'

'But we can't pretend it's not there. You want to dissect it. Lay it out on a slab for everyone to see.'

He curses under his breath. 'I'll record the facts as I find them.'

'You're a scientist, so that's what I'd expect. I don't think in the way that you do.'

He looks outside, then back at me. 'They talk about you at the zoo. They say you have instinct and skill. You get referrals, but mostly you're found by chance. I met Jackson McAdams yesterday. You know him?'

'A little. He shoes racehorses.'

'Around the world. He says you could work anywhere and he doesn't know why you don't. The locals talk about you too.'

'They understand me.'

'I think they cocoon you. You lost your parents. And then there was Thornbrooke.'

'Yes.'

He frowns. 'The anaphylactic episode. It was my fault.'

The butterflies have gone, and now there are bees. Bees with stingers. Thousands and thousands of bees. Is he allergic to bees?

'You should be more careful.' My voice is unsteady. I clear my throat. 'You take risks.'

'With who I kiss?'

'In other ways too.' I'm not wearing a watch, but lift my sleeve as if I were. 'It's getting late.' I pull my cuff over my wrist again.

When he held the ladder, his mouth was wet with rain. Now it's tight with anger. But that was what I wanted, wasn't it?

'That night at my apartment, you said you'd never slept with anyone. Have you had sex?'

'You don't need to sleep with someone to have sex.'

'I don't think you have.'

'Can you tell that by looking at me?'

'I can tell it by sleeping with you.'

The bees in my stomach start buzzing again. They climb to my throat. I force my words through them. 'Stop doing this.'

'We're attracted to each other.'

I take a step back. 'I said *don't*.'

'What? Tell the truth?'

The bees are trapped. They sting my throat. It's swollen and painful. My eyes water. My voice breaks.

'We can't go back.'

'We kiss again. That's how we go back.'

When I shake my head my ponytail, cold and wet, clings to my neck. 'No.'

He yanks at his sleeves, rolling them down. He turns so he's in profile. I see the beats of the pulse at his throat. Are they the same as the beats of his heart?

Thump-thump. Thump-thump. Thump-thump.

I'll never know.

U

Dad made me go back to the psychologist before he went to the hospice.

How did you feel when your brother died?

Unhappy.

How did you feel when your mother died?

Very unhappy.

Were you angry?

For a while. She'd promised she'd stay with me.

It was natural for you to be angry, Jet.

I know that, I've learnt about the stages of grief. But mostly I was sad. Dad was heartbroken. He keeps fighting for my sake.

You know he's not well?

He's exhausted. He'll die very soon. He told me.

It's good to have a plan for afterwards. What's yours?

I'm going to be a farrier.

Is that a good idea, given how your mother died?

I like being with horses; that hasn't changed. And farriers don't only shoe horses, they work out why a horse might be in pain. They try to fix it.

It will be hard physical work.

I'm good with my hands, I'm strong.

You'll finish school first?

I'm not great at schoolwork. And I'll need a job so I can support myself, keep the cottage nice, things like that. Don't tell Dad.

Edward Kincaid wants you to live with him in Sydney.

I want to stay in Horseshoe.

You'll be alone.

I won't have to risk losing anyone else. That's a good thing, isn't it?

CHAPTER
25

A few clients cancelled on Saturday morning because of the rain, so I was home earlier than usual on Saturday afternoon. By the time Sapphie and I had finished with my accounts it was almost dark. We both watched Finn's taillights disappear down the driveway.

'Will he come back?' she asked.

I glanced at the homestead, all the windows dark. 'Not this weekend.'

Gus waves from his front garden as I pull up in front of his house on Sunday morning. He owns thousands of hectares of land but his cottage, with three tiny bedrooms and one living area, is even smaller than mine. I lean over the console to open the passenger-side door.

'Come out of the rain, Gus.'

He smiles and tips his worn leather hat. 'We were in drought a little while back. I'm enjoying this rain while it lasts.'

'There are mushrooms growing in my lawn.'

He gives Banjo, one of Ruby's pups, black and tan like she was, a final pat. 'You stay and mind the house, now,' he says. 'There's a good fella.'

'Your gardens look nice.'

He pulls himself into the cab, carefully placing a bunch of roses, with deadly looking thorns, onto his lap. Then he takes off his hat, tips it up, and puts the flowers in that.

'Maggie would never forgive me, Jet, if I didn't look after her vegie patch and flowers.'

'She must have had a very green thumb.'

'She was good at everything, my Maggie.'

'Married thirty-seven years, right?'

He does up his belt. 'Have I mentioned that before? And not a day has gone by in the past twenty-one years I haven't missed her.'

'You must have loved her very much.'

'We loved each other.' He holds onto his belt as we turn onto the highway. 'There's no missing it when it happens, you'll see.'

I laugh. 'Is that right?'

'Reckon you're a bit like my Maggie. She didn't need to sample this man and that to see which one she liked best. For her it was all or nothing.' He winks. 'Lucky I felt the same way.'

All. *Or nothing.* Am I really like that? 'It was.'

'I really appreciate this, taking me to town on your day off.'

'No problem. I called one of the vets at the zoo. He says he'll meet me there today, instead of tomorrow. Then I'll go to the hardware store.'

'It's still an imposition. Much appreciated.'

Gus knows I listen to audiobooks and insists on listening too. As Dickens's *Little Dorrit* comes through the speakers, he closes his eyes in concentration. When I disconnect fifty minutes later, he frowns disapprovingly. 'I was enjoying that.'

I smile as I turn off the highway. 'We're almost at the hospital.'

He looks around. 'Fancy that.'

'Go to the library, Gus. Choose the book you want and they'll set you up with an audio device.'

'Might have to, the way my eyesight's playing up.' He rearranges the roses. 'I could also do with a horse and cart. Bob Hargreaves drove me home from the pub last night.'

'I offered to pick you up.'

'You were wanted for the trivia, not the transportation. Our numbers were down.'

'I had a quiet night at home.'

'Dr Blackwood wasn't there either. Maybe next week.'

'I think he's going away again.'

'We had a good yarn, last time I saw him. Fiona Hargreaves says he's a clever bloke, doctor this, professor that. He don't act big-headed.'

I pull into the hospital carpark. 'You'll be staying here for lunch, right? I'll be back at two-thirty.'

U

I want to stretch my legs and there's a break in the rain, so Andrew and I forgo the buggy and walk to the giraffe enclosure, a large field near the takhi horses, bordered with moats. We sit on the coat he drapes over a bench, and he hands me a pair of binoculars.

'That's Afaafa over there, the young female in the foreground. As you know, she's pregnant. It complicates things no end.'

'Five months, right? I guess anaesthesia is even more difficult than usual.'

'It's out of the question. Yet treating Afaafa without it isn't going to be easy. She's not keen on getting into the yard, or doing what we want once she's there.'

Giraffes have big hearts, and complex ways to pump blood through their bodies. Knocking them out is a last resort, which is why the zoo handlers do their best, through positive reinforcement, to get them to cooperate.

'Her gait is way off.' I zoom in further. Giraffes have two weight-bearing hooves on each foot like cattle and sheep. In the wild they wear the fronts of their hooves down naturally. But in captivity, even at an open plains zoo, some of them have difficulty doing that and their hooves grow too long. To avoid the discomfort at the front of her foot, Afaafa is sinking back on her heels. 'I reckon I could push her onto the front of her feet with regular trims, but we'd better start soon. Her pregnancy will change the way she carries her weight and that might make things worse.'

Andrew smiles and nods. 'I see you understand. But before we do anything, we need to improve her behaviour in the yard, and we'd like you to be a part of that process. Start slowly, handle her feet, pick up a file but don't use it, paint her toenails if that's what it takes to build up her confidence. But we need to get it done before the calf is born.'

'Sure. I'll take it on.'

'Excellent!' A raindrop falls, and then another. 'Time to go.' We stand and he shakes out his coat, putting it on and fastening the buttons. 'I'll see if Finn has any ideas. He has a lot of experience with African species.'

'Sure.'

'So enthusiastic?' He smiles. 'I have an inkling you two don't get on.'

'Why?'

'He calls you Jemima.'

'It is my name.'

'But used very rarely.'

I'm dry and warm under my jacket. So why do I shiver? 'Where is he?'

'Finn?'

I've made it clear I don't want him, so why am I prying into his life? 'Yes.'

'He went to Scotland briefly to see his family, and then to a university in Durban. He's on the board there.'

We skirt around a group of tourists, walking in an uneven line along the path. 'Did you work with him in Africa?'

'We were on different projects when we met, but were both based at Kruger National Park. I was watching jaguar in the evenings from an observation hut. Finn spent his days on the savanna, anaesthetising rhinos, tagging and getting samples.' He laughs. 'Finn's work was more physically demanding, no doubt about that, but he tended to eat late at night. We often shared a meal.'

'So you know about his ...'

He looks at me curiously. 'Allergies?'

'Nuts.'

'And crustaceans, but that came later.'

What about bees?

When I increase my pace, Andrew jogs a couple of steps to catch up. 'Thanks for taking on Afaafa.'

'I'll do what I can to help her.'

'What time do you pick up your friend?'

'Two-thirty.'

'I'm meeting Luke for lunch in twenty minutes. We're eating at the Golden Goose, that new little restaurant out of town. Would you like to join us?'

CHAPTER
26

The restaurant is crowded, but we're taken to one of the best tables near the window. We haven't even ordered when Andrew gets a call from the zoo. It's obvious he's not needed urgently, but he puts his white cloth napkin on the table and insists he has to leave immediately. As soon as he's gone, Luke sits back in his chair and raises his brows.

'Subtle as a kick in the teeth.'

I smile. 'Do you often meet for lunch?'

'Never. He called this morning. He didn't mention you, so I almost didn't come.'

'It's a good chance to catch up.' I look down at my boots and jeans, and roll up the sleeves of my blue checked shirt. 'I would've gone to more trouble if I'd known I was on a date.'

'You always look good, Jet.' He smiles. 'And I'd like to see you more often, you know that.'

'Maybe we need Andrew to sort us out.' I smooth the napkin over my lap as Luke picks up his menu, a clipboard with a piece of cream cardboard attached.

'I'll have the chicken and leek risotto,' he says.

I don't bother to look at the page. 'I'll have the same.'

The table overlooks hectares of farmland planted with canola. The rows are long and straight and the plants are bright green. When they flower, the field will be buttercup yellow.

'So?' Luke says. 'What have you been up to?'

He's friendly and good-natured. He's pleasant looking and he works hard. It's *normal* to be with someone like him. Our eyes meet and he smiles again. All. *Or nothing.* It doesn't have to be like that, does it?

After we've eaten the main course, the waiter offers to serve coffee on the balcony. The sun, watery and pale, does its best to push through the clouds. The pots overflow with a red-flowered creeper that climbs up the posts. Luke sits on a daybed, bright with orange-patterned cushions, and pats the space next to him. 'This looks comfortable.'

He plumps cushions behind me when I sit. 'Thank you.'

When the waiter arrives, he balances our coffees on the broad timber arms of the daybed. Luke shuffles closer, even though that puts his coffee out of reach. His leg bumps mine. He looks into my eyes. And then at my mouth.

I don't want to give him the wrong idea, to think I'm more ready to get serious than I am. It was only two days ago I kissed Finn. The arm of the daybed hems me in, so it's not easy to inch away.

He frowns and laughs simultaneously. 'I'm thinking that's a no.'

I shoulder bump him. 'I like you.'

'How much?'

'Who knows?'

'At least you're honest.' He picks up his coffee. 'Can I ask you something?'

'Sure.'

'Remember when we saw each other at The Royal a while back?'

'Yes.'

'You left early, and Finn Blackwood left just after you.'

I pick up my cup and saucer, place it in my lap. 'Did he?'

'I left half an hour later.'

'Where is this going?'

He puts one arm along the back of the daybed. 'Finn was charging up the footpath towards me as I walked to my car.' His brows lift. 'I asked him if he'd seen you.'

'Oh. What did he say?'

'Guess?'

I drain my cup. 'I don't think he'd lie. He would have said yes.'

'Thirty minutes, Jet. What were you doing all that time?'

Tangled laces, stolen kisses. 'Nothing important.'

'No?' He stands and walks to the balcony railing. 'Well, that's odd, because I got the impression it might've been important to him.'

I carefully put my cup and saucer on the armrest before joining him. I was trying to spare his feelings. I suspect I've hurt them instead.

'Something did happen between Finn and me, but nothing's happening now. Even so, I don't want to muck you around. I like you, but I don't think I want a relationship, not now anyway.'

He looks towards the daybed. 'So I'm like all the other guys. Just friends?'

'I think we could be good friends. You make me laugh, you're good company, and … it wouldn't worry me to kiss you or anything.'

He laughs. 'Jet, you're priceless.' He holds out his hands. 'How about now?'

'Seriously?'

'I'm not proud.'

There's only one other couple on the balcony, and they have their backs to us. I put my hands on Luke's shoulders and he pulls me closer. Then I press my lips against his. When he wraps his arms around me and kisses me back, I play along. It's not too bad, but …

I step back and take his hands. 'Thanks for that.'

He whistles quietly. 'Any time.'

'I'd better get to Gus.'

The silence is companionable as we walk to my ute. 'Are you going to Sapphie's birthday party the weekend after next?' I ask. 'You can join us at trivia afterwards if you like.'

'Sounds good,' Luke says, as I unlock my car. He opens the door, leaning on the frame as I slide in. 'Dad mentioned he was away.'

I reach for my seatbelt. 'Who?'

'Have a guess.'

'Finn?'

'Got it in one.'

CHAPTER
27

It's after six-thirty, half an hour later than I was supposed to be at the pub for Sapphie's birthday party, when I turn off the loop road and into the driveway.

When I see Finn's car parked up by the homestead, I slow almost to a stop. It's over two weeks since I cleaned out the gutters in the storm. I take a couple of breaths and slowly accelerate, parking in the shed.

Chili, Lollopy and Freckle are standing at the gate, waiting to be let into the home paddock. But Vegemite is nowhere to be seen. The last time he was missing, Finn was at the river, leaping onto boulders and scaling *not quite vertical* cliffs. I leave the ute in the driveway, jump over the gate and half walk, half run across the ground, still soft from the rain. Am I worried about Vegemite, or Finn?

Most of this paddock is cleared. There's nowhere for Vegemite to go except for the trees along the fence line, hundreds of metres away.

It's warm tonight, and I'm sweaty by the time I get close enough to make out his big black nose, poking through the branches of a paperbark tree. He doesn't seem to be distressed.

'What are you doing down here?'

I pat his shoulder briefly before climbing through the fence, picking my way around the undergrowth and looking across the river.

'Finn!' I wrap my arm around the sapling and peer over the edge of the cliff. 'Finn?'

Nothing. So I go back to Vegemite, standing in exactly the same spot as he was. A branch has worked its way through the cheek strap of his halter and is poking out behind his ear. Even so, he should have had no trouble getting free.

'I hope you haven't got dementia as well as arthritis.' I undo the halter and untangle it from the branch, while Vegemite stands perfectly still, as if he suspects he might still be stuck. After I rub around his ears, I put the halter back on again and lead him out. 'You scared me. There's no need to go down to the river.'

Once we're clear of the trees, I peel back his cotton rug and run my hands over his body, checking him out. Besides a nick in one of his legs, and his usual hindquarter stiffness, he seems to be fine, quickening his pace as we walk up the hill to the other horses.

Finn's car isn't at the homestead any more.

By the time I see to the horses, the sun is even lower. When I fetch the key from the box on the pew, the front door is in shadow and I have to feel around to find the lock. I shower and change, then check the mirror to see I'm presentable. My hair falls around my face. Even wet, it's many different shades. *Like a lion.* Besides lip-gloss, I'm not wearing make-up. But my clothes, tight blue jeans and a yellow T-shirt, are clean and relatively new. I shove my feet into sneakers as I rush down the hallway. Then double back for Sapphie's present, lying on the kitchen table. The clock reads seven-thirty.

My stomach rumbles as I push against the dark timber door of The Royal. There aren't many people at the bar, but shouts of laughter and microphone squeaks sound from the lounge. The trivia will be starting any minute. Sapphie is putting on a brave face because she doesn't much like being the centre of attention. She's at the table closest to the door. I hug her tightly.

'Happy birthday. Sorry I'm late. Vegemite got stuck in the paperbark trees.'

She hugs me back. 'Thanks for coming. Go and have dinner. Ma and Pa are in the dining room, searching for stragglers. Can you tell them to come as soon as they can? Gus is having a hissy fit because there are only the two of us at his table. Don't you hurry though, just get here when you've had plenty to eat.'

Mr and Mrs Hargreaves are standing outside the dining room.

'Sorry I'm late.'

Mrs Hargreaves smiles as she looks me over. 'You look lovely with your hair down. It's such pretty hair. Isn't that right, Bob?'

'Quite right, dear.' He points to the dining room. 'It's our treat tonight, being Sapphie's birthday. We can stay to keep you company if you like.'

'Gus's need is greater,' I say. 'You know how competitive he is. Without both of you, he'll never be able to answer the football and movie questions.'

I'm on my way to the bar when a farmer bails me up. He wants to know about a footrot problem he's having with his sheep, but doesn't want to pay for a call-out. Fifteen minutes pass before I return to the dining room.

Lemonade slops out of my glass and onto the floor when I see Finn, alone at the long communal table, leaning on his elbows, his chin propped up on a hand. He's reading a book. Who takes a book to a pub? He has a fork in his other hand, midair with a piece of broccoli dangling from the spokes.

My heart is in my mouth. Does he know I'm here? A light shines above his head. His hair is glossy, and longer than I've seen it. I've only taken one step back when he looks up. He puts down his fork and narrows his eyes.

'Hello, Jet,' Leon says from behind me. 'Pasta, I'm guessing?'

'I … yes, please.'

'Finn had the salmon so it only took a jiffy. Yours won't be long, but I've got to make a new batch of sauce.'

'Fish is okay.'

'No way. I know how much you like my tortellini.'

'They want me at trivia.'

'Gus and the others can wait. You two must know each other, being neighbours and all?'

'Yes.' Finn stands and holds out the chair next to him. There's a parcel on it, neatly wrapped in thick red paper with a hairy mammoth logo. He puts the parcel on the table and smiles stiffly.

'Jemima.'

'Jet,' Leon says. 'Everyone calls her Jet.'

Everyone but Finn. He waits for me to sit and then he sits himself. 'Go ahead and eat,' I say, 'before it gets cold.'

He stabs a carrot, which joins the broccoli on his fork. He still has salmon on his plate, and a mountain of vegetables. Crustaceans were on his allergy list at the hospital. So fish is okay?

'I wanted to talk to you,' he says. No pleasantries, no smile. *We have to go back to how we were.* 'We might as well do it now.'

'Right,' I say, carefully lifting my glass to my lips.

'Your name. Leon commented on it, so do other people. So how about I address you like everybody else on the planet?'

'I guess.'

He nods and spears a piece of fish, putting it into his mouth. I watch his lips as he chews and swallows. What am I waiting for? Blue eyes wide with shock? Shortage of breath? A frantic search for an adrenaline shot?

'Jet?' My name, short and sharp, sounds strange on his lips.

'Yes.'

'What are you staring at?'

'Nothing.'

'Bullshit.'

He eats new potatoes and squash. He pierces a roast tomato with his fork and halves it with his knife. I look towards the doorway, willing Leon to walk through. 'It's Sapphie's birthday.'

He nods towards the parcel. 'The Hargreaves invited me weeks ago.'

I link my hands in front of me on the table. I clear my throat. 'They're very nice people, the Hargreaves. They've fostered a lot of children. Sapphie was the last.'

He looks at me critically as he picks up the last items on his plate, two green beans. 'I asked what you were staring at.'

I jerk my head away. 'Nothing.'

He carefully lines up his knife and fork in the middle of the plate. He turns his chair towards me.

Leon appears. 'Your favourite,' he says, placing a bowl of pasta on the table. 'Enjoy.'

'Thank you.'

He picks up Finn's plate. 'Fiona Hargreaves cooked a cake. If that's all gone, I'll see if I can rustle up some pudding.'

Leon's specialty is apple crumble. Does he use nuts when he makes the topping? Does he slice the nuts on a chopping board? Does he clean it thoroughly afterwards?

My eyes fly to Finn. It doesn't look like the fish has poisoned him. When he leans back in his chair, I look away again. I unfold my serviette, laying it carefully over my lap and smoothing out the creases.

'Are you going to eat?' he says.

I do like tortellini, like Leon said. But the look of it tonight, the texture, the mushroom and bacon pieces, the cheese, it makes me feel sick.

I nod and pick up my fork. Then blow on the pasta as if it's too hot, like Goldilocks did when she was faced with Father Bear's porridge. When I dip my head over the bowl, my hair hides my face. My stomach is tied up in knots.

The smell nauseates me even more than the look of it. My fork clatters onto the table and I push back my chair.

'I'm not hungry.'

'For fuck's sake,' he mutters, his eyes blue and cranky. He picks up my fork, stabs a piece of pasta and puts it into his mouth. Then he takes another piece. He glares as he chews and swallows.

I finally find my voice. 'What are you doing?'

'Don't treat me like a freak.'

My gaze goes from the pasta to his mouth, and back to the food. 'How do you know it's okay?'

His jaw stiffens. 'Leon gave me a choice. Fish or pasta.'

'He knows?'

'I've been here before.' He stabs a piece of mushroom and holds up the fork. He frowns. 'Take it, Jemima. Eat.'

It's not until I have the fork in my mouth that I realise it was in his mouth too. I pull the mushroom off with my teeth and chew slowly, the fork hanging over the bowl. As if he guesses what I'm thinking—he *must* guess—he takes the fork out of my hand and stabs a piece of bacon, putting it into his mouth.

Our eyes meet. 'Say I'd eaten something earlier that you had an allergy to?'

'You never get time to eat. Why were you home so late?'

'I got held up at work.'

'Jet!' Mr Hargreaves appears at the door, puffing a little and waving a piece of paper. 'I've been given special permission to leave the table, as you're a member of our team. We've got Charlotte and Emily. Who was the other Brontë sister? I didn't know there were three of them.'

'Anne.'

He reads from the page. 'Two bonus points if you can name one of her novels, and her pen name.'

'*Agnes Grey*, Acton Bell.'

'Which is which?'

'Sorry, the novel is *Agnes Grey*.'

He writes it down before considering the page again. 'George Orwell's *1984*. When did he write it?'

'1949?' I count on my fingers. 'Yes, I think that's right.'

'Last one.' He reads from the paper. 'Who wrote *Of Human Bondage*?'

'W. Somerset Maugham.'

'Gus thought it might be him. Cheers, love.' He rushes away.

This would be a perfect opportunity for me to go too. I feel Finn's gaze on the side of my face.

'Are you going to eat?' he says.

I have a sip of lemonade. 'I don't think you're a freak.'

'"No, no, no, no, no." Remember that?'

Isn't he as anxious to forget what happened in the shed as I am?
I look desperately towards the door.

'I remember.'

'I'm not a leper either.'

'I know that. There were other things too.'

He holds out the fork. 'Take it.'

I'm unsettled, uneasy. I don't know whether to reach for it or
not. It hovers between us. 'Will you snatch it away again?'

'No.' He gives me a strained false smile. 'I've made my point.'
His eyes are cold. 'Sharing spit won't kill me.'

When he drops the fork onto my plate, I jump to my feet. He
stands too, picking up his book and the parcel, and stalking out of
the room.

CHAPTER
28

Finn's car is back by the time I get home, and the homestead's lights are on. I saw him briefly again at the pub, when he thanked the Hargreaves for inviting him to Sapphie's party, and gave her the present. It looked like a regular rope to me, but it must have been a special one because she was embarrassed about how much it must have cost. Gus invited him to join our trivia table, but Finn told him he had a conference in Sydney next week and had to prepare for that.

I park the ute in the shed, quietly shutting the door behind me, and then drop my bag inside the front door of the cottage. The switch for the spotlight is at the side of the house so I skirt around the pew and turn it on. It shines through the scribbly bark tree in the home paddock, casting oddly shaped shadows over the grass. The moon is high, crescent shaped and slender.

Vegemite is lying down with the other horses. They all raise their heads as I walk through the gate, but Lollopy is the only one who gets to his feet. He walks to me and snuffles my hands.

I thread my fingers through his forelock and tug. 'It's almost eleven, you goose. Are you after a nightcap? As if you'll be fed at this time of night.'

'Jemima.'

'Oh!' I spin around.

Finn closes the gate behind him, shoves his hands deep in his pockets. 'I heard something. I thought I should investigate.'

'I'm saying goodnight to the horses.'

'Do you always do that?'

We walk through the shadows side by side. 'I found Vegemite by the river when I got home. That's why I was so late to the pub. His halter was stuck in a branch. I wanted to see he was okay.'

'The thoroughbred?'

I hold out my hand. 'Stay there. He doesn't know you very well. He'll get up.' I squat by Vegemite's side and rub around his ears. 'His arthritis has been playing up.'

Finn's hands are in his pockets. 'I presume he's on an anti-inflammatory drug,' he says quietly.

'He only used to need it in winter, but it's been chilly for November, and last month was wet. His vet said he might as well keep going with it.'

'He's twenty-eight, isn't he?'

'Yes. But I can't believe I'm still double-rugging him at night. And before you ask, he raced for years. For much too long on the country tracks.' I put my hand inside his rugs at his shoulder. His body is warm. When he turns his head towards me, I kiss his nose. 'Night, boy.'

Finn follows me back to the gate, then opens it and stands back. 'How long have you done this?' he asks.

Is he pretending things are normal between us? How could they ever be? 'Looking after the horses? I've taken the Follyfoot retirees since I started working there. And even before that, Dad always kept an ex-racehorse or two.' I shrug. 'I guess that means forever.'

'It must be difficult when they die.' He glances towards the cottage. Is he thinking of Ruby?

'They deserve to be cared for till that happens.'

'*The friend of age, and guide of youth …*' he quotes quietly.

How long have we been standing here? How did we get so close? When I rush past him, he closes the gate behind us.

'I don't think you're a leper, or a freak.' My words sound unnaturally loud.

'No?'

'I wouldn't use those words, ever.' I jump over a soggy patch of ground so my sneakers don't get muddy. 'But I shouldn't have behaved like that at the pub.'

'Is that an apology?'

When I stop, he stops too. 'It's okay to see things differently, my dad taught me that. And you …' I rub my arms, even though I'm not cold. 'It's kind of the same.'

'Prove it.'

'What?'

He lowers his head. 'Kiss me,' he says gruffly.

The air is cool, but the darkness is suddenly warm. My hands flutter onto his chest. I hold onto his shirt and stand on my toes. Our mouths touch for an instant. But then I remember …

'No!'

'For fuck's …' He grasps my shoulders. 'Stop doing this!'

I push against his chest. 'I ate an Anzac biscuit!' I wipe my mouth with the back of my hand. 'I haven't brushed my teeth.' I lift my top and rub the fabric over my lips.

'So?'

'So!' I shove him towards the light from the cottage and peer into his face. He's not gasping or wiping his mouth. His gaze is steady.

'I thought … it could have had nuts.'

He breathes in and out so deeply I hear it. He runs his hands up and down my arms. He dips his head and murmurs in my ear.

'Anzac biscuits have oats, not nuts. I thought all Australians knew that.'

I push against his chest. 'Stop it!' My voice breaks. 'This isn't a joke!' I spin on my heel and run up the steps of the verandah.

'Jemima!'

'It's not fair! You … you …'

He growls as he grasps my hand and yanks me towards him. 'Enough,' he mutters. He kicks off his shoes and wrenches open the fly-screen door. When he tightens his grip and tugs, our forearms press together, skin against skin. My heart turns a somersault. The hall is a mess because I left in such a hurry. There's a lunch box on the chair and a halter and lead rope trailing from the hat stand.

He pushes my bedroom door wider, and opens the spare room door. 'What are you looking for?'

'The bathroom,' he snaps. 'Where is it?'

He follows my gaze and walks determinedly to the end of the hall. He switches on the light. My work clothes are sticking out of the laundry basket. There's a towel on the floor.

'Finn? What are you doing?'

There's a sink and bench, with a mirror behind them. He turns me around so I'm facing the mirror and then he stands behind me, so I'm trapped between him and our reflections. My cheeks are pink. My eyes are wide.

My toothbrush is sitting on the sink top, in a mug with a tube of toothpaste. He wets the toothbrush and squeezes toothpaste onto it. He holds it in front of us.

'Did you eat nuts today?' he says.

Our eyes meet in the mirror. I shake my head. 'Not since that night in the park.'

He nods. Then presses his lips against my temple. 'That gives me hope.'

'Are you sure about the biscuits?'

He growls again. 'Fiona made them. I asked her.'

I nod. 'Okay.'

'Did you eat lobster for lunch?'

My hands bunch into fists. 'This isn't funny!'

'Did you?'

I shake my head again. 'No. But …'

'What?'

'It doesn't matter.'

He holds up my toothbrush. 'I'm going to put this into my mouth. So are you. Say what you want to say.'

I feel his heartbeats against my back. 'Sapphie saved me a piece of chocolate cake. I ate that too.'

'Fiona made it. No nuts.'

I'm still hemmed between him and the sink as he brushes his teeth, methodically and efficiently. I fill the mug with water.

'Thank you.' He rinses and spits out, then puts the brush under the running tap and squeezes more toothpaste onto it. 'Your turn.'

I take the brush and clean my teeth, trying to be tidy like him. He hands me the same mug of water he drank from, and I spit out too. But before I have a chance to rinse the brush, he tugs it out of my hand.

'My turn again.' He brushes thoroughly, as if sharing a tooth-brush is perfectly normal. And as he brushes he rests his other arm across my breasts. He leans over my shoulder to rinse. He rests his chin on the top of my head and wraps both arms around my front. Our eyes lock.

'Are you happy now, Jemima Kincaid?'

'Kissing Luke was way less stressful.'

He spins me around, lifts me up and plonks me on the bench. 'When the fuck did you do that?'

'I don't know …' My voice wavers. 'A couple of weeks ago.'

His hands clench on my waist. 'Why?'

'I … It would be unfair to Luke to answer that.'

'Unfair to …' He speaks between his teeth. 'You said you'd kiss me before. You didn't.'

He's coiled like a spring. I'm not sure I've seen him like this. Cranky, but passionate. He looks at my mouth.

I want to kiss him so much it hurts. Could I forget about Thornbrooke, just for a night? Forget about losing him, just for a night? Could we go back?

'You kissed Luke,' he says. 'You're obviously capable of it.'

'Are you challenging me?'

'Why not?' He narrows his eyes. 'I haven't kissed anyone since we met.'

We're close but I lean closer. I wrap my arms around his neck. I kiss him, soft and wet, slow and sweet. Our mouths slide and slip. I pull back a little.

'You taste of peppermint.'

He nuzzles through my hair and kisses my neck. He touches my pulse with his tongue and my heart skips a beat. He nibbles the rim of my ear. He razes his teeth down my neck to my shoulder.

I lift a hand, rest it on his cheek. His bristles are rough. 'You haven't shaved for a couple of days.' I slide my hand into his hair, the thick soft silkiness of it. 'Your hair is longer than it was.'

His gaze is heated as it lingers on my face. Desire, sweet and familiar, flows through my body. He lifts my hand to his mouth and kisses my wrist, the base of my thumb and my palm. He touches my lip with a fingertip.

'I missed you.'

'I don't know why.'

He shakes his head. He lowers it and mutters. 'Kiss me again. I dare you.'

I breathe an aching, needy sigh into his mouth. He threads a hand through my hair, holding the back of my head. Our lips meld and our tongues meet. I want to be closer. Frantic little sounds come out of my mouth.

'Finn?'

He slides his hands under my shirt and splays his fingers wide. He kisses me again, his erection against my knees.

When our teeth clash, he lifts his head. He puts unsteady fingers against my lips. He mutters.

'Too fast, we're always too fucking fast.' He rests his forehead on mine. His breathing is rapid. 'We need to talk.'

'Can't we just do this?'

He mutters as he pulls off my sneakers, and runs his hands up and down my legs, pushing against my knees with his hip until I open them. He stands between my thighs and links his hands around my waist.

I close my eyes. I breathe in his scent, the warmth of his body. I run my hands over his chest and kiss his throat. His muscles clench and tighten. Through his T-shirt, I feel the disk that hangs around his neck. I circle it with my finger.

'Wrap your legs around me,' he says.

He carries me to my bedroom. The contact between our bodies warms me inside and out; his smell and touch intoxicate me. He lowers me so my feet are on the ground, and turns on the lamp, and then we tumble onto the bed. He smiles as he pins me down with his leg and pushes my hair from my face. He kisses me again, with long slow strokes of his tongue. I wrap a leg around his hip, drawing him closer. His erection is hard against the inside of my thigh. I feel the heat of his skin through his shirt. It takes me an age to open his top two buttons because of the tape on my fingers. I tug at the fabric.

'Take it off.'

He undoes two more buttons at the front, then the cuffs, and yanks the shirt free of his pants. He pulls it over the top of his head and tosses it onto the floor. When he leans over me again, the disk swings between us. I take it in my hand.

'Off?'

'Yes.'

I trail my hands over his chest, his skin warm and smooth, as I gather up the leather cord. He's leaning on his elbows, but lowers his head. I take the disk off, dropping it onto the side table. I trace his collarbones and sternum. His muscles are hard, well defined. But I knew that from the day we first met.

'You have good confirmation.' My voice sounds different, soft and breathy.

He groans a laugh as he rolls onto his side. 'Thank you.'

When he slides his hands under my top, I moan in relief. He draws back a little. 'I want to see you.'

We pull my top over my head. He dips his head and kisses my nipples through my bra. It's a soft bra, like a bandana with straps.

'Can we turn off the light?'

'Then I can't see.' His voice is husky and warm.

I'm not aware I'm biting my lip until he pulls it free with a finger. He presses my hands against his chest again, then fiddles around at the back of the bra, as if searching for a clip.

'It just pulls off,' I say.

He lifts the fabric over my head, then softly runs his hand over my breasts. All I can see is the top of his head. My breasts are small and I have no cleavage. I'd like to cross my arms.

When he looks up, his lips are parted, eyes are bright. He cups my face. 'You're beautiful.'

His kiss, long and slow, heats my blood and takes away my shyness. He trails his lips over my nipples, nudging them with his tongue. He circles and teases, soft and then firm.

'Finn?' I stroke his hair, arch my back and pull him closer.

He takes one nipple into his mouth while gently stroking the other. And then he swaps breasts, circling more firmly with his tongue. He swaps again. The ache inside me intensifies, thrumming from my breasts to the tops of my thighs.

He lifts his head. 'Jem?'

'Mmmm.'

'Have you had sex?'

'I …' I shake my head. 'I've kissed a lot of men.'

'Anything else?'

'I know the theory.'

'Is that a no?'

'Yes.'

He takes a very deep breath as he sits, and then swings his legs off the bed. He plants his feet on the floor. His back is as toned as his front. I run my fingers over the muscles. 'Finn? What's the matter?'

He's breathing deeply. 'I want to be close to you, Jem, really close. You know that.'

'I guess.'

When we lie down again, he feathers his hands over my breasts and abs, the dip in my waist and the bump of my hip. He undoes the top button of my jeans and pulls down the zipper. I lift my bottom and he tugs the jeans and my underpants off. I'm naked. And ...

He likes me like this. I see it in his eyes, his softly parted lips. When he kisses me again, his tongue in my mouth searches deeply. The tingling in my breasts is an ache; the ache between my legs is heavy and hot. His hands are gentle then firm. When I press myself against him, he lifts his head and groans.

'Finn?'

He brushes his lips against mine. He's serious and intent, beautiful in the shadows. 'You want this?'

My breasts are pressed against his chest. I kiss him hard on the lips. 'Yes.'

He trails his fingers over my stomach. His hand slides lower again, touching between my thighs. I tense.

'Look at me.' His eyes are bright blue. His breaths are short. His fingers gently explore. 'You feel so good. So soft, so wet, so ...' He groans.

I grasp his arm, squeezing it tightly. 'Yes.'

He strokes slowly and cautiously, more gentle than he has to be. He shakes with restraint. I open the button on his pants but he shifts closer, pinning my hand between us.

'Not yet,' he says.

He kisses my breasts again. He trails a meandering path to my mouth. His tongue keeps time with the movements of his fingers, gliding and darting until I writhe against his hand. When he slides a finger inside me I press down hard to keep it there. My body clenches around it, drawing it in then releasing.

'Finn!'

He kisses me until the tremors subside and I go limp in his arms.

U

When I open my eyes, he's on his back and I'm sprawled across his body, my head on his chest. The blanket cocoons us. I stretch and yawn. When I look up, our eyes meet. His are regular blue now, not hot-and-hungry blue. His lip twitches. 'Tired?'

I yawn again. 'Did I go to sleep?'

He kisses my nose. 'You did.'

'For how long?'

He hesitates. 'It's almost two.'

'What!' I sit bolt upright. 'You didn't … Do you want …'

'Sex?' He blows out a breath. Then settles me against his side, rests a possessive hand on my hip. 'I'm too fucking noble.'

'What?' I try to sit again.

'Stay there, baby.' He groans as he adjusts the blanket. 'I'm in enough pain already.'

'What's the matter?'

He hesitates. 'You don't want to know.'

'Do you mean …' I slide my hand over his hip.

'Yes.'

I rub my cheek against his chest. 'Sorry.'

He kisses the top of my head. 'I'm booked on a six-thirty flight tomorrow morning. I have a function in Sydney, and meetings all day Monday. Then I fly to Perth.' When he trails his fingertips over my shoulder and down my spine, I snuggle closer. 'I'll be back in Dubbo Friday morning.'

'Right.'

'They're expecting me at Follyfoot.'

'Mr Hargreaves asked you to speak in February, didn't he?'

'He invited me to spend some time there, to look around. Will I see you?'

'Yes.'

'Good.' He tips up my chin. 'You'll talk to me, won't you? You'll ask me how my week was. And I'll ask about yours.'

'Like normal people?'

'Like a regular couple.'

'I guess.'

He settles my head on the pillow and then sits on the side of the bed. He shrugs into his shirt and tucks it in, runs his fingers through his hair.

When he turns to me I sit too, gathering the blanket around my front. I speak through a yawn. 'I'll get up.'

He wipes hair out of my eyes. 'No need.' He brushes a kiss on my mouth. 'You've already cleaned your teeth. Anyway, you're falling asleep again.'

'Thinking you know everything, it must be exhausting.'

His lip lifts. 'I'm open about what I want.'

'Maybe you have less to lose.'

'I don't agree.' His eyes are suddenly shadowed. Navy-blue-black. 'Thornbrooke, Jem, it won't be forever.'

'No?'

He slowly shakes his head. He mutters against my lips. 'No.'

My hands grasp his shirt and pull him closer. 'Finn? You could stay.'

'You think I don't want to?' He lifts my hands to his mouth and runs his lips carefully over my neatly taped fingers. 'I don't want to rush you. And one night's not enough.' We kiss again, a goodbye kiss, long and bittersweet. 'I'll call. And I'll see you on Friday.'

His footsteps are light on the verandah. They crunch on the path. The wind whistles softly through the leaves of the red gum.

Can we have more than one night?

'Friday,' I whisper.

U

When he calls at nine the next morning, I'm bent double, shoeing a horse at a riding school. He leaves a voicemail.

Jem. It's Finn. I'm in Sydney. I hope you slept better than I did. Call me.

I send him a text with an image of a horse.

He calls again on Monday night.

Jem. I'm about to board a flight to Perth. Are you well? Send me something.

I reply by text with an icon of an aeroplane.

On Tuesday he leaves another voicemail.

I'm told it rarely rains here in November, but it's raining today. Is there a Burns poem for that?

I dictate a voice recording into my phone and send it.

The Winter of Life.

He responds.

How does it go?

I send another voice recording.

> *But lately seen in gladsome green.*
> *The woods rejoic'd the day …*
> *Thro' gentle showers, the laughing flowers*
> *In double pride were gay …*

CHAPTER
29

A glint of sun on metal, filtered by the trees, shimmers from the homestead. It's not likely to be Finn's car because it's only Wednesday evening, but my heart rate speeds up anyway. As I drive quickly around the bend, the shrubs, spouting new shoots, scrape against the ute.

It's Caruthers's truck. I ate lunch, but haven't eaten since. Is that why I feel lightheaded? There's no sign of Caruthers as I reverse into the shed, then walk up the path to the homestead's verandah. I take the steps two at a time. The wisteria around the posts is flowering, big purple blossoms and heavy perfume.

I jump when Caruthers appears around a corner, his hat clenched in one hand. He masks his surprise with a thin-lipped grin. 'G'day, Jet.'

'What are you doing here?'

'Just a friendly visit.' He takes his phone out of his pocket and glances at the screen. 'It's after six, I thought you'd be here earlier.'

'This is Edward Kincaid's house. You have no right to snoop around.'

'Nice place.' When he puts on his hat, it shadows his face. 'Just having a stroll. Why're you so toey?'

'What do you want?'

He rests his hands on the railing and does a standing push-up. The muscles in his chest and biceps bulge, straining the buttons of his shirt.

'Morrissey asked me to come.'

'He should talk to me himself.'

'So there's proof you're getting together, lining up your stories? Like I said last time, best he keeps his distance, keeps things private. That way, anyone gets suspicious, you got nothing to tell them.'

'Why does he trust you?'

'We go back a long time, me and Darren.'

'Say what you have to say.' I look over my shoulder 'I have things to do.'

'Don't be like that, Jet.' He looks me up and down. 'You been working all day. We could put our feet up, have a beer for old times' sake.'

It was over thirty degrees today, but I always wear long-sleeved shirts for work. They protect me from the sun and in other ways. When I climbed into my ute to drive home, I rolled up my sleeves and undid a few buttons down my front. There's nothing much he can see but … I'm alone. He's not overly tall but strongly built. He must weigh thirty kilos more than me, maybe more. He grabbed my wrist when I saw him at Follyfoot.

I cross my arms. 'Say what you've come to say.'

'None of this is personal. You're a great girl, everybody knows that.'

'Say it!'

A kookaburra, the bird that hunts from the red gum, calls out long and loud. Usually his friends join in, but not today. He's alone too.

'A week or so back, Edward Kincaid and Morrissey bumped into each other in Sydney.' Caruthers hooks his fingers through his belt. 'Blackwood was getting somewhere, that's what Kincaid said. Morrissey played it cool, but it made him uneasy.'

'Getting somewhere? That could be anything.'

'He said Blackwood was testing the blood, but he was looking at other things too.' He points to the cottage, then to the homestead. 'You living so close and all, Morrissey wants to know if you can shed some light.'

The homestead's lounge room faces the verandah. What's inside the blue cardboard box on the desk? Does Finn know? Did Caruthers see it?

'I don't know anything.'

'Morrissey's a little worried about the supplements Schofield mixed up, the vitamins. Know much about them?'

That last morning at Thornbrooke, Mike said I should go to my room, in the quarters behind the stables, and pack my belongings. I didn't have a case, just a duffle bag stuffed with clothes and toiletries. I put a framed picture of Mum, sitting astride Chili and smiling down at Dad, at the top. By the time I got back to the stables, Mike was throwing the box of smashed bottles into the rubbish. Morrissey was in the office sorting paperwork, and Schofield was on the phone, arranging for the horses to be taken away so he could do the autopsies.

'No,' I say.

'Kincaid hasn't spoken to you, or Blackwood?'

'I haven't talked to Edward in a couple of months. I haven't said anything to Finn.'

He rocks back on his heels. 'But you've seen him, right?'

I'm certain he knows the answer to his question already. 'Yes, around.'

'I had a beer at The Royal on the way, caught up with the barman. You and Blackwood, he reckons you're mates.'

I grip the verandah rail tightly. 'We're not.'

'So why'd you eat together?'

Did we eat together? He ate salmon and vegetables. He took two pieces of pasta and a piece of bacon from my plate and ate that too. He put a mushroom on my fork, and I ate that. Then we came home and cleaned our teeth.

Caruthers lifts his chin. His eyes are slightly bloodshot. 'You going to answer my question?'

I move quickly, dodging his arm when he holds it out to block me. My boots are loud on the steps. I speak over my shoulder.

'It was Sapphie Brown's birthday, that's why we ate together.'

'Wait!'

He catches up, walking by my side to the shed. I skirt around my ute and open the back.

'Does Morrissey pay you to do his dirty work?'

'Helping out a mate? That's not dirty work.' He leans an arm against the ute, with his boot on a tyre. 'You never answered my other question. Did Blackwood talk?'

'He didn't tell me anything.'

'I'm watching you, Jet. You get information, you come to me.'

'I thought I was supposed to keep quiet.' I cross my arms again. 'Now you want me to report what I hear?'

'You got it.'

'Get lost.'

I turn my back and drag the toolbox towards me. I rifle through the contents, praying that he'll go. I shut my eyes, doing my best to focus on the lists in my head. It's Thursday tomorrow. What clients do I have? What shoes will I need? What time should I leave? What route will I—

He rams his chest against my back. I'm pinned against the tray. Air shoots from my lungs. My chest seizes up. I wheeze.

'Get off me.'

'Ask nice.'

My hands are trapped at my sides. I push back with my leg, trying to lift it. 'Piss off.'

I feel his breath on the back of my neck. 'Watch your language.'

'I said piss—'

He shoves his knee into the back of my thigh. My shin crashes into the tow bar. I cry out. My vision blurs.

He grabs one of my wrists and then the other. He holds them both in his hand, the one with the eagle tattoo. He squeezes so tightly my eyes fill with tears.

'You gotta learn some respect.' He reaches over my shoulder with his other hand, taking the hammer out of the toolbox. 'You asked if Morrissey pays me? Sure he does. So I'd better make sure I earn it.'

Sweat trickles down my front. 'What do you want?'

'You're keeping things back.'

'I don't know anything, I swear it.'

He throws the hammer high in the air and catches it. He twirls it in his hand, spinning it like a baton. And then he opens his fingers. The hammer falls, crashing into the toolbox.

'Please let me go.'

'When I'm good and ready.' He picks up a wrench and holds it in front of my face. He lays his hand flat and moves the wrench slowly up and down, as if assessing its weight. When he jerks his hand towards my face, I flinch. The wrench falls. It bounces on the tray, clipping the backs of my hands.

'Whoops-a-daisy,' he says. 'A girl like you, who works in a trade? You need your hands. You gotta take more care.'

He leans over my shoulder again and changes his grip on my wrists. I feel his gaze on my body and the dampness of his sweat through my shirt. I smell it. Bile, bitter and sharp, climbs up my throat. I swallow it down.

He picks up the clinch tongs. 'You have nice tools, good quality.' He holds his hand at the apex of the handles and runs his thumb around the inside of the pincer. He throws the tongs high in the air and they land, jaws open wide, on the tray.

'I can't breathe.'

He eases back a little. 'You going to stay where you are? Do as I say?'

'Yes.'

'Good girl.' He lets go of my hands. 'How's that?'

I grasp the tray. 'Thank you.'

He shoves his forearm between my shoulder blades so forcefully that I yelp. 'Don't get too comfy. I'm not done yet.'

He searches through the toolbox again and picks up a paring knife. 'What's a girl like you doing with a knife like this?'

The blade is burnished silver. He angles it towards me; it catches the light.

He doesn't need the advantage of weight, not if he has a knife. He holds it between his thumb and fingers. He tosses and catches it. He makes a fist and holds it in that.

I keep my hands perfectly still. I brace my feet, drop my shoulders, bend my elbows and …

He steps back so suddenly I stagger, hitting my hip on the tray. When he throws the knife, it curves in an arc and then drops into the box. I hear footsteps on the concrete, a bang on the bonnet.

'Turn around.'

I do as he says. 'Get out.' My voice is high and shaky.

He tips back his hat. 'When you saw me at the pub, you didn't remember me, did you?'

He's still blocking the exit. My hands are shaking, so I push them into my pockets. I breathe deeply, force myself to concentrate and think about my tools. I know where they are. I know how to use them. I know what to reach for if he comes for me again.

'It was dark,' I say. 'I hadn't seen you in years.'

He shrugs. 'I remembered you. You worked hard, you kept to yourself. You weren't like the other girls, messing around with the blokes. I liked that, respected it. People don't blame you for killing the horses. It'd be a shame to spoil that, wouldn't it?'

'I don't know what happened.'

'I'm not saying the vitamins were the problem, but if they were, you got the doses mixed up. You're not too bright with reading, that's what Morrissey says. You gave the horses too much. And too much of anything can kill. That's what he'll say.'

'Yes.'

He jerks his head towards the house. 'I know where you live.' He glances at my ute. 'I know you've got good gear. You're going to keep your mouth shut about the cover-up. That's right, isn't it?'

'Yes.'

'And you're going to keep this visit to yourself, no blabbing to Blackwood or Kincaid.'

'No.' I say the word, but my throat is so tight that no sound comes out.

He puts his hand to his ear. 'What was that, Jet? Didn't hear it.'

I swallow. 'I won't tell them you were here.'

'That's more like it. Because if you do, Mike gets a visit.'

'I said I wouldn't talk.' The trembling in my legs is getting worse. I put a hand on the ute to steady myself. 'I won't.'

His eyes are cold. 'That's my job done then.' He takes a couple of steps towards the door. But then he turns and points to the toolbox. 'That was just a bit of horseplay. No harm done, right?'

Blood has seeped through my jeans and the denim sticks to my shin. I angle my leg to hide it. 'No harm done.'

'Good girl.'

By the time I hear the bumps on the cattle grate, I'm shaking so much it rattles my teeth. I hold tightly to the tray but my legs won't support me, so I sink to my knees and slide to the concrete. I rest my elbows on my knees, lowering my head. I retch but there's nothing to throw up. I taste blood from a cut on the inside of my lip. When did I do that? I sniff and swallow but tears pour out anyway, gushing down my face. I squeeze my eyes shut. I bite a nail.

But then I remember this isn't a dream.

CHAPTER
30

Thornbrooke, Jem, it won't be forever.

Finn kissed me on Saturday night, and then he spoke those words. And for the next three days, I hoped that they were true. I hoped Schofield and Morrissey had done nothing wrong. I hoped Mike and I had nothing important to hide. I hoped Finn would have nothing to find. On Sunday, Monday and Tuesday, I clung to my hopes. And to the promise of Friday.

Morrissey came two days ago.

No more hope. No more promise.

I swallow down the sadness as I turn off the road and pull into the carpark at Follyfoot. Chili, in the float behind the ute, impatiently stamps his feet.

'Hold on, boy. Not long now.'

Would Caruthers have hurt me? Will he hurt Mike or anybody else? What would I say if I went to the police? My shin is cut and bruised from hitting the tow bar. I have bruises on my hips. I have a tight knot of fear in the pit of my stomach. If I were blamed for what happened at Thornbrooke, it would be my word against Morrissey's. How far will he go to protect himself? He's respected, articulate. *He doesn't lose letters, words, sentences, paragraphs.*

He's aware that I do.

If the horses were poisoned by the supplements, the police would have to investigate. Mike got his first traffic infringement when he was sixty-three. He was a few kilometres over the speed limit, but the shame of it lasted for months. Being an accessory after the fact, or worse, isn't on his bucket list.

I'm loosening the bolts on the ramp when I see Finn striding towards me. I've wrapped tape around three of my fingers. I curl them under my palm as I step back from the float.

'Finn.'

When he touches my hand, heat, sharp but sweet, shoots up my arm. I take a jerky step backwards, out of his reach.

He slowly lowers his hand to his side. 'Jemima.'

'How was your week?' My words come out in a rush.

He hesitates. 'Chaotic. I flew back overnight.'

His clothes are city clothes, dark pants and a blue collared shirt, with the sleeves neatly rolled to the elbows. His hair is shorter, newly cut. He runs a hand through it. He has a long angry mark on his forearm.

'Jem? Is everything all right?'

'What did you do to your arm?'

He looks at the mark and shrugs. 'Nate was in Sydney. We climbed together. Rope burn.'

'A cliff?'

'It was an indoor climb.'

'Right.' I gesture to the float. 'I want to get the horses out.'

He frowns. 'Now we've exchanged pleasantries?'

'I'm running late.' I skirt around him to the door of the float, climb the steps and untie Chili and Lollopy.

'I'll lower the ramp,' he says.

I back Chili down the ramp first, handing his lead rope to Finn, who attaches it to a thin piece of string hanging from the float. I go back for Lollopy, stroke his neck. His coat is still thick, but not as woolly as it was in winter. I guide him down the ramp, tying him next to Chili.

Finn unbuckles Chili's rug. 'I tried not to call in daylight because I knew you'd be working,' he says quietly. 'When I phoned on Wednesday night, you didn't answer.'

'I mightn't have had reception. You know it's patchy.'

'There was no response on the landline either. I left messages.'

After Caruthers had gone and I'd cleaned myself up, I drove to the Hargreaves and slept in Sapphie's old room, making an excuse about possums in the ceiling. I slept at home last night, with the spotlight near the shed shining down the driveway. Even though Caruthers told me he wouldn't come back. *So long as I did as I was told.*

I look towards the hills in the distance, green gums and early morning mists. Like I told Sapphie, Mum taught me what to do when I had to make a speech—memorise the words.

'I have something to say.'

Finn pulls off Chili's rug, folding it neatly and storing it in the float. When he faces me again, his eyes are narrowed. Suspicious.

'Go ahead.'

'You said Thornbrooke wouldn't be forever.' I speak quietly. 'I suspect it will be. I could have answered your calls, or sent a voicemail or emailed, but I thought it was best to say this face-to-face. There is, there *was*, an attraction between us. I felt responsible for what happened in the park. That's why I worried about your allergies. But that's all I felt. I'm happy alone, no matter what you think.'

He speaks between his teeth. 'Are you saying it's over?'

'How could it be anything else?'

'What the fuck are you hiding?'

'Nothing!'

'Bullshit!'

'What you're doing, it won't bring the horses back.'

'I care about the truth.'

'So find it out. But not with me.'

'I want to find it together.'

'On your terms. You always think you're right.'

'What about you?'

'I know what I want. And I know my failings. I don't think I'm indestructible.'

'What? How is that relevant?'

'I …' I shake my head. 'Forget it.'

'Jet!' Laurence rides up on his scooter. 'Darcy's ready to roll. They're waiting for Lollopy.'

I brush past Finn, fumble with Lollopy's lead rope. 'Tell them I'm on my way.'

♘

The children at Follyfoot like Finn. He's a vet. He's good-looking and, although he's not smiling much today, he's patient and attentive. Even Andreas, who's having one of those days where he screams at the top of his lungs, lets Finn lead his horse.

It's after eleven and I'm sweeping the concrete slab when Magda, her curly black hair pushed off her face by a brightly coloured headscarf, appears through the dust with a bottle of water.

'Keep drinking, Jet.' She looks up, shielding her eyes from the sun. 'Another hot one today.'

'Thank you.' I walk to the tap and wash my hands, splash water on my face and retie my ponytail.

'Jet!' one of the volunteers shouts out, a middle-aged woman wearing a hot pink sunhat. 'Can you come over here?'

When she leads Lollopy to a shady spot, under the branch of a grevillea tree with spiky golden flowers, I follow.

'I think he's feeling the heat,' she says. 'He keeps pulling towards the gate.'

Darcy is crouched low over Lollopy's neck, almost lying down. His hands are threaded through the pony's mane. In addition to the woman with the pink hat, Darcy has two other volunteers and a physio walking with him. When I squat down low and gently touch his arm, he turns his head towards me.

'Hey, Darcy. You're riding so well today.'

His smile is crooked; his eyes light up.

'But I need to have a chat with your pony. You okay with that?'

He smiles again, tightens his fingers on Lollopy's mane.

I run my hands through Lollopy's forelock and down his neck. He's warm under his mane, but no more than I'd expect. His eyes are bright and he searches my pocket for a treat. I squat again, holding his bridle either side of his head and kissing his nose.

'Keep walking, lazybones.' I tilt my head and meet Darcy's eyes. 'He used to do the same to me when I was your age. Be firm with him, Darcy. Don't be afraid to squeeze your legs really tight so he knows you mean business. Give him a nudge with your heels to keep him going. The exercise does him good.'

The physio massages Darcy's leg. 'Another ten minutes would be ideal, but we can finish earlier if you think it's for the best.'

'Lollopy gets a treat when his work is done and that's what he's angling for. Darcy knows what to do now. He's in charge.'

I watch Lollopy walk away, the physio's hands on Darcy's thin frame, encouraging him to sit a little straighter.

'Jemima?' Finn says.

I spin around. 'Sorry. Were you waiting for me?'

His shirt has a dirty mark on the front, probably horse slobber. His pants and neatly laced shoes are covered in dust. His arms are crossed defensively over his chest. I'd like to wrench them open, throw myself against his body and kiss his angry mouth.

'I'll be in Horseshoe tomorrow week,' he says. 'I can't get out of it.'

'Gus's working bee?'

'Yes.'

'Jet! Is this better?'

'It's great.' Chelsea trots around the barrels on Cascade. 'Try to keep your heels down even further. Your toes should line up with your knees and hands.'

Laurence walks past on Chili, with a volunteer either side. 'How's my style?' he asks.

I give him a thumbs up. 'Really good.'

He laughs. 'Yeah, pull the other one.'

Finn and I walk from the arena together. 'I might see you next week,' I say.

He nods abruptly, joining a group of volunteers near the fence. They laugh at something he says.

My throat was scratchy when I woke up this morning. Or maybe the lump in it is permanent? I swallow as I bend over my toolbox, checking I have everything.

The hammer, the wrench and the knife.

CHAPTER
31

When Gus yanks open the door of the ute, I jump and hit my elbow on the steering wheel. 'Ow.'

'Why didn't you tell me you were out here?' he says.

'I was ten minutes early. I didn't want to rush you.'

'What? You think I'm not raring to go? Aren't you?'

I haven't seen or heard from Finn since I saw him at Follyfoot over a week ago, but his car was parked at the homestead when I got home from work. It had gone when I left twenty minutes ago. Will he be at the pub? He's bound to be.

'I always look forward to your working bee.'

Gus gives Banjo a final pat and climbs in next to me. 'Why've you got the aircon on? It's freezing in here.'

'I was hot.'

'What?' He does up his belt and then rubs his arms. 'With the temp down ten degrees? I can't believe December's just round the corner. Crazy weather.'

'I had a cold last week.' I put the car into gear. 'Maybe that was it.'

He cocks his head. 'What's that you're listening to?'

I disconnect my phone. 'Not much.'

'It was poetry, wasn't it?'

'Burns.'

'Which poem?'

'It was an ode, a miserable one.' I pull out onto the road. 'Rain is forecast for tomorrow.'

'Don't change the subject. This poem, you tell it to me.'

I smile. 'You won't like it.'

'Just the first lines, then.'

Oppress'd with grief, oppress'd with care,
A burden more than I can bear,
I set me down and sigh;
O life! thou art a galling load,
Along a rough, a weary road,
To wretches such as I!

Gus hoots a laugh. 'That's miserable all right. Henry Lawson, Jet. Now there's a poet for you. Local lad and all.'

By the time Gus and I walk into the pub, the bar is crowded. 'Go straight to the lounge,' I tell him. 'Everyone will be waiting for you. I'll get the drinks.'

'What? Didn't hear that.'

My throat hasn't been sore for a couple of days, but when I raise my voice it feels tight. 'I'll buy you a beer. Go and do your talk.'

He presses a note into my hand. 'My shout tonight. Get something to warm you up.'

I lift my hair from my neck and twist it. 'I'm too hot already.'

I watch Gus disappear into the lounge. His working bee started decades ago, after he lost his wife. A few of the locals suspected he was suffering from depression, and offered to give him a hand on his property. He kept the tradition going, so he could encourage other farmers to ask for help in difficult times. Tomorrow evening after the work is done, he'll roast a couple of lambs on the spit, and serve homemade brew to anyone brave enough to try it.

Finn is sitting at the back of the room, staring into a glass of water. Gus is sitting at a table at the front, shouting over the noise from the bar. This briefing is another tradition—the locals get told what they'll be doing, and work out what equipment they'll need. I put the beer in front of Gus and sit at a table near the entrance.

'In view of the weather forecast,' Gus says, 'we won't start until eight in the morning.'

'Start what?' someone says, laughing. 'Get to the point. What's on the agenda this year?'

'A few hundred seedlings to plant, for starters. And after that, we've got a big old red gum to be dealing with. It fell across the river months ago, up near the boundary I share with Edward Kincaid, a few hundred metres from the cliff. With the amount of rain we've had, and all the debris that's washed downstream, it looks like Warragamba Dam up there.'

'What gear do you want?'

'I'll have my tractor, but another might be handy. We'll need chainsaws and …'

Sapphie joins me after Gus has finished speaking and people have wandered off to order food or go to the bar.

'Ready for tomorrow?' she asks.

'I've promised to shoe the Honey girls' ponies before I start, but they'll come to me. I'll get down to the river as soon as I can.' I shade my eyes from a wall light. 'That's bright.'

'You okay?'

'Just a bit of a headache, that's all.'

She touches my arm. 'Is there anything else? You're kind of jumpy.'

'Just tired. I'll leave when Gus is ready.'

'He's been talking to Finn for the past fifteen minutes.'

'They get on well.'

'Jet?' She touches my arm. 'I think Finn is jumpy too.'

'Is he?'

'You could ask him to drive Gus home.'

'I don't mind waiting.'

'Jet!' Luke Martin comes up behind me, bends down over my shoulder and rattles my chair. 'We need you for pool.'

Sapphie opens her eyes very wide, so only I can see it, because she suspects Luke is still interested in me. He comes here most Saturday nights, and has agreed to help at the working bee.

I wish I could like him more.

'I'll be leaving soon,' I say.

'We only need you for the final game,' he says. 'There were four of us, but my mate had to go.'

'How about Sapphie?'

She laughs. 'I wasn't brought up on pool like you.' She stands and tugs my hand. 'C'mon, live a little. I'll put some music on.'

When I stand, Luke pumps the air. 'Yes!'

Sapphie shouts to Gus. 'We'll be in the poolroom. Half an hour, tops. Then Jet wants to get home.'

He lifts his beer in salute. 'Right you are.'

The table, full-sized with a green top and stained with countless spills of beer, must be almost as old as the pub. Dad used to bring me here, more and more often after Mum died. I wasn't supposed to be in the public bar, but no one seemed to mind. I'd often sit on a stool near the pool table, calling out the shots like an announcer at a racetrack. It must have been annoying for the players, but they never complained. Dad didn't drink, but he liked the company of the old men, and the family men, and the men with tattoos and long-legged girlfriends. They'd make room for us at the pool table, the bar and the lounge. They kept an eye on Dad as he got paler and thinner.

I'm the first to have a shot at the black. An Elvis song, 'Blue Suede Shoes', blares through the speakers. Only a handful of people were watching when we started, but it's been more or less shot for shot, so now there's a crowd, sitting on stools and leaning on walls. Sapphie has been standing on a chair and shouting encouragement for much of the game. I spy Gus elbowing his way to the front to get a better look. Finn doesn't need to do that; he's tall enough to stay at the back and see everything.

The white ball is positioned in the corner, so it's not an easy shot. I take care in lining up the balls, balancing on one foot and resting a hip on the table, with a leg stretched out behind me. I jab the white with the cue and it curves in an arc, hitting the black with a crack. The black shoots across the table, landing in the pocket with a clunk. There's a shout from the crowd, dimmed by the pounding in my head. I'd better take more tablets when I get home.

'Get back, you lot,' Gus shouts, as he pulls me into his arms and twirls me around. It's a different Elvis song now, 'Hound Dog'. My head starts to spin on the second circuit of the pool table. By the time Gus lets go, I have to hang onto the table for support, blinking and swallowing.

It doesn't take long for the crowd to disperse. Sapphie hugs me goodbye. Finn approaches, with his back ramrod straight and his eyes blue and hard.

'You play well.'

I look around for my hoodie, finally seeing it draped over a stool. 'Dad taught me.'

I'm halfway to the stool when I feel dizzy again. The swirls on the carpet move alarmingly at my feet. I hesitate, take three more steps, and grasp the stool with both hands.

'Are you all right?'

'I haven't been drinking, if that's what you mean.'

Before he can reply, Luke bounds up and takes my hands. 'Great round, Jet. How about I buy you a drink?'

I'm conscious of Finn watching, and other people's glances. I want to pull away but my head is still spinning.

'No, thanks.'

There's a hint of a smile on his face. 'A kiss then? This one's on me.'

The kiss is firm, and on the lips. As I pull away, he smiles again. 'Until the next round.'

I walk carefully through the bar, skirting around chairs and people. As Gus takes his hat off the stand, Finn walks past. He opens the door and strides through, without looking back.

My fingers don't work as they should. After three attempts to fasten the zip on my hoodie, I give up.

Clouds hide the stars and moon. The wind is cool on my face. When Gus loops his arm through mine at the top of the steps that lead to the footpath, it's a relief to have someone to cling to.

CHAPTER
32

The Honey girls' father is keen to help Gus, so drops his three daughters and their ponies at the cottage just after seven. I swallow down a mouthful of milky coffee and grab an apple as I walk to the door. My throat is fine today, but my headache is worse. I'm forced to bend low over the ponies' hooves because the tallest of them is only fourteen hands. My head pounds whenever I straighten.

Mary Honey is the youngest. She has a long, fair plait that reaches her waist, and asks questions all the time, about why all my horses are in the home paddock, what the tractor is doing at the river, and who are all those people down there, making so much noise?

'They're pulling a tree out of the river and chopping it up.'

'How did the tree get in the river?'

Mary's sisters answer most of her questions as I work on her Welsh Mountain cross. I've shod these horses for years. They compete at gymkhanas regularly and their feet are in good condition, but it's well after ten by the time their father picks them up, still laughing and chatting. I turn off the forge, tidy my tools and sweep out the shed. My skin is hot, but I'm cold inside. And my teeth won't stop chattering. I shrug into my waterproof jacket, pulling up the hood. The sun is firmly hidden by thick grey clouds.

It's only a few hundred metres to the section of the river with the fallen tree, and downhill most of the way, but by the time I get close enough to hear the good-natured jibes—about Sunday sleep-ins and breakfast in bed—I'm short of breath.

Gus, sitting on his tractor with his ancient Akubra pressed low on his head, bosses the workers around. Banjo sits behind him, ready for direction, pointed ears pricked. The red gum that obstructed the river has been cut into pieces by chainsaw and, as access is better on Edward's side of the river, most of the logs and branches will be left here. The timber will be used for fence posts or firewood even-tually, but now the larger logs are in one messy pile, the smaller logs and branches in another.

Even though the red gum is out of the way, the debris that's built up in the past few months still blocks the flow of the water.

'May as well finish the job,' Gus says, 'and clear out the rest of it.'

'I'll go and help the others.'

We take ropes and loop them around the larger branches in the river, and Gus hauls them through the undergrowth and up the hill. After an hour or so, the water flows freely, bubbling around the rocks and lapping against the exposed roots of the paperbark trees. When there are only smaller branches to deal with, everyone, besides Gus and I, heads off to plant saplings.

'Jet!' Gus, waving from the tractor, is only just visible. 'Are we done?'

I brush hair out of my eyes. 'Just a few more.'

I'm wearing canvas gloves and struggle to form a slipknot. When I look up, I see Gus trudging towards me.

'What's up with you?' he says, taking the rope out of my hand. 'You're as slow as a wet weekend.'

I glance at the sky. 'That's appropriate, isn't it?'

Gus fastens the rope around the branch. Then he looks up and blinks in surprise—as if he's only just noticed that the drizzle has turned to a downpour. He throws his hands in the air.

'How are we going to cut hay if it doesn't stop raining? I'll be doing it on Christmas Day at this rate.'

My footprints form puddles in the mud. 'It's bound to dry up before then.'

'You're still a bit croaky. How's the cold?'

'Not the best. I'll go home and change soon.'

'Come to my place after that. A few of the ladies are doing something special for lunch, feeding the troops for the afternoon shift.'

I attempt to smile. 'Sure.' The wind blows my hood back as Gus says something else. I lean forwards to catch his words. 'What? My ear is blocked.'

'I'd better get my tractor back home. We'll be needing two of them after the lunch break.'

'I'm fine to clear the smaller branches on my own.'

A few loads later, I drag the final branch to the pile. I open my mouth and yawn, trying to clear my ear. It seems to be permanently blocked now, as if the rain, still falling, is being funnelled directly into it. My body is stiff and achy.

If my bathroom had a bath, I'd soak in it.

I've barely started up the hill towards home when I have to stop at the pile of newly sawn logs to catch my breath. The logs are wet, but I'm pretty much wet through anyway. I sit and rest my forearms on my knees. I tip my head to the side. Stabbing pain shoots behind my eyes.

'Ow!' I press my thumbs against my temples as hard as I can.

Shower. Clothes. Food. Rest. But first I have to get home. I look up the hill towards the cottage, as if seeing it there will give me the strength to get to it.

Finn walks towards me through the mist. What mist? There isn't one. I blink a few times. *Everything* is blurry. The grass at my feet, the logs. My hand when I hold it in front of my face.

'Jemima?'

I jump. How did he get here so quickly?

His clothes aren't wet and dirty like mine. He's dressed in a dark-grey rain jacket and jeans. His hood is pushed back, his hair is damp and so is his face.

Impossibly. Blue. Eyes.

'Why are you here?'

'Sapphie called. She didn't know where you were.'

'Gus knew.'

'He thought you'd be at his house by now. Everyone else is there.'

I look to the other side of the river, peer through the paperbark trees. Besides Finn, I'm all alone.

'Are you going to Gus's for lunch?' he asks.

I was hungry before, but now … There are cowpats a few metres away, circular, soggy and brown. I don't usually notice the smell, but suddenly it turns my stomach. I swallow down the acid that wants to come up.

When I push myself to my feet, my head spins. Finn seems to be even taller and broader than usual. Maybe that's because he's still blurry? He's *increasingly* blurry. He puts his hand on my arm. Even though I don't look down, I know it's a well-shaped hand with manicured nails. It untangles knots in laces. It sets my skin on fire. A sound works its way up my throat. A sob? What's going on? I can't string a thought together.

'Jemima? What's the matter?'

'Why are you clean?'

He frowns. 'I got back an hour ago.'

I was out at six, checking on Chili and the other horses. I shod three ponies. What time did I finish at the river? I can't remember.

I shuffle sideways, but he keeps hold of my arm. Does he want to dance with me, like Gus did last night?

'Is Sapphie at Gus's house? Luke?'

When he lets me go, I put a hand on a log to steady myself. I squeeze my eyes shut and open them again.

'Can you tell them I'll be there in an hour?'

'Why not sooner?'

Broken nails. Shaky hands. He's seen me at my worst too often. It's not weak to be unwell, but I don't want to make excuses.

'You go.' In addition to razor blades, I have a pebble in my throat. There's a screw lodged in my temple and a sack of cotton wool in my head. I blink a couple of times, trying to clear my vision. 'I'll be there as quick as I can.'

'But you don't want to walk up the hill with me?'

'No.'

He doesn't respond, just strides off alone.

I see something from the corner of my eye, a herd of young steer. They must belong to Gus. Now I know why there's cow dung in the paddock.

When the nausea hits again I return to the logs, sit and rest my head on my knees. I gag. Nothing comes up, but my head hurts even more. I suck in deep breaths and cling to the slippery timber.

One of the steers bellows. He's dark chestnut brown and sopping wet, with big round eyes. Could he be the calf that Finn pulled from the river? He's much bigger, but … I add up on my fingers. Liam's birthday is the second of August. Almost four months have passed. Of course he'd be bigger, but would he be weaned already?

Should I try to get the calf back to Gus? Not now. He bellows again. All the steers join in. They move towards me, standing and staring, bellowing, grunting.

When I push myself to my feet, the ground moves. And so does Horseshoe Hill behind the cottage. Everything turns, slowly at first and then quickly, rolling and spinning. What is up and what is down?

I fall.

The sky is dense with clouds, thick and steely grey. Rain falls on my face. The grass is wet beneath my hands.

'Jemima!' Finn leans over me, runs firm hands down my body. He puts his fingertips against my pulse, first at my wrist and then at my throat. 'Can you hear me?'

'Hurts.'

'What hurts? Jemima?'

He said he should call me Jet, because everybody else on the planet does that. But he's not the same as everybody else.

'I like ...' My voice breaks. I try again. 'I like Jemima.'

He cups the side of my face. 'Jemima.' His thumb strokes my pulse. 'What happened?'

'Your dad is Findlay.'

He frowns, but not in an angry way. 'I got the short version.'

'Finn?'

'Yes.'

'It hurts.'

He runs his thumbs across my cheeks. 'Listen to me, baby. What hurts? I can't move you until I know.'

'Head.' I want the pain to escape. Seep into the dirt. Be washed into the river and then out to sea.

'Where?'

I close my eyes.

'Open your eyes, Jem.'

I prise my eyes open.

'Tell me what hurts.'

I open my mouth but nothing comes out.

He loosens the press-studs at my throat and pulls back my hood. He lifts my head a little. His fingers move over my scalp. My breath hitches. I flinch.

'You've hit the back of your head. But that's not the problem, is it?'

He puts something soft under my head. The wind has died down. The paperbark leaves rustle quietly. The sound is gentle. So are his hands.

'You had a sore eye.'

'I did,' he says, pushing back my hair.

'And mouth.'

'Yes.'

'Behind my eye. It hurts.' When I lift my arm, it hovers as if it's not mine. I touch his ear. 'Here too.'

I close my eyes and turn my head one way and then the other. Something trickles down my face. Am I crying?

'Stay with me,' he says.

It hurts to be with him. It hurts to be without him. I should run away. But not today. Not now. Not yet.

His voice is a rumble, loud and then soft. 'Don't leave me, Jem.'

My eyes are so heavy, my head is so sore.

Just for a while, I'll sleep.

CHAPTER

33

Sapphie sits on a chair next to my bed. 'How do you feel?' she asks, putting her hand on my arm. 'You've been asleep for hours.'

My head is fuzzy, my throat is dry. When I stretch out my fingers, something pulls. There's a cannula in the back of my hand, connected to a drip held high by a stand. When I move my toes around, the sheet shifts. My feet are bare but I'm wearing track-suit pants, and the T-shirt I dressed in this morning. The room is warm. There's a tree close to the window, filtering the light from outside.

'Where are we?' I'm lying on a single bed and facing a book-case. Most of the shelves are narrowly spaced but filled with books. Children's books? There's a gap next to my bed, and on the other side of the gap is another single bed. It has a cover of blue-and-white stripes, and in the blue stripes there are galloping horses. At the end of the room there's a desk, half hidden by a wardrobe.

I know this room … an upright chair, the one Sapphie is sitting on, is usually pushed under the desk. Above the desk will be a picture of a horse, a palomino with a golden coat and creamy forelock.

'We're at Kincaid House,' Sapphie says. 'Dr Gupta was reluctant to move you, and thought you'd be more comfortable here than in the surgery anyway. He doesn't think you need to go to the hospital, not if you're carefully monitored.'

I lift my hand again. 'What's the matter with me?'

'The cannula was for intravenous antibiotics because you have an ear infection and your temperature was through the roof. Dr Gupta thinks that's why you passed out. You were also dehydrated, so he's giving you fluids as well.'

'What time is it?'

'Almost four o'clock.' She frowns as she picks up a chunk of my hair. 'Your hair is sticky. It's just dried blood though.'

'Why?'

'You hit the back of your head. The graze isn't a worry, but Dr Gupta is concerned about concussion.'

'It was only a cold.'

'And an ear infection.'

I look at the cannula in my hand. 'You said this was fluids?'

'What did you eat and drink this morning?'

'Coffee.' It seems a hundred years away. 'Water, I guess. An apple.'

'I'll call Dr Gupta and tell him you're awake. You probably won't need the drip any more, now you can drink. But we have to watch you don't fall over again, or throw up.'

I yawn, relieved when it doesn't hurt my head too much. 'I think I'll just sleep. Do I really have blood in my hair?'

'You can have a shower later.'

Next time I wake, Dr Gupta is in the room. He's happy enough at first, and takes out the cannula. But when he sits me up, I sway like a drunk, and there's no way I can stand on my own. It worries him, so he makes me lie down and checks me over again.

'The infection could be affecting your balance.'

'I was lightheaded last night, and I felt sick.'

'Consistent with an ear infection.'

'Where was I when I hit my head?'

He purses his lips. 'You don't remember?'

I close my eyes. I was down by the river. Finn walked away and … 'I was in the paddock, wasn't I? Near the logs.'

'Dr Blackwood saw you collapse.'

'How did I get up here?'

'Finn called for help,' Sapphie says, 'but by the time it had arrived, he'd carried you to the homestead.' She squeezes my arm. 'A bit Mr Willoughby, hey?'

I remember talking to Finn. What about? 'When can I go home?'

'Tomorrow at the earliest.' Dr Gupta holds up a hand, as if anticipating my response. 'The less you do in the next twenty-four hours, the better.'

'It's a nice room, Jet,' Sapphie says. 'And there's a bathroom down the hallway. I've already spoken to Ma. You know what she's like. She's preparing something nutritious, light, and suitable for an invalid.'

I'd like to argue, but when Dr Gupta helps me to sit so that I can go to the bathroom, I'm so nauseated that I can't stop retching. He and Sapphie each hold an arm and guide me to the toilet. There's a mirror above the sink.

My face is chalky white, making my eyes a darker shade. A chunk of hair, stiff with blood, sticks out of the side of my head.

'Ew. Can I wash it?'

'Wait until you are steadier on your feet,' Dr Gupta says.

They sit me on the bed and then lie me down. 'Thanks,' I mumble, shutting my eyes in exhaustion.

'Jet?' Sapphie whispers. 'Are you awake yet?'

I force my eyes open. I yawn. 'Sure.' I can see even less through the window now. 'Is it still raining?'

'Pouring.'

'What time is it?'

'After seven.'

Most of the light in the room is coming through the open door to the hallway. Sapphie is perched on the other bed. When she offers a glass of water, I prop myself up on an elbow and drink.

'My head feels a lot better,' I say, lying down again.

'That's good.'

'You're missing Gus's dinner.'

'I couldn't party while you were dying.'

An image of the gardens at Dad's hospice slips into my mind—the different types of roses and the flowering bulbs.

'I know you wouldn't do that.'

Sapphie puts her hand on my arm. 'What a thoughtless thing to say. I'm so sorry.'

'Are you a mind-reader?' I wipe a hand across my eyes and sniff. 'I don't know why I thought of Dad.'

'You were there.'

'There were so many times he could have died. They were the frightening ones, when I wasn't prepared to lose him yet.'

'Ross hid it well, how sick he was.'

I squeeze her arm. 'Stop looking so sad.'

'He told me you used to sneak into his room late at night, but you only ever cried when you thought he was asleep.'

I roll onto my side, facing her. 'When he had trouble breathing, when he needed oxygen to keep his heart going, I was too afraid to sleep.' I yawn again. 'Go home, Sapphie. I'll be fine when I wake up.'

The next time I wake, Sapphie is standing at the end of my bed, smoothing down my covers. It's dark outside. I hear a rumble far away.

'Are you still here? Is it going to storm again? You hate driving alone at night even when it's clear. Go home before it gets worse. I'll be fine, honestly.'

'How are you feeling?'

I stretch. 'Much better.'

'If you collapsed again, I wouldn't be able to carry you.'

'I'm not going to collapse.'

'We don't know that. You can't be left alone.' She glances towards the wardrobe. 'That's why Finn is here.'

'What?'

Finn stands. 'Jemima.'

He must have been sitting at the desk. I struggle onto an elbow, my heart racing frantically. 'How long have you been there?'

He holds up a book. 'I was reading.'

'In the dark?'

'Finn is a vet,' Sapphie says, 'which means he knows about medical things. After Dr Gupta saw how shaky you were, he was going to send you straight to the hospital. But then he said that, as long as Finn was here, it should be okay.'

'I don't want—'

'You either stay here with Finn,' Sapphie says, 'or go to the hospital. Because if you don't, Ma won't sleep, and neither will I.'

I dig my elbow into the bed, trying to lift myself higher. Lights flash in front of my eyes. I feel nauseous again. Sapphie puts a hand on my arm. It's a light touch, but the weight of it pushes me onto my back.

'Your dinner's in the kitchen, and I've put toiletries in the bathroom.'

'I'll be—'

'You always look after yourself. I know that, and so does Finn. It's only one night.'

We had a night in his apartment. After we kissed at the cottage, I thought there could be more nights, but …

'Please, no, Sapphie.'

'Just for tonight, Jet. Not negotiable.'

Sapphie looks apologetically at Finn. When he rubs the back of his neck, his T-shirt pulls tight across his chest. He said *tell me what hurts* when I was lying on the ground.

Can't he understand that just looking at him hurts?

CHAPTER
34

I listen to Sapphie's footsteps in the hall. She opens the front door, closing it quietly behind her. Finn walks to the side of the bed.

'Can I get you anything?'

'Thank you for picking me up, for bringing me here.' I pull the sheet higher, up to my chest. My nails are so short that there's no room for dirt. Even so, they're grubby. 'It's kind of you, but ... I don't think you should do this.'

He smiles stiffly. 'You want nothing to do with me. I'm aware of that.'

Thornbrooke, Caruthers, a kiss that almost killed him. There are so many reasons to agree with what he says.

'So why are you here?'

'You're unwell.'

I swallow. 'Please, Finn.' My voice is shaky. 'Everything's such a mess.'

'For now, we put that aside.'

'I want to go home.'

'That isn't possible.'

I push myself up to a sitting position, much more slowly than last time. When he turns on the bedside light, I see blood on the pillowcase. 'Oh.'

'I'll change it later.'

I study my hands. I bunch up my fingers to hide them from both of us. 'I can wash it when I get home.'

'I could have prevented your fall. I regret that I didn't.'

'You weren't to know.' My voice wavers. I squeeze my eyes shut. 'I don't mean to be rude.'

He holds out a glass of water. 'Drink, Jemima.'

I reach for the glass, carefully so we don't touch.

'I hope Gus isn't too worried about me.'

'He said he'd visit tomorrow. Luke offered to come, but he'd had a couple of beers with lunch.' He shrugs. 'Hence my involvement.'

Hence? Who says hence? I give back the glass and smooth the sheet over my legs. 'This isn't a good idea.'

'I have no hidden agenda. I have no desire to make things worse.'

He has no desire for me. And why would he, when I've pushed him away so completely?

I have no idea where the tears come from. But they're relentless. Finn steps closer but when I hold out my hand, he stays where he is. I cry onto my fingers, onto the sheet. When he puts a box of tissues on the bed, I scrub at my cheeks.

And then, when I'm finally quiet, he squats next to the bed. 'Would you like another glass of water? Or juice? Something to eat?'

I shake my head. But that makes me feel sick. I rest my forehead on my knees and take deep breaths. 'I'd like to have a shower.'

'You should eat first.'

I touch the blood in my hair. 'No.'

I hear him moving around in the bathroom. When he comes back, he holds out his hand.

'I'll walk with you.'

I sniff and wipe my nose, then shuffle to the side of the bed and lower my feet to the floor. I focus on the desk because the colours in the room—white furniture, pale blue walls, hardwood floors and a brightly coloured rug—are all mixed up in a blur. I stand, still holding on to the bed. But then I sway.

He swears and reaches for me, putting his arm around the small of my back. He wraps his other arm around my front, supporting me at the waist.

'I think I'm going to throw up.'

He pulls me closer. 'Lean on me.'

'I have to; my legs won't hold me up.'

'I'll take you back to bed. I'll call Dr Gupta.'

'No.' I close my eyes and will down nausea. 'Shower.'

He holds me upright as I put one unsteady foot in front of the other, like I'm walking on a tightrope. And finally we reach the threshold to the bathroom, a small space with a toilet and sink, and a shower with a glass door. I need to pee. And wash my hair. But I have no idea how to achieve either of those things.

He shuts the toilet lid and eases me onto the seat. He squats by my side. 'I'll help you to undress.'

My voice is a croak. 'I can do it.'

His jaw clenches. 'How?'

My balance is even worse than it was when Dr Gupta and Sapphie helped me to the bathroom. My hands cling onto the toilet seat either side of my thighs.

'You had an apple for breakfast. What did you eat last night?'

'Something at the pub.'

'You had a soft drink. You didn't eat.'

I look into his eyes. 'Oh.'

'I have a suggestion. Eat first, then shower.'

'No.'

He mutters under his breath. 'I'll help you to undress.'

'No.'

'Jemima … Why do you think I'm doing this? Do you think I'd take advantage of you?'

He smells nice. He has fresh clothes and clean shiny hair. His hands are gentle but strong. I'm aware of all of those things because, even as sick as a dog, I'm attracted to him.

'I'm sorry.'

'You damned well should be.'

'Don't …' My voice breaks. 'Please don't shout.'

'I didn't shout.'

More tears. They trickle down my face in pathetic little rivulets. I'm afraid to look at him as I wipe my face with my sleeve. He pulls out a stream of toilet paper and hands it to me.

'Thank you.' I blow my nose. 'I'm sick. That's why I'm crying.'

'Perhaps I raised my voice.' He speaks softly, reassuringly. 'I won't do it again.'

Is this how he talks to his megafauna, his rhinos and hippos and elephants, when they're unwell? He wraps a towel around my shoulders. Then he squats, and loosens my hands from the toilet lid. He holds them tightly.

'I'd like to get your arms out of your T-shirt and then take it over your head. Is that all right?'

I nod.

After my T-shirt is lying on the floor, he stands. 'If you put your arms around my neck, I'll lift you to your feet. You can take off your trackpants.'

By the time I sit on the toilet seat again, all I'm wearing under the towel is a black crop-top bra and sensible black undies.

'Toilet?' he says. 'Can you manage?'

'Yes.'

'Hang onto the cistern while I lift the seat.'

He turns his back and spends an age adjusting the water temperature in the shower. The bathroom is steamy by the time I flush. I perch on the edge of the seat.

'I'm ready.'

'I'd put a chair in the shower, but you might fall out of it.'

I leave my towel on the tiles and crawl into the spray, pulling the glass door shut behind me.

'I promise I won't stand up. Can you pass the toiletry bag?'

He hands it to me. 'Call out when you're finished. I'll leave a towel within reach.'

As the warm water falls against my shoulders and back, I begin to think more rationally. I overheard his birthdate when he was in the hospital. He's just turned thirty-one. He's seen me naked already. And he must have seen a lot of other naked women. Seen them and had sex with them. So why make such a fuss? I strip off my undies and crop top and methodically soap myself. I wash my hair, tentatively lathering the bump on the back of my head. I lean against the wall after I put the conditioner on and look at the label on the back.

I've bumped my head. I have an ear infection. I can't stand up without help. Finn is waiting on the other side of the door and I'm an emotional wreck. There are so many reasons it should be impossible to read the instructions on the bottle. But … after a while they're perfectly clear. The conditioner should stay in my hair for exactly five minutes. I've counted to two hundred and seventy when Finn taps on the door.

'Are you all right?'

'I won't be long.'

I clean my teeth in the shower and then turn off the tap. I open the door and pick up the towel, wrapping it around my shoulders. All I see is his legs when he walks in—black jeans and bare feet. He bends to straighten the bathmat. Our eyes meet.

'You okay?'

'Yes. Can I have another towel please?'

The towels aren't very big. I secure one around my waist, and one under my arms. But my shoulders are bare for only a moment because he throws another towel around my neck.

'Dry your hair with that one.' He holds me by the elbows and pulls me to my feet. When he loosens his hold, I sway and he tightens it again.

'How do you feel?' When I hesitate, he frowns. 'I called Dr Gupta. He said the balance issues are most likely attributable to the inner ear infection. But if you're still nauseated after eating, it could be concussion. He'd want to check you out.'

'I'm lightheaded, but I don't feel as sick as I did.'

We're walking slowly to my bed when he steers me to the other one. 'Sit here,' he says. 'Keep your bed dry.'

Is the other bed his bed? Will I have to face him across the divide? I look at the bed I was in before. It's neatly made.

'You changed my pillowcase.'

As I sit, he points to a pile of clothes. 'Sapphie organised them. Can you manage?'

'Yes.'

It's like playing house—with a room full of tension. While he takes clear wrap off two plates and sorts out cutlery, I towel-dry my hair and rummage in my toiletry bag for a brush and lip balm. There are underpants but no bra, and my crop top is wet so I can't wear that. I pull on pale yellow pyjama shorts with a white polka-dot pattern, and a matching top with an appliqued crescent moon and the words 'Nighty Night' on the front. The pyjamas have white cotton cuffs at the elbows and thighs.

When Finn turns, a tray in his hands, I'm pulling on pale blue socks. Why is it so cold in November?

'We'll eat on the bed you're sitting on,' he says.

His gaze is usually so direct. It's odd, the way he looks past me. Is it because I'm wearing pyjamas? Because I offended him earlier?

I attempt a smile. 'I could sit at a table.'

'This is safer.'

I wriggle backwards and lean against the wall, and he hands me a plate and a fork. Mrs Hargreaves has made a version of niçoise salad—tuna, egg, olives, tomatoes, peas and beans. When Finn sits next to me, he's so far away that there's room for another person between us.

Last time we ate together he told me he wasn't a leper or a freak. After that we cleaned our teeth. And then … I take a deep breath.

'Mrs Hargreaves knows about your allergies, doesn't she?'

He spears a chunk of tuna, frowning as he puts it into his mouth. 'Yes.'

'Why can you eat fish but not crustaceans? Why eggs and not nuts?'

'Is this your idea of dinner conversation?'

'I'm not much of a conversationalist.'

'With me, no.' He points to my plate. 'Eat, Jemima.'

I pick up a tomato and take a tiny bite. I want to eat so I can go home, but my throat is clogged with unhappiness and tension and—

'What is it now?'

When tears well in my eyes, I squeeze them shut.

'For fuck's …' I feel the movement of the bed when he gets up. And by the time I've scraped a hand across my eyes, he's holding out the tissues. I snatch them and blow my nose while he sits next to me again, much closer this time.

'Jemima?'

'What?'

'I'm sorry.' He picks up my fork, spears tuna and a bean and holds it out. 'Truce?'

The fork hangs between us. 'I don't know what's wrong with me.'

'You're not well enough to run away.' His mouth lifts at the corner. 'It must be difficult, going against your nature.'

'Are you laughing at me?'

'I wish it were that easy.'

When I take the fork, he puts his plate back on his lap. We eat in silence, but it's not too uncomfortable. I'm hungry, and I think he is too. After a while, all he has left are peas and beans. The peas are all on one side of his plate, corralled by a line of beans. He sees me staring.

'I don't like peas,' he says.

'Mrs Hargreaves grows them. They're fresh, not frozen.'

'I dislike them either way.'

'What about the beans? I saw you eating beans at the pub.'

He stabs a bean with his fork and puts it into his mouth. 'I eat the beans last.'

'So the peas don't escape while you eat the rest of your food?' When I smile, he stares at my mouth.

'Now you're laughing at me.'

'Do you like the beans best? Is that why you eat them last?'

'Yes.'

One of my legs is bent up on the bed. I turn so I'm facing him side-on, stab one of my beans and hold it out. 'I'll swap you one bean for five peas.'

'Deal.' He takes the bean and eats it. Then, scooping up a forkful of peas, he deposits them onto my plate.

'That's a lot of peas. I only have two beans left.'

'I'll take whatever you've got.'

Our eyes lock. My heart turns a somersault. *No, no, no, no, no.*

He's the first to look away. He scoops up more peas and puts them onto my plate.

'Thank you,' I whisper, as I give him my beans.

When our plates are empty, he collects them without looking at me, but, just before he walks through the door, our eyes meet again. His expression is thoughtful. And it hasn't changed much by the time he gets back and hands me a mug of coffee. He pulls the chair close to the bed and sits, facing me with his forearms on his thighs. I focus firmly on his hands, wrapped around his mug.

'Tell me about your family,' he says.

CHAPTER
35

Doesn't he have enough information? What would Caruthers say if he saw us like this?

But … It's too early to go to sleep. And if I walk out, I'll probably fall. Finn will call Dr Gupta.

Just like him, I wrap my hands around my mug. 'You know plenty already. Tell me about your family first.'

'You've spoken to my parents.'

'In your speech at the zoo, you said they lived in Glasgow.'

'I imagine they always will. They're both fifty-five, they've been married for thirty-three years. We're close.'

'Do you have any brothers or sisters?'

'I have a sister, she's twenty-six.'

'Like Sapphie. What's her name?'

'Fern.'

'Is that a Scottish name?'

'Not really. My mother read it somewhere.' He looks down at his mug. His lashes are thick and dark. 'It's appropriate. Fern is an environmentalist, and a lawyer.'

'She must be interested in what you're doing now.'

'She doesn't approve of keeping animals in captivity.'

'Even in open plains zoos that support conservation?'

'They're slightly less offensive to her. She approved of the work I did in Africa.'

'After your speech, someone asked you a question about Africa. You said you missed it.'

He looks away, but when he lifts his mug to his lips, our eyes meet again. The expression on his face is fleeting. Pain? Regret?

'I miss it less than I used to.'

'What do you miss most? The environment? The danger?'

He frowns. 'The challenges.' He puts his mug on the floor. 'Your colour has improved. How do you feel?'

'Much better, thanks.'

'May I ask you some questions now?'

'Why do you say "may" and not "can"?'

He blinks. 'I'm asking your permission.'

'You don't speak anything like your parents.'

He opens his mouth and then closes it again. 'I went to a boarding school in England.'

'You got a scholarship. How old were you?'

'I was ten.'

'Were you forced to lose your accent?'

'No.' He shrugs. 'But I imagined changing the way I spoke might improve the way I communicated. I was good at mathematics, not the humanities. I wanted to be understood, to fit in.'

'Did you do fencing and rowing?'

'Yes. And I played cricket and rugby. But mostly I studied.'

He grew up with his nose in a book. Could I be attracted to anyone less like me?

'Jemima?'

I lift one knee and balance my mug on it. I blow on the surface as if it's much too hot. 'Yes.'

'Is it my turn to ask questions?'

'I might not answer.'

He leans further forwards in his chair. 'I went back to the cemetery. Fiona Hargreaves was there and explained the significance of the flowers on your family's graves, how important they've become to everyone who visits.'

I like the way Finn speaks, his careful choice of words. 'Liam was only two days old. I didn't really know him. I …' I take a gulp of coffee.

'You lost the brother you expected to have. You would have felt your parents' loss too. You were eleven?'

'Yes.'

'And fourteen when your mother passed away.'

'I like to remember her how she was.'

He frowns, tilts his head to the side. 'I don't want to upset you again.'

'You may as well get it over with. Were you here when Sapphie and I talked about Dad?'

'You were with him when he died.'

'I didn't want to be anywhere else.'

Our knees touch, just for a moment. I'm not sure who moves away, him or me. Maybe it's both of us.

'I think you've spent so many years …' He frowns again, as if not sure whether to finish his sentence.

'What? I'm bound to have heard it already. Dad made sure I saw plenty of therapists.'

'Being independent, it's important to you.'

'I'm better on my own. I worked that out a long time ago.'

'Edward told me he'd made overtures, before and after your father's death. He invited you to live with him in Sydney.'

'I wouldn't go.'

'Why not?'

'The people who come from here, the Hargreaves, Gus, Sapphie, they're my family.'

He hesitates. 'You were only seventeen.'

'Almost eighteen.'

'Edward implied you had something you were afraid of in Sydney, that's why you wouldn't join him. What did he mean?'

'He thought I was afraid of going to a new school. Maybe I was. But I wanted to be a farrier. I had an apprenticeship.'

'So why work at Thornbrooke?'

'I had to pay off my ute. And Thornbrooke was closer to the racing stables where my boss worked. It was closer to college too. I went there every Friday for classes, exams, learning support, things like that.'

He leans forwards like he wants to ask a question. Does he know I have dyslexia? Edward might not have said anything, but it's no secret that Sapphie helps with my bookwork and Magda does my orders at Follyfoot. Leon always makes a point of reading out the dinner specials, and Gus snatches trivia questions out of my hands straight away. When I wrote the note in Finn's apartment, he asked what I'd thanked him for. *Pyjamas. Toothbrush.* After we kissed at the cottage, I sent him icons and recordings, not words.

Of course he knows.

He clears his throat. 'Jemima? How many hours a week did you work at Thornbrooke?'

'Only weekends, but I could stay there on weeknights when I needed to.'

'Edward's father must have owned Thornbrooke when you were there.'

'He'd had a stroke … he wasn't very well. I never really saw him.'

'He left Morrissey in charge.'

My legs are folded to the side. The bruise on my shin is an angry shade of blue. 'What day is it again?'

'Sunday.'

It was a week and a half ago I saw Caruthers. 'Is this what you've been leading up to? What happened at Thornbrooke?'

He stands, picks up the chair and puts it behind the desk. It's not a large room, but he paces up and down between the beds. There's a crease between his brows; his mouth is tight.

After a while, he pulls up in front of me, crouches and rests an arm either side of my legs.

'Tell me what happened,' he says.

I look over his shoulder, out of the window. At first I think there's nothing to see. But then, reflected in the light, I make out the rain, countless little drops, on the glass. The raindrops join up and trickle to the windowsill.

'Why are you afraid?' he says. 'You can trust me with the truth.'

If he leant forwards, he'd press against the bruise on my shin. Would it hurt? 'When will you go back to Switzerland? Or Kenya? Or is it Scotland?'

'Why do you want—'

'Tell me!'

He sighs. 'I'll be in Dubbo until February.'

'And then you'll leave Thornbrooke behind you. That's what I want too.'

CHAPTER

36

I force a yawn. 'I'd like to go to bed now.'

I'm much steadier on my feet than I was, but he shadows me to the bathroom and insists I leave the door ajar while he waits outside. I pee quietly and brush my teeth quickly.

He watches silently as I hold on to the side of the bed and carefully sit. He pours me a glass of water from the jug and puts it on the side table, then picks up the tray and walks to the door.

'I won't be long.'

'I'll be fine on my own.'

'Once you're asleep, I'll leave you.'

I listen to the kitchen sounds, dishes clanking in the sink and cupboard doors opening and closing. The pump starts up. Finn must be taking a shower. Rain whispers on the slate roof and against the window. Puddles will form in the dips in the paths, water will fill the dam. The river near the cliff will gush over the rock that divides it. The pump noises soften to a whir. Soon he'll be back.

But not for long. In February he'll return to the life that he had. Thornbrooke and Finn. All mixed up. But he's been kind to me tonight. I should thank him.

I shuffle to the end of the bed. There's no paper on the desk, just Finn's novel and a handful of pens in a pottery cup. The bookcase is filled with children's books. They're all brand new, but some of them look familiar. I'm sure I had identical copies when I was a child.

On the top shelf there's a colouring book, with drawings of aeroplanes, trucks and tractors. The final page has a picture of a fire truck, but the reverse side is blank. I carefully tear along the seam. I don't overthink things when I form the letters, willing the words to come out right. I put the note on the side table. It looks okay to me but ... I hope my writing is legible and there aren't so many mistakes that he won't be able to make sense of it.

> Finn,
>
> Thank you for looking after me.
>
> You said you shouldn't have left me before I fell. It was me who told you to go. Thank you for coming back.
>
> Your mum is probably happy you don't live in Africa any more. I think she worries about you. Do you know Burns's 'The Mother's Lament'?
>
> Sorry for crying all night. I haven't cried so much in years.
>
> I can't help you with Thornbrooke. There are lots of reasons.
>
> Jemima

I'm under the covers, facing the wall, when light from the hallway seeps into the room. Finn walks between the beds. I hear the rustle of paper.

'Jemima?' I hold the covers more tightly around my shoulders when my bed dips. I feel the warmth of his body against my back. He touches my arm. My limbs feel suddenly heavy.

'You fuck with my mind,' he says quietly. 'You know that?'

I daren't move.

'As soon as I give up, you give yourself away. That's what brings me back.'

I breathe in through my nose and out through my mouth, willing him to go. Or stay.

'I don't think you're asleep.' His hand slides up my arm to my shoulder. 'I've been gone twenty minutes, and you wrote a lot of words in that time. More words in a row than you've ever said out loud.' He runs his finger around the rim of my ear. His voice gentles. 'Open your eyes, Jem.'

I shut my eyes even tighter. I shake my head. 'Go away.'

'After I've responded to your note.' The paper rustles again. 'Verbally, because you've used most of the page, and it'd be a shame to spoil the fire engine on the other side. I wish you'd turn around.'

I shake my head again.

'In paragraph one you thank me. No need.' He runs his hand over the bedcovers. 'Are you warm enough?'

'Yes.'

He puts his hand on my forehead. 'But not too warm?'

'No.'

He lifts his hand. 'Paragraph two. "Thank you for coming back." Is that what it says?'

'I'm sorry you had to carry me all that way.'

He tucks strands of hair behind my ear. 'Better me than somebody else.' He runs his finger along my jawline. He strokes the nape of my neck, pulls hair out of my pyjama top and smooths it over the collar.

Without warning there's a lump in my throat. I open my eyes and address the wall. 'When you were sick, I walked out. Did you hate me for that?'

His hand stills. 'You want to forget that night. That's what I hate.'

We can't go back.

'Paragraph three.' His weight shifts when he reaches over my waist and rests his hand on the bed. His forearm touches my hip.

'My mother worries about me,' he whispers. 'Is that what you've written?'

'Yes.'

'You mention a Burns poem. Is it "The Mother's Lament?"'

'Yes.'

'It's one of Mam's favourites.'

'It's very sad.'

'Can you recite it?'

> Fate gave the word, the arrow sped,
> And pierc'd my darling's heart;
> And with him all the joys are fled,
> Life can to me impart.

'Burns's poetry,' he says. 'How do you know it so well?'

'My primary school librarian, Mrs McNab. She was crazy about him.'

He leans more firmly against my back. 'You refer to Africa. One day I'll tell you about it.'

I close my eyes again. 'You don't have to.'

The paper rustles. 'Paragraph four. You haven't cried like that in years. Since your father died?'

I push myself into a sitting position, turn and face him. His hair is damp. One of his legs is on the floor and the other is on the bed, bent at the knee. He's wearing a dark T-shirt and trackpants.

'We were happy when he was alive, really happy. I only cried afterwards.'

He folds the note carefully and puts it on the table. 'Why did you write to me?'

'To settle things between us.' I shuffle backwards. I straighten my pyjama top, cross my arms. 'Are we all good now?'

He slowly shakes his head. 'We're a million miles from good.'

'Please, no more questions. I can't—'

'Not tonight. Just …' He tilts his head to the side and reads what's written on the pyjama top. *Nighty Night*. He smiles. 'Get some sleep.'

A drip of water is about to fall from his hair, where it comes to a point beneath his ear. It will land on his T-shirt, joining all the other drips that have dampened it already. He's so close. I think about the hardness of his body, his warmth and strength.

I catch the drip just before it falls. Then sit back on my bottom. My index finger is wet. I put it into my mouth. When I see the shock on his face, I freeze.

'What?'

'Jemima?' He croaks my name. His eyes are midnight blue, almost black. He holds out his hands and I take them instinctively. I rest our fingers, tightly linked, on my knees, on top of the covers. We stare at our hands as I desperately think of something to say.

'Your hands …' I clear my throat. 'You have nice hands.' I spread his fingers out and trace around them, like he traced the rim of my ear. 'Your nails are nice too.' I touch each one. I'm looking down but he must see my smile, because he touches the dimple at the side of my mouth.

'What are you thinking?' he says.

'The tips are exactly the same length, like you measure them with a caliper.'

Our hair touches as he inspects my hands, running his finger over the short stub of nail on my thumb. The skin at the top is split and red.

'They shouldn't be as bad as they are,' I say. 'I've hardly had time to sleep.'

He trails a knuckle along my bottom lip. 'You must have particularly sharp teeth.'

I hold his wrist, put my thumb on his pulse and count in my head. 'This is too fast.'

'Jemima, I ...' He takes a deep breath. 'Last night, Luke wanted me to know that you'd kissed him. What were the circumstances?'

'To let him know I could. And ... to see if I liked him enough.'

'Did you?'

I look down, shake my head. 'No.'

'I wanted to smash him in the face.'

'Oh!' I search his eyes. 'You would never do something like that.'

'I wouldn't. But it shocked me to think it.'

'Finn?'

He's still frowning. 'Yes.'

'Your allergies aren't a weakness.' When I smooth the hairs on his arm, his muscles tense under my fingers. 'I should have put that in my note.' I count on my fingers. 'It would've been paragraph six.'

'You have an excellent memory.'

'Do you remember how I kissed you at the cottage?'

He lifts my chin, breathes softly on my lips. 'I'll never forget it.'

'I could kiss you again,' I say quietly, snaking my arms around his neck.

He draws back. 'No, Jem.'

There are a thousand reasons not to kiss him, but they all fly out of my head. He'll be gone in February. We're alone. It's almost midnight.

I stroke his hair, tidy it behind his ears like he does mine, even though there's no need. 'You're nothing like Luke.'

'No?' His gaze slips to my mouth. 'Why not?'

I could fall in love with you.

CHAPTER
37

When I press my mouth against his, he stiffens. But when I pull back, he moans.

'I should let you rest,' he says, searching my face as if looking for clues. He touches my mouth with his fingertips. 'So soft.'

I speak through his fingers. 'Are you worried about catching my cold?'

'Not that.' He lifts his other hand too, and cups my face. 'I'll take anything you've got.'

'So I can kiss you? Or …'

He touches the dimple near my mouth with his thumb. 'Why are you smiling?'

'*May* I kiss you?'

His lip lifts. His eyes soften. 'Yes.'

When I touch the tip of his tongue with mine, he takes hold of my waist to pull me close. I push the bedcovers out of the way and splay my hands across his chest. I feel the thickness of his biceps and the tension in his forearms. He groans when I plant kisses down his neck. I nuzzle against his throat, bite his earlobe, slide my hands under his T-shirt. I trail my thumbs along his collarbones. His skin is warm and smooth and firm. I can't see his nipples but I feel them. He bites my bottom lip, taking it into his mouth. He kisses me deeply, liquefies my bones. My heart thunders hard in my chest. He lifts his head and looks into my eyes. He slowly shakes his head.

'You're unwell.' His voice is gruff. 'Enough.'

'I started it.' My voice is even huskier than his. I lay my palm on his cheek, his growth of beard. 'It makes me feel better.'

He smiles. And then we kiss again, more carefully, with softly opening mouths and gently mingling breaths. When he shifts me on his lap, I feel his erection, hard and long, against my thigh. He buries his face against the side of my neck and kisses a path to my throat.

'It doesn't stop, Jem. Wanting you.'

He cups my breasts through my top. He runs his thumbs over my nipples, one and then the other. He dips his head and kisses them through the fabric, teasing with his mouth, his tongue. He kisses his way up my neck again.

I tingle all over—from my lips and breasts to the tops of my thighs. I thread my fingers through his hair and hold on to him tightly. I stroke his jaw. When he turns his face into my hand, his breath is hot on my wrist. I run my hands over his back. I pull at his T-shirt.

'Take it off.'

He looks at me with bright blue eyes and messed-up hair. He lifts his shirt over his head.

He's not wearing his disk. I stroke where the leather cord and circle of metal should be. When I touch his nipples, flat and dark brown, he hisses in a breath. I do it again, circling with my thumbs.

I run my hands up to his shoulders. I hesitate, feel his tension, and look into his eyes.

'I like your body.'

He swallows. He nods. 'That's … good.'

I feather my fingers over his abdomen. The skin is smooth and stretched tightly over the muscles. A strip of dark hair leads from his navel to the top of his trackpants, sitting at his hips. He sees me looking at it and closes his eyes. He makes a noise in his throat and hauls me back onto his lap. I like the feel of his erection under my bottom, the power and promise of it. I stroke his chest as we kiss, then I follow the line of hair. His body is hard, his skin is soft. His breaths are ragged, caresses firm. The night air is cool but he's warm.

He growls, rolls me onto my back and leans over me. I run a finger over the rope burn on his arm. I kiss it. It's brown now, much darker than his skin.

'You should be more careful.' A sting of tears. I blink them back.

'Jem?' He feathers his thumb across my cheek. 'Baby?' He kisses my eyes. 'What's the matter?'

I wrap my arms around his neck. I pull him close. I see the flecks of grey in his eyes and the inky black of his lashes. 'Nothing.'

We kiss again, carefully at first, like we have to start over. But soon all I'm aware of is the touch of his hands on my body and the scent of his skin and the noises we make, whispered words and sighs. Our kisses go on forever. I never want them to end. I feel his need, his desperation, his …

He wipes hair from my face. He closes his eyes. He swears and rolls over, so he's lying on his back. He pulls me onto his chest. His breaths are harsh.

'Finn?'

'You're sick and—'

'I'm better.'

His smile is strained. 'Bullshit.'

'But I am.'

'We have to sort things out.'

I slam my hand over his mouth. 'Not that!'

He holds my wrist and stares into my eyes.

'Last time we kissed, you said you wouldn't go further.' I swallow. 'That was unfair.'

He tugs my hand from his mouth. He runs his hand down my back, lingers on the curves at my waist and bottom. We roll onto our sides again.

He kisses my chin. 'I *might* have gone further. But you fell asleep.'

I shove him in the chest. 'Prove it!'

He slowly shakes his head. 'Fuck, Jem,' he mutters, as he feathers his hand over my breasts, skimming my nipples with the pad of his thumb. His hand glides over my hip, then slides beneath my pyjama pants. My heartbeats quicken and my toes curl up.

He frowns like he's having trouble remembering. 'I touched you here, didn't I?' His hand slips between my thighs and strokes. I grab his arm.

'Yes.' My voice is a squeak.

He mumbles against my neck. He kisses a delicate meandering trail, stroking and teasing, over my breasts. He moves down the bed, lifts my top and rests his head on my stomach. Our eyes meet. He smiles.

'Should I go further?'

My hands are in his hair. I clench them. 'Yes, please.'

His breath is hot and damp on my skin as he eases my pyjama pants and undies over my hips and takes them off. He mutters endearments as his hands skim over my skin.

I'm restless and needy. 'Finn?'

He puts his hands beneath my knees. 'Bend them for me.'

He kisses a path up the insides of my thighs. His lips are warm. He strokes gently with his fingers again, circling and teasing.

'This all right?' he says.

'Mmmm.'

He murmurs and whispers. He kisses and licks to where I want him most. He's careful and tentative, then firm and assured.

'*Please*, Finn. Yes.'

He teases and tempts so my climax builds slowly. But when it happens it's long and it's sweet. Afterwards, he plays and soothes until I'm totally spent. He crawls up my body and sits against the bedhead. He pulls me onto his lap, untangles my hair and kisses me again.

I yawn and nuzzle his neck. There's still a thrum in my body, something else I need.

'Finn?'

'Shhh.' He strokes my hair, threading his fingers through it. He straightens it out, just like he did with my laces. 'You have beautiful hair.'

'Lion hair?'

'Yes.'

I put my hand on the side of his face. 'We haven't finished yet.'

He shakes his head. 'I feel guilty enough already.'

I slump back on his chest, complain against his throat. 'I bet you were never in trouble at school.'

'I wasn't.' He reaches over me to pick up my clothes. 'Lift up.' He pulls on my undies and pyjama pants.

'Thank you.' When he tightens his arms, I put my hand on his heart. 'I wish it was always like this.'

He cups my face and lifts it. Kisses me possessively. 'It could be.'

I'm barely awake when he settles my head on the pillow and murmurs against my forehead.

'You need to sleep.'

He picks up his shirt and pulls it over his head. He rakes a hand through his hair. He bends and kisses me briefly on the mouth.

'Finn.'

'Sleep, Jem. I'll leave our doors open. Call out and I'll come.'

CHAPTER
38

I kick off the sheet because I'm hot. I pull the covers up to my chin because I'm cold. When I look at the ceiling, the bump on my head hurts. When I face the wall, my ear hurts. I lie on my side and see the other bed.

Finn isn't there and that hurts my heart.

Did my mother ever feel like this, loving my father while knowing that one day she'd lose him? Even though, in the end, she never did.

Dad said I should forget the way Mum died, how scared she must have been. He told me she would have been happy, because in her last conscious moment she'd looked into my eyes. We were on the verandah at the cottage when he said it, sweeping up the leaves that had piled up over autumn. A kookaburra laughed from the gum tree, and others joined in.

'What about *your* eyes, Dad,' I said. 'Wouldn't she have wanted to look into your eyes too?'

He gently tugged my ponytail. 'She would've seen my eyes, because I passed them on to you.'

'Is that how it works?'

'Sure it is.' He leant on the broom and looked into my eyes. 'You've got my eyes and your mum's eyes.'

'Mum had blue eyes.'

'They had bright sparks in them, golden sparks, just like you've got.'

When I started to cry, Dad sat me down on the pew. 'You know how much I loved your mum,' he said. 'I couldn't have loved her more. And I miss her.' He put his hand on his heart. 'I miss her like you wouldn't believe. But she lived two good lives. One with her feet on the ground and one flying high on a horse. She died doing what she loved.'

'Like it says on her headstone.'

'You tell me what it says.'

Abigail Laney died at thirty-nine, doing what she loved. She was married to Ross Kincaid and had two beautiful children, Jemima and Liam.

Not long before my father died, he looked into my eyes. I suppose he saw the bright sparks there, the golden sparks.

♖

What did Blackjack see? The tethering ring had pulled out of the wall and he'd fallen onto his side. He was thrashing around and I couldn't get close, but after a while, legs stretched out and head thrown back, he died just like the others. I could hear Rosethorn rolling in his stable. 'I'm coming,' I'd shouted.

When I'd stroked Blackjack's muzzle, so soft and dark, the tips of my fingers were sticky and red. I scrubbed them on my jeans, tried to get them clean. My thumb was cut under the nail and I couldn't stop the bleeding. I put it into my mouth.

'Jemima, it's all right.' Finn's hand envelops mine, pulling it away from my mouth. 'Wake up, baby, you're dreaming.'

It's noisy in the room, it's … I swallow the whimpers, the gulps and the sobs.

He squats on the floor next to my bed. He tidies my hair, spreads it out on the pillow.

I hiccup a few times, and sniff. 'Did I wake you?'

He wipes his fingers across my cheeks, slippery with tears. 'I haven't slept.'

I come up on an elbow and rub my eyes. My thumbnail hurts. 'I'm sorry. You'll be tired.'

A washed-out sunrise peeps through the window. I carefully sit and put both feet on the floor.

'I have to go to the bathroom.'

He fastens a button on my pyjama top and then, even though my balance is back, he walks me to the bathroom, carefully monitoring my footsteps. When we get back to the bedroom, I sit on my bed and he sits on the other one, so we're facing each other. His hair is slightly tousled.

He points to the side table. 'Would you like a glass of water?'

'Yes, please.' I drink slowly and empty the glass. 'I feel much better.'

'Your ear?'

'A bit blocked.' I put my head to the side. 'It doesn't hurt any more.'

'Would you like more water?'

'No, thank you.'

He crosses the space between us and sits next to me. He picks up my hand and threads our fingers together. My skin heats up when I think about last night. I didn't want him to stop.

He's serious, concerned. 'We need to talk, Jem.'

'Is that why you can't sleep?'

'We have things to settle. Especially now.'

I shake my head. 'It's not like we …'

'What?'

'You've had relationships, haven't you? Long-term relationships? Sexual relationships?'

'Yes.'

'How many?'

His hands slide up my arms to my shoulders and he turns me towards him. I keep my eyes down.

'I'm thirty-one, Jem.'

'Ten women? Twenty?'

'I don't … maybe.'

I hear a whinny. Vegemite?

He takes my hands again. He lines them up; he presses his palms against mine. An ache, warm and intense, seeps through my fingers to my heart.

I have to harden it.

Thornbrooke. Commitment. Peanuts. There are so many ways I could lose him.

He pulls our fingers apart, links them together again. 'We have to do better, Jem.'

'No one calls me Jem.'

'It's my name for you.' He lifts our hands and kisses my thumb. 'May I hold you?'

For my sake, or his? Does it matter? I pull back the sheet. I lean against the wall and bend my knees, wrap my arms around them. He lies on his back, taking up most of the bed.

When he holds out his arms I don't hesitate, lying on my side with one of my legs between his, and my head on his chest. My cheek rests in the hollow between his neck and collarbone. He strokes my hair. He takes my hand and holds it tightly.

I squeeze back. 'Are you afraid of what I might do?'

'Always.'

His T-shirt is soft on my skin. He smells nice.

His voice is a rumble. 'Trust me a little.' He whispers a kiss on my head.

'It's difficult.'

'Tomorrow you'll do better. We both will.'

His heartbeats are just like him, strong and certain, calm and steadfast. They thump beneath my cheek.

CHAPTER
39

A watery sun breaks through the clouds, casting soft-edged shadows on the bed. Finn said he hadn't slept. He's sound asleep now. I listen to his heartbeat one more time before I ease myself out of his arms. But I don't have the will to move away yet, so I lie on my side and study his profile. He appears younger than his age when he sleeps.

His eyes flicker. He rolls onto his side, facing me. And then he's fast asleep again. I put my hand on his cheek.

He shifts, wrapping an arm around my body. 'Jemima,' he mumbles.

When his breath is steady and deep, I move even closer. Our legs tangle up. I run my fingers through his hair and smooth it down. His face is warm between my breasts. He's so much bigger and heavier than me but lying like this I can keep him safe, I can make him happy.

I can pretend I'm not frightened. Of trusting him. Loving him. Losing him.

Just five minutes, then I'll go.

Only three minutes have passed, maybe two, when I hear a car door slam. What time is it? I ease my body from the warmth of his. He rolls onto his back. He's restless, he frowns. But then he's still again.

He must have washed my clothes. They're clean and dry, neatly stacked on the desk. I put my weatherproof jacket over my pyjamas and pick up the note I wrote, putting it into my pocket. I gather the other clothes and tiptoe to the door.

One more look. Finn is still asleep. He said we should talk. But first I need to think. I hear footsteps on the steps.

When I open the door, Edward's hand is in midair, ready to knock. It's not surprising his eyes widen. My pyjama pants are shorter than the length of my jacket. Almost all of my legs are on show, from the tops of my thighs to my feet.

'Jet? I didn't expect you to be up and about yet. How are you feeling?'

How did you know I was sick? Why are you here? 'I'm much better, thank you.' I run my fingers through my hair, combing out the knots. The bump on the back of my head is tender. 'I just woke up. What time is it?'

He looks at his watch. 'Five past eight. Finn wasn't expecting me until twelve, but I left Sydney earlier than expected. I stayed in Mudgee last night. I sent him a text.'

'I guess he's still asleep.' *In rumpled sheets with messed-up hair.* 'Dr Gupta set me up in one of the bedrooms and asked Finn to keep an eye on me. He didn't tell me you were coming.'

I look around Edward to my cottage. The verandah is covered in leaf litter that must have blown in with the storm. I'll clean up, put a load of washing on the line if the weather holds, and invite Gus over for tea. If Sapphie visits at lunchtime, I'll help her with her flowers. I have plenty to do, plenty to keep me occupied until Edward goes away. Until I have Finn to myself. *We have to do better.*

I hold the bundle of clothes to my chest. I press against the wall. 'I guess you'd better come in. Finn will wake up soon.'

'I presume he's told you the latest on Thornbrooke?'

'We haven't really talked about it.'

'I might as well fill you in then.'

I take a deep breath as I put the clothes on the floor. 'I'll make you a coffee.'

Edward follows me into the kitchen and sits on a stool at the kitchen bench—a slab of polished granite at least three metres long.

'Finn has ruled out a genetic defect with the stallion and colts,' he says. 'There seems to be nothing that predisposed those particular horses to heart failure.'

When I close my eyes, little sparks flash into the darkness. *Persephone. Poldark. Blackjack. Rosethorn.*

I walk to the other side of the bench, where the appliances are kept. 'That's good for the stud, for the bloodline.'

'He has various other tests to finalise. You're aware the horses were fed vitamin supplements?'

I've cleaned the coffee machine plenty of times, but never actually used it. I push buttons, keeping my back to Edward. When my hands are steady, I fill a cartridge with water and slot it into the side. 'Yes.'

'We have no samples of the supplements, which were, apparently, inadvertently destroyed.'

'Schofield was in charge of the supplements.'

'He provided details of what they contained. Some of the components, while not prohibited substances, could have proved lethal if inappropriately administered.'

I take milk from the almost-empty fridge and pour it into a metal jug, then place it under the frother and push the button.

Edward raises his voice over the noise. 'Can you add to what we know of the supplements?'

I put mugs under the spout. The machine grinds the beans and fills the mugs with coffee.

'No.'

'So we only have Darren Morrissey's version of events.'

I pour in the milk. 'I suppose so.'

'Are you aware that he and Finn met in Perth the week before last? And they've spoken since.'

I bite the inside of my lip as I push Edward's coffee across the bench. 'No.' I find a small cardboard box near the cooktop and recognise my name. I hand the box to Edward. 'Are these antibiotics? This says I take one capsule morning and night, doesn't it?'

He nods.

I'm not in pain, but my movements are stiff and awkward. Am I a puppet on a stage, putting on a show?

Edward sips his coffee. 'As the stud manager, Morrissey bore ultimate responsibility for the loss of the horses. Yet he's rarely, even after Dr Schofield's death, attempted to defend his own actions. I've always wondered about that. Rumours have circulated for years.'

I put the antibiotics in my pocket, secure the flap. 'It was thought to be something in the feed; he accepted that.'

Edward places his mug on the bench. 'Morrissey has informed Finn that he kept quiet in order to protect your reputation. He said the horses died because you, inadvertently, gave them an overdose of the vitamin supplement.'

My coffee slops over the side of the mug. 'What?'

'Morrissey said this need go no further than Finn and me. He suggested that, in order to protect you, we should abandon the inquiry into Thornbrooke.'

I sit on the edge of the stool and consider the bruise on my shin, the mark Caruthers branded me with.

'Will you do that?'

'It's too late.' Edward clears his throat. 'Did you overdose the horses?'

'No!'

'What was Mike's involvement?'

'He had nothing to do with any of it.'

'You appreciate Finn's tests might detect an overdose, if that is what occurred?'

I hold my mug tightly to keep my hands steady. 'Finn can do whatever tests he likes.' Even if I could lift the mug to my mouth, I'm not sure I could swallow. I push the stool back from the bench. 'Why didn't Morrissey raise this earlier?'

'He said he wanted to leave the past in the past, as you did.'

I move the coffee closer, push it away. 'I have nothing to say.'

'According to your mutual friend, you've been afraid that the truth would come out. That's why you refused to talk to Finn.'

I'm suddenly hot. Then cold. 'What friend?'

'Morrissey told Finn that someone visited you at the cottage.'

The hammer, the wrench and the knife. 'I don't ...' My voice trails off. I have no words.

'You informed this person that you would never speak about what happened, and neither would Mike. Morrissey told Finn it was one of the reasons he agreed to talk—he was certain you wouldn't own up.'

I have to get away. *I have to think.* I spin around.

A door shuts. I hear footsteps on the floorboards. Finn appears in the doorway, still wearing the dark grey T-shirt and trackpants he slept in. His hair is damp at the front, like he's splashed water on his face before pushing back his fringe. He frowns at Edward. In five long strides he's standing in front of me.

I take a jerky step back but not quickly enough. He puts his hands on the tops of my arms.

'Jem? Why didn't you wake me? What the hell is going on?'

When I say nothing, he turns to Edward. 'How long have you been here?'

'Half an hour. I've told Jet about your meeting with Morrissey.' He raises his brows. 'I'm surprised you hadn't apprised her of it.'

'I said I'd handle this.'

I twist away. 'It's been handled. I know what you think, both of you.'

Finn scans my face. 'How do you feel?'

'I'm fine.'

'You don't look it. Have you had anything to eat?'

The last thing I ate was a pea from your plate. The ache in my chest intensifies. 'I'll have breakfast at home.'

I want to leave, but I'm not sure I could get to the door. Finn. Edward. Morrissey. Caruthers. Even if I run, one of them will find me. I sit on the stool again, reach for my mug. The coffee is cold, untouched.

Finn puts a bowl, milk, cutlery and two boxes of cereal in front of me. Neither of them is muesli. *No nuts.*

'Eat something,' he says.

'No, thank you.'

His mouth firms. 'Toast?'

'No, thank you.'

He makes himself a coffee and sits next to me. 'You said you know what I think,' he says. 'In what respect?'

When I press my lips together, Edward answers for me. 'In respect to Morrissey's claim that the horses died of an overdose.'

I turn to Finn. 'Last night you said you wanted to talk. Now I know why. You saw Morrissey when you went to Perth.'

'Yes.'

'You didn't think to tell me that?'

'I wanted to discuss it in person.'

'You saw me two days after, at Follyfoot. And yesterday.'

He smiles stiffly. 'Neither time was appropriate.'

When he leans closer, the top of his arm almost touches my shoulder. His arms are muscular, strong. I know the feel of them under my hands.

'You should have told me.'

'You know now,' he says. 'Could you have made a mistake?'

'If I couldn't read the chart that day, I would have asked for help.'

He sips his coffee. 'I'm still running tests. Nothing has been determined.'

'You don't believe me.'

'I didn't say that.'

'If I was tested on what I could read and what I couldn't, I'd fail.'

He looks over my head, making eye contact with Edward. What are they communicating? Do they need a demonstration?

I reach into my pocket, taking out the note I wrote last night, and walk to the other side of the bench. I hold the note at arm's length. And then I hold it up close. It doesn't surprise me that the words, *my* words, bounce around in an incomprehensible jumble.

'I wrote this about ten hours ago,' I say, putting the page in front of Edward. 'I can remember what I wanted to say, but the words

I actually wrote make no sense to me now. They might not make sense to you either, given the spelling will be wrong and the word order mixed up.'

Finn stands abruptly, scraping back his chair. He holds out his hand. 'That's mine. Give it to me.'

'I wrote it.'

'Don't do this.'

'Why not?'

He glares across the bench. 'Why do you think?'

Edward looks from Finn to me. 'What on earth is going on?'

'You and Finn share information,' I say. 'You might as well see this too.'

Edward reaches into his pocket and takes out his glasses. 'Do I read it or not? Finn?'

He nods stiffly. 'If that's what Jemima wants.'

I'd call the picture on the back of the note a fire truck. Finn called it a fire engine. *We have nothing in common.*

'How many spelling mistakes?' I ask.

'You, paddock, Africa ...' Edward says, frowning in concentration. 'Lament? Other words I could probably make out, but only with difficulty.'

'See?'

'Edward.' Finn speaks between his teeth. 'I wish to speak with Jemima alone.'

Edward picks up his coffee. 'Very well, I'll wait in the lounge room.' He turns at the door, raises his brows. 'I'm not a fool, Finn. Did you sleep with Jet last night?'

'Yes.'

'No!'

After Edward closes the door behind him, Finn walks around the bench. He picks up the note.

'This belonged to me.'

'I wrote it.'

'You could have made your point another way. Why give it to Edward?'

'Why not? Like I said, the two of you share things.'

He rips the note in half, and then rips it again. 'And you share nothing.' He crushes the pieces of paper in his fist. His eyes are darkest blue. And then they're almost black.

I hold on to the bench, my fingertips white. 'Can I go?'

'No!'

'Then say what you want to say.'

His back is ramrod straight. He unclenches his jaw. 'Morrissey blames Schofield for the constitution of the supplements and the autopsy fiasco. He blames you for measuring the dosage incorrectly. You say that's wrong.'

'It is.'

He stalks across the room. He looks out of the window, towards the river. 'Mike arrived after the deaths. Within an hour, he'd taken you from Thornbrooke. I asked you months ago, I made a point of it. Were you and Mike aware that Schofield and Morrissey were concealing something?'

My heart is stuck tight in my throat. 'We didn't know what was in the supplements.'

'If you and Morrissey conspired, are conspiring now, to hide what happened, *that's* the problem. Do you understand that?'

'Yes.'

'Did you collude? Have you seen Morrissey since?'

'No.'

'Have you had any communication with him?'

'No.'

He speaks between his teeth. 'I don't believe you.'

'Think what you like.'

'You don't trust me? Even after last night?'

'Last night was …' I let go of the bench. 'Things are different in daylight.' I straighten my shoulders. 'Why didn't you tell me about Morrissey? You assumed it was true, didn't you? That it was my fault?'

'I didn't know what to think. I still don't.'

'In which case, you don't know me.'

'What the hell is that supposed to mean?'

'I could never make a mistake like that and not own up. I could never be that dishonest.'

'Then talk to me now! Tell me what you know.'

After Mum fell from Abacus, when she was on the ground and I stared into her eyes, I couldn't hear a thing. But then her eyes closed, and all the sounds came back. Two paramedics talked to each other. A third was on the phone and talked into that. The people surrounding us talked. One of the officials told them to stand back. Someone, a woman, was talking to Abacus. She sobbed as she led him away.

After we went home, Dad, the counsellors and the social workers talked. Gus, the Hargreaves and Mrs McNab. Everybody talked and talked and talked until all I could hear, all over again, was silence.

I look over Finn's shoulder. It's shady near the river but the grasses in the paddocks, wet from last night's rain, shimmer in the sunlight.

'When the horses died, I had no idea what had happened, or what I should do about it. At first Morrissey and Schofield controlled things. Now Edward controls it, and you. I'm the one who watched the horses die. I'm the one with bitten nails.' My voice breaks. 'But I've never had control over Thornbrooke.'

I look straight ahead and carefully put one foot in front of the other as I walk to the door.

'Jemima?'

I freeze, my hand on the doorknob. 'Yes?'

'All I ask is that you trust me.'

I face him, the door at my back. 'When we first met, I didn't want to talk about Thornbrooke. Mostly it was because the horses were gone, finding out why was never going to change that. And … and because of the memories.'

He frowns. 'Yes.'

'Now there are other reasons too. You talk about trust. Why can't you trust me when I say that some things are out of my hands, some things I can't tell you about?'

He walks to the bench and picks up my mug, then slams it on the granite. Coffee flows over the top, circling the mug like a muddy brown moat.

'If you walk out now, it's over,' he says. 'You're on your own.'

The carpet in the hallway has parallel lines. I walk along one of them until I reach the bedroom with the twin beds and the galloping horses quilts. The bottom sheet is creased and the top sheet lies crumpled on the floor. I swallow a sob and swipe a hand across my eyes.

'I'm better alone,' I whisper.

CHAPTER

40

The sun is still shining when I turn off the highway and drive into Warrandale late on Thursday afternoon. It's well after five, so the businesses in the pretty main street, except for the pub, are closed.

We arranged to meet in the courtyard, shaded for most of the year by a giant peppercorn tree like the one at Kincaid House. Mike is sitting at a square timber table, nursing a beer, but jumps to his feet when he sees me. He pulls out a chair.

'Sit down, Jet. I've bought you a glass of lemonade. Do you want something to eat? How are you feeling?' He looks at me closely. 'You sure you should be driving?'

'I'm fine, Mike. I'll be back at work tomorrow.' I sip through the straw. 'I don't need anything to eat, but thanks for the drink.'

'I thought you were taking more time off.'

'Four days was enough. Thanks for helping out with my clients.'

'Jackson's wife Ariella is due any minute, so he was on leave. He did the heavy work, while I looked after his phone and handed him tools, all he'd let me do. We only took on the urgent cases, and the owners we reckoned were arseholes.'

'I don't have many of those.'

'More than your share fair, we reckon.' He winks. 'We turned up late and charged extra, so they'd know to appreciate you next time.'

'I'll call Jackson and thank him.'

Mike rotates his ankle. 'He was happy to help.'

'How are you feeling? Is your hip worrying you?'

'I'm good.' He wipes froth from his mouth with the back of his hand. 'You're the one who's been crook. I hear Dr Blackwood helped you out. How's it going with him?'

'It was good of him to have me at the homestead.'

'But you didn't drive here to tell me that, did you?'

I stir the ice in my glass, creating a whirlpool. 'Morrissey told Finn that I overdosed the horses.'

'What?' He bangs his hand on the table. 'Mongrel.'

'I think Finn might believe him, but he's finishing his tests on the blood anyway. There's still a chance nothing will come out of this. Maybe he won't find out whatever it is that Morrissey is hiding. Everything will be just like it was.'

'You didn't overdose the horses, Jet. You have to tell him that.'

'I did, but I can't prove anything.'

'That's not the point.'

'I told Finn I've had nothing to do with Morrissey since it happened.'

'That's the truth.'

'A stretch of the truth.' I take another sip. 'Last time I saw you, I told you I'd seen Jason Caruthers, that Morrissey had sent him to warn us off.'

'That's right.'

'I saw him again. He said if we didn't keep quiet about Thornbrooke, we'd regret it.'

'What?' Mike scratches his head. 'Beat us up or something?'

'He … That was part of it.' I stretch out my leg under the table. The cut on my shin has healed and the bruise is fading fast.

'Who's he to make threats? If he's talking about overdoses, it's time we started talking about stitched-up autopsy reports.'

'Not yet.' I lower my voice when the barman wipes the table next to ours. 'If we've done something against the law, if the police are brought in, of course we'll have to tell them what happened. But why pre-empt that? The police might not be interested, they might not believe us, and then we'd have to deal with Morrissey.'

'It's breaking the law that keeps me up at night,' Mike says. 'Not some bully boy.'

'Take care, anyway. Like I told you when I called last week, if you see Caruthers at the door, don't open it. Avoid him until this is over.'

'I don't even know who he is.'

'He's not that tall, but he's strong, like he goes to the gym and lifts weights. He fancies himself. He has a tattoo on his arm.'

'Oi!'

'What?'

'What's he been up to? You're scared of the bloke.'

'I'm wary of him. You should be too, at least until Finn's done his report and we know where we stand.'

'You still getting nightmares?'

I put my hands under the table. 'You know I am.'

'It's not what your dad would have wanted, Jet, you getting all this stress. You should be happy and settled by now, having babies.'

I smile. 'That's very old-fashioned, Mike. I have a career. Anyway, you've never settled down with anyone.'

'I had my chances, but it wasn't for me.' His craggy face creases in a frown. 'I'm not sure I can say the same for you. Your mum and dad,' he crosses his fingers and holds them up, 'they were so close it warmed the heart to see it. Never a doubt they would have stuck together if things hadn't turned out as they did.'

'They loved each other a lot.'

'But they took their chances, they must've done, 'specially with your dad's illness and all.'

'I'm not much of a risk-taker, Mike. And you know better than anyone how messed up I was—after Dad died, after Thornbrooke. I had to pick up my pieces and put them back together.'

'And that's what you did.' Mike drums his fingers on the table. 'But say a couple of pieces got left behind? There's no shame going back to pick them up. Remember the psychologist lady I told you about? The one who helps the emergency services blokes? Have you thought some more about talking to her?'

I sip through the straw. 'I don't think I need that.'

'No?' He points to the tape on my fingers. 'Well, I reckon you do. You take my advice. I take yours. That's the way it works.'

I line up our glasses on the table. 'I'd better get going. Thanks for the drink.'

Mike tightens his belt as we walk through the courtyard. A few years ago, he'd shoe ten horses a day, often more. Now he looks … frail.

I loop my arm through his. 'Are you looking forward to Mr Chambers's Christmas party?'

'Saturday fortnight, right?' He grins. 'Something else to strike off my bucket list. Got your costume sorted?'

'I might need your help with my hairpiece.'

'No problem.'

'You can give me the psychologist's details when I pick you up. But you have to give me your word to be careful in the meantime, to lock your doors day and night.'

He squeezes my arm. 'You got yourself a deal.'

CHAPTER
41

The following Thursday, Andrew greets me at the entrance to the zoo. The gates to the public are closed because it's only eight o'clock, but the sun is high in the sky and warm on my back. Afaafa is my first client of the day, so I don't have to change my clothes.

I lift my collar and put on my hat. 'Hey, Andrew.'

'Thanks for coming, Jet. I know you'll be busy in the lead-up to Christmas. Fancy a walk to the giraffe enclosure?'

This is my favourite time to be at the zoo, with the animals wide awake, keen for a meal, and the keepers and maintenance staff rushing around. We walk alongside the Savannah Lake, an oval-shaped stretch of water with an island in the middle.

'Afaafa's improving,' Andrew says.

'The keepers are doing a great job, getting her more accustomed to the yard.'

'Have you met Catriona, our new vet?'

'Briefly, at the café. She wants to specialise in giraffes, right?'

'Of course, Finn introduced you. She's interested in what you're doing with Afaafa, so hopefully she'll join us. As a matter of fact …' He points to the rhino enclosure on the other side of the moat. 'I *think* that's her with Finn.'

A four-wheel drive is parked under the trees, facing a tract of land that's closed to the public. Through the trees I see two adult female rhinos and a calf.

'Finn has concerns about the calf,' Andrew says. 'He's not gaining as much weight as we'd like. You know we lost a young rhino a few years ago? It devastated the whole zoo community.'

'Are they just sitting there, watching him?'

'Diagnosis by observation.' He raises his brows. 'Patience is important in the work we do, and it's a quality Catriona already has. She's keen to learn, but lacks experience in the field, particularly with the larger animals. I've been letting her tag along with Finn. She missed him yesterday. He's been unwell.'

'What happened?' My voice is sharp.

Andrew raises his brows. 'He has a cold.'

'Right.'

I warned him I'd make him sick before I kissed him. He said, *I'll take anything you've got.* I swallow down the sadness.

'He's better than he was,' Andrew says, as we slow our pace to watch two young spider monkeys scamper up a tree on the island, before leaping to another one.

'That's good.'

'You assumed his illness was related to his allergies, didn't you?'

I shrug. 'Yes.'

'He hardly ever mentions them. Yet you knew about them months ago, when, so far as I was aware, you hardly knew him.'

The lemurs have long and furry black-and-white striped tails that stick up in the air, or twist around the branches.

'We get training for emergencies at Follyfoot. Maybe that's how it came up.'

'The first and only anaphylactic attack I've witnessed was Finn's.'

'What!'

He looks over his shoulder, back at the rhinos. 'I told you that Finn and I worked together in South Africa? I can't remember what we were celebrating, but we had a party. The camp was hundreds of kilometres inland, but someone arranged for a seafood delivery. The chef was Norwegian, and cooked a traditional meal, crayfish served with mayonnaise and lemon wedges.'

I whisper. 'Oh, no.'

'Finn had always stood out. He was prodigiously clever and capable; we thought he was as strong as his rhinos. It was an instantaneous reaction, and frightened the life out of all of us. He gave himself adrenaline.'

'Was it enough?'

'Ultimately, but it was touch-and-go, and we were in the middle of nowhere. Later we talked about who'd have done a tracheostomy.' He grimaces. 'There were a number of vets and scientists there, but none of us was keen.'

♘

Rivulets of sweat trickle down my back as I throw my file in the box and straighten. So why do I shiver when our eyes finally meet? Finn's shirt is dark blue. His sleeves are rolled up, exposing his arms, more tanned each time I see him. When I lower my head, my hat shadows my face and the V above the button of my shirt.

'Jet,' he says stiffly.

'You're doing well,' Catriona says, smiling appreciatively. She's not overly made up, but her lips shine pink. 'I'd like to sit down and talk about this some time. I know a lot about hoof construction, but treating injuries, remedying problems like Afaafa's, is a whole new ball game.'

'Sure … if you think it would help. Though I only really know the practical side—how to relieve pressure on the foot, balance the gait, things like that. The theory I'm not so good at.'

Andrew laughs. 'Your diagnostic capabilities are second to none, Jet. There's plenty of theory in that.' He glances at Afaafa's hooves. 'She looks better each time I see her.'

When I started working here, I thought all the female giraffes looked pretty much the same. Now I can tell them apart. Afaafa has a particularly delicate head, and her eyelashes, long and thick, match the darker colours in her markings, russet to deep golden brown. She's taller than the other females, and she's snarky. Some days she cooperates; others she won't let me touch her. But once she's made up her mind to play nice, she's easy to work on. She put a foot on the block immediately today, reaching expectantly for her carrot while I crouched and trimmed her hoof.

'Trudy's doing an amazing job.'

The giraffe keeper grins. 'You're not bad yourself. Quiet, confident, a light touch and quick. Afaafa appreciates those qualities.'

I smile. 'Thanks.'

Finn is deadly serious. But then again, he's not too well. He's been holding in coughs for the fifteen minutes he's been here, and keeps walking away to blow his nose.

When the keepers supervise Afaafa's trek back to her herd, the rest of us watch her progress. Her gait is much better than it was.

Our group is walking past the rhino enclosure when one of the keepers pulls Andrew aside. When he asks me to wait for him, I stand in the shade of a gum. The trunk is broad and shedding strips of bark. A female rhino grazes in the distance. The male is separated from her and stands in the shade. When he moves his feet, the dust stirs around him. The wind picks up, hot and dry. I hold my breath when Finn and Catriona stroll towards me. They stop for a moment. She puts her hand on his arm and laughs as he bends down to say something. Then she walks to Andrew and the keeper.

Finn throws a backpack onto the ground. 'Jemima.' He has a blocked nose. His hands are in his pockets, his shoulders are stiff. We both watch silently as he flattens a bump in the dirt with his boot. He glances at me before looking away.

'Does he know you?' I blurt out.

'Who?'

'The male rhino. The bull.'

He frowns. 'He'd know my scent.'

'Do you mind the way the animals get used to people?'

'What do you mean?'

'The way they're trained with cooperative reinforcement.'

'It avoids anaesthesia and restraint.' He glances at me again. 'It's possible for us to work safely around them.'

'But what you said in your speech ... the rhinos in Africa are free, they're wild. It's different here. The keepers have regular contact with the rhino calves, so that they'll remember them when they're adults.'

'I ... why are we discussing this?'

'You were the one who came over here, and then you didn't say anything, so I had to talk.'

'You accuse me of not communicating?'

When his gaze goes to my hands, I imagine what he's thinking. *She keeps her feelings to herself. She has trust and commitment issues. She gave me a cold. She bites her nails.*

'Is that why you walked over here?' I ask. 'To insult me?'

'How did I ...' He releases a breath. 'I have most of the results I require to finalise my report.'

My heart hammers. 'Edward will be happy.'

'But I won't be in a position to release the findings, even to Edward, until the New Year.' He looks intently at the rhino. 'What I'm about to say is confidential.'

'Right.'

'Do you recall Nate Gillespie? He works for the UN.'

'You were with him at the clinic when Mike and I were there. You climb with him.'

Finn massages his forehead, shields his eyes from the sun. 'He has an interest in something I've come up with. I have to consult with him again before anything becomes public. We're meeting towards the end of January; it's the earliest he can do.'

That's six weeks away. Will Caruthers come back to Horseshoe and ask what the delay is all about? My throat hasn't been sore for over a week. So why does it hurt to swallow now?

'Right.'

He rubs his forehead again.

'Do you have a headache?'

'Yes.'

'Are you going to Scotland for Christmas?'

'Yes.'

The male rhino is standing in silhouette, his horns clearly outlined. He's not physically attractive; he's beautiful because he's powerful. Finn is powerful *and* physically attractive.

He moves further away, as if to make sure there's no chance we'll touch, and picks up his backpack. The wind whips my hair across my face. I push it back and put my hat on again, pulling the brim down low. Looking at Finn, thinking what might have been, it hurts as much as it ever did.

There are gums in the rhino enclosure, but much larger trees on the other side of the fence. What is it like on a savannah in Kenya?

Or Tanzania? Finn said the colours are similar to here, the browns and greens, wide-open spaces and bright blue skies.

'Jemima?' When he steps in front of me, his gaze slips to my mouth. Desire, swift and unexpected, warms my body, takes my breath. He drops his backpack at his feet again.

'What do you want?' My words come out in a rush. I glance at my watch. 'I have to get back.'

'I want you to answer a question. Honestly.'

I cross my arms. 'I might not have helped you. But I wasn't dishonest.'

His eyes are cold. 'There's a fine line.'

You untied my laces. You held me. 'Yes.'

'You had opportunities to tell the truth.'

To mumble words into your mouth when I kissed you. 'Yes.'

'A week ago,' he says, 'you did tell the truth. You never had control over Thornbrooke, at the time or afterwards.'

I jerk my head to the side. Clouds collect on the horizon. 'Yes. I mean, no.'

'Can you tell the truth about something else?'

Our eyes meet again. 'Maybe.'

'What happened at the homestead …' His eyes are on my mouth again. 'It could have gone much further.' His voice is low and rough. 'Did you have an ulterior motive?'

'I don't understand.'

'In respect to Thornbrooke, to revealing what happened, I'm a threat. Were you keeping your enemy close?'

Finn would never hurt me physically. But it feels like I've been punched. Air rushes from my lungs. I push words through the tightness in my throat.

'Are you accusing me of using you?'

'Were you?'

When he kicks a stone, it skitters across the ground towards Andrew and the others. One of the men looks up.

'You think I'd use sex as a bargaining chip?'

'I deal with facts. You avoid me, you push back, you lie.' He narrows his eyes. 'Yet you sleep with me. It can't be ruled out.'

'I guess not.'

'I should have had sex with you months ago—to get you out of my system.'

Catriona shouts out. 'Finn! Are you coming? We're heading back now.'

I take a few shaky steps backwards. 'Go.'

He spears his fingers through his hair. He picks up his bag again. 'The Chambers's Christmas function,' he says. 'I saw Mike's name on the list. Will you be there with him?'

'Yes.'

'It's likely I'll see you then.'

I walk away before he has the chance to. *Not if I see you first.*

CHAPTER
42

The Christmas party at the Chambers's home, a large property a few kilometres south of Warrandale, is held in mid-December every year. Mr Chambers is on the board of the zoo, so a lot of the senior staff are invited, along with major sponsors like Edward, and well-off stud owners and farmers. For the past few years, Mike has been invited too, and I've come along as his plus one. Except for last year, when he wasn't well enough to make it.

He's pacing the porch when I pull up in front of his house. 'We'll be late,' he says, as I jump out of the ute and open the passenger door. When I reach for his arm he brushes me aside, takes the handle and lifts himself onto the passenger seat, twisting carefully as he sits.

'We have the same argument every year,' I say, climbing back into the car and fastening my seatbelt. 'Arriving a few minutes after the start time doesn't make us late.'

He grunts. 'In my day, it was good manners to greet the host on the dot.'

I smile at his outfit—long brown shorts with sandals, and a cream shirt with string laced through eyelets at the front. His white hair is brushed off his forehead and sticking up in spikes.

'You make a very good Barney Rubble.'

He winks. 'You're a fine Pebbles Flintstone.'

There's a prehistoric theme for this year's party. I'm wearing a short white denim skirt that's frayed at the hem and sits low on my hips. My bright orange singlet top is cut off in zigzags at the waist, and my hair is in such a high ponytail that the ends only just brush my shoulders.

Mike rifles in his bag, pulling out a short length of metal worked into the shape of a bone.

'As requested.'

I hold the bone in my hand. 'I didn't expect you to go to this much trouble. It's stainless steel, isn't it? That's so difficult to work with.'

'Iron would've been too heavy. You'd have got a headache.'

I pull an orange ribbon from my pocket and tie the bone to my hairband. Then I check the mirror on the back of the visor. I always use sunblock, but I've worked outside a lot this week and my face is lightly tanned. I'm wearing blusher and dark-pink lip-gloss. I'm not sleeping as well as I could, but the outfit is comfortable, and I look okay.

'If you keep preening like that,' Mike complains, 'the party will be over before we leave Warrandale.'

This is one of the few parties Mike is invited to that isn't a community event. Meaning he doesn't feel compelled to erect the tents, stand behind the BBQ and tidy up afterwards. Even though he always leaves early, afraid of outstaying his welcome, he looks forward to it, which is why it was on his bucket list. He missed it last year. He might miss it next year as well.

I give him a shaky smile. 'Are you looking forward to the buffet?'

'What are you getting all soppy-eyed about?'

'Nothing.'

He harrumphs. 'Any news on Thornbrooke, then?'

I grasp the steering wheel tightly as I turn onto the highway. 'We won't know anything else until late January. If anyone brings it up, please don't mention Morrissey.'

'Mongrel. Why should we protect him?'

'As far as I know, he only told Edward and Finn that it was my fault. I can live with that. You haven't heard from him, have you? Or Caruthers?'

'Nope.'

'Finn will write about what he finds. Try not to worry about what might and might not happen.'

Mike grumbles some more but by the time we turn off the road and drive over the cattle grate to the Chambers's tree-lined driveway, hundreds of metres long, he's brightened up again. An attendant directs us through a gate to a paddock close to the homestead. We're only ten minutes late, but Edward's car is parked here already, and so is Finn's. I focus on putting on my sandals, and tying the long leather laces that crisscross my legs. I tie the bows loosely at my knees so I'll be able to undo them easily. When my skirt rides up to the top of my thighs, I pull it down a little lower.

Mike squints at my feet. 'Is that nail varnish, Pebbles?'

I smile as I link my arm through his. 'Yes, Barney. I wanted to look my best for you.'

The spacious kitchen and informal dining areas, which lead onto the wide verandah that surrounds the homestead, are modern additions. Edward intercepts me and kisses both cheeks when I walk to the buffet table.

'Good evening, Jet. You look charming.'

'Thank you.' He's wearing a cream suit and a colourful woollen scarf. 'Who are you?'

'Someone who can travel back in time.' He holds out his arms. 'Doctor Who.'

'Of course.' I straighten my top. 'I'm Pebbles Flintstone.'

He raises his brows. 'So I gathered.'

I pick up a plate. 'I came with Mike, he's Barney Rubble.'

'I presume you'll spend Christmas with the Hargreaves?'

'They're always very welcoming.'

'Nevertheless, you have a standing invitation to come to Sydney, should you ever wish to avail yourself of it.'

'Thank you. You're always welcome at the Hargreaves, too.'

He raises his eyebrows. 'I understand you've spoken with Finn regarding his report? The delay is unfortunate.'

There's a lot of seafood—baked salmon, oysters and prawns—in addition to traditional Christmas food. Finn is sitting next to Catriona, at a table of ten. She's wearing a tight green jumpsuit with a feathered cape, but I'm not sure what she's supposed to be. A very attractive Pterodactyl? Finn is the only person eating a sandwich, and the only one not dressed up. He's wearing a creased linen shirt, starkly white against his hair and skin. He catches me staring and watches as I scoop salad leaves and turkey breast onto my plate. When I leave the buffet, I walk to a table on the other side of the room.

How could he imagine I could pretend an attraction that I didn't feel?

After dinner I find Lorenzo, the dietician from the zoo, and his wife Luisa and their baby Marco, sitting on a chaise longue on the verandah. Marco is eight weeks old now, with fluffy dark hair and chubby little thighs. He refuses to sleep after Luisa, tired and tearful, has fed and changed him, so I offer to walk him around while she and Lorenzo have something to eat. The baby wriggles and cries at first, bringing his knees up to his chest, but after a few minutes he settles, and I walk him to the old part of the homestead—a gun-barrel hall with intricate plaster arches, and a grand lounge and dining room—where it's cool and quiet. He grizzles again for a while, then hiccups twice and promptly falls asleep, his warm little body tucked against my shoulder. I yawn as I walk into the library. All I can hear of the party through the thick brick walls is a gentle hum and an occasional shout of laughter.

There's no artificial light in the room, only distant garden lights and moonlight, so it takes a while to adjust my eyes to the shadows. I'm careful where I place my feet as I walk to a bookcase and bend at the knees to select one of the large glossy books. I squint at the words on the front. Toulouse? Truffles? I think it's a French cookbook.

When I lean back in a big leather armchair, Marco stirs. He opens his eyes, dark brown like his parents', and blinks. But then his eyes flutter closed again. My mother had blue eyes. Dad's eyes were brown, and so are mine. Is that how it usually works? Finn would know about recessive genes, about which colours trump which. I push away my unsettling thoughts and rest my chin on the top of Marco's head. I listen to his rapid little breaths.

My eyes spring open when I hear footsteps in the hall. I can't see who it is because the back of my chair faces the door, but someone walks into the room and switches on a lamp.

'Maggie has set you up, I understand, with the internet password and so on.' It's Mr Chambers. 'Take a seat at the desk, make yourself at home.'

'I apologise for troubling you,' Finn says. 'I'd arranged a call with my parents, but don't have reception out here.'

My heart skips two beats out of three.

'It's no trouble at all,' Mr Chambers says.

The door clicks shut.

Marco is still sleeping soundly. I wriggle carefully to the edge of the chair and stand slowly. By the time he sees me, Finn is sitting behind the desk with an iPad propped up in front of him, the bay window at his back. It's like he's moving in slow motion when he gets to his feet. He stares, looking me up and down. I wasn't self-conscious before, but now … my skirt is very short and so is my top, so there's a lot of skin showing. And I have a stainless-steel bone in my hair, held tight by a bright orange ribbon. I hold Marco even closer.

'Jemima?'

'It was quiet in here.' I look down at Marco, his face soft in sleep. 'I'd better get him back to his mum.'

There's a tap on the door. 'Jet? Is that you?'

'Come in.'

The moment Luisa puts her head around the door, a call comes through on Finn's iPad. He looks from Luisa to me. And then back at the iPad.

'I'm sorry, I have to take this.' He touches the screen. 'Hello.'

'Finn? Is that you?'

It's Annie, Finn's mother. I recognise her voice from when Finn was in the hospital.

'Yes, Mam, it's me.'

'I can't see you.'

Finn blows out a breath as he sits. He touches the screen again.

'There you are!' Annie says. 'You're getting quite a tan, aren't you? Are you over your head cold? Can you see me?'

I imagine Annie waving.

'I can see you, Mam. Can you hold on a minute? I have to go to another room.'

'No,' I hiss. 'We're leaving.'

Luisa tiptoes into the room, gesturing to Finn to keep talking. She smiles gently at Marco.

'Are you ready to come back to Mummy?' she whispers.

'Finn?' Annie says. 'What's happening there?'

'It's fine, Mam. How did the surgery go?'

'The doctor said it was a *teensy* little lump, but he has to do more tests. He's sure it's not "C", but wants to be on the safe side. You know Dr Tan, don't you? He's a very clever doctor but a terrible fusspot. Your father and I are sure the lump is nothing. That's right, isn't it, Findlay?'

'We took comfort from the doctor's reassurances,' Findlay says. 'But it's been a worrying day all the same, son. A worrying week, in fact.'

'I'm sure it has, Dad. I'm sorry I couldn't be there.'

'It hardly hurts at all,' Annie says. 'It was keyhole surgery, you see. Just a few stitches.'

When I pass Marco to Luisa, he wriggles and squirms. She bends her knees as she bounces up and down, trying to settle him.

'Have you managed to get an earlier flight?' Findlay asks. 'We don't want to put you out, mind.'

'I leave tomorrow morning,' Finn says.

'That's great news, son. Another set of ears will be useful on Monday, when your Mam goes back to the doctor.'

'I'll be there in time for tea on Sunday,' Finn says.

'Tea be damned,' Findlay says. 'It'll be grand to share a pint, and with any luck a dram.'

Marco lets out a muffled cry and then falls back to sleep. Luisa whispers loudly as she tiptoes to the door.

'Jet, you're an angel. Thank you.'

I'm walking towards the bookcase to return the book when I hear Annie again.

'Jet?' she says. 'Jet Kincaid? Is she there with you, Finn?'

When I turn around, Finn is rubbing the back of his neck. 'Mam. I don't think—'

'She is there, isn't she? *Please* put her on. I've so much wanted to thank her for all that she did.'

Finn turns to me, mouth tight. 'Would you mind?'

'Of course not.'

Finn pulls up another swivel chair and sits next to me with the iPad between us on the desk, angled towards me. His mother is pretty, with large round eyes and wavy brown hair. Her face is plump; her skin is pale and smooth.

'Jet,' she says, 'how nice to see you at last. Look at her, Findlay, isn't she lovely?'

I touch the bone and ribbon. 'I don't usually wear my hair like this.'

'You look beautiful, dear, and so … *Australian* looking. I thought you might be a sturdy lass, being a blacksmith, but you're only a slip of a girl. How did you hold Finn up when he collapsed? He weighs a ton,' she smiles affectionately, 'just like his father.'

'I'm stronger than I look.'

'I can't tell you what a comfort it was to Findlay and me, being so far away, knowing you were with Finn at the hospital. He was a wee little bairn the last time he had a reaction like that, and the doctor said if we hadn't lived so close to the hospital, we would have lost him. Breathing through a tube down his throat …' She shudders. 'I've never got over it, have I, Findlay?'

Annie must have moved the iPad because Finn's father appears. I blink. This is what Finn will look like in thirty years' time. A few frown lines, grey hair at the temples. Findlay smiles at his wife.

'No, Annie, you've never got over it.'

'And you looked after him, Jet,' Annie says, 'when he was daft enough to discharge himself from the hospital. I don't know how we would have got through the night if we hadn't known you were there. Thank you, dear, from the bottom of each of our hearts.'

Findlay clears his throat. 'For once in her life, Annie's not exaggerating.' He smiles at Annie and she beams back. 'We're both very grateful to you, lass.'

'It wasn't any trouble.'

'A whole night without sleep?' Annie says. 'You must have been exhausted.'

Finn is watching me instead of the screen. What is he thinking? That we should have had sex that night, all those months ago, so he could have got me *out of his system* more quickly?

'We didn't know about the crayfish,' Annie says, 'until the hospital told us it was on the list.' She frowns. 'Finn? Where are you? I'm still not happy about that, am I?'

I move the iPad so it's facing both of us. 'No, Mam,' he says.

'Especially after what happened in Mozambique. You had given your word, telling us you'd be more careful.' She shudders. 'It wakes me up at night still, thinking what could have happened. Isn't that right, Findlay?'

'Calm yourself, Annie. There's naught to worry about now.'

'Sometimes I'm not so sure,' she says. 'Is there anything else I don't know, Finn? Anything else you haven't told me?'

'Nothing,' he says.

He speaks with such *certainty*. Even though he doesn't always take the care that he should.

'Are you sure about that?' The words are out before I can reel them in.

He curses under his breath. 'Yes,' he hisses.

'Finn!' Annie says. 'What's going on?'

His lips are so tight he can't answer.

'Jet, dear. Is there something we don't know?'

'I didn't mean to worry you, Annie. I'm sorry. It was nothing, really.'

'Now, now,' Findlay says, 'let Annie and me be the judge of that. Say your piece, lass.'

I take a few deep breaths. 'It's just … I just wonder … there are so many plants that are native to here. I'm sure Finn is very careful, but say he had an allergy to one of them without knowing it?'

'That's a good point,' Annie says. 'Finn! Are you paying attention? Which ones in particular, Jet?'

'Plants with pollens, I suppose. Or flowers, I guess.'

Finn grabs the arm of my chair, swivelling it around to face his. When our knees collide, heat, sharp and intense, shoots up my legs. He rolls his chair backwards. He glares.

'Have you lost your mind?'

You saved the calf.

You cared for Ruby.

You quoted Burns.

You undid my laces.

You held my hand.

We slept together.

Not once, but twice.

I lost my mind on the day we first met.

'Finn?' Annie says. 'What did you say to Jet?'

'Nothing,' Finn snaps.

Seeing him struggle for breath could never be *nothing*. 'Other people worry,' I tell him, 'even if you don't.' I face the screen again. 'Is he allergic to bees?'

Finn sucks in a breath. 'What the …'

I turn to him. 'Well?'

We stare at each other. He tips back his head and closes his eyes. He mutters, 'You're doing it again.'

'What?'

'Giving yourself away.'

Findlay clears his throat. 'It was thoughtful of you, Jet, to consider Australia's flora, and Finn will seriously take into account all that you have said.' He points to the screen. 'I've got that right, aye, son? To spare your poor mam worry?'

Finn speaks through his teeth. 'Yes, Dad.'

'Good lad.' Findlay smiles. 'But with regard to bees, Jet, you can rest easy. Finn's not got a problem with bees.'

'Good.' I nod. 'That's … good. Thank you.' I line up a stapler and hole puncher. I bite hard on my lip to stop any more words shooting from my mouth.

When Finn presses mute on the iPad, I watch Annie's mouth moving, but there isn't any sound. She frowns into the screen and turns to Findlay.

'Pollens and bees?' Finn says, as he angles his chair towards me again. 'What the fuck are you up to?'

I squeeze my hands between my knees. 'You say you're careful. I think you should be more careful. Otherwise … ' I clear my throat. 'I wouldn't want you to die like that.'

'Are you really so concerned?'

'Last week, you accused me of keeping my enemy close.'

He narrows his eyes. 'That was different.'

'You also said that if we'd had sex, it would have got me out of your system. Well, guess what? I don't even *want* to have sex. Especially not with you.'

I see movement. The iPad. Finn must see it too. Annie isn't on the screen any more and neither is Findlay. A dark-haired, fine-boned, blue-eyed woman has taken their place. She's the female version of Finn. She must be Fern, his environmental lawyer sister. She smiles a knowing smile.

'Fuck!' Finn says. 'Fuck!'

I check the iPad. It's muted, just like I thought. She can't have heard anything. But then she smiles again.

'Fern,' Finn says, 'you're not to say a word to Mam.' He lowers his voice. 'Don't you *fucking* dare.'

She moves her hands—rapidly, meaningfully, mouthing words as she does it. Finn signs back. It's a conversation, punctuated by Fern's laughing eyes and Finn's muttered curses.

After a particularly pointed sign from Finn, his sister grins and raises her middle finger. She mouths more words as her hands dance between them. She's smiling, her blue eyes mischievous, when he stabs at the iPad, blanking the screen.

I sit further back in the chair. 'Is your sister ...' I link my hands in my lap. 'Was she lip reading?'

'She has no hearing.' He slams the iPad shut. 'Her other senses? Her steel trap mind?' He swears under his breath. 'Fucking second to none.'

We sit silently side by side at the desk. This library is almost as large as the lounge room at Kincaid House. It has the same dark timbers, antique desk, high ceilings and candelabra light fittings. It's very different from my cottage. It will be different from the council house that Finn was raised in. Until he got a scholarship to a posh school in England. Lost his accent. Studied at Oxford. Travelled the world.

He has likeable parents. But I suspect their ordinary world, my world, isn't his or his sister's any more. I hear Mike talking to someone in the hall. Is he looking for me? He's afraid of staying too long. And aware it'll take me well over an hour to get home. He didn't finish school. He works with his hands. He's from my world too.

'Your sister has eyes like yours.'

Finn grabs my chair again, swivelling it around. He holds the arms to steady it. He's wearing black jeans. My legs are bare to the tops of my thighs. They're only millimetres away from his.

'My mother,' he speaks quietly, but his eyes are angry blue, 'will question me about pollens for the next twelve months.'

'She worries. She thinks you're keeping things from her.'

'Things she doesn't need to know.'

'That's for her to decide. She shouldn't find out in the middle of the night that you have an allergy to crayfish. And what was Mozambique all about?'

He mutters under his breath. 'Why do you care?'

'You accused me of using you!' I lower my voice, pull up my singlet strap. 'Which is pretty rough, since you're the one who's had all the relationships. What was it? Ten, twenty, you didn't even know. As if I could use you anyway.'

He opens his mouth and slams it shut. He lifts a hand and gestures to my leg, my midriff and the zig-zagged rips in my top.

'You have no fucking idea,' he mutters.

Our eyes meet again. And all of a sudden … He's no longer angry. His eyes are bright and dark. My skin heats. I'm short of breath. My lips part. So do his.

We both jump at the knock on the door. Mike walks in, followed closely by Catriona. She looks from me to Finn as we push back our chairs and stand. When Finn shoves his hands in his pockets, she smiles a little stiffly.

'Are you ready to head off?' she says. 'You've got an early start tomorrow morning.' She smooths Pterodactyl Lycra over her hips. 'And I've promised you a lift to the airport.'

Finn picks up his iPad. 'Yes.'

'Were you looking for me, Mike?' I say.

'That's right.' He considers Finn suspiciously. 'What's going on here?'

'I was looking after Marco. Finn had to take a call.' I take Mike's arm. 'Let's go.' I nod jerkily at Catriona and Finn. 'I hope you have a nice break.'

'You have my number,' Finn says.

And why would I use it?

I can't hear what Finn and Catriona talk about as they follow us down the hallway, but she's laughing up at him as Mike and I say goodbye to Mr Chambers. Finn has had ten or twenty lovers. *Maybe twenty-one.*

Intimacy and desire. Love and commitment. I have to push them away.

Back to where they were before we met.

CHAPTER

43

Before I go to the Hargreaves's on Christmas Day, I always visit the cemetery, but this is the first time I've brought Chili with me. It seemed like a good idea early this morning, when I saw him looking expectantly over the fence, as if I'd promised him an outing. But leading him three kilometres along the side of the road in thirty-five degree heat, and manoeuvring him through graves with randomly placed headstones, crosses and statues wasn't easy. There's no shade. And after weeks of sweltering days, the grass between the rows of graves is flat and yellow, so there's nothing for him to eat. When he peers forlornly at me, I rub around his ears.

'I thought you wanted to come.'

Mrs Juniper's grave has a vase near the headstone, filled with faded silk roses. When a hot dry gust blows over the hill, the flowers shift and flutter. Chili shies sideways, landing centimetres from Liam's cross.

'C'mon, boy, it's time to move on.'

I lead him to the church, tying him to the wrought-iron fence near the grey gums. He picks at the meagre shoots of grass that grow in the shade, turning his head to the side to reach under the rail.

'That's better,' I say, patting his dark chestnut coat and adjusting the fly veil over his halter.

Why did I bring him? To visit Mum? If she's around, she can see him anywhere. It's odd it's taken me so long to understand how wrong I was, how selfish, to hang on to Chili after Mum's death. I should have agreed to do what Dad suggested and give him away. I knew I'd never ride him myself. Dressage bored him on competition days, but he couldn't wait to get started in cross-country or showjumping; he seemed to enjoy the buzz and applause of the crowd. Mum had to hold him back when he flew too fast at the fences; that was his only fault.

He stamps his foot, trying to rid himself of a fly at the top of his leg. I swipe it away, then lean against his shoulder. When he raises his head, I breathe into his neck.

'I never got to the Olympics either, but at least I had a say in that. I'm sorry, boy, for holding you back.'

I return to the graves; Liam, Mum and Dad. In winter and spring, their plots stand out because of the daffodils, jonquils and freesias. But they're also distinctive in summer. It takes hours for Mr Hargreaves, kneeling on a cushion, to bunch and tie up the leaves once the flowers are spent. He insists this improves the following year's crop. They do get better and better, so I don't have the heart to tell him not to bother.

I sit on the railway sleeper that marks the third row. Other locals will come to the cemetery later, when the sun is lower and the heat of the day has passed. But, for now, I'm the only one here.

'Follyfoot's had a good year,' I tell my family. 'Chelsea's a standout, and little Darcy's doing great. I've been getting more work at the zoo. Mike and Andrew introduced me to Precious—she's an elephant. I had an ear infection, Mum. But I got over it. Mike got an invitation to Mr Chambers's party again, and we dressed as Barney and Pebbles. And Dad, you'd be happy about all the audio books I've downloaded. They've got poetry readings on Spotify now, even the old Robert Burns ones I learnt with Mrs McNab.'

When tears spring to my eyes, I close them. I've known Finn for half a year. Does he have to be a part of *everything* I do?

I blow three kisses. 'I love you.' I walk up the hill towards Chili, who raises his head and whickers.

Years ago, there'd be twenty people for lunch at the Hargreaves's small brick-veneer house. Now there are over fifty because their foster children bring their own families. Most of them stay overnight. Sometimes they pitch tents in the garden, or park caravans out on the road. But often they cram into one of the bedrooms, or bunk on the porch at the back of the house. It takes over half an hour to thank everyone for having me and say goodbye, so it's almost five when I shoulder my bag and follow the dusty path to the side street where I parked. I'm wearing a long cotton skirt and a white lacy top; the sun is hot on my back.

By the time I round the bend and see Caruthers, it's too late to double back.

'G'day, Jet.'

He's leaning against the door of my ute, dragging on a cigarette. His truck, facing the wrong way, is parked so close to my car that the front bumpers touch. He straightens, throwing his butt onto the bitumen and extinguishing it with the heel of his boot. He's wearing jeans and a loud Hawaiian shirt. His light-brown hair is shaved at the sides.

'What do you want?'

'The barman at The Royal said you'd be here.' He grins. 'Nice Chrissy lunch?'

I'm safer here than I would be at home. Even so, there's no one within shouting distance. I place my bag at my feet in case I need my fists. 'I asked what you wanted.'

'Like that, is it? That's a shame.'

'Are you going to move your truck, or do I come back later?'

'With reinforcements?' He holds out his hands. 'Against little old me.'

'Tell me what you want!'

He leans against the ute again. 'Darren Morrissey got no joy out of Edward Kincaid.'

'He told him I'd overdosed the horses.'

'He thought it was worth a shot.' He crosses his arms, bulking them up even more. 'The hold-up. What's that all about?'

'With the report?' I shake my head. 'I don't know.'

'You know what I reckon?' He drawls his words. 'Always best to tell the truth.'

'People go away at Christmas, maybe that's it.'

He stares at my top, the rise of my breasts. 'You look real pretty in that outfit, Jet, real Christmassy.' A trickle of sweat rolls down the side of his face. 'Your mate Blackwood hasn't said anything? You sure about that?'

'Yes.'

He pounces, grasping the tops of my arms. His fingers dig into my skin. It's impossible to raise my hands or my knees. He tightens his grip and I cry out.

'You're hurting me!'

He lifts me up; my toes scrape the ground. 'So far, Jet, you and Mike, you're doing okay.' Besides beer and smoke, I smell onion on his breath. 'But you still got to keep your traps shut. You got that?'

My eyes water. 'Yes,' I croak.

He cocks his head to the side. 'What was that, Jet? Don't be afraid to speak up.'

'Yes!'

'Because if you don't do what you're told …' He shakes me, then lets go so suddenly that I stagger backwards, stopping short when I hit the ute side-on. 'You're gonna pay for it.'

I rub my elbow. 'I get it,' I croak.

He holds out his hand. 'Greetings of the season.'

I stare at the eagle tattoo, the narrow eye and curved sharp beak. And jump when a lizard, a wide-bodied blue tongue in a hundred shades of grey, appears out of the undergrowth. She looks left and right, before plodding back to the shade. A horn sounds, happy goodbye beeps. I watch silently, painfully swallowing, as Caruthers withdraws his hand and climbs into his truck.

A shoulder strap has slipped down my arm. When I pull it up, I see the marks of his fingers, the red and blue stains on my skin.

My hands won't stop shaking, so I'm clinging to the steering wheel as I turn into the driveway. When my phone rings and I pull over, I see that it's Finn. If I answer, I'll burst into tears. So I let the call ring out. But as soon as I get the message beep, I listen.

Jemima, it's Finn. Merry Christmas. I'm in Scotland, but leave for Switzerland after New Year, and will be there for a couple of weeks. My report is almost complete, but as you know, Nate Gillespie won't be available until later in January. I'll send through the meeting details as soon as I have them. In the meantime, if you have any concerns, or if there's anything else … call me.

What would he say if I told him about Caruthers? He'd tell me to go to the police. What if they didn't arrest him? Even if they did, they're unlikely to lock him up. Mike and I would be in the same position we're in right now. Maybe even worse. Once Finn's report is done, all this will be over.

As I walk to the river in the late afternoon, the sun, a big golden ball, hovers over the hill. The crickets are raucous behind me. The grass at my feet is dry, a washed-out shade of green. Vegemite ambles next to me, but then heads back to the gate.

Instead of walking towards the boundary, where it's easy to get to the water, I follow the path to the cliff, sitting on my bottom and wriggling to the edge. Did Finn really climb down there? And up again. Now he's in Scotland, enjoying Christmas with his family. What if he'd died in the park? How would Annie, Findlay and Fern have survived? What a terrible Christmas. I take a shaky breath and listen to his message again. He's far from indestructible, but he's safe and well right now.

The water is low, and flows at a meandering pace around the rock that divides the river. Finn said *later in January*. How many weeks? I back away from the edge and stand, leaning against the sapling and stretching out my legs. I only have a bar of reception.

'Gus, it's Jet. Happy Christmas. Did you have a nice day? How long will your family be staying?'

'They're leaving tomorrow for their beach holiday. My son is upset because I won't go with them, but what can I do, with all the work that needs doing round here?'

'Can you do me a favour? I'm not sleeping too well. Do you think Banjo or Patty would mind spending nights at the cottage? Just for a while.'

'I've seen your lights on. Are you missing a bit of company, with Dr Blackwood being away?'

'Like I haven't been alone for ten years? The ear infection mucked up my sleep, that's all.'

U

For the first two evenings, Gus brought Banjo to the cottage on his tractor. But after that, just as Gus had predicted, Banjo came to me on his own. For the past three weeks, he's slept on an old saddle blanket on my verandah, because Gus says that's what he's used to. I don't think he rates being a guard dog. When I say goodnight and rub his tummy on Thursday night, he sighs with resignation, his glossy black tail banging slowly on the boards.

The sun has barely risen on Friday morning when I sit on the pew and pull on my boots. I whistle and Banjo leaps, sitting next to me and cocking his head as he waits for instructions.

'Big day today, boy,' I say, stroking the tan fur on his chest and rubbing under his chin. 'I get to find out what Finn knows about Thornbrooke.' When I rest my arm across his back and kiss the top of his head, he tolerates it, but I can tell he wants to get back to Gus. Just like Ruby wanted to get back to work when she was a pup. 'Time to let you go, Banjo.' He pricks up his ears. 'Thought you might like to hear that.'

We hop from the pew together. He trots ahead to the gate, scrambling over it, sitting and staring at me. Vegemite, Chili, Freckle and Lollopy are in the home paddock, waiting to be let into the paddock by the river. If I stand on my toes, I can see the pile of logs where I fell. That morning is a blur in my mind, but the evening is clear. It warms my body. It hurts my heart.

How does Finn remember that day? Does he ever think about it? Does it slip into his dreams at unexpected times? I'll see him in town at ten o'clock this morning. I won't be dreaming then—of things not meant to be.

The sun is hot on my neck and shoulders, so I push my hat low and then tip it back. 'It's Gus's birthday, Banjo, which means you'll come here with him tonight. I've got a full day's work, but Sapphie will be here with the cake.'

His eyes, golden in the sunshine, are bright with expectation. He knows what happens next, but he waits for the signal. I point in the direction of Gus's house, a kilometre across the paddocks and out of sight.

'Home, Banjo!'

Within seconds he's a black-and-tan blur.

CHAPTER

44

The doors to the foyer slide closed behind me. Finn, dressed in a suit, stands at the bottom of the town hall staircase, messaging on his phone. I'm sure his blue-and-silver tie is the same one he had on when gave the speech in Dubbo. He looks up, straight into my eyes.

I was dressed as Pebbles Flintstone the last time I saw him. Today I'm wearing work clothes—jeans, worn boots and a checked blue shirt. I'd never wear a suit, even if I had one. So why … I straighten my shoulders and lift my chin. My hands and face are clean because I came here straight from home. My hair is shiny; my ponytail swings when I walk.

He pulls the tie undone, winds the length of silk around his hand and puts it into his pocket. He undoes the top button of his shirt, then runs his hand around the back of his neck. He usually does that when he's frustrated, or angry. But he doesn't appear to be either of those things. He looks cool and calm, in control.

He holds out his hand. 'Jemima. Thank you for coming.'

We shake hands like strangers, his grip firm but brief. 'I want to get this over with. So does Mike.'

I hadn't noticed that Edward was in the foyer, but he joins us immediately, kissing my cheeks. He's wearing his country outfit, neat chinos and a striped shirt. Nate Gillespie, also wearing a suit, walks down the stairs. He smiles as he holds out his hand.

'Jet Kincaid,' he says, 'fantastic to see you again.'

'Hi.'

Nate has slightly broader shoulders than Finn, but Finn is taller and his facial features, his cheekbones and jawline, are much more clearly defined. Has he lost weight?

We walk up the stairs to the meeting room. It has a large table in the middle and a lot of upright chairs. Nate directs us to our seats, me next to Edward, and Finn across the table, opposite me. Nate sits at the end of the table and takes out an iPad.

'Finn and I are meeting my colleagues here at twelve,' he says, looking at his watch. 'We have quite a bit to get through beforehand. Do you mind if I set the agenda?'

I shake my head. Edward smiles politely. Finn shrugs. 'Go ahead.'

'For starters,' Nate says, 'I figure Jet and Edward may be wondering why I'm here?'

Edward raises his brows. 'The thought had crossed my mind.'

'Well, how about I put your mind at rest?' Nate hands out business cards. They're thick white cardboard, with a plain black font.

'Thanks.'

'I work on a team, with representatives from the US, Asia and Europe, that's been set up by a United Nations committee. We investigate arms trafficking, money laundering, illegal drug networks and organised crime. They all have transnational elements, hence the UN involvement.' He leans back in his chair. 'I'm here because Finn came across something that goes beyond Thornbrooke.'

Edward whistles quietly. 'I see.'

Nate nods towards Finn. 'You want to get the straightforward part out of the way?'

I listen carefully to what Finn says, about the various serum samples he located, his methodology, the way he consulted with colleagues in Sydney, Pretoria and Geneva, and worked closely with a chemical pathologist. I listen to the way he speaks, how rarely he gives away his heritage. His voice is deep. His lips are well-shaped. When we slept at the homestead, he told me we could do better.

'The horses died within two hours of each other,' he says, looking pointedly at me. 'Which gave credence to Morrissey and Schofield's story that an outside food contaminant was responsible. The conclusions they came to were also backed up by what they said was in the supplements: minerals, salts and other elements, none of them banned substances.' He hesitates. 'But there was something else I found in the samples, months before the deaths. It took time to identify what this substance was. But once I had, Nate got involved. A particular strain of the substance was on the market at the time the horses died. We're certain it was this that killed them.'

Edward clears his throat. 'There was no overdose?'

'No,' Finn says. 'Morrissey lied—he knew Jemima wasn't responsible. But others suspected that she might have done something wrong. Now we have proof she had nothing to do with the deaths.'

I hold onto the table. I'm suddenly lightheaded. 'I knew I didn't give them too much, but ... that's good.'

Finn frowns. 'Are you all right? Should we take a break?'

When I shake my head, the room spins a little. 'I'm okay,' I say.

'What was this mystery substance?' Edward says.

'It was a sub-class of MDMA, or Ecstasy, a stimulant. We believe Schofield was masking its administration by mixing it with other things.'

'But the horses weren't even racing,' Edward says.

'Yet,' Finn says, 'and it was early days for the drug. We think Morrissey and Schofield were experimenting with horses, like the colts, that weren't tested as regularly as others would have been.'

'Why wasn't it identified earlier?' Edward asks.

'At that time, there was no routine MDMA test for horses, let alone tests for the sub-class of drug that Morrissey was supplied with. Even now, that particular drug doesn't show up without a specific test, a series of tests, and the technology for doing that was only developed recently.'

'So why bother to fudge the autopsies?'

Finn sets up his iPad. 'The most likely scenario is that the horses died from the drug's toxic effects on their organs, which would have caused circulatory collapse and asphyxia. Death caused by the mythical food contaminant might have presented in a different way. I'll send my data through.'

Edward turns to Nate. 'How exactly do you fit in?'

'Finn and I go way back,' Nate says. 'He contacted me when he worked out what the substance could be. Our pathologists got together and what do you know? There were commonalities between the substance he'd identified and one I have an interest in.'

'This drug is widely used?'

'It's worth millions, hundreds of millions, in the drug trade annually.'

Edward sits back on his chair. 'I see.'

'We're not sure what Schofield's motivation was,' Finn says. 'Perhaps he thought, once the horses were racing, knowing how they responded to the drug would prove useful.'

'He knew his pharmaceuticals,' Nate says. 'We suspect he had a drug problem himself. He thought he'd do a little experimentation.'

Edward throws his pen on the table. 'He used my father's stud as his lab.'

'With Morrissey's backing,' Nate says.

'Why experiment on Rosethorn?' Edward says. 'He was simply at stud.'

Nate shrugs. 'Who knows?'

'Schofield and Morrissey asked Jemima to place the orders for the legal substances,' Finn says. 'Schofield mixed them with the illegal one, and Jemima administered them.'

'Each horse had its own recipe,' I say quietly.

'Did Morrissey and Schofield blame you at the time?' Finn says. 'Is that why you left?'

'I didn't know they'd done anything wrong, but Mike suspected they'd blame me. It would have been my word against theirs. Mike was trying to protect me, that's all.'

'He destroyed the supplements, didn't he?'

'I … I don't want him upset. He's scared of getting into trouble.'

When Nate extends his hand, it lies on the table between us. He has a scar on his knuckle. His nails are neat like Finn's.

'We have no interest in you, or Mike,' he says.

I take a deep breath. 'After Mike smashed the bottles, it looked like we had something to hide—even though we didn't know what it was. Mike is scared we're accessories after the fact, or something like that. He hates the idea he did something wrong.'

'He regretted doing it?'

'Once he'd had time to think things through, yes. It was so out of character for him; he never tells lies.' My voice wavers. 'He said going to jail wasn't on his bucket list.'

Nate smiles sympathetically. 'I got access to telecommunications records. Morrissey and Schofield, they didn't make it to Thornbrooke in time, did they?'

I shake my head.

'You were on your own.'

'It would have looked bad for Morrissey, leaving me with twelve stabled horses to care for. And acting like he was there … it meant he and Schofield could put their spin on the deaths.' I swallow. 'It also meant I didn't have to deal with anything. It seemed … everything seemed a good idea at the time.'

It's a large room. No one is speaking. Even so, there's too little air. When I stand, Finn stands too. He holds out his hand, like he's afraid I might fall down.

'The horses that died …' My voice is soft and shaky. 'Those horses had names. Persephone. Poldark. Blackjack. Rosethorn.' I swallow. 'They had names.'

Nate finally breaks the silence. 'How about we take a break? I'll order in coffee and tea, cookies or—'

'No!' I sit on my chair again. I trace the grain on the table. 'No, thank you. I have to get to work.'

Nate nods slowly. 'Then how about I finish what I have to say?'

'Please do,' Edward says.

Nate tells us that even though Schofield and Morrissey were unimportant in terms of the quantities of drug they purchased, Morrissey has the potential to help Nate with an investigation in Malaysia. Nate needed a link between the sub-class of drug used on the horses and a crime syndicate he's interested in. Now he might have it.

'I interviewed Morrissey yesterday,' Nate says. 'He knows a connection has been made between him and the syndicate, and he's desperate to avoid any contact with it. He wants our protection. He's terrified.'

'That's why he's been scaring me,' I whisper.

Nate frowns. 'What did you say?'

'You have him locked up, right?'

'Yes.'

I nod. 'Okay.'

'Let's go back a little. You said Morrissey scared you? Recently?'

'He got someone to threaten me.'

Finn stiffens.

Edward turns in his chair and touches my arm. 'What on earth?'

'I was told to keep my mouth shut.' I rub the tops of my arms. 'This man, he threatened to hurt Mike too.'

'Did he harm you?' Finn says.

'Not much. But he said it would get worse if I talked to anyone.'

'For ...' He mutters a stream of curses under his breath. 'Tell me what happened.'

'I'd prefer not to talk about it.'

'Jem ...'

I trace the grain on the table again. 'He grabbed my arm the first time. After that, he just pushed me around ... a bump on my leg, some bruises.'

'I saw your shin. Did he do that?'

'It's healed now.'

His jaw clenches. His gaze slides to my hands. I link my fingers together to hide the tape. 'When was the last time?'

'Christmas Day, but he won't do it any more, not if Morrissey's locked up.'

'Morrissey won't apply for bail,' Nate says. 'Not after what happened to Schofield.'

Edward sits straighter in his chair. 'Wasn't he killed in an accident?'

'Maybe he was, maybe he wasn't,' Nate says. 'Either way, it shook Morrissey up. The drug that killed the horses also led to the deaths of innocent people. Morrissey must have had an inkling of that, which is why he acted as he did. A food contaminant in grain is unfortunate, but not particularly controversial. If Morrissey had blamed Schofield after his death, or said anything about the horses being doped, questions would have been asked. That was a risk to Morrissey in multiple ways.'

I push back my chair. 'The police have Morrissey. That's what's important.'

'You're important too,' Nate says. 'Who was it, Jet? Who threatened you?'

'He was doing Morrissey's dirty work. He won't be interested now.'

Finn mutters under his breath. 'Tell him, Jemima.'

'You must give Nate the details,' Edward says.

I have to call Mike. I have clients to see. I have to get home for Gus's party. That's what I have to do. I look at Edward. Nate. Finn.

'No.'

Nate and Edward talk over each other as I walk to the door. Finn pushes back his chair and walks towards me.

'You have to report this,' he says.

'I don't have to do anything. I want nothing to do with Morrissey.'

'I understand that, but—'

'No.'

When he touches my elbow, my heart rate goes up. 'May we speak privately?' he says.

'It's over, all of it.' I step back. 'I took the morning off. I have to get to work.'

'Please, Jemima.'

When someone knocks on the door, I reach for it like a lifeline, opening it wide. A woman and two men stand outside. They must be Nate's colleagues. Lawyers? Police officers? UN investigators? The woman is tall and attractive, dressed in a suit. Her shirt is white and silky, with small pearl buttons. There's a laptop under her arm. The bag at her feet is bulging with documents.

She will have access to plenty of words. Could I borrow just a few of them?

'Give us two minutes?' Nate says, stepping in front of me and shutting the door.

'Somebody hurt you,' Finn says. 'You can't pretend that didn't happen.'

'Yes I can.' I reach for the doorknob again. 'I want to call Mike. I want to tell him he doesn't have to worry now, that he won't go to jail.'

'Jem.' When Finn rests his hand on my arm, the warmth of his touch goes straight to my heart. I twist away, yank open the door.

The woman in the suit is waiting outside with the men. She picks up her bag and smiles. 'All done?' she says brightly.

Why can't I smile back? Because Thornbrooke may be over, but I'm not over Finn?

Will I ever be like I was? Able to look at the sky without thinking of him, the shades of blue in his eyes.

Happy to be on my own.

CHAPTER

45

It's after six when I turn off the highway to the loop road that leads into Horseshoe. Was it only twelve hours ago that I sat on the pew, chatting to Banjo as I pulled on my boots? It feels like much longer.

Gus has left his tractor in the paddock. The other guests have come by road, parking close to the homestead so they don't block the doors to the shed. Sapphie's car is here, and the Hargreaves's. Gus's cousin, and the friend Gus visited in hospital, have driven here from Dubbo. There are three four-wheel drives. One of them is Finn's.

He closes the gate to the home paddock and walks directly towards me. 'Jemima.'

'Finn.' He's changed into jeans, a T-shirt and boots. His hair is damp. He pushes it back from his forehead. I harden my delicate heart. 'Did Gus invite you to his party?'

'After I told him the Honey family had parked me in, yes.' He attempts a smile. 'He assumed you'd forgotten to tell me about it.'

'Are you visiting for the weekend?'

'I'm here to see you.'

'I've said all I'm going to say.'

'Are you referring to the threats?'

'It's over.'

'It's not,' he says. 'But that can wait until tomorrow.'

I reach into the ute for a file, wedged behind the gas bottle. It's just out of my grasp. He leans over me, picking it up easily. He was careful not to touch me, but my heart rate goes up anyway. When I face him again, I look straight ahead, at the rise and fall of his chest. His breathing is steady.

'I missed you, Jemima,' he says quietly, 'every fucking day. Did I mention that?'

I snatch the file and throw it into the toolbox. 'So why not take the time to tell me what was happening?'

He frowns. 'It was only a hypothesis until last week. I was waiting on data from the bloods, and Nate was sifting through information on the drug ring.'

'You could have said something.'

'If we'd known about the threats, it would have been different. As it was, we were afraid that Morrissey would suspect we were onto him, and disappear. Mike was off limits, you were evasive.' He crosses his arms. 'I called on Christmas Day.'

'Why? If you weren't prepared to tell me anything?'

'I wanted to hear your voice. You didn't call back.'

'When Morrissey said I'd overdosed the horses, you believed him.'

'Bullshit.'

'You're a scientist; you look at probability. You must have thought there was a chance of it.'

He blows out a breath. 'Are you accusing me, or excusing me?'

'I don't know …'

He walks a few paces away, comes back again, holds out his hand and drops it to his side.

'Giving the incorrect dose,' he says quietly, 'could only ever have been a mistake. Even so, you'd never have forgiven yourself. I didn't want you to carry that guilt. Other than that, I didn't care whether you'd done it or not.'

'What? Even if I hadn't owned up?'

'It was a traumatic event.'

'But … it would have been dishonest.'

His lip lifts. 'You and honesty are complicated.'

'They are not!'

He hesitates. 'Can we talk about this later?' He points to the cottage. 'Everyone is waiting for you. I've taken the horses to the small paddock at the side of the cottage. Are you still rugging Vegemite?'

'You accused me of keeping my enemy close. Isn't it dangerous to be here?'

'I can't help myself.'

A flock of cockatoos fly overhead and the kookaburras start up. I hear Sapphie's shout and Gus's throaty laugh.

'Give me the rug,' Finn says. 'Then go up to the house.'

I brush past him, skirt around the barrow and fetch the rug. When I hand it over, our hands touch. My heart skips a beat.

He searches my eyes. 'We have to do better.'

I lean a little closer. 'You *really* didn't care whether I'd done it or not?'

'No.'

I hear the truth in his voice. I see it in his eyes.

Truth is important to him. I've known that from the start.

We have to do better.

The sky is a washed-out blue, not quite day and not quite night, when I walk up the steps to the verandah. Banjo wags his tail, joining me on the pew. I hear Mrs Hargreaves through the fly-screen door.

'Would you like another sausage roll? Or a chicken pie? They're only bite sized. Jet made the fruit salad first thing this morning, and there's plenty more in the fridge. I took the Anzac biscuits out of the oven just before I left home.'

'I'll miss you, boy,' I say, rubbing under Banjo's chin as I kick off my boots. I stand and watch Finn, throwing the rug over Vegemite's back. 'He said he'd missed me. What do you reckon?'

It takes fifteen minutes to shower and dress in clean clothes, a singlet top and old denim shorts, and walk barefoot into the living room. Finn leans against the wall near the kitchen, listening to Gus's cousin ramble on about the price of a steer. The youngest Honey girl leaves her sisters to join me, and chats excitedly about Sunday's gymkhana. Everyone talks at once as Gus opens his presents. Sapphie and I bought him a new Akubra hat. He tells us he'll keep it for special occasions, like when he goes into town.

'I'm sorry I was late, Gus.'

He smiles as he slams the hat on his head. 'It was nice of you to make a fuss in the first place, you being so hard at work.' He nods in Finn's direction. 'Now your neighbour's back in the homestead, Banjo might lose his security job.'

'He can go home with you tonight.'

Mrs Hargreaves is collecting plates. 'I've put all the leftovers in the fridge, Jet.'

'Thank you.' When I whistle, everyone stops talking. 'Who's ready for the birthday cake?'

Finn's thigh brushes mine when we kneel and scoop up wrapping paper. Our arms press together as we stand side by side at the sink to rinse the dishes. When I lick chocolate frosting from the side of my hand, I look up and catch him staring. So, by the time the guests say goodnight and Gus heads home with Banjo at his heels, I'm even more of a jittery bundle of nerves than I was when I came through the door.

Sapphie whispers when I walk her out. 'Finn is still in the kitchen, but said he'd be heading off soon.'

'Thanks for organising everything.'

She hugs me. 'I'll be here around nine tomorrow. I'll take Chili out.'

I yawn. 'I'll be leaving early, so might not see you until Sunday.'

The screen door slams shut as I shake the tablecloth over the verandah railing. After the Hargreaves's taillights disappear, I kick leaves off the verandah and toss the water from Banjo's bowl into the garden. Besides a dim light coming from the side entrance, the homestead is dark.

I'm almost at the door when it opens and Finn props it wide with his boot. Our eyes meet over the threshold. He holds out his hand. 'Jem?'

Does he want me to take his hand? Or follow him into the house? I'm mulling over that when he leans forwards, sliding his hand down my arm and threading his fingers through mine. Our palms are pressed together, our forearms touch. Warmth, soft and sweet, spreads through my body.

'Come with me,' he says.

CHAPTER
46

What are we without Thornbrooke?

I tug my hand free as we sit next to each other on the sofa. He glances at my face, then rests his forearms on his thighs.

'I'd like to ask you something,' he says, 'before I go back to the homestead.'

I link my hands neatly in my lap. 'Yes?'

'Will you have dinner with me tomorrow night?'

I blink. 'What do you mean?'

'Saturday night. A meal. Anywhere but Horseshoe, or Gus will find us and pull up a chair.'

'But … why?'

He straightens. 'It's what people do. It's how they get to know each other.'

'But we already know each other.'

'In some ways.' He glances at my legs before jerking his head away, as if guilty. When I cross my arms, he looks at my nails. He frowns.

I hold out my hand. 'Do you want to take a closer look?'

'Don't.'

'I thought you wanted to get to know me.'

He grabs my hand and sandwiches it between his. 'You dream of the horses that died?'

'Yes,' I say quietly.

'I know a lot about them now.'

'I guess you would, their blood, their genes.'

'I also know their names. Persephone, Poldark, Blackjack and Rosethorn.'

He knows too much. I shut my eyes tightly, talk through the stiffness in my throat. 'The dreams. They'll get better now I don't have to talk about Thornbrooke. Or avoid talking about it.'

'Or worry about Mike. I'm sorry it took so long.'

'I'll see a psychologist anyway. Mike knows her, she helps the emergency services men and women.'

He turns my hand and lays it palm up in his. When he traces around my fingers, up and down and in and out, my heart jumps about.

'I want to be open with you,' he says.

'To show me how to do it?'

'In the hope you'll learn to trust me.'

'Why do you need that?'

'Just trust me when I say that I do.'

'Can I ask you something?'

'Of course.'

'How is your mother? Were her test results okay?'

He squeezes my hand. 'She's well, Jem. The lump was benign.'

'She said it would be, but I worried about it.' I take a deep breath. 'Can I ask you something else?'

'Anything.'

'You miss Africa, don't you? You'd like to go back there?'

'I don't miss it like I did.'

'When we were at the Christmas party, Annie said something about Mozambique. What was that about?'

'Something happened while I was working there.' He shrugs. 'It rattled her.'

'Tell me.'

'It's not important.'

I pull my hand away. 'You said I could ask you anything.'

He mutters something, but then he leans forwards again and focuses on the rug. 'I'd just got my doctorate, and was working in Mozambique for an anti-poaching organisation. It gave internships to Canadian post-grad students, and three were assigned to me. We visited a village near the border with Tanzania. It was a day trip. We were meant to be back by three.'

'But you weren't? What happened?'

'The area we went to was remote, but politically stable. Or so we thought. We were ambushed by anti-government rebels.'

'Oh!'

'I managed to radio for help, but then we were taken away. It took a week of negotiations to get us out.' He glances at me. 'We were fed a cashew-based gruel. I couldn't eat.'

I link my fingers tightly together. 'Couldn't you say something?'

'The students were petrified. I was in charge. I knew the region well and could communicate, more or less, in the rebels' language. If they'd found out I was essentially the weakest in the group, it would have been used against us. At best, there would have been more pressure on the negotiators to accede to the rebels' demands. At worst, they could have forced me to eat. I said nothing.'

'Did your families know what was going on?'

'They were formally notified after we were released.'

I touch his arm. When he turns to me on the sofa, his knee is against my thigh. 'You didn't eat all that time?'

'I drank what I could.' His face softens when he looks into my eyes. 'It wasn't that bad.'

'A whole week?'

'The rebels were given an amnesty. I drove us out. End of story.'

'No wonder your mother was rattled.'

'I tried to keep it from her, but she knew I'd lost weight. She cornered the High Commissioner and grilled him. She's far more ferocious than she appears. He caved within minutes.'

'The crayfish at Kruger came later?'

'How do you know about that?'

'Andrew Martin told me.'

'He talks too much.'

'You miss Africa because it was dangerous.'

He runs his hands up my arms to my shoulders. His fingers clench as if he's scared I'll run. Even though I hardly know where to run to any more.

'I meant what I said before,' he says. 'I missed you.'

'I don't know what you want.'

'I want to go out to dinner with you.'

His breath is unsteady; his colour is high. His eyes are fiercely bright. He doesn't look like he wants to go out to dinner. He looks like he wants to have sex.

'Can we go to bed?'

He stiffens. 'What?'

'I want to sleep with you again. To get you out of my system.'

He frowns. And then he smiles. 'Touché.' He shakes me gently. 'Dinner.'

'Bed.'

He groans. 'I haven't had sex since we met. If I sleep with you, we'll have sex.'

'You haven't had sex since August?'

He takes a deep breath. 'No.'

'I meant we'd have sex. Not sleeping.'

He takes my face in his hands. 'Seriously, Jem, you're killing me.'

I touch his silky hair. 'We could have dinner another time.'

'When do you finish tomorrow?'

'My last regular client is at twelve, but I promised Andrew I'd see Afaafa on the way home.'

'If we meet at the zoo, we can drive back here together. We'll see to the horses, then go out to dinner.'

'I guess.'

'Is that a yes?'

I pull him to his feet. 'Yes!'

He runs his hands down my body, gripping my waist, my hips. 'I didn't plan to do this.'

'You didn't write it on your whiteboard?'

When he growls against my mouth, I stroke his cheek. But then, before he can change his mind, I draw away, take his hand and tug.

CHAPTER
47

He throws himself backwards onto the bed, dragging me with him. And when I laugh, he flips me onto my back. I bury my hands in his hair and yank down his head, grinding our lips together. He stills for an instant. But then he takes over my mouth like he's starved of the taste of me. I'm starving too. When I tug at his shirt, something rips.

'Oh!' I push against him and sit. We're both breathing quickly, with shaky hands and thumping hearts. I undo his top two buttons. When he tries to help, I push his hands away and open the rest, kissing a trail down his front.

He pulls my top over my head, nuzzles my breasts, then rolls me onto my back and unzips my shorts, pulling them down with my undies and throwing them onto the floor.

The bed dips as he sits on the edge. He strips off his shirt and takes off his socks. He turns towards me, with passionate eyes but a serious mouth.

'I don't want to rush you,' he says.

I sit too, trailing my hands over his shoulders, arms and chest. He touches the side of my breast, strokes it with the back of his hand.

'I started this,' I say.

'I want you to be certain.'

'I am certain. I think, I think …' I touch his nose. 'I think you have a very handsome face.'

He laughs. 'And you're fucking beautiful. Your eyes, nose, mouth, body, everything.'

'Thank you.'

'You didn't believe a word I said, did you?'

I shake my head.

'Playing pool in skintight jeans, you're beautiful. In a hat and boots, with dirt on your face, you're beautiful. That Pebbles outfit? *Jesus*. What was Mike thinking, letting you out in public like that?'

I circle his navel before walking my fingers to the button of his jeans. His erection bulges under the fabric. When I lay my hand on it, he groans.

'Do you always wear clothes to bed?'

He kisses my shoulder. 'No.'

'Just when you sleep with me.'

'Yes.'

'Why?'

He hesitates. 'Tell me how you feel.'

'About what?'

'Me, Jem.' His eyes are warm. 'Besides how my face looks, tell me how you feel about me.'

I pull up the sheet so I'm covered to the waist. 'I feel … I want to have sex with you.'

'That's it?'

I bring my knees up to my chest and wrap my arms around them. 'I haven't had sex with anyone else, but I want to have it with you. Doesn't that tell you how I feel?'

He rubs my back. 'Are you cold?'

'Just exposed.'

He scoops up the cotton blanket from the foot of the bed and drapes it over my shoulders. 'I could tell you how I feel about you.' He speaks slowly, precisely. 'But I don't know how you'd react if you knew.' He takes my hand and turns it over in his, tracing the line that runs across my palm to my wrist.

'I just want ...'

He breathes deeply. 'You have no idea what you want.'

'I do!'

'What?'

'To sleep with you.'

He tips his face to the ceiling. 'Fuck.'

'You didn't swear so much at first.'

He closes his eyes, mutters. 'I didn't need to.'

'I'm sorry.'

He growls as he gets to his feet and pulls down the zip of his jeans. He puts his wallet on the side table then picks it up and rummages around. I look away when he strips off. But when he sits on the bed again, one of his knees bumps mine. I look down, see his erection, and suck in a breath.

'Jem? I want your agreement.'

I swallow with a gulp. I nod. 'Right.'

He holds out his hand. 'Give me your word. Dinner tomorrow.'

I line our fingers up—his perfect nails, my broken ones. 'I promise.'

I'm not sure how long we kiss, but we're both warm and shaky by the time he lifts his head. He strokes my arms. He runs his hands up my legs. He touches my breasts, kisses them, sits back and touches them again.

'I could look at you forever,' he says, nudging my legs open and circling between them with his thumb. I arch my back and press against his hand.

'*Finn*.' My voice is husky and low. 'I think we should do it now.'

'I love your colours.' He groans softly as his fingers slip in and around me.

I swallow. 'Please do it now.'

He smiles unsteadily. 'You're small, Jem.'

'I think … you're not, are you?'

He shakes his head. 'I don't believe so.' He kisses my mouth, loops his tongue around mine and sucks. 'So fucking sweet,' he mumbles.

'Now, Finn.'

He nuzzles against my throat. 'I'm afraid of hurting you.'

I fear tomorrow, next week, and in ten years' time. But not tonight. I touch his cheek. 'You won't.'

His eyes close as he lowers his head. He kisses me deeply. His erection sits hard and unyielding between us. I have another look. How on *earth*?

He takes my hand. 'Touch me if you want to. It might make it easier for you.'

When I trace the ridges, the delicate skin and the hardness, he draws in his breath and clenches his hands into fists. His face is all angles. His cheeks flush even more. I run my thumb softly over the moisture at the top.

'Oh, fuck.' When he reaches for a condom, I wriggle down the bed. I remind myself of the facts. He knows what he's doing. I want this. I want him.

I try to smile when he lies down on his side next to me.

'I think it'll be easier if I'm on top,' he says. 'Is that okay?'

I push his hair back. 'I trust you.'

He groans a laugh. 'This is not a good time to hear that.'

I bend my knees and he lies between them. One gentle nudge and then another. It's uncomfortable and ... With the third nudge my muscles tense up. My heels dig into the bed and my thighs press together.

'I'll pull out,' he says.

'Please don't move.' I put my hand between us. He's hardly even in. 'Just ... wait.'

When I lift my hips, forcing him further inside, he moans. 'I'll hurt you.'

I bite the inside of my cheek so I don't cry out. If I'd had more practice, it would have been easier. It would have—

'Ow!'

'I'll pull—'

'Don't! It stings, that's all.' I grasp around his waist and hold him where he is. 'Just wait a minute. Just ... wait.'

His arms shake. He presses his head into the pillow. He counts under his breath. He lifts his head. He whispers.

'I'm sorry, baby.'

'Why do you call me that? I'm not a baby.'

He mutters. 'You think I don't know that?'

'I'm not sure I like it.'

'You can say it to me.'

'Baby?'

He lowers himself onto his elbows, slowly and carefully so he doesn't push further inside. He smooths hair off my face. I wriggle under him. I'm not as sore as I was.

His lip lifts. 'I dare you.'

I breathe the word slowly into his mouth. 'Baby.'

He smiles against my lips. 'You can do better. More conviction.'

This time I draw out the 'a'. 'Baaaby.'

He stares at the dimple near my mouth. *Really* stares, as if he's never seen it before.

He presses his thumb into the groove. He runs a fingertip along my bottom lip. He traces the seam between my lips. And when I open my mouth a little, he lowers his head and follows the path his finger took with the tip of his tongue. He's *too* gentle. I wrap my arms tightly around his neck and kiss him back properly. My body sinks into the mattress. I soften. He shifts, moans, slips further inside me. I feel a stretch but that's all. I lift my legs and join them around his hips.

His voice is a murmur. 'I want you, Jem.'

I look into his eyes. 'I'm scared to want you.'

At first his movements are slow and drawn out, careful and cautious. But he can't hold back for long. The intensity builds. Our bodies heat and sweat, our breaths are loud, our movements frantic. Until finally, our arms and legs bound up, we find what it is that we need. For him it's release. For me it's something else. My body is heavy, weighted and warm. I hold him inside. I keep him safe.

CHAPTER

48

*The grass, early autumn gold, is soft beneath my feet. Finn runs behind
me but his shadow is in front. My arms are out wide and the wind blows
through my hair. I laugh as I leap his shadow. I hear him call my name.
Jemima.*

*I turn but he's gone. And so is his shadow. How did I lose him so quickly?
I look up at the sun, still shining brightly. It blinds me and I close my eyes.*

*I'm in the stables at Thornbrooke. Blackjack is hanging from the lead
rope; twisted neck and frightened eyes. When I tear at the knot, my fingers
slip and slide. I put them in my mouth to stop the bleeding …*

My tears drip silently onto Finn's chest. I pray he won't wake up.
That he'll never—

'Jemima?'

I wipe my face with the backs of my hands. My fingers sting.
I try to roll away but he pulls me back. He circles my wrists with
long firm fingers. He looks into my eyes. His face is a blur.

'What's wrong?'

'Blackjack.' When I hold back a sob, I hiccup. 'I shouldn't have tied him up.'

He runs his lips over my cheeks, collecting the tears. He tightens an arm around my shoulders and clamps my legs between his. He takes my hand and sucks a finger and then another. He must taste the blood. I pull and tug but he won't let go.

'Let me,' he whispers. 'You think I care?'

I squeeze my eyes shut as he folds me into his arms.

I tiptoe through my room as the sun sneaks through the curtains. It must be after six. I'm going to be late. I'll have to put tape on my thumb before I do up the button on my jeans, or it'll bleed again.

Finn is asleep on his back. His lips are softly curved; his lashes are dark on his cheeks. He stirs, rolls onto his side and stretches out an arm. He stiffens. And then he sits bolt upright. He sees me in the shadows and mutters under his breath. He holds out his hand.

'Jem.'

I open a drawer and take out a pair of socks. 'Finn.'

'Come here.' I tuck in my shirt and sit on the edge of the bed. I pull on a sock. By the time I straighten, he's close behind me. He puts his hand on my shoulder, moves my collar out of the way and kisses the side of my neck. Desire, hot and sweet, shoots to my toes. 'You should have woken me.'

'Why?'

He reaches to the side table for his watch and puts it on. It's important to him, the exact time, not the time that comes through the window. Other than his watch, he's naked. He's tousled. I'd like to touch his body, stroke his cheek. I'd like to kiss his cranky mouth.

'Can you turn this way, please?' I do as he asks, put my feet on the bed and pull on the second sock. They have horseshoes on them. A present from Gus. When I look up, Finn puts his finger under my chin and raises it further. 'Are you not a morning person?'

'No.'

He kisses me hard on the mouth. 'That's the third time we've slept together.'

'I guess.'

He takes my hand and holds it firmly, lifting my thumb to the light and examining it. 'Did you go back to sleep?'

I shake my head.

'Do you remember what you promised last night?'

I nod.

'Say it.'

'I'll meet you at the zoo. We'll come back here, see to the horses, then go out for dinner.'

'Like a regular couple.'

When I don't reply, he squeezes my hand. 'You're running late, aren't you? Leave the horses, I'll see to them.'

'Thank you.' I pull my hand free. 'Sapphie will come at nine. She knows what to do with Vegemite.'

When our eyes meet, memories flash through my mind. His taste and scent. The words he said, the look in his eyes, the way he felt inside me. I'm not sure who moves first, but all of a sudden I'm in his arms.

'How do you feel?' he says, pulling me closer. 'Are you sore?'

I shake my head. 'Are you?'

He laughs. 'No.' He kisses the top of my head. 'I'll send you a text at lunch.'

I run my finger down his cheek as he fastens the button on my jeans. 'Finn?'

'Yes?'

'I think … Everything about us. We're so different. Are you sure about dinner?'

'Yes.'

'You're already bad-tempered.'

'I'm merely concerned.'

'We'll argue.'

His eyes are unsettled like clouds in a storm. 'Trust me.'

He works with wild animals. He writes thousands and thousands of words. He fastens buttons, untangles knots. I take his hands and fold down his fingers. I run my lips across his knuckles. Before he can see the tears in my eyes, I jump from the bed and leave him.

CHAPTER

49

Like a regular couple. Finn wants me to trust him. He didn't want a one-night stand. But he didn't say things were forever, either. Gus told me months ago what it was like for him and Maggie.

All. Or nothing.

Am I like that too? Am I in love with Finn?

The road ahead is straight, with a mirage of heat at the end. The paddocks are dry and dusty. Either side of the road, herds of cows shelter under gum trees.

What's it like in Switzerland? Mountains and pine trees.

Scotland? Biting winds, barren moors and stocky Shetland ponies.

Just before nine, I pull over in the long tree-lined driveway of Mandy Flanagan's stud and call Mike.

'Just checking up on you,' I say. 'How did you sleep?'

'Like a log. You?'

'Pretty good. I'll come by next week. Do you need anything?'

'Nothing I can't get for myself.'

'Call if something comes up.'

'Should I write Dr Blackwood a note?'

'What for?'

'To say thank you. I could do it from you and me.'

'If you like, but he wouldn't expect it. He wanted to find out the truth.'

'Have you called the psychologist yet?'

'I'm seeing her next week.'

'Good to hear.'

'Mike, remember when you said I might have left pieces behind when I put myself together? Do you really think I did?'

'You're a good girl, Jet, but ...' He whistles. 'You remember what your dad used to call you when you were a mite?'

'His wild colonial girl.'

'That's the one. I know you're all grown up, but a leopard don't change its spots. Sometimes you got to do what comes natural, have a bit of confidence. You get what I mean?'

Trust.

Fear.

Loss.

Finn might break my heart.

But maybe it's time to be brave.

♘

I listen to Finn's message as I walk to the giraffe pen: *Jem. I'm at the rhino yards. Meet you at the clinic at three. Let me know you get this. Finn.* I send back a text with an image of a giraffe.

It's one-thirty when Andrew catches up to me in the buggy. He parks near the elephant enclosure, takes off his hat and fans his face.

'I appreciated the rain we had last year,' he says, as we walk side-by-side, 'but nothing since. I've had enough of this heat.'

'What do you expect in the middle of summer?' I push back my hat and smile. 'They're saying it'll rain next month.'

Afaafa is already in the yard. She's halfway through her pregnancy, but her shape looks much the same. It's wrong to think that animals, especially wild animals like giraffe, share human feelings. But Afaafa gazes at me with soft brown eyes. She appears to be happy to see me.

'Hey, girl,' I mutter under my breath, 'it's good to see you too.'

'Pardon?' Andrew says.

I pick up my toolbox and sort through it. 'Nothing.'

'You'll continue to look after her for as long as she tolerates it?'

When a keeper holds out a long stick with a carrot on the end, Afaafa reaches for it, putting one of her front feet, bent at the knee, on the block in front of me. She'll never trust me a hundred per cent, maybe not even ten per cent, but we have a connection now, like I have with my horses, and Finn has with his rhinos.

I pick up a file, specially shortened to make it easier to work on her foot. 'Sure I will.'

An hour later, as Andrew and I walk back to the elephant enclosure, I see Precious near the moat. She walks towards her smaller night yard and the tree that shades it, her trunk swaying gracefully.

'She's moving well,' I say. 'No problems with her toenail?'

'It seems to be fine.' He smiles. 'She's looking this way.'

'She'll be wondering why Mike isn't with me.'

When we reach Andrew's buggy, I roll up my sleeves and undo a couple of buttons, flap my shirt around to let in some air. 'That's my workday done. You go ahead, I might walk back the long way.'

I stretch out the stiffness in my back as I join the couples and families meandering along the bitumen pathway. I pass giraffe, blackbuck and addax on my right, and ostrich on my left. Last time I was here, there were four white rhinoceros in the enclosures. Today there's only one female and the male. Walking through the 'staff only' gate and following another path, I see why that is. The mother rhino and her calf are in the smallest rhino yard, used for animal observation and treatment. The yard is square and the metal fence is a couple of metres high.

Finn and Catriona have their backs to me and are watching the rhinos through the railings. Justin, a work-experience student, is leaning against the railings near the shed, and doesn't see me either. He's standing on his toes on a crate, holding his phone towards the rhino calf, and talking. I guess he's making a video. He's very tall for seventeen.

Aditi is one of the largest rhinos at the zoo, and the biggest female by far. She has a giant grey head with a wide square-shaped mouth, and one large and one small horn. The skin above her front legs folds in creases. Her calf Chimbu is only six months old. He has a small horn on the end of his nose, and a bump where his second horn will grow. His hairy oval-shaped ears twist left and right like antennae. When Aditi lies down, Chimbu gambols around her as if wanting her to get up and play. A cloud of dust forms at his feet.

Finn and Catriona talk with their heads close together. She's wearing a similar zoo outfit to mine, but her shirt is tucked in, and her breasts fill it out. She doesn't have to roll her pants up at the ankles or stuff them into her boots. She laughs at something Finn says, and the way she puts her hand on his arm suggests …

Catriona likes animals and is friendly and clever. Finn likes and respects her. I have no reason to dislike or resent her unless …

I'm jealous.

'Hello, Jet.' One of the keepers, Fritz, stands next to me. 'Here to manicure rhinos?'

'Provided they're anaesthetised.'

He laughs. 'I saw you with Andrew before. Who are you waiting on now? Finn? He and Catriona have been here for hours. They should be winding up soon.'

'I'm supposed to meet him at the clinic.' I cross my arms, uncross them. 'I was running early, but … I don't want to disturb him. I think I'll head back now.'

I've only taken a step when I see Justin grasp the top rail of the fence. He glances quickly at Finn and Catriona, still deep in conversation, before climbing up the bars and straddling the top.

Fritz stiffens. 'Bloody idiot,' he mutters. 'Hey!'

Justin ignores the shout, or doesn't hear it. He still has his phone in one hand and it's trained on Chimbu. The calf is only a few metres away, snuffling the ground between the fence and his mother.

When Chimbu looks up, Justin leans to one side to capture the image. Fritz shouts again, louder this time. Justin starts, loses his balance and, as if in slow motion, tumbles into the yard.

A lot of things happen at once. Finn and Catriona stop talking. Chimbu trips over his feet to get to his mother. Aditi scrambles upright and faces Justin, crouched on the ground and holding his leg.

'Help!' he shouts, his voice breaking. 'Help!'

Finn, on the other side of the fence, walks towards Justin. 'Keep your voice down,' he says firmly but calmly, his eyes fixed on Aditi. 'Don't move.'

He doesn't clamber up the fence like Justin did. He takes two steps back and leaps to the top. Within a heartbeat he jumps to the ground, landing on his feet and facing Aditi.

When I gasp and jump forwards, Fritz holds out an arm and blocks me. 'Wait.'

Aditi looks at Finn. Then her gaze swings away and goes back to Justin. She lowers her head and snorts, taking a step towards him. Stripes of sunlight, long and sharp, shoot through the railings onto the ground.

I can't hear what Finn is saying as he talks to Catriona, standing on the other side of the fence, but she nods a few times before walking away. She talks quietly into her radio. When Fritz joins her, he points out that I'm here and she gestures to the shed.

'Get the portable steps, Jet. Quick as you can.'

Aditi looks no less threatening by the time I get back. Catriona takes the steps out of my hands and she and Fritz put them up against the fence. I'm standing out of the way, but hear Finn's voice clearly.

'Justin,' he says. 'Do exactly as I say.'

'My ankle,' Justin says, clutching his leg.

'Hold onto the fence. Pull yourself up. Move slowly.'

'But what about—'

'Do as I say.'

Using the rails for support, Justin pulls himself upright and stands on one leg. Fritz climbs the steps on the other side of the fence. Another keeper appears, and climbs up next to Fritz.

'Turn your back on Aditi,' Finn says quietly to Justin. 'Lift your arms.'

The keepers lean over the fence and take hold of Justin's arms.

Aditi takes a step towards Justin, and then another. Chimbu, by his mother's side, mirrors her movements. Aditi swings her head and …

'Get him out!' Finn shouts, running in front of Aditi, before dropping and rolling along the ground. The rhino pulls up short, disoriented, as the keepers haul Justin over the fence. But when

Finn gets to his haunches, Aditi pivots towards him. Her body quivers with tension. She lowers her head.

The keepers climb the steps again. 'Finn,' Fritz says, his voice soft but tense. 'Get over here.'

Finn's eyes are on Aditi. 'I'm working on it,' he says.

The keepers are metres away. Finn takes a sideways step towards them. An ambulance siren wails. Catriona swears under her breath. My chest is so tight that it hurts. My hands are unsteady so I cross my arms to still them.

Another keeper arrives and stands behind the gate. He's carrying something. A tranquilliser gun? When he loosens a bolt on the gate, Chimbu skitters sideways, away from his mother. But that brings him closer to the keepers on the steps. He spooks again. Now he's between the fence on one side and Finn on the other.

Aditi charges.

Finn sprints across the yard and leaps onto the fence. He clings to the rail and swings in an arc, bringing one leg over the top. When Aditi crashes into the fence, Catriona cries out.

Finn hauls himself over the bar and falls to the ground.

I reach him first. He's on his back. His eyes are closed, his lashes dark. I crouch by his side, my arm hovering. I touch his hand.

'Finn?'

Yesterday he shaved. Not today. I rest one hand on the side of his face and the other on his chest. I feel for the beats of his heart. Blood seeps through his pants and into the dirt.

'Finn?'

I'm sure I speak out loud. So why is it so quiet? Catriona runs towards us, drops to her knees and feels for Finn's pulse. Andrew leans over me. When did he get here? He takes my arm and pulls me out of the way.

He's on one side of Finn. Catriona is on the other. They know what to do. What *not* to do. Justin is sobbing. Fritz holds the radio to his mouth. Lorenzo arrives, gesturing with his hands.

I see everything but hear nothing.

I've been here before—on the day my mother died.

It's not often that so many people make so little noise.

I crouch by the shed. The ambulance arrives. All the sounds come back.

Andrew tells the paramedics that Finn knocked himself out, though not for long. Catriona tells them that Finn has a gash in his leg and it will need stitches, but in the meantime she's bandaged the wound to slow down the bleeding. I hear Finn's voice, asking questions and answering them. The paramedics check Finn out and confirm what the others have already said. They re-strap his leg. Justin's ankle gets strapped up too, and as soon as that's done he hobbles to Finn and sits on the ground. When he presses his sleeve against his face, Finn grasps his arm and talks intently. Justin nods and sniffs.

There's something about the tall paramedic that ... He walks from the ambulance, wheeling a stretcher along the path towards Finn. He's staring at me, too. He takes off his cap, shoving it into a pocket.

'Jet?' he says, grinning. 'It is, isn't it?'

I lift a hand. 'Hey, Simon.'

'We have to stop meeting like this.' He jerks his head in Finn's direction. 'He gives you a spot of trouble, your bloke, doesn't he?'

Last time the ambulance was called, I'd kissed Finn to death. 'Yes.'

He winks. 'You reckon he's worth it?'

He thinks we're a couple. Are we?

'Jem!' Finn calls out. 'Come here!'

Simon laughs. 'Get over there, Jet, before we take him away.'

Finn's face is so pale. His eyes are so blue. His bandage is white. And red.

If I lost him, what would be left of me?

When I kneel by his side, he searches my face. 'Jem?' He frowns. 'Why are you here?'

'I finished early. I came to meet you.'

'When?'

'A while ago.'

'You're as white as a sheet.'

'You too.'

He holds out a hand. 'Take it.'

I shake my head as I push his arm back to his side. 'You have to go to the hospital.' I undo the top buttons of his shirt and pull out the disk, carefully smoothing the kinks in the cord and laying it on his chest.

'Dinner?' he mumbles.

'Not tonight.'

His eyes flutter closed as Simon straps him to the stretcher.

'Finn?'

'All good,' Simon reassures me. 'He's had a shock, lost a bit of blood. Just having a snooze.'

I touch the disk. 'You'll check with the hospital, won't you, before they do anything? I don't think he's allergic to medicines, but some people have allergies to iodine, don't they? Can you make sure …'

'We'll take care of him, love. Don't you worry about that.'

I stand back as Simon pulls levers and raises the stretcher. Catriona walks towards us, Andrew by her side. She touches Finn's arm and smiles at Simon. 'I'll travel with him.'

Simon glances at me. 'Jet? I've only got one spot free.'

What can I tell him?

I've learnt about love. All. *Or nothing.*

I've known about loss for a very long time.

'Catriona saw what happened, she was standing closer.' I push words through the tears in my throat. 'She can explain things better to the doctors, medical things.' I roll down my sleeves, fumble with the buttons on the cuffs. 'I'll come to the hospital later. I'll see him then.'

CHAPTER
50

The sky is dusky blue, streaked with red and gold, when my phone rings at seven on Sunday morning. I turn off the tap at the trough before I answer.

'Jet Kincaid.'

'It's Finn.'

'How do you feel? Why are you up so early?'

Silence. 'You were in the hospital waiting room yesterday. Why didn't you come to my room?'

'Andrew said you were asleep.'

'Not until the evening.'

'The doctors were in and out. So was Andrew. And Catriona. Justin's parents too. I thought you'd be sick of visitors.'

'They're doing my discharge now. When can I see you?'

'I … Sapphie's here today.'

'So? What's the matter, Jem?'

'You should rest. I can explain. I'll do it soon. I promise.'

It's late on Wednesday afternoon and I'm on the verandah, sitting on the pew and eating an apple, when Finn drives past the cottage. My hair is sweat-salty. I put on the first shirt I saw in the half-light this morning, a faded moss green, worn thin at the elbows. The cuffs are undone. The tape on my thumb was white this morning. Now it's dirty grey.

He only limps a little as he walks from his car and stands at the bottom of the steps, his hands shoved deep into his pockets. His eyes are twice as dark as the cloudless sky behind him. His lips are tight.

'I was giving you time,' he says. 'I got sick of waiting.'

My chest is in a vice and someone is turning the handle. I throw my apple core into the garden.

'I thought I'd see you at the Follyfoot function next week.'

'You owe me an explanation.'

'Andrew said your leg is getting better.'

'You haven't returned my calls.'

I look beyond him to the horses, waiting at the gate. 'I let you down. I knew you'd be angry.'

He walks up the steps. 'Can we do this one item at a time?' He sits next to me on the pew, close but not touching. 'Thornbrooke.'

'It's over.'

'It's not. The man who assaulted you, has he threatened you again?'

'No.'

'Who was it?'

'Hasn't Morrissey told you?'

'He won't give Nate a name. He claims it was a misunderstanding; there was no intention to harm you.'

'I knew it would be my word against Morrissey's and the other man's.'

'He hurt you.'

'Getting shinned on a tow bar? That happens a lot. You don't get locked up for pushing someone around.'

Finn frowns. 'You could have applied for a court order, compelled him to leave you alone.'

'Nate might have lost Morrissey if I'd done that. Not that I even knew he was after him. I was afraid of Morrissey, that he would retaliate against Mike and me. I didn't know what your report would say.' I clear my throat. 'I was scared.'

He shifts on the pew, raises his hand and drops it. 'Finish this, Jem. You have to go to the police. Mike agrees. He had no idea what had happened.'

'Why did you tell him?'

'You were hurt!' He lowers his voice. 'He couldn't remember the man's name.'

'I didn't report it when it happened, that wouldn't look good. The bruises have gone.'

'I saw your shin. Nate and I will back you.'

'Morrissey is locked up. There's no reason for anyone to hassle me now.'

He stands abruptly and walks to the railing, like he's too wound up to sit any longer. 'You only gave Mike half the story. Why?'

'I didn't want him to worry.'

He turns, shoves his hands into his pockets again. 'Like he doesn't worry already? Like the town doesn't worry about you already?'

'Is this something else you want to talk about? Your second item?'

'Call it what you like.'

'Get it over with, then.'

He makes an effort, holds onto his temper. 'People liked and respected your parents,' he says. 'They have a great affection for you. But they also feel responsible. You left here once, to stay at Thornbrooke.' He blows out a breath. 'And look what happened there.'

I lift my chin. 'Some good came out of it. I started working for Mike.'

'And that's all you wanted?'

'Yes!'

His lips firm. 'I met your first boss a few weeks ago. He told me he didn't need another apprentice, but there was something about you he couldn't look past. You were curious and meticulous. You worked hard.'

'He was good to me.'

'He said he contacted you a year after Thornbrooke, he wanted to take you back. He's highly respected in racing. He makes good money; he's in demand here and elsewhere. Mike encouraged you to get broader experience. Why didn't you?'

'Mike's a good farrier too.'

'For over fifty years, he's worked within a two-hundred-kilometre radius.'

'There's nothing wrong with that.'

'I agree. But Mike wasn't your first choice.'

'I do interesting work at the zoo.'

'And how did that come about? You're too young to have worked your way up. Did you network with professionals, or board members, or sponsors like Edward? No way.'

'Andrew supports me.'

'He pores over journals and radiographs, you look at movement, and diagnose on instinct. You're good at what you do, exceptionally good. But he found you by chance.'

'I'm no good at selling myself, is that what you're saying?'

'It's more than that. Andrew knows that if he asks too much, puts too much pressure on, you'll walk away.'

I consider the fading mahogany stain on the pew, the flakes of peeling varnish. I sit again, perch on the edge. 'Are you enjoying this? Picking over my pathetic little life?'

'It's a good life, Jemima. But there's more.'

A flock of pink-and-grey galahs fly overhead. Squawking and screeching, they swoop over the shed and down to the valley.

'And you'd know all about that, wouldn't you?' I swallow. 'Your life is different, it always has been.'

'My childhood was working poor and mind-numbingly ordinary. I went to school and haunted the library. I dragged my family to the zoo. Every summer, to shut Fern up, we stayed in a god-forsaken campground on Scotland's west coast. It wasn't anything special.'

'I don't read books. I left school early. I didn't go to university.'

'You're intelligent. I know that, so do you.'

'I don't want to change like you did, straddle two worlds.'

'I never said you had to.'

I sit further back on the pew, lift my feet onto the seat, bend my knees and wrap my arms around them. 'Have we finished?'

He shakes his head. 'No. I want to talk about what happened on Saturday.'

'I'm sorry I didn't see you at the hospital. I felt ... there were too many people.'

He sits next to me, wincing when he stretches out his leg. 'You were upset when I got hurt. It was unfortunate you were there to see it.'

'Justin was in trouble. You did the right thing; you did exactly what I'd expect you to do. And maybe ...' my voice catches, 'maybe it was good I saw it, because it made me face the truth. You don't need to go to Africa to find adventure. I think you'll find it whatever you do,' I wave towards the river, the cliff, 'and wherever you go. And that's not a bad thing. It's the way you are.'

He narrows his eyes. 'You don't like the way I am?'

'Like I said, we're different. I knew that already. But seeing you with the rhinos, and with the people you work with, Andrew, Catriona ...'

'You're giving up.' His voice is flat and hard.

I sit further forwards on the pew again, holding the seat tightly either side of my legs. 'I made a mistake.'

He shifts on the seat. 'For fuck's sake.' His eyes are so blue. Concerned and blue and ... He misses the blue skies in Africa. He thought this might happen. He didn't want to rush me.

I jump to my feet, walk to the railing. 'Please don't make it worse.'

'Worse than this?'

The shadows from the gum are lengthening, stretching over the straggly yellow grass. 'I'm better on my own.'

'Bullshit.'

I face him, run my hands down my jeans. 'This is my home. I'm happy here, happy with my life.'

'I haven't asked you to leave it.'

'One day you would. Or you'd be the one to leave. You'd get bored or miss adventure too much, or ...' My voice catches. I clear my throat. 'I don't like change. I don't take risks.'

He stands. Now his eyes are stormy blue. 'Not even calculated ones?'

I rub my hands down my jeans. 'I've tried to explain.' I turn and face the valley. Freckle and Lollopy are foraging for grass. Vegemite, at the gate, stamps his foot. I shake my head. 'I'm sorry.'

He curses under his breath as he walks behind me, to the far side of the verandah. He grips the railing with both hands.

'Friday night, what was that to you?'

On Friday night I was happy. It wasn't for long, but I was trusting and brave and adventurous.

'You know what it was.'

'And now you tell me it's over?'

My shirt smells of smoke. It's creased and faded; there's a stain on the front. His shirt is fresh and clean. It'll smell of soap powder.

I cross my arms. 'Yes.'

He turns. And in four long strides he's standing in front of me. 'I want you to give me a chance. It's not much to ask.'

'I don't regret ...' Tears clog my throat. 'I don't regret Friday. Or the other nights.'

He holds out a hand. 'Take it.'

I ignore the ache in my heart. I take a step back.

He brushes past me and walks down the steps two at a time. He pulls up short and spins around. He looks me up and down, from my tangled hair to my dusty brown boots.

'You're a coward.'

His words fly around me like a dust storm in summer, drying my tongue and taking my breath. When I open my mouth to defend myself, not a single word comes out.

What would I say anyway?

I was a wild colonial girl. I had dreams. I took chances.

I could do anything.

Not now. Not any more.

Finn has driven away by the time I walk from the home paddock, pushing a wheelbarrow of manure to dump on the compost pile.

I finish my chores and return to the cottage. A piece of paper is folded neatly in half and wedged in the fly-screen door.

Edward sometimes writes in simple language, thinking it will make it easier for me to read. Finn writes in the same way that he speaks. He must know I have the type of dyslexia where sometimes I can read and sometimes I can't. He would have looked dyslexia up, researched it, assuming he didn't know about it already. He would know dyslexia is different for everyone who has it.

I swipe away tears with the back of my hand.

I know him, just like I said on Friday night.

Jemima,
Please call Nate (I enclose his card), or me, with any concerns regarding Morrissey and the man who assaulted you.

My lease is up. Accordingly, I've left the keys to Kincaid House on the nail behind the shutter.

I'll see you at Follyfoot on Friday week.
Finn

CHAPTER
51

The Follyfoot arena is buzzing with children, horses and volunteers. Visitors sit in the stands with sponsors, waiting for the display to begin.

Lollopy, his bushy black forelock concealing his sparkly red headband, is tied to the float next to Chili and patiently waiting. 'Won't be long, boy,' I say, as I tighten Chili's girth.

I'm about to lead the horses to the arena when I see Finn, twenty metres away with a jacket flung over one shoulder. Mike, selling raffle tickets by the gate, calls him over, and he gets out his wallet. He's with Catriona, and there's another woman too. They all buy tickets. Catriona waves and walks away, but the other woman links her arm through Finn's. She's tall, with shiny dark hair. When he turns his head to speak with her, she looks at him intently.

Finn isn't limping any more, but his gait isn't quite right yet. He slows when he sees me, and so does the woman. She's very attractive, wearing jeans, low-heeled boots and a silky green shirt. There's something familiar about her face. She looks like …

She's Fern, Finn's sister. She butted into the Skype call he had with his parents. Her eyes open wider. She elbows him hard in the ribs.

'You're Jet Kincaid, aren't you?' she says, holding out her hand. Her voice is deep, a little stilted. 'I'm Fern Blackwood.' She has a beautiful wide mouth. Her eyes are as blue as Finn's.

When I fumble with Chili's lead rope, Finn takes it out of my hand.

'That's right,' I say, as I shake her hand. 'Jet.'

She winks at her brother. 'Wait till Mam hears about this.'

At the Christmas party, I'd told Finn I didn't want to have sex, *especially* not with him. Fern read our lips, and raised her middle finger when he told her to keep quiet. A blush moves up my neck and warms my cheeks.

'Jemima,' Finn says, nodding stiffly. 'How are you?'

Will loving him ever stop hurting? 'Fine, thanks.' I make an effort to smile. 'Mike forced you to buy raffle tickets, didn't he? Sorry about that.'

I hold out my hand for Chili's lead rope, folding down my fingers so the tape isn't as obvious. 'I'd better get these horses to the kids.'

When our hands touch, my skin heats again. I can't look at Finn, or his sister.

'The display will start soon, then the speeches.' My words run together. 'Later on there's a BBQ. Have a good night.'

'Thank you,' Fern says, as Lollopy nuzzles her palm.

Finn nods abruptly. 'Thanks.'

Was it a decade ago that we slept together? Or a year, a day, a minute? What would he do if I leant against his chest?

Thump-thump. Thump-thump. Thump-thump.
I'm certain he'd push me away.

Most of the Follyfoot children sit at the front of the stand, watching as the more experienced riders show off their skills. Laurence rides Chili for the final time, telling anyone who'll listen that this is his last year at Follyfoot, but he'll continue to volunteer on Fridays. Chelsea rides confidently on Cascade, cantering around the arena and trotting over the low cavaletti jumps with her arms out in front, to the side, in the air, to show how good her balance is. I swear her legs have grown longer in the break.

After the display, I lead Chili back to the float and pull off his saddle. 'How'd you like to work with Chelsea? She's desperate to go to pony club, and to compete, and Cascade's not up to that. I'd miss having you at home, and so would Sapphie, but we're thinking of finding you agistment near Dubbo. That way, Chelsea could take you out all the time, and you'd get to go to shows again.' When I take off his bridle, he rubs his head against my shirt, leaving a mark. I scratch around his ears, then smooth down his forelock. 'Thanks for that.'

Finn stands on the hay bales stacked in the arena when it's time for him to speak. He addresses the children and their parents, promising to keep his talk brief and saying that, probably like them, he has difficulty concentrating when he's hungry and can smell sausages on the BBQ. He starts with a game, 'What Am I?'

Australian.

Carnivorous.

Long tail.

Strong jaw.

Endangered.

Marsupial.

Black fur with white markings.

Found in Tasmania.

He's only halfway through the list when the kids start shouting 'Tasmanian Devil', but he pretends he can't hear them until he's done. By the time I walk to the back of the stand and find a seat next to Andrew, Finn has asked the children to put their hands up, so he can answer their questions in turn.

He tells them about Devil facial tumour disease, and the important work scientists do in working out what causes the cancer and how it spreads. Conservationists have helped to protect the species by isolating a healthy and genetically diverse population, and letting them breed on an island off the coast, until it's safe for them to go back to the mainland.

Andrew nudges my arm. 'He's good with all age groups, isn't he? We'll miss him.'

'He's going then?'

'He's got the funding to stay, but yes … he'll be around for another month or so, but then he's moving on.'

I swallow. 'That's a shame for the zoo.'

Finn tells the children he's never had the courage to get on a horse, and then he asks them what it is he's missing out on. The younger children tell him horses are big, and friendly, and gentle, and physiotherapy hurts much less when you do it on a horse. The older children tell him they like the challenge of being up high and going fast, and doing things other people can't. Finn tells them that the connection and respect they have for the horse will stay with them forever. He knows that, he says, because that's what he felt when he saw his first rhino, and that's the way he feels still.

'A rhino stabbed you in the leg!' one of the children shouts out.

Finn shrugs. 'Aditi wanted me out of the way. She was protecting her calf. It was my fault.'

'No hard feelings, then?' a parent says.

Finn laughs. 'I wish I'd run faster.'

The children all have a physical disability; some of them have intellectual and learning difficulties. When Finn says the horses will teach them to do good things in their lives, it's easy to see that he means it.

I'm about to load the horses into the float when Finn steps off the path. Fern is not far behind him, talking to Andrew.

'We have an early flight to Tasmania,' Finn says.

I untie Lollopy and lead him to the back of the float. 'Thanks for coming.'

He glances at the tape on my index finger. 'How are you?'

I hold up my hand. 'This, you mean?'

'Yes.'

I loop Lollopy's rope around my arm and undo one of the bolts. 'Knowing what happened at Thornbrooke is helping. The psychologist thinks so too. I should have thanked you earlier for that.'

'I regret how difficult it's been for you.'

I'm dreaming less. And when I do, I'm working on turning my thinking around. It wasn't my fault the horses died. If I'd been able to call others in, it wouldn't have made a difference. Blackjack's twisted neck? I won't forget that, but the memories will fade. Fade like before.

Before I met Finn.

I run my hand under Lollopy's mane. 'Thanks, anyway.'

Fern joins us, still smiling warmly. Hasn't Finn told her I'm a coward? When she touches his arm, he turns towards her. Her long, graceful fingers fly through the air, hovering and darting. He signs back, just as assuredly as her. From time to time, they glance at me.

At the end of their conversation, she pokes him in the chest. 'Well?' she says.

He shakes his head, a short, sharp motion. He frowns. 'No.'

I blurt into the silence. 'Have fun in Tasmania.'

'Finn and I are climbing over there,' Fern says, poking Finn in the ribs. 'So long as he can keep up.'

'The stitches came out today. I'll strap my leg.'

'Mam was worried about snakes and spiders,' Fern says to me. 'She didn't factor in,' she counts on her fingers, 'an anaphylactic shock, a goring and a bashing.' She faces Finn again. 'Did they ever catch those men?'

He touches his lip, traces the scar. 'I'm still looking.'

She laughs. 'Looking where?'

He holds out his right hand. 'His fist was too close to see the detail, but one of them had a tattoo,' he runs a line from his thumb to his index finger, 'right about here.'

One of them had a tattoo …

What would Finn do if I told him it might be Caruthers? He'd go to the police. I could go to the police, but …

Caruthers would deny everything. Morrissey would probably back him.

If I'd told Finn at the start what I knew about Thornbrooke, he might never have been hurt.

I was messed up about Thornbrooke when Caruthers frightened me. I'm still messed up … but less than I was.

Caruthers has been looking for work. Didn't he give me his number? He won't be hard to track down.

It was Sunday morning before I worked up the courage to call Caruthers. I left a message, and a few hours later he called back. He was working in Queensland, but was driving home at the end of the week. We arranged to meet on Saturday afternoon.

When I pull off the main road, just before the turn-off to Dubbo, it's after four o'clock. Even so, the carpark spots are taken, so I leave my ute on the broad grass strip between the service road and the toilet block. Locals and visitors come here every week to buy freshly grown produce. I go from stall to stall, filling a cardboard box with fruit and vegetables, so the stallholders know I'm here. I buy a coffee from the cart, then sit on one of the benches that surround the picnic tables and rummage for a handful of strawberries, laying them on a napkin. A shadow takes shape as I wrap my hands around the coffee cup and blow through the spout in the lid.

'G'day, Jet.'

The hairs on the back of my neck stand on end. 'Jason. How was Queensland?'

He sits on the bench opposite. 'How'd you know I was there?'

'You told me you were working up north.'

He slaps his forehead. 'Got it! Big night out with the boys last night.'

'Thanks for stopping by.'

'Pretty surprised to get your call.'

I straighten my arms but keep hold of my coffee. The table is close to Rosa's stall. She's eighty at least, but wiry and tough, and her grandson John is with her. He works in the fields and markets and his arms are just as beefy as Caruthers's.

'I'm not one to hold grudges,' I say.

'Thanks for keeping your mouth shut. Really appreciate it.'

'I was curious about Morrissey. Have you seen him?'

'In jail? No way.'

'He tried to set me up.'

When Caruthers picks up a strawberry, the eagle on his hand opens its beak. 'I didn't ask questions, just helping a mate, needed the cash. Only a bit of horseplay, like I said.'

'Thanks for leaving Mike alone.'

'I have my standards. Young kids and pensioners, I wouldn't rough up neither of them.' He forages through the box and takes a plum, tossing it high in the air and catching it with one hand. It reminds me of what he did with my tools. My mouth is dry. I swallow.

'Well … thanks anyway.' My phone is in my front pocket, hard against my hip. Will it record through my jeans? I didn't think to test that. 'Morrissey must have done something serious if he's in jail. You sure you don't know what it was?'

Caruthers moves his jaw around. His teeth are large and stained by cigarettes. 'Haven't got a clue.'

'Because all you do is horseplay, right?'

'You said no grudges.'

'Just curious.'

He pinches the bridge of his nose. 'Morrissey never paid my doctor's bills, that pisses me off.'

'What doctor's bills?'

'Busted nose.' He puts the plum in his mouth and talks through the pulp. 'Morrissey put me onto a bloke he said was from the city. All I planned to do was rough him up a bit, give him a scare. Where'd he learn to fight like that? In a bloody cage, I reckon.'

I carefully open my fingers and let go of my cup. I flatten my hands on the table. I focus on my breathing. *One. Two. Three.*

'Right.'

'He cracked my brother's rib and twisted my mate's arm something awful. After that, it was on for young and old.' He slaps the table. 'Self-defence and all that.'

A wasp, long and thin with two sets of wings, hovers over a punnet of raspberries. Finn isn't allergic to bees. Is he allergic to wasps? It wasn't a bee or a wasp that blackened his eye and split his lip. It was three men on a dark night in a backstreet.

I lift my cup to my lips, as if I'm capable of drinking without choking. 'Are you talking about Blackwood?'

Caruthers's arm stills in midair. When he spits out the plum stone it flies past my face, bounces twice on the table and falls to the ground.

His smile is wide but fake. 'What's that to you?'

'I … nothing.'

He takes another strawberry, holds it up between us. He digs out the stalk with a twist of his thumb. 'These are good, Jet. Real sweet and juicy.'

I push the other strawberries towards him. 'Take them.' I stand and pick up my box. 'I have to go.'

He takes my coffee cup, lifts it up and down. 'Why'd you buy this if you weren't going to drink it?'

I look behind me, straight into the sun, so he's just a blur when I face him again. 'I should have bought a cold drink.'

He presses the spout to his mouth. 'Might as well take advantage, then.'

Halfway to the ute, I pause, put my foot on a tree root and pretend to adjust my hold on the box. Caruthers is standing near the mango stall, resting his hip on the counter and drinking my coffee. A truck on the main road chugs up the hill. Two cars overtake it.

My arms are aching by the time I get to the ute. I balance the box on my knee, pull my keys from my pocket and push the remote to unlock the doors. Two beeps. Footsteps behind me. Caruthers's aftershave. When he grabs my arm and swings me around, the box drops to the ground and fruit and vegetables scatter at my feet.

I yank my arm free. 'What do you want?'

His bulky chest and arms block my view of the stalls. He looks left to the service road, fifty metres away. And right to the toilets. There's no one within sight. He pants into my face.

'You think I'm stupid? What's going on?'

I remind myself that it'll be closing time soon, that someone is bound to walk past. I thread the ignition key between two fingers, like a claw. There's warmth in the air but I shiver.

'I don't know what you mean.'

'You're not the only one calling—some jerk keeps hanging up. And someone paid my mate a visit, wanted to know where to find me.'

'That's news to me.'

'Blackwood. Why'd you ask about him?'

'I was curious, that's all.'

He holds out his hand. 'Give me your phone.'

I take a step back. 'No!'

He grabs my arm again, his grip so tight that his fingers turn white. I swing my other arm wide, jabbing him in the neck with the key.

His eyes widen in shock. He lets me go. The key drops onto the dirt.

'Jem!'

Only Finn calls me that.

He charges down the slope from the service road, jumps over a log retaining wall, sprints across the grass and tackles Caruthers around the thighs, bringing him to the ground with a crash. He bends over him and rams a knee between his shoulder blades. Caruthers writhes face-first on the ground, swearing and spitting, as Finn pulls back his head with one hand and twists Caruthers's arm behind his back with the other.

'Enough!' Caruthers croaks.

Finn yanks even harder. 'I'll fucking break it.'

Nate, breathing hard, catches up. 'Whoa there.' When Nate grabs Finn's arm, he pulls it away.

'Fuck off.'

'Finn! Ease up!'

Glaring, Finn lets go of Caruthers. But when Caruthers drags himself to his knees, Finn stomps onto the small of his back, forcing him onto the ground again. Caruthers moans.

Nate, muttering under his breath, shoves Finn out of the way. He takes Caruthers's arm and yanks him to his feet, holding his arms behind his back as he walks him away.

CHAPTER
53

Finn lays his hand on the side of my face. It's a tentative touch. He's shaking.

'What the ...' His jaw is clenched. He's lost his words.

It's only been a week. How could I have missed him so much? I drag my gaze away, to the dusty fruit and vegetables, the upturned cardboard box. 'I have to pick them up.'

When I squat on the ground, he sits next to me, carefully putting his leg to one side.

I leave the plums, raspberries and strawberries for the birds, but we collect everything else, dust them off on our pants and stack them in the box. I sit sideways in the front seat of my ute as Finn paces up and down in front of me. He's favouring his leg.

'You refused to give us a name,' he says. 'And then you do this?' He rubs around the back of his neck. 'Would you care to explain your reasoning?'

I take a deep breath. 'Fern said something at Follyfoot, about you being bashed. That's when I worked out that what had happened to me might not be a one-off, that Caruthers could have hurt you too.' I remember my phone and pull it out of my pocket. The recording icon, a jagged red line, bounces about. I press the double parallel lines. 'He admitted everything, more or less. I taped him.'

'You what?'

'I taped—'

'I heard what you said!'

I sit further back and hold out the phone. 'Should we give it to Nate?'

He snatches it out of my hand. 'Don't move.'

A stallholder sets up a pair of folding chairs and hands me a bottle of water. He sits with me as two police cars turn off the highway and park in the service road. Three officers take Caruthers away in one of the cars, and a fourth officer stays behind. She talks to Finn and Nate and makes notes. After a while, Nate walks towards me.

When the stallholder gets up from his chair, Nate nods politely. He smiles as he sits opposite and holds out my phone.

'The recording might not be admissible as evidence,' he says, 'but it could prove useful anyway. I sent it to my phone.'

'I don't want it. Can you delete it?'

'Already have.' He looks towards Finn. 'They want Finn and me to go to the police station. It's a domestic matter, so my UN connection doesn't sit well with them.'

'Did Finn recognise Caruthers?'

'Sure did, tattoo and all. The police will get a statement from Finn later tonight.'

'Will I have to give one?'

'Tomorrow morning will do for yours. I'll ride shotgun. They'll want the full story.'

'I don't know how I'll go.'

'I reckon Caruthers will put his hand up for the assaults, because he won't want to be connected to Morrissey in other ways. The drug syndicate that Morrissey and Schofield dealt with, that's heavy-duty crime.'

I rub my arms and wince. Another bruise from Caruthers. 'How did you know we were here?'

'Sheer dumb luck.' He grimaces. 'That's what freaked us out. We wanted to get the guy who'd assaulted you—with or without your help. And we figured there might be a connection between what had happened to you and Finn.'

'I only added two and two together last week. Caruthers couldn't meet until today.'

'I've been on to him for a while. Caruthers had the link to Thornbrooke, and a reputation with his fists. Finn only got back from Tasmania last night, so I asked him to tag along as I followed Caruthers, hoping he'd make an ID. We'd been tailing Caruthers for an hour when he turned off here. We couldn't believe it when we saw your ute.'

'I hope you didn't think I was his sidekick.'

Nate laughs. 'Armed with a key? You wouldn't hurt a blowfly. Everyone knows that. Which reminds me.' He holds out my key.

'Did you wash it?'

'You didn't break the skin.'

'Oh.' I shudder as I take it. 'That's kind of a relief.'

He holds in a smile. 'He *might* have a bruise.'

'So much for self-defence.'

'We knew things were bad when you went for him.'

I rub my arms again. 'I'm no fighter.'

'That's what Finn said.' He blows out a breath. 'Using much more colourful language.'

'Let me guess. "What the fuck is she doing?"'

'Way more cursing, but that was the gist.' He tips his head to the side. 'He might've had a point, Jet.'

I watch the taillights of the police car as it turns onto the highway. Finn is alone now. His head is down. He's pacing again.

'If I'd told Finn about Morrissey at the start,' I say quietly, 'he might never have been attacked. I was trying …' My voice catches. 'I was trying to make things right.'

Nate touches my arm. 'By putting yourself at risk? I'm not sure Finn saw it like that.'

'I was careful, meeting in a public place.'

Nate raises his brows. 'You know Finn well, right?'

I nod. 'Pretty well.'

'He and I met on a mountain in Switzerland, years ago. On the end of a rope, in the field, at his desk, he has a reputation.'

'He's good at whatever he does.'

'He's unflappable. He's reasoned and rational. He's dead calm in a crisis. But …' he raises his brows, 'an hour ago he lost his cool. Why do you think that was?'

I clear my throat. 'He was concerned, that's all.'

'What Finn did, what he wanted to do to Caruthers, was totally out of character. Caruthers was unarmed. He couldn't defend himself. He was never going to escape.'

I study my dusty boots. 'What are you saying?'

'When I asked Finn whether there was something between you and him, he almost blew a gasket.' He glances over my shoulder and raises his brows. 'He's still letting off steam by the look of him.'

As Finn walks towards us, I stand and fold my chair, leaning it against a tree. 'I think he's hurt his leg again. Can you ask him about it?'

Nate shrugs. 'Sure. I hadn't noticed.'

I fold the other chair too, then open my back door to check the cardboard box won't fall off the seat when I brake. By the time I turn around, Finn is standing next to Nate.

'I told the officer we'd be there by six,' Finn says.

Nate looks at his watch. 'In which case, we'd better get going.' He turns to me. 'You okay to drive home?'

I hold up my key. 'Yes.'

Finn walks around me and slams the back door. 'I want five minutes first.'

I feel Finn's gaze on the side of my face. I turn to him, my feet slightly apart, arms crossed.

'Thank you for your help. I'd better get home. I have to bring the horses into the—'

'Home paddock.' He glares. 'I won't keep you long.'

Six months ago, on the weekend he moved into the homestead, he wanted to talk about Thornbrooke. When I knocked on the front door, he opened it. His eye was black, his lip was split. I told him I couldn't stay, because I had to bring the horses in. He looked at his watch and said it was only four o'clock.

'Why are you so angry about this?'

'Why do you think?'

'I should have gone to the police.'

'Or talked to me, or Nate. But that's not why I'm angry.'

'Are you going to explain or not?'

He smiles stiffly. 'You care about me. That makes me angry.'

'What?'

He looks away, towards the road. Some of the cars have their headlights on, others haven't. He's breathing so deeply I see the rise and fall of his chest. His light blue shirt is hanging out of his jeans at his hip. He looks at me again.

'You care about me. That's why you refused to leave me after I collapsed in Dubbo, even though, back then, you didn't even like me. That's why you faced Caruthers, even though you were afraid of him. That's why you warned my mother about pollens and bees.'

'I don't know what you mean.'

He narrows his eyes. 'You wrote those notes because you care about me.'

'What?'

'The first note told me you had dyslexia. I think the other note was even more of a test. You wanted to make sure your writing, what it represented, didn't matter to me.'

'I didn't think of it like that, but ...' I swallow. 'Maybe that's true.'

'You let me get physically close because you care about me. That's why you slept with me, had sex with me.'

'Why are you doing this?'

'I'm getting there. You push me away because you're frightened you'll lose me. That means you care.'

The words hang between us. I open my mouth, but shut it when nothing comes out. I try again.

'Losing you ... I know about loss.'

'The anaphylaxis, what I do for a job, is difficult for you.'

'When you collapsed.' My voice is croaky. 'You were wrong. I did like you then.'

He slowly shakes his head. 'The night before we slept together—the third time—I said we had to get to know each other. You said we already did. I think you were right.'

I undo my cuffs, and then do them up again. 'We might not know everything.'

'So I'll make myself clear.' He tucks in his shirt. 'It goes both ways. I'm afraid of losing you too.'

'What?'

He points to the stallholders, packing up their tents. 'What happened today scared me. The amount of time you spend on the roads, that scares me. You get less support in your profession than I get in mine. That scares me too. But do you know what scares me most?'

I swallow the lump in my throat. 'No.'

'I'm afraid that I've lost you already. Before we've even got started.'

I squeeze my eyes shut. But when I open them again, nothing has changed. His fists are clenched. His jaw is set. His eyes are blue and shadowed.

'You think I'm a coward.'

'In respect to Thornbrooke and everything associated with it, no.'

'I think …'

'Don't tell me we're different!'

'We are! I'm nothing like Catriona!'

'What?'

'You have plenty in common!'

He hesitates. 'I'm not afraid of losing her.'

'She likes you, that's obvious.'

He frowns. 'I told her weeks ago, at the Christmas party, that nothing was going to happen.' He waves towards the service road. 'She and Nate went out last week.'

'Oh.'

'Jemima? Is there anything else?'

The wind has picked up. It rustles through the leaves and blows my hair around. 'It's just that …' I push the hair out of my eyes, put strands behind my ears.

'Yes?'

I look towards the carpark. Rosa is walking to a van, carrying a box. When John runs after her and takes it out of her arms, she pats his cheek.

'After Dad died,' I say quietly, 'after Thornbrooke, I had to put my pieces together again.'

'What pieces?'

'The ones that make me strong.'

He frowns. 'I don't want to change you.'

'It's difficult.'

He runs a hand through his hair. 'I leave in a week.'

A week. A month. A year. A decade. A lifetime.

I'm afraid that I've lost you already. Before we've even got started.

I look down at my hands, linked tightly together. There's no strapping tape today, but sometimes there will be. Finn knows that. Finn knows me.

Just like I know him. He's not indestructible. He's not always in control. When he held his hand against my cheek, it trembled.

I take a deep breath and blow it out in a stream. 'It's Gus and Maggie's wedding anniversary tomorrow. I mean, it would have been.'

'I see.'

'When Mum was alive, she used to invite Gus for dinner at the cottage. After Mum died, Dad would take us to the pub every year. Now it's just Gus and me. Gus likes you. You rescued his calf. You were there when Ruby died.'

Nate shouts. 'Finn! We gotta go!'

Finn's eyes are fixed on my face. 'What are you saying?' He has a smudge of dirt on his cheek.

'You wanted to have dinner together.' A magpie, his white markings stark, hops over the ground towards the fruit. 'I know Gus will be there, but …' The bird plants his feet in the dirt and cocks his head to the side. 'You could come too.'

CHAPTER
54

The sun, a fuzzy ball of yellow, hides behind the clouds. It's early Sunday morning, and cooler than it's been. I look behind me, towards Horseshoe and home.

'Let's get this over with,' Nate says, combing his fingers through his messy blond hair.

'I didn't sleep too well.' We're close to the police station now; I see the white cars parked out the front. 'Did Finn give his statement last night?'

'Sure did.'

There's a bottlebrush tree near the front steps. Two rosellas, blue, green and orange, peck at the bright red flowers. I pull a leaf from the tree. When I join the ends in a circle, it doesn't snap, it bends.

'C'mon.' Nate touches my arm. 'They're waiting for us.'

'I thought I'd put this behind me.'

At the top of the steps, he holds the door wide. 'Turn around, lift your knee and smash it in the nuts.'

One of the detectives is large, gruff and middle-aged, and the other looks too young to grow a beard. They tell me Nate can stay. 'Do you need any more support?' the young one asks.

I sip from the glass of water. 'As long as you can do the writing and Nate can do the reading, I'll be okay.'

The young detective takes notes, while the older one asks questions.

Caruthers threatened you?

Yes

What happened the first time?

He grabbed my wrist to get my attention.

That was at Follyfoot?

Yes.

The second time?

He pinned me against the ute.

What else?

He showed me a hammer, a wrench and a knife.

Talk us through one by one.

He spun the hammer around.

He threw the wrench. It fell on the tray and bounced. It hit my hand.

He picked up the clinch tongs.

What clinch tongs?

I forgot. The jaws were open.

Tell us about the knife.

He turned it slowly.

You have to be more specific.

The sun caught the blade.

The third time? Christmas Day, wasn't it?

He took my arms, lifted me up.

Did you resist?

He held on too tightly.

And yesterday?

He grabbed my arm. I dropped the box.

Give us some background on how this all started. Thornbrooke. What's that all about?

Four horses died, Persephone, Poldark, Blackjack and Rosethorn …

U

Gus's tractor is parked in the home paddock when I get home, and he's sitting on the pew, his old hat tipped to the back of his head. Banjo is lying at his feet but jumps up to greet me, darting down the steps and running in circles.

'Hello, Gus. Happy anniversary. Is everything all right?'

He stands. 'I saw Sapphie out riding Chili. She said you had to go to the police about something.'

I squat, and stroke around Banjo's pointed ears. 'It's hard to keep things quiet around here.' Banjo licks my face.

Gus harrumphs. 'How'd it go then?'

'I think I did all right. They have a lot of evidence against the man they're interested in, which means he'll probably confess. I shouldn't have to go to court.'

'Was Dr Blackwood there too?'

'No. But yesterday I invited him to join us for dinner. I hope that's okay with you.' I stand and put my hands in my pockets.

Gus lowers his hat and clears his throat. When he smiles, the creases around his mouth deepen even more.

'He's a fine man, Jet. My Maggie would approve.'

CHAPTER
55

Gus hitched a lift into Horseshoe hours ago, so I arranged to meet him at the pub. I drive to the gardens and park under the trees. The grass near the rose beds, watered from the bore tap, is an oasis of green in a sea of patchy yellow. There's a rumble in the distance. Thunder? A large drop of rain, ragged round the edges, falls onto the footpath. It hasn't rained since November.

A group of local children gather outside the supermarket, taking wrappers off ice creams and putting them into the bin. So it's only as I step around them that I see Finn, standing outside the pub. Thoughts tangle up in my mind. I want him so much. I need to be brave.

All. Or nothing.

I do my best to smile. 'You're early.'

'You're late.' He opens the door and stands back. 'Gus is waiting in the dining room.'

The table is set for three. Finn and I sit next to each other, and Gus sits opposite. I order tortellini and the men order steak, and for forty-five minutes Gus and Finn talk about cattle, and Maggie. When Gus blows his nose and scrapes his eyes on a napkin, I find him a fresh one at the bar. By the time I get back, Gus is smiling again and nodding enthusiastically. Sapphie comes to the table and pulls up a chair.

'From Jet and me,' she says, giving Gus a small bunch of banksia roses with green leafy stems. The flowers, tiny and delicate in soft shades of yellow, are made of crepe paper, petal by petal.

'I only did the cutting out,' I tell Gus. 'Sapphie did everything else.'

Gus's eyes get watery again. 'Maggie's favourite flowers,' he says, turning to Finn. 'They grow a treat at the cemetery, and on the porch at home.' He holds the flowers reverently. 'What a sight for sore eyes.'

'You can't get them wet,' Sapphie says. 'So leave them here for Jet to look after while we go to the bar.' She takes Gus's arm. 'Pa wants to buy you a beer.'

After they've gone, Finn sits forwards in his chair. 'Jemima?'

My gaze goes from the narrow V of skin above his top button to his chin, mouth and nose. I look into his eyes. 'Finn?'

'Would you like to write me a note?'

'What about?'

There's a cheer from the poolroom, laughter at the bar. A breeze whispers in through the window. Finn frowns as he picks up the flowers. He studies them closely, puts them down carefully. He angles his chair towards mine and rests his forearms on his knees. There's strength in his hands, his shiny, well-shaped nails.

'I'll take anything you've got.'

When I hold out my hand, he takes it, threading our fingers together. 'Gus has a theory,' I say. 'He thinks some relationships are all or nothing.'

He squeezes my fingers. 'Better or worse? Richer or poorer? Sickness or health? That suits me.'

I move our hands from his lap to mine. 'The third time we slept together, I had a nightmare.'

'I remember.'

'But before that, I had a dream. We were running next to each other. I could see your shadow, but then it disappeared. I should have gone back and looked for it. I should have known you'd be there somewhere. I should have trusted my instincts.'

His lip lifts. 'Yes.'

'I'll try to do better.'

When he frees our hands and cups the side of my face, I lean into his hand. His thumb brushes over my lashes, the dampness.

'You said you'd put your pieces together,' he says, 'and that's what made you strong. You're independent, solitary. You're tough and smart and tenacious. Your strength is why I want you.'

'I didn't want to rely on anyone.' When I kiss his palm, I feel the pulse at his wrist. 'But I didn't have you. I was missing a piece.'

Big fat raindrops plop onto the footpath as I face Finn and Gus. Gus's flowers, safe in a plastic container, are stuffed beneath his coat.

'You don't mind if Finn drops you back, do you?'

''Course I don't,' Gus says gruffly. 'You do what you got to do.'

When Finn kisses my mouth, lust shoots straight to my toes. 'Drive carefully,' he says. 'I'll see you at home.'

I grab his shirt, creasing it, and kiss him again.

He mutters against my lips. 'Don't keep me waiting too long.'

Rain drums against the shop awnings. It rushes down the gutters and cascades into the drains. As I cross the road, it drips down my back. The windscreen wipers slide back and forth, washing away the dust and bugs of summer. There are no cars in front of me and no cars behind.

There are no lights at the cemetery either, just the lopsided, faded sign at the turn-off. I follow its arrow to the parking spaces by the tiny stone church. Another two shingles have slipped into the gutter at the base of the ridge. The clouds obscure the moon, but some of the beams get through. They light the rocks, mottled with paint, that mark the grave near the fence, and the pebbles on the path. Liam's cross shines too, timber bleached to a soft dove grey. I run my hand over it, slippery with rain.

'Hey, baby brother.' I feel for the uneven nail heads and the out-of-kilter join. 'Our dad, he barely knew a hammer from a screwdriver. But he did his best.'

Dad's headstone is made out of local granite like Mum's. He chose it himself, long before he died, so I wouldn't have to do it. He told the stonemason what to write.

Tears and rain blur the inscription, and there isn't much light. But I can read the words.

Ross Kincaid is in love with Abigail Laney. He is a father to baby Liam, and to Jet, the most precious girl in the world. He wouldn't change a thing. He treasures every day.

There's a dandelion flower growing on Mum's grave. The spindly stem, dripping with moisture, is stronger than it looks. Dad used to say a weed is just a plant that's in the wrong place. When I was small, I picked daises, dandelions and thistles for Mum. She'd trim the leaves and put them in a vase in the kitchen.

I'll be back at the cemetery soon, to see the freesia shoots peeking through the soil. After that, if the rain doesn't last, I'll water the jonquils and daffodils. And after the flowers are spent, Mr Hargreaves will tie the stems into knots. In the summer months,

I'll rake mulch from the gums by the church and sprinkle it over the graves.

So why does this feel like goodbye?

Treasure every day. Every day's a gift.

Finn's business card is in my wallet. Bold black letters on white. He's clever, ambitious, honest, articulate. Vulnerable. *Your strength is why I want you.*

The thunder grumbles loud and then soft. Lightning shines brightly and spotlights the graves.

Liam, Mum and Dad.

They have my back as I walk up the hill.

CHAPTER
56

I keep an oilskin coat on a hook in the shed, but I'm so wet there's no point in putting it on. As I run up the path to the cottage, water streams into my shoes.

Finn limps when he runs down the steps of the verandah. But his gait evens out as he walks across the grass. When he opens his arms, I don't hesitate. He lifts my hair and kisses my neck. I listen to the beats of his heart.

But then I pull back. 'Now you're wet too.'

When he kisses my mouth, I wind my arms around his neck. Our lips meld through raindrops, our tongues touch, I shiver. He lifts his head. 'You're cold.'

'No, I'm not.'

'I missed you.'

'I should have stayed at the church and ...'

'What?'

'More of the tiles have slipped. The roof might leak.'

'It has to be fixed tonight?'

'Tomorrow will do.'

His lips firm. 'I'll hold the ladder.'

'It's not very high.'

He tips up my chin with his knuckles. 'You do my head in, you know that?'

I touch his face. His eye where it was bruised. His cheekbone and jaw. His firm and serious mouth. I spread my fingers over his chest.

'We can look out for each other.'

He kisses me again, a hard, possessive kiss that heats my body and softens my limbs. Even through the rain, I see the brightness in his eyes.

'Commitment,' he says. 'You understand that, don't you?'

I stand on my toes and take his face between my hands. 'Because you care about me?'

'Yes.'

'When you untied my laces, I knew then.'

'What?'

'I cared about you.'

He takes a deep breath. 'You didn't think to communicate that earlier?'

When I sit on the pew, he sits next to me and pulls my feet onto his lap, untying my laces even though they're not tangled. He yanks off my shoes and takes off his own, lining them up side-by-side.

'Will we live together?' I ask.

'Yes.'

'Where?'

'Where we'll be happy.' He shrugs. 'Let's start with Horseshoe.'

'Are you sure?'

'I can travel when I have to.'

'You don't want to live in Scotland? What about "My Heart's In The Highlands"?'

He whistles. 'You do appreciate how freakish this is, don't you?'

I hold in a smile as I peel off my socks. 'I really liked that one.'

'Go on then.'

> *My heart's in the Highlands, my heart is not here,*
> *My heart's in the Highlands, a-chasing the deer;*
> *Chasing the wild-deer, and following the roe,*
> *My heart's in the Highlands wherever I go.*

I rest my chin on my knees. 'Well?'

'I'm a conservationist. I don't hunt and I don't fish unsustainably. I also like blue skies.' He kisses me firmly. 'My heart is here.'

When I fetch the key from the pottery box that sits at the end of the pew, he mutters under his breath, locking the door behind us as I flick on the lights.

He takes my hands. 'They're cold.'

I snake my arms around his waist. 'You always think you're right.'

'Bull—'

When I pull down his head and press my lips against his, he widens his legs so our heights are more even. My tongue tip circles his. I move closer, against the press of his erection. When I open the top few buttons of his shirt and feel his skin beneath my hands, he groans.

'I've waited, Jemima,' he says, 'for a very long time.'

I undo another button and pull his shirt out of his jeans. He feels and smells so good, he tastes good too and …

I pull back. His eyes are so dark. 'You saw what I ate tonight, right?'

He growls. 'Yes.'

'Just making sure.' I tighten my arms again. 'I like to kiss you.'

He lifts me so high I'm balanced on my toes, and then he shepherds me backwards through the bedroom door. We kiss in the shadows. But then he draws away and switches on the lamp.

'I like to see you,' he says, pulling off his shirt.

I run my hands over his shoulders and trace his collarbones down to his sternum. I lift the leather cord and disk over his head, wind it around my hand and place it on the side table. I circle his navel, and follow the line of hair to his belt. He picks up my hands, studying my fingers and kissing them one by one.

'I'll try to do better,' I say.

'I want you to be happy, that's all.'

We take off my shirt and lift my bra over my head. He pulls me close, watching for the moment when my nipples touch his chest. He moans, dips his head and nuzzles against my neck.

'Finn?' My voice is croaky. 'Can we go to bed now?'

He smiles a lopsided smile and holds the waistband of my jeans, yanking them down and following with his mouth. If he weren't holding my bottom so tightly, I think I'd collapse. I see him between my legs in a hazy foggy blur. I hear him, murmuring under his breath.

'Finn ...'

He looks up, smiles. Then strips off the rest of his clothes and backs me onto the bed. As soon as I sit, I notice his leg. There's a transparent plaster on his calf. He has a scar, an uneven red line, which he must have got in the rhino yard. At one end of the scar are a few fresh stiches.

'What happened?'

'It's nothing.'

I yank the sheet up over my thighs. 'Tell me!'

He lifts me by the waist, throwing me backwards so I'm sprawled on the bed. He crawls up my body slowly and deliberately. His hands brush my thighs, hips, stomach and breasts. My heart jumps around. I want him inside me; I tremble with need.

'Tell you what, Jem? How much I want you?' His erection lies warm between my legs.

I moan and open for him. 'Yes.'

When he laughs, I remember. 'No!' I push against his shoulders. 'Your leg. What happened?'

He rolls onto his back, taking me with him. 'I ran too hard yesterday. The surgeon patched me up this morning. It's nothing, except ...'

'What? Why are you smiling?'

He bends his legs at the knees. 'You go on top.'

I carefully sit, straddling him. 'Like this?' When I lean forwards, my breasts touch his chest.

'Yes,' he says, kissing me. 'And this.'

His fingers play softly, gently and deeply. Weak with longing, I move against his hand. 'Finn, I think ...'

'More?'

'Yes.'

He holds my hips and adjusts our positions. In one long thrust, he slides inside me. My breath hitches.

'I'm sorry, baby. It's just ... you okay?'

I run my hands through his hair, wet with rain, and his chest, damp with sweat. I take deep breaths, accept his length and width.

'I think so.'

He cups my bottom and lifts me, going even deeper. He talks in fits and starts. 'When my lip bled, I knew.'

I touch his cheek, his jaw, and his mouth. 'What?'

'I didn't want anyone else. Only you. Ever since.'

I need him to move quicker and harder. I bite his shoulder. I whimper. 'That early?'

'Yes.'

His touch heats my blood. His kiss steals my thoughts. His words take my breath. I climax and cry out his name. He holds me close, shudders against me, and moans his release. When he sleeps in my arms, our hearts share a rhythm.

Thump-thump. Thump-thump. Thump-thump.

The wind blows gently, rattles the window. The rain falls softly, slides down the glass. We lie on our sides, facing each other. I trace his mouth with a fingertip. I push back his hair. His body lies warm and hard against mine.

His eyes open slowly. He smiles when he sees me. 'Morning,' he mumbles.

'Hey.'

'What time is it?'

I glance through the gap in the curtains. 'Five-thirtyish.'

He strokes my breast. 'Early.'

Our eyes meet. 'When you mix blue and brown, do you always get brown?'

He stills. He opens his mouth and shuts it again. I stiffen. But before I can jump from the bed, he grabs me around the waist.

'What did you mean by that?'

'It doesn't matter.'

'Were you talking about eye colour?'

'I … yes.'

'The brown is generally dominant.' He speaks quietly. 'I'm glad about that.'

'I was … forget it.'

'Were you referring to our children?'

I open my mouth to deny it, but … 'We should be honest with each other.'

'Always.'

He nuzzles my breast, circles my nipple with his tongue. He groans softly when it puckers. He licks and plays.

I stroke his hair. 'We could have a baby. Or two. Sometime in the future. If we can.'

He lifts his head. His lips are wet. 'I love you, Jem. How could you imagine I wouldn't want that too?'

I push against his shoulders until he rolls onto his back. I lie across his body, put my head on his chest.

'You want to talk rationally, don't you? In a *considered* way. Like a regular couple.'

He laughs and tidies my hair. 'I don't want regular. I want you.'

When I trace the muscles in his abdomen, his fists clench. When I stroke his erection, his toes curl up.

'I should be with a safe man, someone like Luke.'

He growls like a bear, and flips me onto my back. He throws his leg across my hips, pinning me down.

'Your stitches!'

He speaks through his teeth. 'What did you say?'

'I didn't mean it.'

He touches my cheek. He frowns into my eyes. 'I love you, Jemima Kincaid. I won't leave you. I want children.'

I wrap my arms around his neck and kiss his cranky lips. I bury my face against his neck and breathe in his scent. 'I'm sorry.' I push back his hair.

He narrows his eyes. 'Do you have anything to add?'

The rain has eased, and the sun, soft peachy-gold, sneaks through the curtains. The horses will be at the gate, waiting to go into the paddock by the river. The kookaburras call out, impatient for daylight. The Honey girls catch the school bus at eight; I promised to shoe their ponies at seven.

I wriggle out of his arms and sit with my legs to the side. I study him seriously, in the same way that he studies me.

He touches my cheek. 'Jem? It's okay. I've known for so long, it's easy for me. You don't have to—'

I kiss his mouth. 'I love you, Finn Blackwood.' I run my lips over his eyes, one then the other. I slide a finger down his nose. 'And I promise that I'll keep you safe.'

ACKNOWLEDGEMENTS

I was nine years old when I was given my first pony, so it was around this time that I began to appreciate the crucial role that farriers play in not only the soundness of a horse, but their long-term health and wellbeing. One of the highlights of writing this novel was spending many hours on the road with Michael Fruin, DWCF Master Farrier at Fruin Forge. Michael and fellow farrier Blake answered all of my questions with patience and good humour, and gave me fascinating insights into this highly skilled profession. Michael also works with other hoofed animals such a giraffes and elephants and his knowledge, together with insights shared by zoo handlers and keepers, were invaluable. I take full responsibility (and plead creative license) for anything I might have missed.

Dyslexia is common, but extremely complex, and I did my best to ensure it was portrayed, in terms of the story, realistically. Thank you to Vani Gupta, speech pathologist and writer, who provided valuable feedback. Thank you to Dr Margaret for your assistance in regards to the (many!) scientific and medical issues that arose as I was writing this novel. Any errors are mine alone, and creative license.

Early pages of this book were workshopped with my friends in the Turramurra Writing Group. Thank you to Cathleen Ross, Kandy Shepherd, Isolde Martyn, Elizabeth Lhuede and Christine Stinson, and a particular thank you to Carroll Casey, who gave me the confidence to persevere with the teardrop bulbs in the cemetery. And many thanks to my fellow Ink Wells, particularly Pamela Cook, Rae Cairns, Laura Boon, Joanna Nell and Michelle Barraclough, each of whom endured months of endless whining about where this book might end up if I didn't finally finish it.

Thank you to my wonderful publisher, Jo Mackay. You, and my fantastically supportive and insightful editor, Annabel Blay, have made this novel even better than I—who love my characters to death—could ever have hoped it might be.

To my dad, Philip Watson, and my uncle, Sandy Morrison, thank you for sharing your intimate knowledge of all things Robbie Burns. To my gorgeous daughters Philippa, Tamsin, Michaela and Gabriella, thank you for your love and support. Finally, thank you to my sons Ben and Max, two fine young men and heroes in the making.

Turn over for a sneak peek.

Starting from Scratch

by

PENELOPE JANU

Available January 2021

CHAPTER

1

Most people see colours, but sometimes I think that I see them more clearly.

I've worked at the long timber bench at the farmhouse for the past two hours, pressing crepe paper petals into shapes so they're ready to form into flowers. *Gompholobium grandiflorum*. Large Wedge-pea. The petals, in four shades of yellow, are lined up neatly in rows.

Saffron, lemon, amber and gold.

When a gust of wind rattles the window and sneaks through a gap in the frame, scores of petals fly into the air and fall to my feet like sunbeams. As I collect the petals and put them into a shoebox, I imagine Gran at her old kitchen table, the surface obscured by reams of crepe paper.

'Don't be so particular, Sapphie,' she'd say, as I fussed over shade and sequence. 'It's the imperfections that make the flowers perfect.'

I pack away supplies—glues and tapes, forestry wire and scissors, the yellow-coloured crepe I've cut into strips and the moss-green pieces I'll shape for the foliage. A screech shoots through the silence. Possums in the red gum. I wish they'd eat there every night and leave the orange trees alone.

Another gust of wind, stronger than the last, rattles the window again. The latch is fastened but the timber is weathered and the screws are loose. One day, when this farmhouse is mine, I'll replace the windowsill and fill in all the gaps. I'll hang curtains to keep out the cold, plaster the gaps in the cornices and repair the rotting skirting boards. One day …

I turn off the overhead lights and lock the front door behind me. A butterscotch moon, low in the sky, throws shadowy light on the gardens—camellia trees, azalea bushes and tangles of bare branched mid-winter roses. The trunk of the red gum is palest pink, the low-lying branches heavy with foliage.

When the breeze catches my hood and pulls it back, the air is cold on my face. I thread loose hairs through my plait and secure it under my collar. My breaths are white as I step through the shadows on the porch. I could walk by road to the school where I teach and live, but I prefer to hike cross-country. High silky clouds, grey and teal, obscure the pinprick stars.

Tree roots have lifted cracks in the path at the side of the farmhouse and the water tank near the raised bed of herbs is ringed with rusty stripes. Ten empty pots, stacked in a wobbly tower, lean against the greenhouse. Was it Barney who hid the marijuana plants behind the tomato vines and trellis? My heart sinks. I don't want it to be him, or any of the teens and children who come to the farmhouse to help with the horses or just hang around, but Barney has shown particular interest in the vegetable gardens in the past few months.

I glance at the compost bin. The plants were mature. Was it safe to uproot them, cut them up and shove them in there? Tomorrow I'll add worms to the bin and fill it up with horse manure.

Skirting around the mandarin and cumquat trees, I bypass the horses napping near the yards and slip between the rungs of the wide metal gate. The track through the paddock is fairly straight and the grass is low and scrappy. More difficult to navigate is the scrub that borders the creek; I push back the branches, jump over a ditch and skirt around thistles. The creek is low and the meandering flow, black in the shadows, is interspersed by ridges of rock. I jump over two shallow crevices before leaping over the band of deeper water to land on my feet and scramble up the incline.

I'm still crouched low, my hands on the ground, when I see a man walking through the paddock from the direction of the school. He's dressed in city clothes. His shoulders are broad. He's tall. If I stand, he'll see me. Does it matter? Horseshoe Hill is my home. I haven't done anything wrong.

As I push myself upright, I touch a dandelion weed, the long, fleshy leaves soft on my fingers. I recall the marijuana. Barney is only fourteen. I don't think he smokes or drinks. Was he cultivating the weed for somebody else? This track leads directly to the farmhouse. Is the man sneaking in to check out the crop?

I scramble back to the creek bed, running along the bank before tackling the incline again. There's little cover on this side of the creek, only two gum trees. The closest tree isn't very tall, but there's a much larger tree next to it. I stand on a boulder and leap to the first tree, taking hold of the branch and swinging a leg over the bough, before hoisting myself onto it and sitting astride. I wriggle to the trunk, wrapping an arm around it and standing. The adjacent tree's lowest branch, narrow and straight like a bar, is higher than the one I'm on, and only a metre away. I bend my knees and jump, grasping the branch with both hands before looping my legs around it. The branch, bowing under my weight, tilts towards the ground. Yikes.

Hanging by my legs and arms, I shuffle towards the trunk. It's too wide to wrap my arms around, but the knobbly remnants of a long dead branch provide a handhold. I grasp it as I pull myself up and sit, legs dangling beneath me. I check my phone. Almost ten o'clock. I peer through the leaves.

The man is only twenty metres away. His coat falls past his thighs; the collar is turned up. I can't make out his features, but I think that he's young with short dark hair. He doesn't have the look of a teenage druggie and, as he's not shady and thin, or thickset and threatening, he looks nothing like the dealers I've seen. But … there's something familiar about him.

When he stops at the end of the track and looks in my direction, I hold my breath. He shouldn't be able to see me. My hair is dark brown, I'm dressed in black and grey and obscured behind the tree trunk. But just in case, I yank up my hood, pulling the toggle tight so it sits above my mouth.

I hear steps through the undergrowth, branches pushed aside. Silence. My heart thumps hard against my ribs.

'Hello!'

His voice is deep. Does he know I'm close? Why else would he call out? Should I answer? If he's walking around in the dead of night with criminal intent, I have no interest in talking to him. He might not know exactly where I am and even if he does, my branch won't hold his weight. I feel for my phone again. Reception isn't great, but I can threaten to call for help if I have to.

He scrambles down the bank to the creek and walks alongside it, his eyes on the ground until he reaches my tree. He stops, turns and looks up. The moon sneaks through a crack in the clouds and shines on his face. My breath catches.

Matts Laaksonen.

A strong jaw, high Nordic cheekbones and deep-set, intelligent eyes. A crease through his brow when he frowns and a twitch to his lips when he smiles. A scar on his chin.

It's a face I could never forget.

'Who are you?' he asks.

A wave of unhappiness tightens my throat.

The girl who loved you a lifetime ago.

'Come down,' he says.

The school is hundreds of metres away, securely locked up for the night. The old schoolhouse where I live is even further. In the distance, I see headlights, a truck on the loop road. It's probably Freddie, who's often late home from the markets.

Matts scrambles up the slope and pulls a phone from his pocket. When he activates the light, the bright silver beam triples my heart rate. Should I stand on my branch? It would hardly make a difference.

'Sapphire?'

His shoulders are broader than they used to be. The stubble on his face is even and neat.

I sit taller and loosen the toggle on my hood. I draw it back, pulling out my plait and flicking the long end down my back. I blink against the glare. 'Turn off the light, Matts.'

He puts the phone in his pocket. 'Why are you up there?'

'Why are you down there?'

'I came to warn you.' He crosses his arms.

'What about?'

'Not now,' he says. 'Get down.'

One of my hands is on the tree trunk. The other is on the branch near my leg. I wriggle my fingers, stiff with cold. I want to get down, but—

'How did you know I was out here?'

'I looked for you at the school. I was sent to the farmhouse.'

'By who?'

'The hotel barman.'

When I'm teaching children to sound out words, I draw out the letters. I elongate them. *Ba ... aa ... rr ... mm ... aa ... nn.* Matts does the opposite when he speaks. His native language is Finnish. He's fluent in English, but his words are short and sharp.

'Did my father send you?'

He can't reach the branch, but steps as close as he can. 'How did you get up there?'

When I don't answer, he looks from my tree to the other tree, then speaks through his teeth. 'Still taking risks?'

'Calculated ones.'

'You can't go back that way.'

I glance at the ground, three metres down. It drops away steeply. I'll have to swing wide, and drop to higher ground. Even so ...

'I'll manage.'

'You'll hurt yourself.' He takes a few steps down the incline and braces himself. 'Jump, Sapphire. I'll break your fall.'

'Leave me alone, Matts.'

'You haven't changed, have you?'

'It's been eight years. How would you know?'

There's a rustling in the leaves above me. A ringtailed possum scampers headfirst down the tree trunk. When I yelp and pull back my arm, he freezes. His coat is speckled grey, his startled eyes are bright.

I put my hands on the branch either side of my legs as I inch away. 'I'm on your tree, aren't I? It's okay. I won't hurt—'

The branch dips sharply and I lose my balance. I fall.

If I'd jumped, I would have landed on my feet. Matts would have stopped me falling down the slope. As it is, my arms flail in mid-air as I try to right my body. But I don't have time. I don't—

I'm moving too fast for Matts to catch me so I land on my back and tumble helter-skelter down the slope towards the water.

'Sapphire!'

Pebbles and gravel dig into my skin. My chest burns and I fight to suck in air. My eyes water then tears trickle down my cheeks and into my ears.

He crouches by my side and runs his hand, barely touching, up my arm. 'Are you winded? Take small breaths. Fill your lungs slowly.' He puts a hand on my shoulder and frowns. 'Don't move.'

He takes my wrist and feels for my pulse. When he looks at his watch, his breaths are steady. His eyes are dark like storm clouds. He smooths hair from my face and it sticks to my cheek.

'Ow.'

He frowns again. 'I'm sorry. It's grazed.' He shrugs out of his coat and lays it over my body, tucking it closely around me from my neck to my toes. 'Breathe, Kissa.'

Kissa is Finnish for cat. When I was a little girl, he said I was a pest, but tolerable. Only he wouldn't have said tolerable. What did he say? That allowing me to follow him around was far less trouble than forcing me to leave.

'I want to check nothing is broken.'

I squeak a response.

He carefully presses down the right side of my body—shoulder, ribs, hip, knee and ankle—his touch impersonal and clinical. His hand goes to my left side. He feels down my shoulder and arm. I flinch.

He frowns. 'What? Did I hurt you?'

There's scar tissue on my inner arm. And other scars as well. 'No,' I croak.

When he's finished looking for broken bones, he sits back on his heels. The shadows shift. I shudder. I suck in tiny breaths. His shirt is long sleeved, but cotton. He must be cold.

'Can you move your hands?' he says. 'Your feet?'

I feel the weight and warmth of his coat as I stretch out my fingers and rotate my ankles. 'Yes,' I whisper.

'Your head. Your back and legs. Do you feel pain? Numbness?'

'Just … winded.'

He watches as I draw air into my lungs, and bend and straighten my legs until they feel like mine again. When I attempt to get up, he puts firm hands on my back and waist and shifts me onto my side.

'Stay there.' His phone buzzes. 'Laaksonen.' He speaks in Finnish, just a few words.

I roll, without help this time, onto my hands and knees. I smell eucalyptus, dust and leaf litter.

Matts stands easily and holds out his hands.

I shake my head. 'I can get up by myself.'

'Prove it.'

We're at the base of the slope. The creek gurgles next to us; the trees tower above us. Where is the possum? I dig my heels into the ground, draw up my knees and rest my forehead on them—as if I'm lightheaded, as if I need to think. I *do* need to think.

'Give me a minute.'

The air is cold on my cheek. I tentatively touch it; sticky with blood. The children in my class range from seven to ten. I'll tell them I climbed a tree because I had to … what? Spy on someone? I could have stood on the ground and hidden behind the tree trunk. That would've been adequate. Sensible. Why go to so much trouble?

I look up, straight into his eyes. Slowly shaking his head, Matts kneels, rearranges his coat around my shoulders and fastens a button.

'What a stupid thing to do,' he says, as he unclenches my fingers and brushes stones from my palms.

'Ow!' I snatch my hands back and press my palms against my knees. He frowns and, muttering under his breath, he stands again, undoing the buttons of his shirt and shrugging it off. He's wearing a white T-shirt underneath. I blink when he grabs the hem with both hands and pulls it off.

'Matts? What are you—'

He's slender but strong. Even in the half-light, his pectoral and abdominal muscles are clearly defined. Holding the T-shirt between his knees, he slides firmly muscled arms back into the sleeves of his shirt. I look away.

'Wait here,' he says.

His coat hugs my back as I rest my head on my knees again. His footsteps crunch on the gravel. Within a minute he's back and holds out his T-shirt, wet but neatly folded.

'Clean your hands and face.'

The fabric is soft. When I hold it to my cheek, it smells fresh. His shirt is buttoned again and neatly tucked in. My skin is suddenly warm.

'Thank you.'

Besides the wind in the trees and occasional movement in the undergrowth, it's quiet. I take care with my hands, ignoring the stinging as I brush the dirt away. The fabric is smudged with blood. I don't want to give it back but I don't want to hang onto it.

As if he reads my mind, he takes it from me. I clumsily undo the button and hold up his coat. 'Thanks.'

'Keep it.'

A shiver passes through me. 'I'm okay.'

After shoving the T-shirt into a pocket, he puts the coat back on. He holds out his hands and I take them. I wait for my hands to hurt again, but all I'm aware of is the press of his palms against mine. A second passes. Or is it a few? Our hands have grown. We're adults now. His touch feels the same, yet different. Slowly and carefully, he pulls me to my feet. He's still much taller, but our height differential is far less than it was. When I tug to free my fingers, he tightens his hold. He checks that I'm steady on my feet before he lets me go.

I nod stiffly. 'Thank you.'

The clouds shift. They're thinner than they were—gossamer sheets of iridescent pearl. Light catches his hair and turns the tips gold.

There are golden eagles in Finland.

Kotka is Finnish for eagle.

That's the name I gave him.

Other books by

PENELOPE JANU

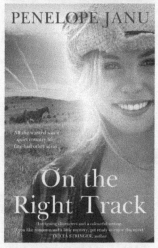

talk about it

Let's talk about books.

Join the conversation:

 facebook.com/romanceanz

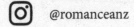 @romanceanz

romance.com.au

If you love reading and want to know about our
authors and titles, then let's talk about it.